Manchon Moon

The Telepathic Alliance
Book II

Tanya M. Parr

iUniverse, Inc.
Bloomington

Manchon Moon
The Telepathic Alliance Book II

iUniverse books may be ordered through booksellers or by contacting:

iUniverse
1663 Liberty Drive
Bloomington, IN 47403
www.iuniverse.com
1-800-Authors (1-800-288-4677)

ISBN: 978-1-4620-0440-9 (sc)
ISBN: 978-1-4620-0441-6 (ebk)

Printed in the United States of America

iUniverse rev. date: 4/5/2011

PROLOGUE

After dealing with the Federation and the men that came with Ritage, Logan and the others return to the stronghold. Cassie and the villagers, along with Leyla's group gather outside in the compound. They all gather around the discipline shed as Eric Ritage is led out. Before saying anything out loud, Thayer mentally asks Logan if Cassie knows about his relationship with Hillary Quinn. When Logan confirms that she does, Thayer steps forward.

"Eric Ritage. You are charged with the murder of Hillary Quinn. Without just cause, you shot her in the back when she was delivering a gift to Cassandra Blackwood from my wife and her father."

"I wasn't the one that shot her, and even if I was, she had no business even being there. The people in the Blackwood house were under Earth Security protection. Quinn didn't have the proper clearance to go near them or the house for any reason." Ritage states glaring at Logan and Cassie.

"And you're a liar Mr. Ritage." Cassie says glaring back at him. "I saw you pull the trigger, and I saw the look on your face as she collapsed in my arms." she says remembering the shock of what had happened right in front of her and barely able to keep her tears at bay.

"What are you complaining about? I got rid of Knightrunner's whore for you. You should be thanking me." Ritage sneers at her, not even realizing that he had just admitted to the crime.

"Why should I thank you for murdering an innocent woman, who did what she could to help me and my family? I didn't begrudge her the night she had with Logan. I'm glad that he could give her such a wonderful experience before you murdered her."

"Enough of this!" Logan snarls taking a step towards Ritage. "He's just admitted to killing her. On her behalf, I claim the blood-rite."

Thayer looks around to the others who all nod their agreement that Logan has the right, because of both his physical and mental ties to the dead woman. "You have the right to avenge Hillary Quinn." Thayer tells him, but then holds up his hand when Logan steps forward. "I think that the woman and children should not be present for the retribution that you will take out on him." he looks to his mate. "Leyla, would you take them to the ship and show them more of the holograms of Calidon and Manchon?"

Nodding her agreement, Leyla and the older women lead everyone to the ship. Once the door closes behind them, the men close the circle around Ritage.

"How will you take your revenge?"

"By sonic knife." Logan pulls his blade from his belt.

"You have to allow me to protect myself!" Ritage shouts backing up only to be pushed forward again by the men behind him.

"Why? You didn't allow Hillary the chance to protect herself." Logan growls back at him and then lunges forward cutting through Ritage's upper right arm. "She didn't even see it coming, didn't know it was coming until it was too late." He lunges again and this time gets Ritage across the chest, causing him to cry out.

"It was an accident! I thought my gun was on stun!" Ritage pleads holding his chest.

"Don't try to lie to me Ritage. I know you too well." Logan laughs viciously as his blade cuts the other man across his rib cage. "You planned on killing someone that morning. Who was it you really planned to kill Ritage? Me perhaps?" Logan jumps forward and Ritage turns away and receives a cut down his back.

"YES! YES!" Ritage screams as he falls to his knees. "but you sent your whore instead." he says knowing that if he says the right things, Knightrunner would end the torment, the pain, and just finish him off. He couldn't stand the pain any longer. When a sonic blade cuts through the skin it leaves a resounding in the nerves that can take hours to die away. "If they hadn't disappeared I would have killed the Blackwood bitch too. After me and my men had some fun with her first." he pants in pain.

Logan lets out a primal growl and plunges his blade deep into Ritage's back, twisting it several times before pulling it out. Ritage falls forward with one final scream, but is dead before his body even hits the ground.

Logan drops his knife and looks up into the sky, letting out another primal scream of pain and anguish so loud that it can be heard even deep within the Calidonian ships. When he looks down again, Cassie is standing in front of him. He falls to his knees in front of her and wraps his arms around her waist, burying his face in her stomach.

Cassie hugs his head to her and gently strokes his hair. *Let it go now love. There's no need to hang on to the anger any more. You did what you needed to do. Her murder has been avenged. She'll rest peacefully now. She wouldn't want you to suffer any more then you have.'*

The other men have moved away to give them the privacy that Logan needs to regain control after such an emotional release. They all realize that Ritage had forced Logan to end his life before he was ready, but they also knew that it was better this way. Logan's anger could have taken him over the edge into madness. Each of his blows had caused more and more anger to build and they knew that if it wasn't contained he could have eventually turned on anyone else, even his beloved Cassandra.

Thayer stops near the house and turns back to look at his friends. He was glad that Logan and Cassie had finally gotten together. If they hadn't, right now Logan's very sanity would be at stake and they might have had to end his life as well. He wasn't sure if he could have done that to his life long friend. It was time for Logan to go home, back where he could heal and regroup, back to his family.

CHAPTER ONE

Cassie runs her hands through Logan's hair and tugs gently when she reaches his nap. "How long did you say this trip would take us?" she asks kissing his cheek.

"At our present speed, we should reach Manchon in about two weeks. If we were going at top speed, we'd be there in less than a week." he tells her running his hands down her back.

"Do you think that I'll have any trouble on Manchon?" Though Thayer had assured her before they left that she would be treated as an honored guest, Cassie couldn't rid herself of the feeling that something was going to happen to her not too long after they arrived.

"No, you won't have any trouble. You're the Calidonian ambassador. You'll be protected by the royal family because of your emotional connection to Thayer and Leyla." He moves her slightly away so that he can see her face. "What's wrong love? What has you so worried?"

"I don't know." she admits shrugging her shoulders wrapping her arms around his neck.

"Well, lets see if I can take your mind off whatever it is that's troubling you." he leans over her and begins kissing her deeply. Within seconds Cassie pushes away her misgivings and concentrates on being with Logan.

⌇

"Because Thayer's oldest aunt didn't have a girl child, and her only son had such a weak psi level, the seat of power went to his uncle. Daviman was a good King, but he refused to pick one of his concubines to be his lifemate." Logan explains to Cassie the recent complexities of Thayer's family rule. "Though Daviman had several daughters, only one was qualified to become queen. Because she is not a lifemate child though, Thayer's other aunt was made queen when Daviman became ill and passed away. From what we learned from Thayer's mother Royanna, his aunt Liasky died in child birth, which meant that Royanna was next to become Queen. Because of her position as Grand Master Healer, Royanna didn't feel that she should become Queen unless it was absolutely necessary."

"But wouldn't such a situation make it necessary?" Cassie asks in confusion.

"Yes under normal circumstances it would, but her decision was based on the fact that there was no one to take over her place as the Grand Master Healer. By a special law, she was able to pick the niece most qualified to take her place on the throne, until another Grand Master can be found and trained. At that time she would take over as Queen and hopefully find a lifemate or a life-bond mate and produce another heir to the throne."

"But isn't she too old? I mean, she must be in her late fifties early sixties by now. And what about Thayer? What if he was to return?"

"Most women on Manchon can give safe births well into their sixties, sometimes even into their seventies. It's probably because our longevity is about triple of that on say Earth. As for Thayer, its hard to say. Under our laws, once someone leaves Manchon, unless they have been given a special royal sanction, they can never return. Because no member of the royal family had ever left the planet before, I don't know what decision would be made in his case." Logan thinks over the possibilities of such a thing happening and shakes his head, unable to picture it. "Like I said, Royanna was able to choose Niccara Rican to take her place until she can take the crown. Nicca was crowned Queen several years ago with Royanna as her chief advisor. From what I heard from the few Majichonie I've seen over those years, she's made a good Queen."

"You seem quite proud of her." Cassie says watching him closely. "It also seems you're very fond of her." she adds with a touch of anger that causes Logan to look at her sharply.

Noticing that its not a true anger, he reaches for her hand and lifts it to his lips. "Yes, I guess I am proud of her, and yes I am fond of her also. Not the way I'm fond of you though my love." he assures her looking into her eyes. "The year before I left, Nicca and I became very close Cassie." he squeezes her hand tightly as she tries to draw away from him. "She was my first lover. My feelings for her ended when I left. Where she was my first lover, you are my last."

Cassie looks into his eyes, seeing the truth of his words buried deep within them. She smiles softly at him to show that she believes what he's told her. She hadn't had such feelings of jealousy when she knew of his night with Hillary which had only been a short time ago. His time with Thayer's cousin had been years ago before he even knew of her.

He returns her smile and then gets serious again. "Now that that's settled, we need to go over the laws and customs of the Majichonie. We can't have you accidentally offending anyone." For the next several hours, Logan goes over the laws and customs of his people, and explains how each affects the different classes. He also explains how the healing gift has always decided who should rule. How for the last two hundred years, the Rican family has given birth to the strongest healers ever on Manchon. That in itself has been strange, because in all of the history of Manchon, no one family has ever held the royal seat of power for so long a time.

"Has their rule been good for the Majichonie?" Cassie asks.

"Yes. When they became the ruling family, they kept the different sects from killing each other off. There are fewer fights now then at any other time in our history. Now that Thayer has come into his true powers, even though he is not on Manchon, even that fighting will now ease."

"Why or how would Thayer's abilities effect people in such a way?"

"Both him and Leyla are peace to all telepaths. Their abilities will constantly soothe away any anger or hostility that may enter our minds. Soon no telepath will be aggressive to another or anyone else for that matter." he explains.

"But what about the Alliance? It will act aggressively to aide and protect others. How is that going to bring peace?" Cassie puts to him. "I agree that we need the Alliance, but there must be some other way."

"Not until the Federation can deal with people in a more fair and just manner. Until then we will act with aggression only when it is needed. Only a select group will act from each planet in the Alliance." he assures her. "It won't last long."

During the rest of their first week, they go over everything several times and write up the things that will be in the Alliance agreement. During the second week, Logan teaches Cassie some self-defense moves, both physical and mental. He wants her to be prepared to defend herself if anything should happen while he wasn't with her. Though she would have guards he didn't want her to only depend on them to protect her.

When they get closer to Manchon, they review everything they went over the previous week. Satisfied that she has everything well in hand, Logan contacts Manchon to let them know who they are and when they will be arriving. They wouldn't want the planet's defense system targeting them. He begins the communication in Majichonie giving his status to the controller.

"Resser ketect purs resser dala Torian. Kete fants Tanian Niccara doli Kazita Catived Royanna." ("Royal messenger of the royal son Thayer. Message for Queen Niccara and Grand Master Royanna.")

"Time of landing?" the communications officer asks him.

"Approximately eighteen and a half hours."

"We will inform the Queen and the Grand Master of your arrival. Who is the messenger?"

"Logan Thurda Knightrunner, private bodyguard to his royal Highness Prince Thayer Robus Starhawk of Manchon, King of the planet Calidon."

"Very well Lord Knightrunner. We will inform them and your family of your arrival. I am sure that they will all be happy to see you again sir." the officer tells him.

"Thank you. Manchon runner X2598 out." Logan shuts off the communicator and turns to Cassie as she enters the pilot's cabin. "Got everything packed away love?"

"Yeah. It's incredible how much that bag Leyla gave me can hold. I got all of my things and all of yours into it without any trouble." she tells him in amazement.

"It must be one of those new stretch bags. They're suppose to be able to stretch to four times their normal size."

"Well they do." She sits down on his lap. "How long before we reach Manchon?"

"A little over eighteen hours. You ready for something to eat? It's been a while since we had anything to eat."

"Not really. There is something else that I'm ready for though." she pulls his head closer and whispers into his ear. "Think we have time for that?" she asks sitting up.

"Oh, I think that we can spare the time." Logan grins at her and runs his hand up her leg.

Cassie returns the grin and then stands up and takes his hand. She pulls him up and leads him out of the pilot's cabin, and down to their sleeping cabin.

When the time finally arrives for them to prepare for the landing, Logan calls out to Cassie. "We'll be landing in fifteen minutes Cassie. Come in here after you put the bag by the door. I want you to see Manchon before we break atmosphere."

Within moments Cassie joins him and gasps at the sight on the front screen. Manchon has clear skies of the palest blue that she had ever seen, while the rivers and larger bodies of water appear to be a light and medium shade of purple. Logan explains that because of the mineral content in the rocks and soil, the waters only appear to be purple, when they're actually a brilliant blue.

"It's beautiful Logan. I can't see how you could have willingly left this." she says in complete awe of its beauty.

"It wasn't easy, but my place was to be always with Thayer." he tells her looking at his home world. "I've been Thayer's bodyguard since he was twelve and I was fifteen. I was given the choice of staying here or going with him. He's always been like a brother to me and the choice was easy. Except for my training with the Federation of Planets, I've always been near for him. If this business with the Alliance wasn't so important to all of us, we'd be back on Earth with him and Leyla right now."

"My father would have liked it if we had stayed on Earth." Cassie says softly, as she remembers her father's objections to her leaving so soon after his release. She had been a little hurt at first that he hadn't seemed to understand her need to be with Logan.

"But why do you have to go? Knightrunner can take care of setting up the link and Leyla can send one of her people to represent their interest."

"That's true Da, but I want to go. I want to be with Logan, to see his home. You can understand that Da."

Denral looks at his oldest child and sees the pleading in her eyes for him to understand her need. "He's the one, isn't he?"

"Yes he is Da. As soon as everything is set up, we plan to be lifemated." she sees the pain and fear in his eyes. "It will be fine Da. Leyla says that Logan and I are totally compatible, and Thayer agrees. You know that they would never let me do anything that might cause me harm. Thayer even plans to arrange for you and the others to be brought to Manchon for the ceremony."

"But you'll be so far away lass. Can't you wait here for him? Surely he can understand us wanting to be together after our separation?"

"He does, but this is my choice Da. I have to be with him. Please don't make me choose between the two of you. I couldn't stand to lose either one of you. We'll be together again Da, I promise."

Denral notices that his continued objections to her leaving are causing her great pain and distress. "All right honey. You go with your chosen mate, but don't you go getting joined without your family being there."

"Thank you Da, I won't." she hugs and kisses him.

"You may want to sit down now Cassie, we'll be landing at the palace in a few minutes." Logan warns her noticing that she has drifted off.

Cassie shakes her head slightly, focusing on the screen before sitting down in the second pilot's seat. Watching their approach, she notices that the village of Mistrican surrounds and blends into the palace. It was hard to tell exactly where the one ends and the other begins. They head for an open area on the northwest side of the palace gardens, where five other ships are sitting. Three runner ships and two A class cruisers. Logan sets them down near the two cruisers and shuts down the engines.

"Let's go, our escorts will be here in a few moments. If I'm not mistaken, we'll have a royal escort right to the Queen and Grand Master." he smiles at her as he stands up and offers his hand. "Except for greetings, don't talk to anyone or answer any questions until we're with Nicca and Royanna."

After pulling her to her feet, they walk to the door and Logan picks up the bag with their belongings, then opens the door. As they step off the ship, four guards walk around the rear of the ship.

"Valma Logan."

"Thank you Sheyome. It's good to be home." He shakes hands with the front guard. "Prince Thayer sends his love to his godchild."

"Thank you Logan. Queen Niccara and Grand Master Royanna await you in the Queen's private audience chamber." Though she would like to ask him about the pale woman with him, Sheyome holds her tongue and leads them into and through the palace to where the Queen awaits.

Knocking on the door, Sheyome opens it when she hears the Queen call out. She steps in and announces, "Lord Logan Knightrunner and his companion." She steps aside for Logan and Cassie to enter the chamber.

Logan leads the way to where the Queen and Grand Master are seated, hiding his shock at the way Niccara looks. He places his right hand over his heart and bows to the Queen. "Your Majesty."

"Welcome home Logan." Nicca stands and steps away from her chair to place her hand on his head. "You need not bow to me Logan. We are old and close friends are we not?" Logan straightens up and smiles at her, still surprised at how fragile she looks.

"Thank you Majesty. May I present to you Cassandra Blackwood. She is here on behalf of your cousin Prince Thayer Robus Starhawk, who is now King of our sister planet Calidon."

Cassie holds her skirt with her left hand and places her right over her heart as she curtsies. "Gelnolous resser Tanian Niccara lubri remi calib Torian doli fab orma Tanian Leyla." (Greetings royal Queen Niccara from your cousin Thayer and his wife Queen Leyla.)

"Thank you for bringing his message to me. You are welcome here. This is my aunt, my cousin's mother, Royanna Rican-Starhawk." Nicca turns slightly and nods to her aunt. "She is also my chief advisor and our Grand Master Healer."

Royanna steps forward and kisses both of Cassie's cheeks. "Valma Cassandra Blackwood. May our home become your home."

"I'm sure that it will your Highness. Manchon is a very beautiful world, and I feel a sense of peace here that I have never felt at home on Earth." Cassie informs her quietly.

"Would you care to rest before we discuss the reasons for Logan's return home and your visit Miss Blackwood?" Nicca asks, stressing the word visit.

Cassie looks at the older woman and sees something in her eyes that she can't quite put her finger on. "Actually..." she begins only to be stopped short as Logan speaks over her objections.

"Actually Nicca, that would be a good idea. This is Cassie's first trip off Earth, and we just spent two weeks in space. Not to mention what we went through prior to our trip here." Logan cuts in. *'Don't argue about it Cassie. Something isn't quite right with Nicca. I want to find out what's wrong with her before we discuss too much about the Alliance.'*

"Yes, my legs are feeling a little shaky, and I'm feeling a little light headed." Cassie agrees.

"Fine, I'll have one of the maids show you to the chamber you'll be using." Nicca mentally calls one of the maids. "Logan, your private chambers have been aired out and prepared for you already." she tells him with a smile.

"That was very thoughtful of you Nicca, but a separate room for Cassie won't be necessary. She'll be staying with me." Logan tells her smiling down at Cassie who is looking up at him. Both miss the look of anger that passes over the Queen's features.

Royanna sees it though, and frowns slightly, knowing that it was not a good sign.

Just then one of the inner chamber doors opens as there's a knock at the outer door. Sheyome opens the outer door as Nicca turns to the young man entering through the other door. "Yes Daemon, what is it?" she snaps startling the young man.

"Sorry to interrupt atma, but the Minister of Justice says that he must speak to you most urgently." Daemon Heorte apologizes looking first at Logan and Cassie, before resting his eyes lovingly on the Queen.

"Very well Daemon." Nicca says to him with only a trace of irritation, before turning back to the others. "Business calls. Truloka will be your personal maid Miss Blackwood. Now if you will all excuse me." With that she quickly turns back to Daemon and they leave the room followed closely by a man that steps out of the shadows at one corner of the room.

Logan opens his mouth to speak, but is stopped by a shake of Royanna's head. *'Say nothing here. We will talk in your chambers.'* she tells him mentally.

Logan nods. "Truloka, Miss Blackwood will be staying with me in my private chambers, so we'll arrange a small chamber for your use in my suite. All right?"

"Yes my Lord." Truloka agrees quietly.

"I'll come with you and you can tell me more about my son and his mate." Royanna tells them as they head towards the door. "Your father and sister will see you at your welcome home celebration this evening. Chevala had to go to the edge of the village for a consultation and your father decided to visit old Roushta, since he's in the area where Chevala is visiting."

"No doubt he also wants to keep an eye on her and all the young men that usually follow close behind her wherever she goes." Logan says with a laugh.

"True. It also doesn't help your father's peace of mind that someone let it out that your sister is still a maiden. He fears that one of her suitors may try to force their attentions on her." Royanna says with a sigh.

Logan frowns at this information as he leads the way through the corridors to his suite. After he opens the door, he dismisses Sheyome and the other guards. "I'll talk with you later Sheyome. I have a private message for you from Thayer."

Sheyome nods and signals the others to depart. "Until then Logan. My Lady Royanna, Mistress Blackwood."

"Please call me Cassie."

"Thank you Mistress Cassie." she bows to all three before leaving them.

Logan allows the ladies to enter first before following and closing the door. "Truloka, will you take our bag into the sleeping chamber? There is a small chamber across from it that will be yours. When you've put the bag in our chamber, go and gather your belongings and bring them here."

"Yes my Lord." Truloka looks at Royanna who nods to her. "My Lord, I have a small child. May I bring her here also?"

"Of course you can. I have no objections. Cassie?" he looks at her.

"Yes, bring your daughter Truloka. It will be nice to have a child around." and she smiles at the younger woman.

"Thank you my Lord, Mistress." she takes the bag to the sleeping chamber and then comes back out. "Did you wish for me to unpack for you Mistress?"

"No, that's all right Truloka. You go and get your daughter and things. I'll take care of our things." Truloka curtsies and leaves, closing the door very quietly behind her.

"Why don't we sit down?" Logan suggests and indicates the sitting area. "Can I get either of you something to drink?" he asks after Cassie and Royanna are seated and he walks over to the small drinks counter.

"I'll have a glass of fruit juice Logan."

"I will too." Cassie agrees smiling up at Logan. He smiles back and pours out the drinks.

"So Miss Blackwood, what exactly is your relationship to my son and his mate?" Royanna asks after seeing the loving exchange between this woman and her dearest friend's son.

"Please call me Cassie. Leyla and I were raised together, and our families have always been close. We consider each others parents as aunts and uncles." She smiles up at Logan again as he hands her a glass. "Leyla and Thayer met almost three years ago I think it was. He gave her a lecture on voicing her opinions about Earth's politics in public. Not long after that, they started dating." she stops to sip at her juice.

"What type of woman is your friend?" Royanna asks also sipping at her juice.

"Leyla is a very loving and caring person. She'll help anyone that truly needs it. Over the years, she has helped several telepaths learn to control and improve their abilities. My family has always known about our own abilities. We're all twins, but until a few years ago, we could only use them with our own twin and once in a while with others in our family. Leyla has taught all of us to communicate with other telepaths as well as use our other abilities."

"And what do you think of her Logan?" Royanna asks turning to look at him.

"She's everything that Thayer needs in his life. Leyla has always accepted him for himself, nothing more. His psi has even gone up since their joining." he tells her with pride in his friends accomplishments. "They've adopted a young Calidonian girl who was in danger when they first arrived on Calidon. Salis bonded with both of them immediately, and Thayer is very proud of her."

"Have you met her?" When Logan nods Royanna asks to see her. Logan opens that part of his mind to her, and after a few moments she sits back and smiles at him and Cassie. "Yes, he has every right to be proud of her. Both she and Leyla are very beautiful. I look forward to meeting them both one day soon."

"Royanna, I must ask you. What's wrong with Nicca? I feel that something isn't right with her. There's a, I don't know, a type of evil presence that seems to surround her."

Royanna shakes her head and sets down her glass. "I don't know what it is Logan. Since Drogen Firnap showed up, it seems as though her whole personality has undergone a drastic change."

"Who is this Drogen Firnap?" Logan asks with a frown. Before Royanna answers, Cassie excuses herself to put away their things, sensing that this part of their conversation is not really something that she should hear right now. As soon as she's gone Royanna answers his question.

"We're not really sure. He just appeared about two years ago. He introduced himself to Nicca and she accepted him right away." Royanna shakes her head. "Since then, I've noticed that her biorhythms have been changing. In the past few months the change has been even more noticeable, as has her emotional swings. Even Daemon Heorte her consort, has felt the change. He still plans to lifemate with her, but I don't think it a wise idea right now."

"Do you think that she's capable of making this decision concerning the Alliance?" he asks knowing that Thayer has already told his mother the basics of the Alliance.

"Right now, yes. But in a few months, who's to know." She closes her eyes as one of her assistants contacts her. Just as she opens them again, Cassie returns. "I have to go now. One of the stable boys has gone and gotten himself kicked in the side. I'll see the two of you later at the celebration." she says standing.

"All right Royanna. I'll fill Cassie in on what you've told me." they walk her to the door. His concern for Nicca has grown greatly in the past few minutes, and he wonders if Royanna was right to continue to trust her judgment.

CHAPTER TWO

Thurda Knightrunner is sitting in his friend Roushta Barbertin's parlor discussing the latest findings on Avdacal, Manchon's largest jungle moon. "The creatures are highly aggressive, and show some signs of human intelligence." Roushta tells him as they sip their flincen drinks.

"But where did they come from Roush? Until almost three years ago, we never saw these creatures. Nicca went to Avdacal not long before she was crowned and never saw them." Thurda points out.

"I know. It's like they just came into existence." Roushta agrees shaking his head. "Wherever they've come from, they've started to breed. Pertela counted at least twenty young."

"Were they able to capture any this time?"

"Yes, an older male and female just before the end of the mission, which came to an end a little over a week ago if I remember correctly. They seemed to try to speak, but Pertela said that their tongues are slightly forked and it was hard to try and understand what they were saying or trying to say. She said that the female cried, and that when it did it sounded almost human. When they went to sedate the creatures to calm them, they became agitated and started to change somehow right in front of them. They quickly gave the sedative and the creatures bodies almost instantly burst into flames. Nothing was left to be examined, and no one could pick up any sign of an essence release. Everything releases it's essence when it passes over."

"That is strange. What about the botanists that we had up there? Did they find any signs of them?"

"No, not even a piece of equipment could be found. It was like they'd never even been there. Tholton seems to think that the creatures may have in some way had something to do with their disappearance."

"How so? If they were responsible, then the equipment would still be there or some place that we could trace them to." Thurda points out reasonably.

"Yes, yes, but what other explanation is there? No ship has been reported there since the supply ship that took them new supplies."

"Yes, and what about that? The pilot said that someone or something attempted to wave him off as he was landing. Then when he and his crew unloaded the supplies, they were attacked by what they thought were the botanists who were growling and snarling like wild beasts." Thurda reminds him, still unable to believe the pilot's account of what happened.

"I've been wondering about that too. Until we know what happened to them and more about these creatures, no one will be allowed to stay on Avdacal for more than forty-eight hours. If that long." Roushta tells him. "We'll keep sending out groups every two weeks to check on these creatures, but I think its safer that they don't stay there any longer than two days."

"I agree, that would be wisest." Just then there's a knock at the front door and Chevala enters and shortly joins them.

"Good afternoon Roushta." she says kissing her father's friend on the cheek and then her father's. "I hope that you two are all finished, because I'm here to snatch my father away from you." She tells them smiling down at both of them. Whatever they had been discussing had bothered both men considerably. She had felt their unease when she entered the house.

"We're done my dear." Roushta tells her, feeling his cheeks redden at her show of affection. "We've just been going over the Avdacal reports that Pertela and Tholton brought me earlier."

"Good." Chevala looks at her father. "Royanna just contacted me. Logan's arrived and is in his suite at the palace. She's told him that we'd see him at the celebration this evening, so we'd better head home and get ready." She looks back at Roushta. "You are coming tonight aren't you?"

"Of course I am. I wouldn't miss my godson's homecoming celebration for all the flincen on Manchon."

They all laugh knowing that Roushta only drinks the light alcoholic beverage occasionally, and then only when he was with friends. Thurda and Chevala say their good-byes and head for their home nearer to the palace.

⁓

"I don't know Logan. It doesn't feel right to me." Cassie says as she finishes getting ready for the night's celebration of Logan's return home. "What if her emotional swings interferes with the Alliance? It could very well endanger all of us with the Federation. We're going to have a hard enough time getting them to accept the Alliance without having to worry about Nicca instigating some type of confrontation."

"It won't come to that sweetheart. If it looks like she's losing control, Royanna will take over the seat of power." Logan assures her, coming up behind her, he hooks up her necklace for her and then wraps his arms around her waist. "Chevala would then take over more of the duties of the Grand Master Healer, though she hasn't reached that level in her training. She's as close as anyone to taking over that position."

Cassie leans back against him and looks at their reflection in the mirror. "All right, but it still doesn't feel right. I have the feeling that something's going to happen. Something bad."

"We'll handle whatever comes sweetheart. Trust me." he kisses the side of her neck.

"Mm...you know that I do Logan." she murmurs as she tilts her head more to the side for his kisses.

Logan turns her to face him and takes her mouth to kiss her deeply. Cassie runs her hands over his back, pulling him closer to her. Logan releases her lips and hugs her tightly to him. "I wish that we didn't have to go to this thing tonight. I'd much rather stay here and keep you all to myself in our bed." he tells her with a growl, and nipping at her neck gently with his teeth.

"Me too love, but we have to go." Cassie tells him giving him one last lingering kiss before stepping out of his arms. "Besides, I want to meet your family and friends."

"Well you're definitely going to do that. Come on before I say to hell with it and take you to bed anyway." He takes her hand and pulls her out of their sleeping chamber. As they enter the sitting room, Truloka is chasing her three year old daughter around the room.

"Kimtala, you bring that back here right now." she calls out laughing as her precocious daughter squeals and jumps out of reach, putting her snatched feather duster on top of her head. As she runs past Logan and Cassie, Logan reaches out and snags her under the arms.

"What's this, a new kind of bird?" he asks running his fingers up and down her ribs, causing the child to squeal and wriggle in his arms. "It sure sounds like a bird."

Kimtala catches her breath and says in a high pitch, "No bird! Kimtala."

"Oh no. You can't be Kimtala, she doesn't have feathers, and you do." he tells her, winking at Truloka.

"Kimtala no ga feathers. Momma's duser." she tells Logan pulling the duster from her head with a grin and showing it to him. "See, duser." she says and then proceeds to dust Logan's face with it.

Cassie laughs and Truloka quickly grabs the duster from her daughter's hand. Kimtala looks at Logan in surprise as if to say 'Where'd it go?'. Logan laughs and hands her over to her mother.

"That will teach me to argue with a three year old with a weapon handy." Logan says ruefully, wiping a hand over his face.

"I'm so sorry my Lord. She decided to play keep away with it." Truloka says turning slightly red in the face at her daughter's antics.

"Don't worry about it Tru. He needed a good dusting off." Cassie says with a laugh and Logan sends her a disgusted look.

"I'll remember that the next time I have a duster handy." he threatens and Cassie sticks her tongue out at him before turning back to Truloka.

"Since we don't know when the celebration will be over Tru, you can have the rest of the night to yourself."

"Thank you Mistress Cassie." Truloka says with a curtsy.

"Yes, you can either come to the celebration, or go and visit with your family or friends." Logan tells her taking Cassie's arm and leading her to the door.

"Thank you my Lord. I will take Kimtala and go visit my mother and sisters." She informs him graciously.

Logan nods and leads Cassie from the room. As the door closes behind them, Sheyome and the three other guards step forward. They all bow and then Sheyome takes another step forward.

"My Lord, Mistress. we're to act as your personal guard from now on." she informs them. "The Queen feels that until everyone becomes used to your presence amongst us again, we should stay close by."

"Though I don't feel that it's necessary, I'll agree to it for now Sheyome. I would rather you and the others concentrate your protection on Cassie rather then me though. Her abilities aren't yet quite strong enough for her to totally defend herself."

"Of course my Lord. We'll take you to the banquet hall now." She signals the others to take their positions, and then takes her own position and leads the way.

"I don't know if I like the idea of being surround by guards all the time Logan." Cassie whispers to him looking over her shoulder at the two rear guards. "Wouldn't just one or two be enough?"

"Maybe in time Cassie, but right now they're necessary. They won't be with us all the time love, just when we're out in public." he assures her. "If I know Sheyome, most of the time that they are with us, you won't even know that they're around, unless of course something happens." he says looking over at Sheyome for confirmation.

"That's completely true Mistress Cassie. Unless I feel that it's necessary, neither you nor anyone else will know that we're anywhere near." she agrees.

Cassie gives her a weak smile and hugs Logan's arm tighter to her side. Her sense of danger increasing greatly. She tries to shake the feeling, but it stays with her as they reach the banquet hall. Sheyome leads them straight to the Queen's side, and then she and the guards disappear into the crowd watching everyone and still keeping their eyes on Logan and Cassie. None of them would be too far from either of them should they be needed.

Logan bows and Cassie curtsies, then Nicca signals them to her left side before signaling for silence. The room slowly grows quiet, and then Nicca rises from her throne.

"We have gathered here this night to welcome home Logan Thurda Knightrunner. He returns to us after following and protecting my cousin Prince Thayer for the past fifteen years on Earth. His duty to my cousin is now ended, and we celebrate his homecoming."

Cheers go up around the hall and after a few seconds, Logan steps forward and holds up his hands for silence so that he can make an announcement. Once it quiets down again, he looks around the hall. "Thank you all for this warm welcome, but it is not all that we have to celebrate. Three moon cycles ago, Prince Thayer was lifemated as you all may already know. What you may not know, is that he is now King of our sister world Calidon. He is also now the epitome of his name, he is the Starhawk. His bride and Queen is the FIRESTAR of ancient legend come to life. Peace is once more upon us."

More cheers go up and Logan smiles at those around him and notices the shock on Nicca's face, and the joy on Royanna's. He holds up his hands once again and has to wait several minutes for the people to quiet down again. "I now wish to introduce to you all Cassandra Blackwood, close personal friend to Prince Thayer and his Queen wife Leyla Aeneka Latona. She is here to represent them in setting up a link for Manchon to join a Telepathic Alliance with other planets with our same abilities." He watches as everyone nods their approval and looks Cassie over. "She is also very special to me, and has agreed to become my lifemate once Manchon is established as part of the Alliance." he smiles down at her, sure that he had surprised her with his announcement.

Cheers can be heard once again as Cassie blushes looking up at him. She had not expected him to mention their engagement until later on, and then to his family first. They once again miss the Queen's show of anger, but Royanna and Daemon Heorte do not. Neither does Drogen Firnap.

"On with the celebration!" Nicca calls out. Music starts up and acrobats start performing around the hall. "This is becoming more and more irritating by the minute." Nicca says louder then she intended.

Logan hears the frost in her voice and turns to look at her. She smiles at him slightly, and then turns to Drogen Firnap who has just stepped up next to her. He whispers something in her ear and she bites her lip, before shaking her head. He frowns at her and steps back into the shadows.

"If you'll excuse us your Majesty, I'd like to introduce Cassie to my father and sister."

"Of course Logan. You're seated at table to my left. The meal will be served in exactly one hour." She nods to Cassie and then returns to her throne with Daemon at her side. Drogen stands a couple of feet behind the throne.

"Come on Cassie, I think I saw Chevala standing over near the juice bar." He takes her hand and leads her through the crowd of well wishers. She shivers a little, sure that whatever Drogen had said to the Queen, had to do with her.

As they near the juice bar area, a woman with light brown hair rushes forward and throws herself at Logan, who catches her and swings her around. They hug each other and laugh before Logan sets her back on her feet. "That was some greeting from an old girl like you Chevala." His sister glares at him, but Logan only smiles and adds, "And you're still very beautiful, and a sight for sore eyes."

"I'll give you old you...you...you crazy idiot." she laughs even as she punches him in the arm, then hugs him again. "Welcome home little brother."

"Thanks sis. It's good to be back." He looks around. "Where's father? I didn't see him earlier."

"He's around here somewhere. I think he went to find Roushta. We were both shocked by your announcement little brother. Especially since we had no idea you were going to be making it." She looks pointedly around him to where Cassie is waiting patiently. Logan quickly drops his arms from his sister's waist and spins around to face Cassie. He holds out his hand to her and she takes it.

"I'm sorry love. With the excitement and..."

"It's all right darling, I understand." she smiles up at him and reaches up to smooth the frown from his brow. "It's all right. If you remember, I did the same thing when Da was brought back to us." she reminds him.

"Okay sweetheart." he turns back to his sister with Cassie now close to his side. "Chevala, this is my chosen one, Cassandra Blackwood. Cassie, my sister Chevala." He watches them both closely hoping that his instincts that they will be close is right.

They look at each other for several long seconds and then Chevala steps forward and hugs Cassie. "Welcome home sister."

Tears come to Cassie's eyes as she hugs Chevala back. "Thank you sister." They pull apart and smile at each other. Just then, two older men join them, one with silver hair and mustache and Logan's facial features, only a little softer. The other has light brown hair speckled with gray and soft green eyes.

"Logan!" Thurda says roughly.

"Father." The two men hug and pat each other on the back, then step back a pace.

"Welcome home son." Thurda says shaking his head and looking up slightly into his son's face. "You sure have grown." Everyone laughs since when he had left Logan was already three inches taller then his father.

Roushta steps forward. "How about a Hello for your favorite godparent?" he says smiling up at the tall young man that use to follow him around when he was a lot shorter and a lot younger.

"My only godparent." Logan says giving him a bear hug. "How are you, you old screecat?"

"Fine, fine. Good to have you home again boy. And with such a beautiful young girl on your arm too."

Once again Logan spins around to Cassie, only to find her and Chevala smiling indulgently at him. He feels his face getting warm and holds out his hand to her again.

"You better watch it Cassie, it looks like its becoming a habit of him forgetting you're near." Chevala tells her jokingly, not knowing that this second forgetting of her presence in as many minutes, has disturbed Cassie more than she wants it to.

Logan frowns at his sister, and then pulls Cassie in front of him and wraps his arms around her waist. "That's the last time it's going to happen Chevala." He smiles down at Cassie, then introduces her to his father and Roushta. "Father, Roushta, this is Cassandra Blackwood, light of my heart and soul. Cassie, my father Thurda and my godfather Roushta Barbertin. Both taught me what it's like to love and cherish only one woman."

Cassie steps forward and hugs both men in greeting before stepping back into Logan's embrace. She wonders about the slight frown on Thurda's brow, and the look he exchanges with Roushta and Chevala. Soon they're joined by Royanna and Logan begins to tell them of his life on Earth. Watching the people closest to Logan, Cassie sees the love and worry they all go through as he tells his story. She also sees the love between his father and Royanna. Though nothing has been said, she knows that soon Logan will have to deal with the fact that his father now loves and cherishes another woman. Though it may be hard she believes that he will be better able to accept their relationship after what had gone between him and Hillary. Though he cared for the other woman, it did not take away from his feelings for her. He would understand that his father's new relationship with Royanna wouldn't detract from Thurda's feelings for Logan's mother.

When the gong sounds, Logan leads Cassie to the Queen's table. As they reach it Nicca waves her hand to the right. "We've placed Miss Blackwood on the other side of Daemon, Logan. This will give her a chance to speak with my aunt about Thayer and his new bride."

Logan looks at Nicca for several seconds, and then bows slightly before leading Cassie to her seat. Before seating her he turns her to face him. "Are you all right with this love? If not I could insist..."

"No, I'll be fine Logan. As it happens I have some things to tell Royanna for Leyla." she smiles up at him. "Besides, I'll have you all to myself later on, and we don't want to offend the Queen."

'It's she who's doing the offending by separating us after our betrothal announcement.' he tells her with a mental frown.

'That may be, but two wrongs won't make it right. Now kiss me, seat me, and go sit down in the place of honor.' she tells him lifting her lips to him to kiss.

Logan kisses her deeply, and then pulls out her chair for her. He places his hand on her shoulder before going to the Queen's left and taking his seat.

Nicca nods and the servants start to bring out the platters of food and beverages. After plates are filled, Nicca signals Daemon to make the opening toast. He stands with glass in hand.

"Logan Knightrunner, on behalf of her Majesty, Queen Niccara Mistara Rican, I toast your home coming and give you the title of Minister of Interplanetary Relations."

Cheers go up and Logan bows his head to both Nicca and Daemon, before standing. He picks up his glass to make his own toast. "To her Majesty, in her rule for the people and the signing of the Alliance agreement in the near future."

More cheers are heard, then everyone starts to eat and converse. Cassie comments on the foods to Royanna, and answer questions about her family and Earth from both Royanna and Daemon.

"I understand that you and Queen Nicca are to be lifemated in a few weeks." Cassie states to Daemon as Royanna is in conversation with the gentleman on her right.

"Yes, in three weeks. We've been planning the ceremony for the past two moon rises." he tells her with a wry grin. "Though I would prefer something somewhat smaller then what we're planning. Since Nicca is Queen, the ceremony must be befitting of that position." he says with a look at Nicca.

"Not to mention the position you will be undertaking when you become her lifemate. How do you feel about becoming King?"

Daemon frowns a little and looks down at his plate before answering. "I hope that I will be as good a King as Nicca is Queen. Though the position matters little to me, my love for Nicca is great. I know all will be well for us once we are lifemated."

"Daemon does not give himself much value as the next King, but he will make a good one." Royanna says leaning forward to smile at Daemon. "He has a very loving heart and is a very compassionate person Cassie. He's also been in love with Nicca since he was about sixteen or seventeen."

Daemon blushes and looks over at Nicca. He frowns when he sees her once again in deep conversation with Logan and leaning towards him intimately. Turning back to his plate, he tries to calm his jealousy towards the other man.

After the meal, there's dancing and as guest of honor Logan is obliged to dance the first dance with the Queen. Once they've gone around the floor once Daemon leads Cassie out onto the floor. Soon others join the two couples on the dance floor, keeping well away, so as not to bump into either couple. Nicca uses this time to have a private conversation with Logan.

"I've missed you atmo. I'm so glad that you're back. Things have been happening around here that I think you can handle better than Daemon."

"I've missed you too Nicca, but I think that you're selling Daemon short. He's been your consort for what? About three years now. How much authority have you given him? Do you let him make any important decisions?" Logan asks.

Nicca stares at his chest for several seconds before answering. "No. He's only my consort after all. Besides, he's too young to..."

"Your mother was a consort and younger than you, but your father allowed her the authority to make decisions for both his household and the people. How can you treat Daemon with less respect then your father gave your mother? Especially since he's going to be your lifemate?"

Logan watches the anger and confusion cross her face at his words. She stops dancing and looks up at him. "Maybe I won't take him as my lifemate then." she states and then turns away only to come to a stop when she sees Daemon close by looking at her with his face white and his hurt showing in his eyes. "Daemon, I..."

"Definitely not here, and definitely not now your Majesty." Daemon tells her between clinched teeth, holding out his arm to her. "Your sister Tacara just arrived and wishes to speak with you."

"All right Daemon." she takes his arm and looks at him once more before looking at Logan again. "If I don't see you before the end of the evening, good night and once again, welcome home."

Logan bows to them and as they turn away, Cassie steps to his side. "She hurt him greatly with her words Logan."

"I know love." he takes her in his arms and begins to dance. "She knows it too."

"But why would she say such a thing? From what Royanna said at the table, Daemon has been in love with Nicca for eight or nine years now. Why would she even think such a thing, let alone say it knowing that?" Cassie wonders with confusion and hurt for the young man who has shown her nothing but kindness.

"I don't know sweetheart. For some reason she's confused and uncertain. There's something going on in her mind that doesn't make sense. I gently touched her mind earlier, and it was like there were two minds inside her head." he tells her.

The music ends and they leave the dance area to get something to drink. They stop and talk to some of Logan's friends and then join Chevala and Royanna near the juice bar where the two are quietly talking together.

"Logan, what's wrong with Nicca? She had the strangest look on her face a few minutes ago when she was speaking to her sister." Chevala asks handing Cassie a glass of juice.

"She said something she shouldn't have, and Daemon overheard her and was hurt by it. Right now she's feeling guilty about it, and for hurting him." Logan tells them sipping at his own drink.

"Not again." Royanna sighs, frowning as she looks over to where Nicca and Daemon are standing talking to a couple of lesser lords. "I hope that it wasn't as bad as when she called him a ketedt dai (messenger boy) when she was in a council meeting and he brought her a message from Lady Corpora."

"I'm afraid that it's a lot worse than that Royanna." Cassie says sadly looking at the royal couple and then back to Royanna and Chevala. "She said she may not take him as her lifemate."

Both Chevala and Royanna look at her in shock before letting out collective groans and Royanna shakes her head. "I thought this might happen with your return Logan, but not this soon. I also hoped that her love for Daemon would be stronger than her obsession with you."

"Surely she wouldn't try going after Logan knowing that he and I are to be lifemated?" Cassie asks her in shock.

"Who's to know what she'll do?" Chevala puts in looking kindly at the younger woman. "She's been doing things totally against her true nature in the past few months."

Logan listens, watching Nicca and Daemon with a frown. "I think we need to keep a close eye on any decisions she makes in the future. Something is definitely wrong inside her." he tells them. "They're leaving now. Chevala, would you and father join us in our suite first thing in the morning? You also Royanna. We need to discuss this more, but somewhere more private than a hall full of people."

"All right Logan. I'll go find father and let him know. We'll see you in the morning." Chevala kisses him and then Cassie on the cheek. "Good night."

"Good night Chevala."

"I'll say good night as well. I have some patients to see before I turn in. I'll see you both in the morning."

"Good night Royanna, pleasant sleep." Logan tells her and kisses her cheek in parting. Cassie does also and then watches as the older woman weaves her way through the crowded room.

"Let's have one more dance and then we'll call it a night." Logan takes Cassie's hand and leads her back onto the dance floor. "Though this has been a great welcome home, I've had enough of

27

crowds for one day." he pulls her closer. "Right now I just want to be alone with you in our chamber." They finish the dance and Logan lets Sheyome know that they're ready to go and that they'll meet her and the others by the doors.

* * *

"Daemon, I swear that I didn't mean it." Nicca says standing by her vanity wringing her hands. Daemon is standing at the window looking out into the night.

"I find that hard to believe Majesty. Since you said it with such strength and conviction to the man you've been obsessed with for the past fifteen years."

Nicca bites down hard on her bottom lip, drawing blood. Since knowing of Logan's return, her emotions have been in a state of confusion. She loves Daemon greatly, and knows he loves her just as much. Yet something inside of her wants Logan too. Walking over to Daemon, she gently touches his back. "Please don't be like this Daemon, atmo. I truly did not mean that I don't want you for my lifemate." She wraps her arms around his waist and lays her cheek against his back. "I love you more than life itself atmo. I would gladly give up the throne of power, if that's the only way that I can keep you with me."

Daemon turns within her arms and looks deep into her eyes for the truth. He can see that she does regret her words, that she would give up the throne for him. He puts his arms around her. "I believe you atma, but you must believe this. If you ever do or say anything that will hurt or disgrace me again, I will leave you." He looks at her and gives her a not so gentle shake. "Do you understand?"

She looks at him and realizes that he means every word he's saying. "Yes Daemon, I understand."

"Good, now let's go to bed." He releases her and goes to his side of the bed and removes his robe, laying it across the foot before climbing in. He notices Nicca still standing where he had left her. "Come to bed Nicca. We'll not think of it anymore tonight." Nicca walks to the bed and removes her robe, then climbs in beside him. Daemon takes her into his arms and pulls her tightly against his body.

⟋

"What do you think happened with Nicca and Daemon after they left the hall?" Cassie asks as she gets ready for bed.

"Hopefully she was smart enough to explain and apologize. There's no way she could have missed the hurt her thoughtless words caused him." Logan removes her necklace.

"Are you going to mention to Royanna about the second mind you might have felt?" she asks as she steps away and pulls off her dress, laying it over a chair.

"Mm...yes. I'll suggest that she insist on giving her a full mental as well as a physical exam, in a few days." He finishes removing his own clothes and wraps his arms around her waist, pulling her against him. "That's enough talk about the Queen and her consort. Now I just want to concentrate on you and me and what we're going to do in that big soft bed over there."

Cassie smiles at their reflection in the mirror and then turns to face him. "And just what might that be?" she asks innocently knowing that she will only provoke him to a greater need with her words and her act of innocence. Logan picks her up and she squeals. "As if you didn't know." He carries her to the bed and falls onto it with her still in his arms. He turns so that she lands on top of him and moves his hands to her buttocks. "And if you don't then now you do." he gives her a squeeze drawing her closer.

Cassie moans and pushes against him, trailing her fingers up his chest and shoulders, and into his hair. Logan removes her panties and flips over on top of her. He kisses her deeply even as he penetrates her feminine lips. With a groan, he captures her hips to keep her still. After a few moments he begins to move within her and Cassie moans pushing up to him. They find their rhythm and slowly Logan increases his movements. As they reach their peak, Cassie lets out a keening type of cry, almost that of a bird in victory, and Logan gives a shout of release. He collapses onto her, but is careful to keep most of his weight on his arms.

After a couple of minutes, he slowly pulls out of her and moves to her side, pulling her close. He sets her comfortably on his shoulder and kisses the top of her head. Using his telekinesis, he turns out the lights. Cassie kisses his chest, and wraps her arm around his waist, before drifting off to sleep with a smile on her lips.

CHAPTER THREE

"Tru, we'll be having guests for the morning meal. Have cook send enough food for five please." Cassie asks arranging the flowers that Truloka brought to her earlier.

"Yes Mistress Cassie. Would you like anything special?" she asks setting the table with extra place-mats.

"I'm not really sure. Do you know of anything special that Lady Royanna and Lady Chevala would prefer? Or Lord Thurda?"

"The Ladies prefer fruits and Lord Thurda...well, he'll eat just about anything from Cook's kitchen."

"All right then, order enough fruit for everyone, and have cook add something more for Lord Thurda and Logan." Cassie tells her stepping back to examine the flowers. "Oh, and make sure that you get enough for yourself and Kimtala."

"Yes Mistress." Truloka goes to check that Kimtala is still asleep, before leaving to get the food.

Logan comes out of the bed chamber tucking in his shirt. He looks around at the room. "How long have you been up?" he asks kissing her and nibbling at her lower lip having missed waking with her in his arms.

"Mm...about an hour or so. I wanted to fix up the room a little and Tru found me some flowers to arrange. How does it look?"

"It looks great sweetheart. Where are Tru and Kimtala?"

"Tru went to order breakfast, and Kim is still sleeping."

"Did you order fruit? I forgot to tell you that my sister and Royanna only eat fruit and vegetables. None of the strong healers eat meat of any kind."

"Tru is taking care of everything. I told her to get enough fruit for everyone, and to have Cook add something more substantial for you and your father."

There is a knock on the door, and Logan goes to open it. Chevala and his father come in and they all hug in welcome. Before Logan can close the door, Royanna arrives. Greetings are said all around and then Logan directs everyone to the sitting area.

"Truloka is getting the food now, so she should be back in about fifteen minutes." Cassie tells them as she carries over a tray of juice and hands everyone a glass.

"So, what are we here to discuss son?" Thurda asks after taking a sip of his juice.

"Like I told Chevala and Royanna, we need to keep a closer watch on all of the decisions that Nicca is making father. From what they have said, and from what I myself have observed, there is definitely something wrong inside of her." Logan turns to Royanna. "I want you to insist upon a full mental and physical examination Royanna."

"For what purpose Logan?" she asks looking up at him.

"At the banquet last night, I lightly touched Nicca's mind. What I found leads me to believe that there is a second mind present. I want you to examine her and let me know what you find. If some other mind is now a part of her, we need to know where it came from, and what type of control it has over her."

Just then Truloka comes in with a floating tray bearing their breakfast. After placing the food on the table, she takes her and Kimtala's into their room and closes the door.

"Even if Royanna does find another mind present son, how are we to know where it came from or who's it is?" Thurda points out as he loads his plate after waiting for the women to get what they want.

"We'll have to take it one step at a time. Right now I'm just looking for confirmation on it's presence."

"If what you suspect is true Logan, I'll have to remove her from the throne of power." Royanna reminds him.

"Maybe not right away." Cassie says into the silence. "What I mean is, wouldn't it be better to leave her in control while we try to find out who or what is controlling her? From what I know of your family Royanna, whoever or whatever it is that's controlling Nicca has to be very strong mentally. We need to find this person or thing and somehow get it to release her."

Royanna nods her agreement. "Yes, anyone or anything strong enough to control a member of my family could be a danger to all of Manchon. It's better if we deal with this quickly. How soon do you want me to do the exam Logan?"

He finishes chewing before answering. "Let's wait a few days. We'll watch her and see what happens. I also need to know everything she's done and everywhere she's went over the past five years."

"That's going to be a little difficult little brother. We've got records for the past three years, since she became Queen, but before that?" Chevala shrugs her shoulders. "Nicca did a lot of roaming around during the two years before she became Queen. I think that she even spent a couple of weeks up on Avdacal the year before becoming Queen. Wasn't it father?"

"Yes, that's right." Thurda frowns and looks at his daughter for several seconds. "I maybe wrong, but I think we need to check Avdacal out more thoroughly." He goes on to explain the strange happenings and the creatures recently discovered on the moon.

"Once we've started the negotiations on the Alliance agreement, I want to fly out and check it over for myself." Logan says pouring himself some more juice.

"What will I be doing while you're away?" Cassie asks looking at him with a worried frown.

"You love, will continue the negotiations. Royanna and father will be there to lend you their support. As soon as I'm done looking around, I'll come and help you finish up." He assures her knowing how uncomfortable the politics of their lives made her.

Truloka's bedroom door slams open and Kimtala runs out. "Kimtala, come back here!" They hear Truloka call out.

Kimtala runs into the sitting room and comes to an abrupt stop when she sees all the people. When she hears her mother, she runs to Cassie and climbs into her lap.

"What are you up to little one? You playing chase with momma again?" Cassie smoothes the little girl's hair from her face.

"No more room Cassie?" Kimtala says looking up at her with a smile.

"Kimtala, shame on you." Truloka says stopping at Cassie's side.

"It's all right Tru, we're through with our discussion." Logan assures her. "Besides, she's right. No one likes to be stuck in their room first thing in the morning." He looks over at Kimtala snuggled up to Cassie's breast. "Isn't that right sweetie?" He smiles at the little girl.

"No good. No fun." Kimtala nods her head in agreement and smiles at him glad that he understood her not wanting to be shut up in her room again.

"We'll be going now." Thurda stands and wipes his mouth. "You can tell the council about this Alliance at this morning's meeting. It's scheduled to start in an hour." Chevala and Royanna stand and say their good-byes.

"We'll be there." Logan assures him following them to the door. He starts to close the door and then remembers the guards. "Sheyome."

Sheyome steps out of the shadows, "Yes my Lord?"

"We'll be going to the council meeting this morning."

34

"All right my Lord. We'll be ready." She steps back into the shadows and Logan closes the door.

Cassie bounces Kimtala on her lap and sings her a song she remembers her mother singing to her and her siblings when they were all little. Logan stands there and listens to her, while Truloka listens as she clears the table. Cassie finishes the song just as Truloka finishes the table. Cassie gives Kimtala a hug and then sets her on her feet.

"Now, you behave for your momma and when I get back, if it's all right with your momma, I'll take you for a walk in the garden. Okay?"

"Okay." Kimtala smiles up at her.

"I don't know Mistress Cassie." Truloka chews on her lower lip. "She can be a handful when she's outside."

"Me be good momma. Me be good." Kimtala says going over to her mother and looking up at her. "Please momma?"

"We'll see." Truloka sighs. "Would you like to help me take this back to the kitchen?"

"Yes, yes!" Kimtala jumps up and down then runs over to the food tray and tries to move it. Truloka laughs and shakes her head.

"I'll take the tray and you can open the doors for me."

After they leave, Logan takes Cassie into his arms and kisses her. Suddenly he picks her up and carries her into their room. Setting her on her feet he starts to undress her.

"Logan, what are you doing?" Cassie asks laughing against his lips as she lets him slip her dress down off her shoulders. "We have to be ready to leave in less then an hour."

"We have plenty of time sweetheart. Besides, you need to change your dress. Kimtala got some fruit juice on this one." He tells her as he finishes undressing her and starts on his own clothes.

"What's your excuse for undressing? You didn't even pick her up." She reminds him even as she helps him with his shirt and then his pants.

"I have to change into my Lordly robes."

"Mmm, good reason." They clasp each other and then collapse onto the bed.

Two hours later Cassie is addressing the council. "The point of the Telepathic Alliance is to join all telepathic people and planets, together as a type of watchdog over the Federation." She explains as she looks around at the men and women gathered in the council chamber. "Thayer and Leyla have the ability to unit all of us for the betterment of all life forms."

"What can you tell us about these other planets that will be a part of this Alliance?" One of the council women asks.

"Besides Calidon, there will be two others to join with us right now. They're Panthera and Aquila. The people are peaceful and very protective. The Pantherians are part human, part cat. The Aquilians are part human, part bird. In the past several years they have intermarried and become closer because of these marriages or joinings." Logan answers for her having expected this type of questioning and what would follow it.

"Are we also expected to intermarry with them as well?" Another councilman asks.

"It will not be a condition in the agreement, but neither will it be frowned upon if some should choose to do so." Cassie informs them. "By intermarrying, the Alliance can only be strengthened by such unions. Though it will be hard at first, everyone must accept the changes that are to come."

"You cannot force acceptance my Lady." Roushta warns her. "It is the surest way to cause hatred and discontent."

"No one will be forced to accept my Lord. Though would it not be better to accept, rather then to hate and mistrust? Where no one will be forced to accept, no one will be forced into not accepting either."

"What if a family doesn't wish such a union to take place? Are you saying that they must accept one of these...beings...as part of their family?"

"Only if they wish to keep in contact with whatever family member has made the union." Cassie points out gently. "What do you think will be more important? The family's prejudice against the chosen mate, or their love for the one who's choice it is?"

Murmurs go around the room as Cassie's point hits home. No one wanted to be estranged from their loved ones. Many had already indured such separations and it was painful for everyone not just the families affected. After several minutes, heads begin to nod in agreement.

"When will we be hearing from these other...people?" Nicca questions her. "Will they just show up unannounced, or will we have some warning?"

"As soon as Thayer and Leyla have established all of the details with the ruling families, all of you will decide on when and where you will meet. First we have to establish Manchon's agreement to join and then prepare any terms that you might wish to add to the Alliance. Everyone in the Alliance will have a voice that will be listened to."

"Why should we watch over the Federation? We've never had any trouble with them before. By doing this we'll only be irritating them and then we will have trouble with them."

"No, there won't be any trouble. According to their own bylaws, any group can ally themselves and monitor the Federation's activities, as long as they don't cause unrest amongst the other members of the Federation. Our Alliance will make sure that all life forms are treated fairly and not forced into joining the Federation for any reason. If any other telepaths are found, they will be given the opportunity to join us if they so choose. Over the years the Federation has manipulated many planets for their own gain. This has caused a lot of planets to become destitute because of the high membership costs. This in turn has caused the people of these worlds to sell themselves into service to feed and shelter their families." Logan tells them.

"The only worth our planets have for them, are our special abilities. We cannot allow them to get control over us or anyone like us. To do so would destroy any chances of peace we have." Cassie says with great conviction. Finished, she sits down and takes a drink from her glass of water.

Logan stands up to finish the discussion. "Now that you know the intentions of this Alliance, it is up to you and Queen Niccara to decide if Manchon will join and support the Alliance to the fullest, or be left on it's own." He looks around to all of the council members and then at Nicca. "Remember this when you make your decision. Not only are you protecting our people, but possibly protecting people that cannot protect themselves from being taken over." He warns them before sitting down and taking Cassie's hand in his, giving it a gentle squeeze. There was really nothing else that they could say to sway them to join.

"Thank you Lord Logan for your report." Murmurs start up at Nicca's slight to Cassie and her part in the meeting. Sensing the council's displeasure with her behavior, Nicca addresses Cassie. "Thank you also Mistress Blackwood for your insight into the problems our people may face with this new Alliance."

Lord Roushta clears his throat. "I think that we should break for the noon meal and come back to discuss this afterward your Majesty."

"Very well Lord Roushta. We will break for lunch and continue this discussion amongst ourselves in two hours." Nicca stands and the council stands with her. After she leaves the chamber, murmurs can be heard coming from the council members as they leave the council chambers.

Besides Cassie and Logan, Thurda, Roushta and Royanna stand waiting for the room to empty. When the others have left Logan opens his mouth to say something, thinking that they are alone, only to be stopped by Royanna's mind touch.

'Drogen Firnap is still in the room. He didn't not leave when Nicca did.'

'Where is he Royanna?' Logan asks stepping closer to the table and looking at his papers still spread out on the surface.

'Near the tapestry behind the high seat.'

While still looking at his notes, Logan begins a mind sweep as he picks up his note pad and turns to face the others. He lightly touches the other man's mind and picks up various images of people and some strange looking creatures. One of these creatures is large and golden in color. He pulls back carefully, stepping away from the table. "Let's go and eat. Knowing Nicca, she won't want too much and we'll be back here before the two hours she's given us." He holds out his arm to Cassie and leads her out of the room followed closely by the others.

As they walk from the room, Sheyome and the other guards take up their positions around them. Walking down the hall, Sheyome looks back as Drogen leaves the room. Their eyes meet for only a few moments, but it is enough to cause Sheyome to shiver and look quickly away.

Logan sees her shiver and looks back, seeing Firnap disappearing around a corner, then turns back and looks at Sheyome. *'We need to talk Sheyome.'*

She looks at him and then away again. *'What about my Lord?'*

'About why you're afraid of Drogen Firnap for one. What happened to your parents for another. I think that you know something, and that it's tearing you up inside.'

'You're wrong my Lord. I know nothing.'

'Don't lie to me Sheyome. I know you better then most, even though I've been gone these last fifteen years. You have nothing to fear from me Sheyome. Even though you're a Royal guard, until Thayer says otherwise, you're just as much under my protection as Cassie is.'

Sheyome looks at him and sees that he is totally serious. With her parents missing and Thayer not on Manchon, she is by law under the protection of anyone her guardian feels capable of serving in his stead. Who better for that then the man who has been with her guardian for the past fifteen years and has no doubt learned more than she can ever hope to know about protection in this life time. *'When do you wish to talk my Lord?'*

'*Later this afternoon in my chambers. And Sheyome...*' He waits until she turns her head slightly to look into his eyes. '*No more of this my Lord stuff all right? I'm starting to feel old before my time.*' He tells her with a grin hoping to bring her out of the pensive mood she has fallen into since seeing Firnap.

Sheyome smiles and nods her agreement. They both know that it will take time to break the habit of years of training.

"I'm sure Mistress Blackwood won't mind missing the afternoon session Logan. Will you Miss Blackwood? After all we'll only be going over what you've already covered." Nicca sips her wine and watches Cassie's face for a reaction.

Knowing that the queen has taken a personal dislike of her, Cassie doesn't let any emotion show on her face. "Not at all your Majesty. In fact I was just trying to think of a way to ask to be excused." She says smoothly. "I was thinking that a walk in the gardens might be nice. Besides, I promised Kimtala that if it wasn't too late when we finished, that I would take her out with me."

Nicca frowns at the quick acceptance, but then smiles and nods. "Yes, that sounds like a fine idea. The gardens are beautiful at this time of year." That taken care of Nicca turns her attention back to Logan.

'*Smooth save, Cassie my love.*'

'*Why thank you Logan my dear.*' They both try to hide grins trying to escape after their mental exchange.

Cassie communicates with Sheyome so that she knows of the new plans and then finishes her lunch.

CHAPTER FOUR

Cassie watches as Kimtala chases a butterfly around a rose bush and squeals with delight each time it lands and then pouts when it takes off again.

"Sheyome, what can you tell me about Daemon Heorte?" She asks looking over at the woman walking beside her.

"He loves the Queen greatly, and tries to smooth things over when she insults or offends someone. Though we all know that she loves him, in the past few months she's been treating him badly."

"How do you think he'll do as King?"

"Daemon will be a good King Cassie. He has all the qualities that are needed in a good King."

"Kimtala, not too far away now." Cassie calls out when she sees the little girl run around one of the fountains. "Why do you think the Queen dislikes me Sheyome?"

They stop at a bench and Cassie sits down watching Kimtala splash her hands in the water. Sheyome chews on her bottom lip before sitting down beside Cassie.

"I don't think that she really dislikes you Cassie. Something isn't right with her right now. She's been turning on people that have been her friends for years. Any time someone questions her on a decision, or about her health, she seems to feel threatened. It seems here lately that when that happens whoever it was that questions her disappears." Tears come to her eyes and she turns away. She stealthily wipes away her tears before continuing. "What no one can understand is her lack of concern. Why she never asks about these people. Recently a whole group of botanist disappeared on Avdacal and she never even ordered a search. When Roushta asked her about it, she told him that there was no sense in doing a search since no one had even picked up on a psi distress signal." She looks around the garden, taking in the wonderful smells of the different flowers and herbs. Her small bout of grief now under control.

Cassie looks down at her hands worrying about Logan's plan to have Royanna do a physical and mental exam on Nicca. Could the Queen take offense at this? She sincerely hoped not. She would not know how to explain to Thayer that in some way his beloved cousin was responsible for his mother's disappearance. "We'll all have to be careful not to make her feel threatened then." She tells her looking up at the sky and then over at Kimtala.

"Come on Kim. It's time we were going back in." Her mouth drops open when she realizes that Kimtala has climbed into the fountain and is now soaked from head to toe. "Oh my goodness." Standing, she slowly walks over to the fountain and looks down at the little girl. Kimtala looks up at her and grins. Cassie shakes her head and lifts her out of the water. Concentrating hard, she dries Kimtala's clothes and then takes her hand. "We won't tell your momma about your little swim in the fountain, okay?"

"Okay Cassie" Kimtala smiles even more at her and then swings their hands. "Dry now."

"Yes, you're dry now and you're going to stay that way, right?"

"Right." Kimtala grins liking this new person in her life. She never scolds her bad when she does something that she shouldn't and accepts her promise to do better.

They go back into the palace and back to Logan's chambers. Sheyome enters with them and looks at Logan not saying anything. He picks up Kimtala and swings her around a couple of times.

"Kim, how would you like to go and visit your grandma and cousins for a few days?"

"Momma come too?" She asks looking at her mother.

"Yes, your momma too. Do you want to go?"

"Cassie come too?"

"No Kimmybird, Cassie has to stay here, but I'm sure you could come and visit her for a little while in the gardens."

"Okay, me go see granma."

"Good girl." Logan kisses her cheek and sets her down. "Take as long as you need Tru, to see to your sister's comfort. When she's recovered from birthing and you and Kim have bonded with the baby, will be soon enough for you to return to your duties here."

"Thank you my Lord. Sema was worried because I have only just started working for you and Mistress Cassie."

"Tell her there's nothing to worry about. Whenever your family needs you, you're free to go to them. I remember how important family bondings are at a birth." Logan smiles at her and squeezes her shoulder. "You go on now and I'll have some of your things brought to you at your mother's in an hour or so."

Truloka picks up her daughter and lets her give Cassie a kiss before they leave. As she walks down the hall to the side entrance, she can't help but be grateful that she was now working for the Lord and his Lady. She was sure that the Queen would have refused her request for some time with her family.

After the door closes, Logan suggests that they all sit down. There is already a tray of juice on the table and he pours Cassie and Sheyome each a glass before refilling his own.

"All right Shey, let's hear what you have to say. What happened to your parents?" He asks sitting down beside Cassie and getting straight to the point of her being there.

Sheyome looks down at her drink for several seconds before answering. "At one of the council meetings, mother questioned the Queen's decision to place a colony on Avdacal. Father also questioned it as well, stating that we should first explore the moon and study the plants and animals that are living there."

"That sounds reasonable, considering how little we really know about the moon, even though its been used for camping excursions over the years."

"Yes, well, Queen Nicca insisted that the colonists could do the exploring and whatever else had to be done. Mother and Father then pointed out that none of the people on the Queen's list was qualified to do the work needed. Two days later they both disappeared. That was nearly two months ago, and no one's seen them since." Stopping for a second, she takes a sip of her juice. "About a week ago, I felt... I felt their loss." She looks down at her drink and tries to control a shudder that runs through her at the memory. She still couldn't believe that they were gone, and that she never got to tell them good-bye or that she loved them.

Logan looks at her knowing that she is still going through her grief, but also knowing that she knows something else that may help in his investigation. "What else is there Shey? Why are you afraid of Drogen Firnap? What do you know that you haven't told anyone about?"

Sheyome looks up at him and then over at Cassie, who gives her an encouraging smile. Looking back down at her juice, she takes a drink. Taking a deep breath, she forces herself to tell them the rest. "The last coherent memory they had was of Drogen Firnap coming into the house with a stranger, and some kind of mist coming from Firnap's mouth. I believe that he's the one responsible for all of the disappearances over the past three years. Each time someone disappears, he's gone for a day or two. I don't even think he's human. He may look and act human, but if you look at his face closely, you'll notice that his jawbone protrudes more than a human's does. I know that there are beings that are part human, but I don't and won't believe that he's one of them." She shakes her head as an image of Drogen comes to mind.

"What do you feel when you're around him?"

"I feel that I'm in the presence of something evil and a feeling of fear and hopelessness runs through me."

"Yes, I felt the same thing at the celebration when he looked at me." Cassie shivers as she remembers that look.

"I'm going to go to Avdacal tomorrow and have a look around. I think that Firnap is some how connected with the creatures that Roushta's people have found there." He explains about the images he picked up during his mind sweep in the council chambers. "I'll be back in time for the examination Royanna will be giving the Queen. Shey, I want you to stay in these chambers with Cassie until I return."

"Of course my..." She stops as Logan glares at her and smiles. "Oh, of course Logan. I'll station the others out in the hall except for Libre. He's my dium."

"What is a dium?" Cassie asks in confusion, looking from one to the other.

"It's a companion that shares all parts of your life in the physical and emotional." Sheyome explains. "It's one of our ways to choose a mate."

Cassie nods her understanding and then looks at Logan. "Have you told the others about the creatures you saw in Drogen's mind?"

"Not yet. I'm going to go to Roushta's tonight and get his holo-tapes on the creatures and the last sighting location. Hopefully I won't have to go too far to find one."

"You're not going to try and capture one of them are you? From what Roushta told us this morning they can be very dangerous when cornered." Cassie bites on her lower lip, worrying about him going there alone.

"No love, all I plan to do is watch and see if I can pick up on anything. Hopefully I'll find out what happened to the group of botanist while I'm there."

Over the next couple of hours Logan gets the tapes he needs and delivers Truloka's things to her and prepares the ship he and Cassie arrived in for his trip in the morning. Meanwhile Cassie tells Sheyome all she can about Thayer and his new family and home.

"From the holograms Leyla showed us, Calidon is a softer version of Manchon. I think the lands and waters are pretty much the same in size and mass. There might be more mountains on Calidon though."

"And Torian, I mean Thayer, likes this other world?"

"Oh yes. He and Leyla said they couldn't wait until they got things settled on Earth and with the Alliance, so that they could go home. Leyla's parents will probably be in charge of Earth until a new leader can be found that will restore the peoples faith in government leadership again."

"What will happen if no one can be found?"

"Then I think that Thayer and Leyla will try to find someone from either here or Calidon to take over. Since both worlds have the governorship, I'm sure that they'll find someone. At least now Earth is safe."

Just then Logan comes in with a stack of holo-tapes and the portable unit from their ship. He sets it all down on the sitting room table. "Roushta gave me identification tapes on everyone that has disappeared in the past three years." He explains as the women's mouths drop open at the number of tapes. "I want to study the facial structures and see what I can come up with. Something tells me that it's very important."

He selects a tape and places it in the unit. The image of a young man appears above the unit, along with his personal information. Because of his ability to absorb information quickly, Logan is able to go through nearly two dozen tapes in less than two hours. Stopping to take a break and eat the food that Sheyome has had Libre bring in from the palace kitchens, Logan goes over the list of people with Sheyome to see if she knows if any of them had offended the Queen in some way.

"A lot of them only questioned her on some small issues where her decisions didn't make sense, others commented on how ill she was looking. A few questioned her right to rule in Royanna's place. They felt that the next strongest family should take over the throne of power if Royanna didn't want it."

Logan smiles at this bit of information. "What did my father have to say to that idea?"

"Thurda said that as far as he was concerned, Nicca could stay right where she was and with his blessings." She tells him with a smile and then breaks into laughter as Logan chuckles. Cassie looks at them both with an expression of bewilderment on her face, she didn't see what was so funny. Logan takes several deep breathes and tries to regain control of himself so that he can explain their laughter to her.

"What Shey means my love, is that my father refused to take Nicca's place on the throne of power. My family is next in line to the crown should all of the Rican line die out or be unable to continue to rule." He explains still chuckling at his father's reaction and wishing that he had been here to see his father's face.

Once more Cassie's mouth drops open. "I... You..." She glares at him. "You never said anything about your family being so high up in Manchon's hierarchy Logan Knightrunner."

"Why should I? Both Thayer and I know that his family will be the last to hold the throne of power." Logan looks at her strangely. "Would you want to be queen Cassie?"

"What?! No, thank you. Just being your lifemate will be all that I can handle." She says without guile. "Are you sure that there's no chance...?"

"I'm sure love." Logan grins at her look of utter relief. They finish their meal and go back to the tapes. Before putting in the next tape, Logan looks down at it and then up at Sheyome. "This next tape is of your parents. If I didn't need to refresh my memory of them I wouldn't bother looking at it."

"It's all right Logan. I can handle it." She assures him smiling weakly, hoping that she's speaking the truth.

Logan puts in the tape and quickly studies the couple on the screen, committing their physical description to memory before turning the tape off. Pulling it out he looks at Sheyome who is wiping away a few tears.

"I told Roushta of your receiving their essence and he said to give you this tape." He hands it to her and then gently squeezes her hand. Giving her time to collect herself and to control her grief, he goes through the tapes that are left to view. He decides to look at the report on the botanist first, and then the last one that Pertela did on the captured pair. He puts in the tape and studies it closely, frowning now and then. Something in the report wasn't making any kind of sense to him, and he just couldn't put his finger on it.

Putting in the last tape, he studies it just as closely only this time he stops every couple of minutes to study the images. While he's doing this, Cassie and Sheyome are talking quietly so as not to distract him. Suddenly he shuts off the unit and sits back with a look of utter shock on his face. Cassie, feeling his shock rushes to his side.

"Logan?! What is it? What's wrong?"

At first he just looks at her and then he looks at Sheyome and then back at Cassie. He runs his hand over his eyes still unable to believe what he thinks he saw in the tapes. Without saying anything he stands up and walks around the room. After walking around for a couple of minutes, he pours himself a glass of flincen and turns to look at them.

"I want you both to look at this last tape. Pay close attention to the creatures facial features. Shey I want you to pay close attention to the vocal sounds that they're making." Though he would rather not involve her in this he needed her confirmation of what he thought he was seeing and hearing. He goes back over to the holo unit and turns it on. Stepping away, he goes over to the balcony doors to wait for their response.

Cassie and Sheyome study the tape, watching and listening. They watch it three times and then both women gasp. Sheyome becomes deathly pale.

"By the Great One! This can not be! Loganda, uto ka cial bee ou ari tain." Sheyome is so upset that she converts to the Majichonie language unintentionally. ("Logan, tell me that this is not true.")

Logan has already moved to her side and taken her into his arms, holding her tightly. "I wish that I could little one. I'm sorry honey, but I'm afraid that it is true. Those poor creatures were somehow your parents." He confirms both of their fears not knowing how it could be possible, but having no other explanation.

Suddenly Libre bursts into the room only to stop suddenly when he sees his dium in the arms of Lord Knightrunner, and that man's mate standing beside them with her hands over her mouth and tears coursing down her cheeks.

"Atma, uto ka lypt ou entho." ("My love, tell me what is wrong.") He says to her in Majichonie as he walks over to them.

Logan releases her and Sheyome falls into Libre's arms. She weeps into his shoulder as she tells him what they have just learned. Libre looks at Logan for confirmation, and when the other man nods he tightens his arms around Sheyome.

Cassie wraps her own arms around Logan's waist, feeling the pain and grief running through the other couple. Logan kisses her forehead and pulls it to his shoulder. Once Sheyome has calmed down, the other guards are reassured that there is no danger and that everything was fine, that they can return to their posts, the two couples sit down.

"We can not mention this to anyone else just now Shey." Logan warns her gently. "I'll tell my father, Roushta, and Royanna, but no one, absolutely no one else must know what we have found out here tonight."

"But my Lord, the other families..." Libre begins only to have Logan stop him with a shake of his head.

"No one Libre. We have to find out how this happened and if there's any way that we can reverse it. Until we do, you must keep silent about it."

"We will Logan." Sheyome assures him, having pulled herself together.

"Good. I'll send this all back to Roushta, and he can start studying all the tapes of the creatures and see if he can identify anyone else." He stands and pulls Cassie to her feet. "You two can have Truloka's room. Sheyome, have the others make themselves pallets in here for tonight. I'll be leaving first thing in the morning." Not waiting for any response, he teleports the tapes back to Roushta and quickly explains everything to him.

As he and Cassie go to their room, he contacts his father and Royanna and tells them as well. Once in their room with the door closed, Logan pulls Cassie into his arms and holds her close. He vows that none of this would ever touch them more personally then it had this night.

~

Early the next morning, Cassie says good-bye to Logan in their bedchamber. "Don't take any chances with those creatures Logan. They may have once been human, but right now they're more wild animal then anything else."

"I know sweetheart, but if I can recognize one I'm going to try and communicate. We have to know what caused this change if we're ever to return them to their true forms. We have to establish a way to question them."

"Just don't get too close. Those claws looked really dangerous."

"Cassie, you know I won't do anything to endanger myself or those poor creatures. I'll be sure to keep at least ten feet between us all right?" He pulls her into his arms and kisses her deeply. When he finally releases her mouth, she leans against him and looks up at him.

"I wish you would at least take one of the guards with you like Shey suggested."

"It will be safer and quicker to go on my own. Besides, I want all the guards with you while I'm gone." He counters causing her to frown. "You said last night that you don't feel comfortable around Firnap. With all of them around you, he won't be able to get too close to you."

"Okay, but at least take a stunner with you." She pleads with him very afraid for his safety.

"No. It might kill them just as the sedative did. If I get into a difficult situation I'll port to safety."

Cassie lays her head against his chest and sighs, knowing that it's useless to argue with him any further. "Okay, I'm sorry I've been such a nag. It's just that I have an uneasy feeling about all of this, this morning."

"Everything will be fine love. I'll be back by tomorrow night one way or the other, I promise." He puts a finger under her chin and lifts her mouth back to his. After the kiss he looks into her eyes. "Now, walk me to the ship and then Shey will take you to my father's for breakfast."

Cassie gives him a weak smile and links her arm through his. They walk out of the bedchamber and meet Sheyome and Libre in the sitting room."

After watching the ship disappear, Cassie follows Sheyome and Libre through the gardens and off the palace grounds. As they go through the palace gates, an old woman walks up to Cassie and touches her hand lightly. "Beware of the golden shadow child. She will take all that you hold dear and leave nothing but an empty shell." She shakes her finger at Cassie and then walks away.

Cassie and Sheyome look after the old woman while Libre and the other four guards frown and move closer to Cassie. None of them had noticed her until she was standing beside Cassie and touching her.

"Who was that Shey, and what did she mean?" Cassie asks in confusion still looking in the direction that the old woman had gone and suddenly disappeared. It hadn't been a normal teleportation, but more of a fading away.

Sheyome looks at Libre, and then back at Cassie. "She's known as the Timeless One. When something is going to affect the ruling family, she just shows up and gives some kind of warning. The last time was just before Prince Thayer and Logan left for Earth." She says frowning as she remembers that time.

Many in the Rican family had died and there were not many left that could take over the throne, not many with any real power or strength, that could keep the peace. The Timeless One had come and said that Thayer must leave and that before his return confusion would rule.

Shey doesn't tell Cassie this, but plans to talk with Lord Thurda and Lady Royanna about this latest prophecy as soon as she can, and in private. "We better get going Cassie. Thurda is waiting for you."

Cassie nods absently and begins walking again. "Why would she tell me this Shey? I'm not a part of the ruling family."

"I'm not sure Cassie. It could be because of your bond with Prince Thayer's wife. You are very close, almost like sisters." She tries to explain something that she doesn't really understand herself.

"It still doesn't make any sense." Cassie says shaking her head and looking down at the hand the old woman had touched. On the back of her hand is an old Native American symbol of a thunderbird. She rubs at it and then holds it out for Shey to see. "What is this?"

Sheyome looks at Cassie's hand and then straight ahead. "Its a sign of protection to ward off sadness and unhappiness. She probably sensed your sadness at Logan's going away and wanted to give you comfort." Sheyome improvises, not wanting to worry her new friend with any more information then she was ready for.

'*You should have told her the truth atma.*'

'*Why atmo? So that she can worry about something evil that will try to take away her soul, her very essence?*'

'*So that she will use more caution. You heard Lord Logan, she doesn't yet have the ability to protect herself from such things.*'

'*That's why he made us her personal guards. If we do our jobs right nothing will happen to her. I will not worry her to the point that she's afraid to leave her chambers even with us to watch over and protect her.*'

'*Lord Logan or his father will tell her.*'

'*Then that is their choice, not mine. Besides, what I told her was the truth.*'

'*As far as you told it.*'

'*That was my choice to make not yours! Just shut up about it Libre!*'

They arrive at Thurda's home a few minutes later and Sheyome knocks on the door. Chevala opens it and waves them in. "Libre and the others will wait outside Lady Chevala." Sheyome informs her and then glares at Libre. He nods to her and then to Cassie and Chevala, before turning and standing to one side of the door. The other four guards take up positions around the house.

Chevala frowns and then shrugs her shoulders before closing the door. "Father and Royanna are in the sun room. Please take Cassie in Shey, I have to check on the pastries and then I'll join you." Not bothering to point the way, Chevala goes to the kitchen.

Sheyome leads the way to the sun room with Cassie close at her side. "Should I tell them about the Timeless One Shey?" Cassie whispers.

"If you wish to." Sheyome looks at her and sees the doubt in her eyes. "Would you like me to tell them about it for you? I think that they should know. In some way her words will affect them as well as you." She points out thinking that it would also make it easier to be open about what she had told Cassie of the protection sign.

"If you don't mind. It still makes no sense to me." Cassie agrees as they walk into the room where Thurda and Royanna are seated close together. Thurda stands and greets Cassie with a kiss on both cheeks. "Good morning daughter. I trust that Logan got off well this morning?"

"Yes sir, he did. Good morning Lady Royanna."

"Good morning Cassie, and please, drop the Lady. We're amongst family and friends here and don't have to be so formal." Royanna smiles as Cassie nods and blushes.

Thurda sits her opposite them and invites Sheyome to sit as well. "The same goes for you Shey. No my Lord's or my Lady's while your alone with us. You're family now, and we expect you to act like it."

Sheyome looks from Thurda to Royanna and realizes that they no longer see her as just a royal guard. They now saw her as Prince Thayer's godchild and ward. "I will try to remember, but it will be hard."

"Then we will just have to remind you my dear." Royanna says smiling at her son's godchild. She knew that when Thayer arrived, when he left again, Sheyome would be going with him.

Handing each of the young women a glass of juice, Thurda returns to his seat. "Now, what were you whispering about not making any sense daughter?" He asks causing Cassie to blush and choke on her sip of juice.

Sheyome pats her back and Cassie looks at her pleadingly. Sheyome nods and turns to Thurda and Royanna. "Just after we left the palace grounds, the Timeless One appeared and approached Cassie with a warning." She explains, telling them word for word what was said and about the symbol that appeared on the back of Cassie's right hand. "I told her that it was a sign of protection against sadness and unhappiness." Telepathically she tells them the rest. *I didn't tell her about it also being a sign to protect her soul and essence from being taken by an evil one.*

Thurda frowns at this admission of omission on Sheyome's part. Before he can speak aloud, Royanna stops him. *'She did the right thing Thurda. Cassie is already filled with worry. To add to that now would not be good for her. Something else is bothering her that I don't think she's mentioned to even Logan.'*

'But we must tell her Anna. She must be prepared to fight whatever it is that is threatening her essence.'

'True, she must be told, but we must leave that telling up to Logan. He will know how to explain it so that she will understand completely.'

Thurda nods his head just as Chevala enters with the floating food tray. After serving everyone, she sits down and joins in the conversation. Once again Cassie asks why she was singled out for this warning.

The other four look at each other and then Royanna tries to explain why this could be. "You are linked to my family by three people. First by your relationship with Leyla, and her relationship to Thayer. Your relationship with Logan is another link to my family." Here she stops and looks at Thurda and Chevala before continuing. "When Logan's mother passed on, I received a large portion of her essence or memories. We were very close, almost as close as you are to Leyla. Her essence is what bonds us all together."

"What also bonds our families together, is my love for Royanna, and her love for me." Thurda puts in with a look at her. "When we are life-bonded that bond will become even stronger." He tells her no longer able to keep it secret. Maybe now Royanna would be forced to agree to their bonding.

Royanna frowns at him, but says nothing about his speaking of something that was not yet settled between them. "Even so, that is the most logical explanation that I can think of for your receiving the warning."

"Do you think that I have anything to worry about?" Cassie asks feeling that it wouldn't surprise her if there was. Her feelings of danger seemed to be growing stronger with every passing day.

"What should you have to worry about?" Chevala asks smiling at her. "With Sheyome and Libre to guard you day and night, not to mention my little brother? Only a fool would be crazy enough to try something with those three around you all the time."

They all laugh at the face she makes after saying this. Royanna nods her approval of Chevala's actions as some of the worry eases from Cassie's mind and body.

"Do you have any plans for the rest of the morning Cassie?" Royanna asks after they finish breakfast and Sheyome helps Chevala to clear away the dirty dishes and offers to help with the wash-up.

"Not really. Since there's not to be a meeting for discussion of the Alliance until tomorrow, I thought that I would have Shey take me around the village until it was time for me to meet Kimtala in the palace gardens this afternoon."

"That sounds fine. I was just wondering if you would like to join Chevala and I when we make our rounds this morning?"

Cassie smiles at her and sits a little straighter in her chair. "Could I? That would be great. While we stayed at Thayer's stronghold, I was learning some healing. It was all pretty basic, and didn't really satisfy my curiosity for the healing arts, but the Shaman said that I had a gift for it, as does my youngest sister Merri."

"Then you're in for some pretty heavy learning my dear. Royanna is the best Healer on the planet." Thurda tells her and chuckles when Royanna blushes and then slaps his shoulder.

"Don't let this old cotfox fool you Cassie. Chevala is a good healer in her own right. In fact, she's one of my best students. Between her and Nicca, its hard to say who would be the one to take my place as the next Master Healer. Though they both have more to learn before that happens, they're both evenly matched at this point."

"You mean Nicca's a healer too?" Cassie asks in some surprise.

"Oh yes. Most of the families on Manchon have at least one or two healers in them." Royanna states. "Even though she's Queen, Nicca must still practice her healing arts. It's too precious a gift to let go unused. If ever I should decide to reclaim the throne, she along with Chevala would be the ones most likely to take my place as Master Healer."

"And Nicca would be welcome to it Anna." Chevala says as she and Sheyome come back into the room. "I have no wish or desire to become the next Master Healer. Assistant to the Master is as high as I wish to go."

"Humph. You'll never get anywhere with that attitude Chevy and you know it." Her father grumbles at her.

"I've gotten to where I want to be father, and you must be happy for that. Besides, if I were to become Master Healer, think of how little you would see of me and how bored you would become."

"At least with you as the Master Healer then I would see more of Anna. I wouldn't be bored either." Thurda snaps back grumpily.

Before Chevala can say anything more to provoke her father, Royanna stands up. "That's quite enough you two! I'm still the Master and Chevala is still my assistant until **I** decide otherwise." She glares at them both and then smiles. "Now Chevala, go and get our bags and let's be off. Cassie is going to join us for our morning rounds before she returns to the palace."

"All right Anna." Chevala says quietly before walking to the door. Before going out, she turns quickly around and sticks her tongue out at her father.

"Why you...!" Thurda stammers dumbstruck at her action.

"Chevala!" Royanna gasps just as shocked.

"Oww!" Chevala cries out as she feels two very hard mental pinches to her backside.

Cassie and Sheyome try hard to smother their laughter, but Thurda and Royanna start to chuckle and they all let loose with it.

Chevala meets them in the hall by the front door, rubbing her bottom. "That was not funny." She tells them as she hands Royanna her bag, but there is a hint of a smile on her lips and in her eyes as she says it. Now more then ever she knew that her father and Royanna belonged together. Their minds thought along the same lines.

CHAPTER FIVE

For the rest of the morning, Cassie follows Royanna and Chevala on their rounds of the village. She watches and listens as they treat everything from sprains to internal problems.

"Our first responsibility is to keep the patient calm and to treat all injuries with great care. What may seem to be a simple sprain, could actually be a brake." Royanna explains as they walk through the village. "Over the years we've learned to look into the body and see what is the true problem. Though there are many healers, not many have developed this ability."

They stop at a small cottage where a young boy is sitting outside with his leg propped up on a chair and cushions. Royanna kneels beside him as his mother comes out of the cottage.

"What seems to be the matter Tatori?" Royanna asks the woman as she stops behind the boy's chair.

"We're not sure Master Royanna. He was fine when he went to bed last night, but this morning he complained of pain in his foot, and a numbness moving up his leg. When he tried to stand, his leg wouldn't support his weight."

"What did you do yesterday Matori?" Royanna asks the boy as she looks at the bottom and sides of his swollen foot and ankle.

"I went swimming with Pecari and Saliero down at the river Master Royanna." he tells her quietly trying to ignore the pain caused by her gentle touch.

Royanna nods and signals for Chevala to examine the foot and ankle while she searches through her bag for what she will need to care for the boy.

Chevala carefully looks over the foot and ankle, also noticing several small reddened puncture wounds about his heel and ankle. *'It looks as if he's stepped on a waterpine. There seem to be a couple of the spins still imbedded in the holes around his ankle.'*

'Yes, and we need to get them out soon. If the poison should reach his genitals, it could cause sterility.'

Cassie hears their mental conversation and smiles at the boy. "Hello Matori. My name is Cassie."

Matori looks at her shyly, but then looks quickly back at Royanna when she pulls out a pair of very thin tweezers. "Hel... Hello." He says nervously.

Cassie seeing the tweezers and the boy's nervousness, tries to distract him for what the healers are going to be doing to his foot and ankle. "I'm new here, and haven't seen too many of the sights. Is this place you went swimming good?"

Matori looks up at her. "Yes, very good. We've put up a swing line in one of the tallest trees. If you do it right, you can land right in the middle of the river."

"But isn't the current stronger in the middle?"

"Not that much. My little sister Vajoia can swim it real easy."

"How old is your sister?"

"Vajoia's seven. Father says she swims like a caryfish."

"Oh, and what is a caryfish?"

"It's a fish that swims in the big waters and it has a hole at the top of it's head. They're really fast swimmers, and they help people that are hurt or lost in the water."

"We have animals like that back home. They're called dolphins. Only their not really fish Matori, they're mammals, because they breath air just like we do. They also give birth to live young."

"Do yours sing? Ours sing. Not with words, its more like humming." He explains.

Chevala removes the last spine and puts it in the small pouch with the others. In the mean time, Royanna finishes mixing up an herbal wash to cleanse the wounds so that no further infection can enter the boy's system.

After applying the wash, she closes her eyes and places one hand over his ankle and the other high up on his thigh. A pinkish white light passes between her hands and encircles Matori's leg. The swelling and redness soon diminish, and she removes her hands.

"Okay Matori, I want you to slowly lower your leg to the ground. Count to five and then stand up slowly. Let me know if you have any pain." Royanna instructs him sitting back on her heels and watches as Matori carefully does as instructed. Noticing that he hasn't put any weight on the heel, she instructs him to do so.

Matori bites his lower lip and then puts down his heel. An unexpected cry comes from him and he collapses back into the chair clutching his leg.

Royanna and Chevala both frown, sure that they had removed all of the spines. They look into the heel, but neither can see anything. "I don't understand this." Royanna mumbles to herself. "There's nothing there." Chevala shakes her head also bewildered.

Cassie places her hand on Matori's shoulder and feels his pain. Closing her eyes, Cassie follows his pain to it's source, concentrating on what the bones and muscles look like. Finally she reaches the spot where the pain is coming from. With her eyes still closed, she speaks to Royanna about what she sees sure that she can help to relieve the boys pain. "There's still a spine in there.

It's right up against the ankle bone Royanna. It's tip is pushing against one of his nerves nearly puncturing it."

Royanna looks at Cassie. "Open your mind to me and let me see what you see Cassie."

Opening her mind to her, Cassie shows her the spine against the ankle bone. Royanna pulls out and looks at Chevala.

"She's right. It's going to be difficult to remove though." Again Royanna frowns as she tries to figure out how to remove the spine without causing any damage to the nerves.

Cassie keeps her hand on Matori's shoulder to block the pain that has increased greatly over the past few seconds. "Royanna, I think that I can push it back out the way it came in far enough for you or Chevala to get to it with the tweezers." Not waiting for an answer, she concentrates on the spine and sending it backwards to it's entry point. As she does, sweat breaks out on her forehead. At first the spine resists her mental push, but then slowly begins to move downward. All the while she is doing this, she blocks as much of the pain from Matori as she can. When it finally reaches the point where it can be reached with the tweezers, Cassie stops pushing and keeps a light pressure on it to prevent it from working it's way back up. "You should be able to reach it now Royanna. It's straight down from the bone."

Taking up her tweezers, Royanna gently probes the hole and feels the spine. Slowly and carefully, she pulls it out and holds it up. When she does, Cassie releases her connection with Matori and pulls herself apart from him. Letting go of his shoulder, she nearly collapses to the ground, but Libre is there to catch her as her knees give out. Tatori brings over a chair for her to sit on.

Chevala asks Tatori for a glass of juice, into which she mixes some restorative herbs, before handing it to Cassie. "Drink all of this Cassie. It will bring your energy level back up to normal in a couple of minutes. You have to drink all of it though for it to do you any good. It will also ease the mental stress of using a part of your mind that you're not use to using."

Cassie nods and then gratefully drinks the juice while Royanna puts more of the herbal wash on Matori's ankle. "Ready to try again young man?" Royanna asks after a few minutes smiling encouragingly at him.

Matori bits on his lower lip and doesn't meet Royanna's eyes. Noticing his hesitation Cassie reaches over and lightly touches his hand. "It's all right Matori. I promise that you won't have any pain this time."

Looking into her eyes, Matori can see that she truly believes that the pain will be gone. He nods to her and then takes a deep breath before standing. Slowly he puts his heel down and gradually puts his full weight onto it. When he feels no pain he smiles over at Cassie. "You're right Cassie, it doesn't hurt any more."

Cassie returns his smile with a nod, and then laughs as he flings himself at her and hugs her tightly. She returns the hug and then warns, "Now, be careful when you go swimming. Watch where you're stepping, or wear something on your feet that will protect them. Okay?"

"Yes, I promise Cassie. Thank you for helping me." He hugs her again and then runs off, yelling to some of his friends that are passing by, to wait for him.

Tatori shakes her head and turns to Royanna who is now standing and brushing off her skirt. "I must apologize for him Master Royanna. I give you our thanks for healing him."

"No thanks are necessary Tatori. Just seeing him able to run and play with his friends is enough. Though I must admit, without Cassie here with us today, he might not have been able to do that." The Master Healer confesses as she smiles proudly at Cassie and watches her blush at the compliment.

Chevala gathers up their things and hands Royanna her bag. "I think that Cassie should receive the payment from this patient Anna."

"Yes, I agree Chevala. Tatori, tell Matori that services go to Lady Cassie for his healing."

Cassie looks at them in shock. "Oh no Royanna. I only helped..."

"Nonsense child. If it weren't for you, Matori might not have been able to ever walk again. He might even have lost his foot because of the spine. No, you will receive whatever service Matori feels his foot and being able to walk is worth." Royanna states firmly. "Now, it's time we were off. We've one more stop to make before you return to the palace."

"Yes ma'am." Cassie stands and shakes hands with Tatori. "It was nice to meet you. Good-bye."

Tatori nods and waves them off before carrying the chairs back into the house. She had heard that Lord Logan's chosen mate was very nice. She had also heard that Lady Cassie didn't let the Queen's attitude get to her. Knowing how the Queen had been over the past few years, Tatori wouldn't be surprised to hear that the Queen had done something to anger both the Lady and her Lord.

Watching from the shadows, Drogen frowns and slips away from the wall where he's stood watching everything. His golden queen would not like this one to remain free with such abilities. He must get Niccara to cast her out. The sooner his true queen had control of this one, the sooner she would have her true prize.

He makes his way slowly back to the palace. He could not understand why his golden queen had put Niccara in control. He could have sent her more of the humans then Niccara was. They were behind schedule because of her slowness in providing enough specimens. The transformation took nearly a week, and then they had to wait for nearly another week before the breeders new bodies were mature enough for them to begin reproducing. They needed more breeders, but right now they had more drone workers then breeders, because Niccara was still fighting him on what stock to send.

Soon he would have to talk to his golden queen about her. Maybe she would start letting him pick out the stock for himself without any interference from Niccara. Besides, he was tired of this world and it's people, of the form he had been forced to take. The Golden One had promised him that he could begin breeding as soon as they had enough females. If they didn't get enough soon, he would be too old to breed, and his line would die out with him.

Their last stop is to check on Truloka's sister Sema. Cassie waits outside with Kimtala and her mother while Royanna and Chevala go in to see how far along Sema is.

"Tru, I'm headed back to the palace after this. Why don't I just take Kim with me? We'll have a picnic in the gardens, and then take a carriage ride down by the docks. When we're finished exploring, we'll bring her back here before returning to the palace."

Chevala comes out of the house just then. "I think that would be a good idea Tru. Sema is close to her time and I think that it might be best if Kimtala wasn't here for the next few hours." She looks over at Cassie. "If you could bring her back in say about four hours, I think that the worst should be over. We should be able to deliver shortly after that."

Cassie looks at Truloka who is looking into the house. "Tru, do you agree? If you don't, we can wait out here with you."

A scream comes from inside the house and Truloka notices her daughter clutching at Cassie's hand and burying her face in the other woman's skirt. "No, take her with you Mistress Cassie. I don't think that she can handle any more of her Aunt Sema's screams. Can you little one?"

Kimtala shakes her head against Cassie's lap. "No momma. I sorry."

Truloka kneels down beside her and takes her into her arms. "Don't be little lovebird. You'll get used to such things as you get older and can help more to take your mind off of it all. Go with Mistress Cassie, and have a good time. Remember to do as you're told and to stay close to her always."

"I will momma." The little girl assures her mother and gives her a hug, then takes Cassie's hand once again.

Cassie looks down at Kimtala and gives her a smile before turning to Chevala. "I think that we'll go ahead and go now Chevala. Please tell Royanna that I'll see her this evening at dinner." She stands up and gives the older woman a hug. "Thank you for everything today. I had a great time watching you both work." As she turns away and leads Kimtala down from the porch, Sheyome steps to the other side of Kimtala, who takes her hand.

Sheyome smiles down at her before looking at Cassie. "One of the kitchen maids will be meeting us in the garden with a picnic basket."

"Oh, thank you Shey. I was hoping that it wouldn't take too long to set everything up. I forgot to arrange it last night."

They walk back to the palace with Kimtala skipping between them, swinging their hands. Cassie and Sheyome share a smile at the little girl's happiness. Entering the garden, Kimtala gasps and stops as she sees the picnic that has been set up for them. Releasing Cassie and Sheyome's hands, she runs forward and stops a few feet from where the large blanket is spread out on the grass.

"Oh my goodness!" Cassie exclaims coming to a halt. "This is more then I had planned on Shey."

Sheyome recovers from her own shock at what the maid has brought them. "It's more than I asked for Cassie. I only asked for enough to feed the eight of us."

Just then the Queen and Daemon Heorte come from another part of the garden. "Good afternoon Mistress Blackwood, Sheyome." Nicca stops a couple of feet away from them. "I hope that you don't mind, but I took the liberty of having extra food brought out. When the cook asked about this little picnic, I thought it such a wonderful idea, that I didn't think that you would mind if Daemon and I joined you."

"Not at all Majesty." Cassie says with a curtsy. "I hope that you don't mind that my guards are joining us? They have been very diligent in their duty of watching over me, that they have worked up a good appetite."

Nicca looks at the guards that are hovering close to Cassie's back. Though she would like to refuse, she knows that if she did, they would just continue to hover around. By agreeing, they would get their food and sit a respectful distance away. "Of course I don't mind." She looks down at Kimtala. "And who is this little mite?"

Kimtala moves closer to Cassie and buries her face into Cassie's skirt. "This is Kimtala, my maid Truloka's daughter. Truloka is with her sister preparing for a birth. I offered to entertain Kim for the next few hours." Cassie places her hand on Kimtala's head surprised that Niccara didn't know the child's name since Truloka had been one of her own maids. "Kim, say hello to Queen Niccara and Daemon." Kimtala gives a small curtsy and mumbles into Cassie's skirt. "I'm sorry Majesty. I'm afraid that she's a little shy with strangers." Cassie tells the Queen, though she knows that something else was definitely bothering the child. She had not acted this way when she had first meet Logan and herself. She was by nature an open and loving child.

Nicca waves her hand in slight irritation. "No matter. I'm sure that by the end of our picnic she and I will be good friends." She smiles at Kimtala who just looks back at her not saying anything. Slowly the smile leaves Nicca's face and she looks away from the child.

"Why don't we all sit down?" Daemon suggests knowing that in some way the little girl was agitating the Queen with her refusal to talk to her. After seating the ladies, Daemon signals to the maids to begin serving. Once done the maids step back into the shade of the trees where Libre and the other four guards are seated with their lunch.

"Where did Logan fly off to this morning Miss... May I call you Cassie?" When Cassie nods, Nicca continues. "From what I understand Cassie, he left before breakfast."

Having planned with Logan for such questioning, Cassie repeats what Logan had told her to say. "He decided that he wanted to visit some of the places he had spent time at as a boy before he left Manchon all those years ago."

"Well there are quite a few. But why didn't you go with him?" She asks holding her glass up for more wine.

"Maybe some other time. Right now I want to keep both feet firmly on the ground for a while. Besides, he said something about flying out to Settecas and staying there over night." Cassie gives a small shudder. "I just got done roughing it for several months, and couldn't get up much enthusiasm for even just one night of it."

Nicca and Daemon laugh and Sheyome soon joins them. "If he's looking to rough it as you say," Daemon stammers, trying to control his laughter, "then he's in for a surprise when he gets there."

"Yes, most of Settecas has been colonized over the past twelve years or so." Nicca tells her smiling smugly.

"Well if there's any place to do it, Logan will find it." Cassie assures them.

"Knowing Logan, he probably will." Nicca admits. "Tell us, how did the two of you meet?"

Cassie sips at her juice pretending to think about it when she's really trying to guess at Nicca's reasons for wanting to know such things. She was sure that it wasn't plain curiosity. "Well, Thayer and Leyla introduced us. At first I didn't want anything to do with him. I didn't care for him too much because I thought that he was just like all our other government men. Then once I got to know him, I realized that he was nothing like the others, that he was special. He was always kind to my family, my sisters and brothers, even when they were being pains in the butts. He was always respectful to my father. My sister once said that he had kind eyes, and she was right. There was only one time that his eyes ever really frightened me, and that was the day that he claimed the blood rite." This time she doesn't have to pretend to shudder, a strong one hits her. "There was so much hatred and anger in him that day. If I had just met him that day we never would have gotten together."

No one says anything for several minutes, then Kimtala says in a loud whisper, "Gotta go potty Cassie."

Everyone tries not to laugh, and one of the maids steps forward. "I'll take her Mistress."

"Oh, thank you..." Cassie pauses not knowing the girl's name.

"I'm Neila, Mistress."

"Thank you Neila." Cassie looks at Kimtala. "Go with Neila, and when you come back we'll see about that carriage ride, all right?" Kimtala nods and takes Neila's hand.

'Shey, send one of the guards with them please.'

'Are you sure Cassie? She'll be perfectly safe with Neila.'

'I'm sure. I don't want anything to happen to her because she's close to me.'

'All right, I'll send Libre.' Shey links with Libre. 'Follow them and keep in mind touch with Kimtala Libre.'

'But...'

'Cassie wishes it. I think that she may sense some threat to the child.'

'All right.' A few seconds later Libre stands and follows Kimtala and Neila into the palace.

"Where do you plan to go on your carriage ride Cassie?" Nicca asks sipping at her fifth glass of ereo wine. It is a lot stronger then the flincen, and Daemon has had no luck in getting her to stop drinking it as if it were water this afternoon.

"I thought we'd go down to the docks. Logan told me that they're set up something like the ancient wharfs on Earth, almost a thousand years ago."

"How boring that all sounds. Why don't you go through the Rican Woods? They're quite beautiful this time of the year."

"Maybe some other day Majesty." Cassie declines, having seen a strange gleam enter the Queen's eyes at this suggestion. "It's close to the time that I should be returning Kim to her mother. We'll only have time for a quick look at the docks before we have to take her home."

"Mm." Nicca frowns and then tries to stand. Daemon quickly rises to assist her. "Well then, we'll bid you good day then." Nicca says with a slight slur turning away, and then turning back again. "Oh yes. Will we be seeing you at the council meeting tomorrow morning?" she asks as an after thought.

"Yes you will. Lady Royanna mentioned to me that some of your councilors have a few more questions concerning the Alliance. I'll be happy to answer them if at all possible."

"Very well. Good day."

Cassie and Sheyome stand there and watch them leave as Neila and Libre return with Kimtala. The child goes straight to Cassie's side and takes her hand. "There's a bad man watching us from the door Cassie." She whispers and points to a side door.

When she looks, Cassie sees Drogen Firnap standing there staring at her. They look at each other for several moments before Sheyome steps in front of her to block her view.

"Never look straight into his eyes Cassie." Sheyome hisses a strong warning at her.

Cassie shakes her head as if to clear it and then looks over Sheyome's shoulder. Drogen is gone, but still a shudder runs through her. She kneels down in front of Kimtala. "Don't ever go near that man Kimtala. If he comes close to you, you run to your Momma or another grownup that you trust. Do you understand me Kimtala? Stay away from him always."

"I promise Cassie. Don't be mad at me." Kimtala looks up at her with wide tear filled eyes afraid that she had done something wrong.

"Oh sweetheart. I'm not mad at you." Cassie reassures her pulling her into her arms and holding her close. After a minute she puts her a little away from her and tries to explain. "I just want you to be very careful. I'd be very sad if something happened to you." She smoothes the child's hair and then stands up. "Now, let's go for our ride and have some fun, then I'll take you back to your Momma. We'll even stop and get something for your aunty and her new baby."

Kimtala smiles up at her and nods her head. She thinks to herself that Cassie didn't have to warn her to stay away from the bad man. When she looked at him she could see a blackness and didn't want it to touch her family. She was sure he was going to do something to her family.

CHAPTER SIX

Double checking his charts, Logan prepares to leave the ship for the first of his exploration trips. Roushta had given him the locations of all the sightings for the creatures, and of where the botanists had camped. His first trip would be to check out the camp and the surrounding area. After making sure that the ship's transporter is set to bring him back should he become unconscious, he leaves the ship and secures it. Double checking it's location he begins walking towards the campsite.

As he goes, Logan checks the trees and the undergrowth. When he comes upon a set of tracks, he squats down to examine them closely. Though they're a little larger then normal, he recognizes them as udio tracks. The udio is basically in the same family as the deer found on Earth.

Continuing on, he listens to the animal sounds around him, trying to identify them. Though he can hear them, he doesn't see any of the animal life. When he reaches the campsite, he stops and just looks around for several minutes. Not detecting any movement in the area, he moves through the camp and examines it in closer detail.

As he walks around the camp, he notices several mounds of dirt around the area that have been covered with leaves and bushes. Carefully he removes the covering from one of the mounds and studies it closely. Sensing something buried beneath the dirt, he starts digging. After he has dug about two feet, Logan feels as though he's being watched. Without stopping what he's doing, he does a quick scan of the area around him. Suddenly he hears a growling sound coming from his left and looks up quickly. There is a bluish-green flash as one of the creatures turns and runs off.

Quickly getting to his feet, Logan runs after it. He follows it for almost an hour before it disappears into an underground cave. Probing into the cave, he senses three life forms within. Knowing that it would be foolish to enter the cave without any light to penetrate the darkness, he looks around for some place to hide and watch the cave. Finding a tree with adequate coverage, he ports to a point where he can clearly see the cave and then places a shield around himself so that the creatures cannot sense his presence still in the area. While waiting, he notices several more such caves in the area. He marks their locations in his mind and then turns his attention back to the cave where the creature that he followed had entered.

After nearly a half an hour, one of the creatures comes to the cave entrance and looks around. When it doesn't pick up any foriegn scent, it slowly leaves the cave and sniffs the air around it. Still not picking up the scent, it moves to the area where Logan had last stood and sniffs the air some more. When there is nothing, it looks back at the cave and Logan notices the other two creatures. They come out cautiously, and Logan notices the differences in size and skin tone. The first one is about a foot shorter then the one he had followed to the caves, and it's skin tone is lighter and more of a greenish blue. The second one is no bigger then Kimtala and it's skin is the same as the one it is standing next to.

Logan studies them for a while and realizes that they must be a family unit. Deciding that the larger one must be the male, he studies the female's facial structure, trying to match it to one of the missing women. He then does the same to the male. He is fairly certain that they are possibly one of the couples missing from the expedition. That confirmed, he studies the child. There had been no reports of any children missing, so he looks for any signs that it might be human, but can find none.

Frowning at this discovery, he decides to return to the campsite and finish checking the mound. He was sure that he would find some answers there. Taking one last look at the creature and his family, Logan ports back to the site. Before returning to the mound, he rechecks the area and then sets his mind to pick up the higher pitch of alpha psi that he believes the creatures have. He then finishes digging up the mound. When he's done, Logan sits back on his heels and just stares into the hole not touching anything.

Inside the mound, buried about three or four feet down, is a clutch of eggs. There are five eggs, all the size and shape of footballs. Mentally he reaches out to the embryos inside and discovers that they are at this point mostly human, but are slowly changing into the creatures. Though he would like to remove one for closer study, Logan decides that it would not be safe to do so. Even though he wishes to learn more about them, he has no wish or desire to harm one of their young. He carefully covers the eggs back up with the dirt, and places the leaves and bushes back the way he had originally found them. While doing this, he senses one of the creatures coming, and slows down so that it can see that he is returning it to how it had been before. After a few minutes, he stands up and leaves the camp, returning to his ship. Getting something to eat, he goes to the lounge where he has set up the holo recorder and makes his report.

[I'm going to try to communicate with the family unit in a couple of hours. I'm sure that it was the male that saw me at the clutch. Hopefully he will realize that I mean his family no harm, and will let me get a little closer then I was when I observed them from the tree. There is a good chance that they are one of the couples that made up the group of botanists. I'll need to be closer to be sure. If they are, we will have to do a careful examination of each creature to determine if all of them were at one time human. It is possible that they have already produced young which while in the egg, are more human, but once they hatch they are no longer human.]

Turning off the recorder, he sits back and wonders what Cassie was doing at that moment. If he could communicate with these creatures and get some kind of information from them, then maybe he wouldn't have to stay on Avdacal over night. It surprised him that he had made contact so soon. He had figured that he wouldn't make contact until sometime tomorrow, if then. What had surprised him even more was the fact that the male had not attacked him while he was digging at the mound. Hopefully it had sensed that he was no real threat to it or it's clutch. Shaking his head, he gets up and goes to his cabin to lay down for a couple of hours. There was no telling how long it was going to take for him to get close to the creatures again.

Four hours later Logan is slowly approaching the area of the caves when he is surrounded by six of the creatures. He stops and stands still looking carefully around him. From their size and coloring, he figures that they are all males. When he spots the male that he had seen and followed earlier, he turns to him slowly.

"I mean no harm to you." He hears a growling from the other males, but keeps his concentration on the one in front of him. "You are Chiero Culato and your mate is Shama, granddaughter to my godfather, Roushta Barbertin." The growling stops and Logan looks around. The others are all looking at him in what seems to be total surprise. He returns his gaze back to Chiero. There are tears in the creature's eyes as he looks at Logan and shakes his head.

"N... N... No." Chiero finally gets out.

"Yes Chiero. I know who you are." Logan tells him gently.

"H... Ho... How?" Chiero questions him.

"Your face. Though it has changed, I can still tell that you are Chiero Culato." Logan explains not letting any of his pity show or be projected.

Chiero touches his face and begins to shake his head. "N... N... No hu... hum... human." He struggles to say.

"Yes you are human. All of you are still human." The creatures all step back from him and shake their heads in denial. "Don't be afraid. Now that I know for sure, we can work on a way to return you all to your true forms."

"Dra... dra... drag... ma... man de... de... sss... tro...oy."

"Who or what is this dragman?" Logan asks. Again the creatures shake their heads and step back. Logan moves slowly towards Chiero. "Who is dragman Chiero? Are you afraid of it?"

Chiero looks at the others and gives a type of bark. They look at him and then at Logan. He barks again and they move off into the trees. Chiero looks at Logan and then signals him to follow, before leading him to the cave.

With one last look around him, Logan follows him, staying at least ten feet behind him as he had promised Cassie. As they approach the cave, Shama stands and steps forward. When she notices Logan following behind him, she growls a warning and picks up the child.

Chiero barks and growls at her causing her to look from him to Logan and back again. After watching Logan for several seconds, she relaxes and steps back. Chiero walks over to her and nuzzles her and the child, touching each gently.

Logan comes closer but still keeps some distance between them. He sits down and keeps his hands where they can see them. Mentally he calls out the mobile recording unit so that he can record this meeting. He needed proof for the others so that they could begin working on a plan to help these people.

Chiero goes into the cave and comes back out with a small animal in a cage. He sets it down where they can all see it, and then sits down by his mate. "Dra... dra... drag... man co... co...

me w... we kn... kn... ow." Chiero informs Logan pointing to the cage.

"All right. Now tell me what this dragman is."

Chiero takes his mate's paw and looks up at the sky. Several moments pass before he looks back at Logan. "Sh...she bi...bi...big. Go...go...ld. Ma...ma...de u...u...us t...to dra...drag...man t...too."

"She's big and gold, and she made you into dragmen." Logan repeats and Chiero nods his head in agreement. Logan thinks of the golden creatures that he had seen in Drogen Firnap's mind. "How did she make you into dragmen?"

"No...t ss...ss...ure ho...ho...how di...di...did."

"Why couldn't our other people communicate with you? Do you remember them?" Logan asks, wondering why he was able to do so.

"Mi...mi...nd...ss no...t ri...ri...ght. No...t h...h...ear ch...ch... ange. Tr...try t...to wa...rn th...th...em."

"They couldn't hear your higher psi, and you tried to warn them." Logan figures out. "Could you show me what you tried to warn them about?" He points to his own head.

"Y...y...ou h...h...ear?"

"Yes, I can hear your psi."

"I tr...try." Chiero agrees and moves away from his mate and child. Logan moves closer to him. Once they're in position, Logan slowly reaches out his hand to touch Chiero's temple.

Chiero closes his eyes and tries to picture what he wants to show. Logan closes his eyes too, and concentrates on the images Chiero is sending to him. With the images of warning, Logan also sees what Chiero had not been sure of.

After about five minutes Logan pulls back and sits on his heels looking at Chiero and then at Shama and their child. They could probably reverse the transformation for the parents, but he wasn't sure what they could do for the children they had produced. Standing slowly, he walks back to his original place and sits down again. Chiero moves back to his mate's side.

"Y...y...ou ss...ee?"

"Yes I saw." Logan looks down at his hands and then back up at the family. "I also saw how you were changed into a dragman."

"H...h...ow?" Chiero's face registers his surprise and shock.

"The golden dragman placed a strand of her hair along the back of your neck at the base of your skull, and it imbedded itself there. You were then placed in a type of cocoon to finish the transformation."

"Y...y...ou ch...ch...ange?"

"I hope so. Chiero, I'm going back to Manchon tonight to speak with Master Healer Royanna. Do you remember her?"

"Y...y...ess. Go...goo...good he...he...healer."

"Yes she is. I'll work with her to find a way to change you back." Logan stops and looks at the child. "Chiero, I don't know if we can help your children though."

Shama clutches the child to her and starts to bark and growl at him. Chiero soothes her and then looks at Logan. "Y...y...ou t... try pl...pl...ease?"

"Yes I'll try. By the Great One I promise, I'll try to help your children too Shama."

Shama nods and looks down. Chiero nods then stands up. "Y...y...ou mu...mu...st go n...n...ow."

Logan stands up and holds his hand out. Chiero looks at it and then steps forward to grasp it carefully.

"Fr...fr...ien...d."

"Yes Chiero, we're friends. I'll be back, I promise." They shake hands and then Logan turns and walks back the way he came and sends a mental command for the recorder to return to the ship. He leaves it on to record the area back to the ship. They would need to study the surrounding area to discover if there was any ties to the changes that were taking place. He needed to get back to Manchon and speak with Royanna and his father. They would have to find a way to tell Roushta about Shama and Chiero.

CHAPTER SEVEN

Congratulating Sema on the birth of her son once more, Cassie says good night, and walks outside to wait for Royanna. Sheyome and Libre meet her at the bottom of the stairs. "Are you ready to leave now Cassie?"

"Not yet Shey. Since it's so late Royanna's going to ride back to the palace with us."

"Do you want me to ask one of the maids to take some food to your chambers?"

"Yes, that sounds good. I think just the fruits and vegetables for us, and whatever the men would like." Sheyome nods and then steps away to contact the palace kitchen. "Libre, when we were at Tatori's this morning, did you notice anything unusual?"

"Like what exactly Cassie?"

"Like another presence. I could swear that someone was watching us while we were there." She explains recalling the sensation of being watched from close by, but not seeing anyone. It had made her quite uncomfortable, but she hadn't wanted to say anything to distract Royanna and Chevala from what they were doing.

"It's possible that someone could have been watching from one of the other cottages."

"No, this felt closer. It was as if I turned my head I would have seen whoever it was, or at least their shadow."

"I didn't notice anything, but Shey might have. She was very tense while we were there."

Sheyome returns to them just as Royanna and Chevala come out. "Everything will be ready by the time we arrive Cassie."

"Thank you Shey." She turns to Chevala. "Are you sure that you won't join us Chev? There will be plenty for one extra."

"Thank you, but no. I promised Nacari that I'd spend some time with him this evening."

"No doubt he will try again to get you to become his dium." Royanna teases her with a smile causing Chevala to frown.

"He probably will and I wish he would give up on that. I like him as a friend nothing more."

Libre shakes his head and smiles sadly at her. "I've tried to explain it to him many times Chevala, but I'm afraid that my big brother is quite in love with you."

"Yes, and I'm afraid that I'm going to have to stop seeing him soon if he doesn't accept that our relationship is going no further." She sighs shaking her head. "Well, I better get going. I'll see you in the morning Anna." She hugs Royanna and then Cassie and Sheyome. "Good night."

As she walks down the road, a man steps out to talk to her. Cassie and the others see her shake her head at some question and then nod. The man holds out his arm to her, and Chevala hesitates before taking it. They disappear around a corner seconds later.

"Looks like Nacari didn't trust her to keep their date tonight." Sheyome says to no one in particular.

"Not totally." Royanna states and then walks down the stairs to join them. "I knew about their evening together, and about Chevala's doubts about their relationship. I let Nacari know where he could meet her." She admits to them without shame of her interference. Something had to be settled between them soon.

"You should not interfere Master Royanna." Libre admonishes her quietly.

"Why not? If left to her, she would have put it off and then he'd be following her around for the next week. No, she either has to accept him or make him to understand how she feels. Putting it off any longer will only make it harder for both of them."

They walk to the carriage and Libre helps Cassie and Royanna inside. Sheyome climbs up front followed by Libre, while the others climb onto the back. Picking up the reins, Libre heads them back to the palace.

⟋

"Yes, it sounds like she might have had something planned for you in the woods." Royanna agrees after being told of Nicca's joining them at their picnic and her suggestion. "The trees are so close to the path that barely any light from the sky shines on it. No one travels the path through it without luminous poles day or night."

"I remember Logan telling me that you need a good sense of direction when traveling through them." Cassie recalls pouring more juice. "Though I trust Shey and the others along with their abilities, I would rather go through there with Logan beside me."

"I for one am glad that you didn't take up the idea." Sheyome says with a shudder. "I got lost in there when I was eight. It scared me so bad that I couldn't even port myself out. I haven't set foot in there since."

They finish their meal and move to the sitting area. Neila, who brought the food, asks if they need anything more before she returns to the kitchen and the rest of her duties. She had found it strange that her services had been asked for again by Lady Cassandra.

"No Neila, that will be all. You can put the rest of the fruit in the storage unit though." Cassie instructs her.

"Yes Mistress."

Before she leaves, Royanna calls her to her side and Neila kneels down beside her. She, like all of the staff knew that before they left Lady Royanna, they could expect their memories to be erased of anything that might endanger them. She had no fears of the memory swipe. Lightly she feels the touch of Royanna's fingers at her temple. All of what she had heard is carefully wiped from her memory and replaced with everyday conversation.

"You may go now Neila. See me tomorrow if you still have a headache."

Neila stands and curtsies before going to the float tray and leaving the room. After the door closes, Libre signals the other guards and they all stand. "We're going to keep watch in the hall for a while Cassie."

"All right Libre." She nods to them and they leave closing the door quietly behind them.

"What did you think of the birthing Cassie?"

"It was interesting Royanna. Was the passing around of the baby part of the bonding with the family?"

"Yes, though the true bonding ceremony won't happen for another two days. At that time the godparents will be named and when they have been bonded with the child the family will strengthen their bonds. If anything should happen to the parents, then the godparents will take over the care and raising of the child."

"I wish that I could have been there when Kimtala was born and was a part of her family." Cassie says to no one in particular thinking of how such an experience would have been and the closeness she would have with Kimtala.

Royanna and Sheyome both smile at the wistfullness in Cassie's voice. "Even though you weren't here Cassie, you are bonded to Kimtala." Royanna assures her. "Truloka says that except for myself and Chevala, you and Logan are the only ones that she has ever self-bonded with." Cassie looks at her in surprise.

"Because I'm with you so often," Sheyome adds, "she's also bonded with me."

"Is this good?" Cassie wonders aloud.

"It's very good my dear. Truloka's family usually only bonds within itself. For Kimtala to bond with you means that she feels that you are a part of her family. Such bonds are rare even with other Majichonie, and you are not from Manchon. Kimtala has made of you an honor rarely given to other-worlders."

"Is that why I felt so strongly that she might be in danger at our picnic?" Cassie explains how and what she had felt and about seeing Firnap.

"I have no doubts that's why. You did good to warn her to stay away from him. I just wish that we had some physical proof that he was responsible for the disappearance of our people."

"But what about my parent's memory Anna? It's proof that he was the last to see them on Manchon." Sheyome points out.

"If others had received parts of their memories as well, it would be proof Shey. But no one else did, which means it would never get past the council because they all know that you distrust him."

"Then how do we get proof that he is responsible without placing someone in danger?" Cassie asks the question that has them all worried. She did not want to place anyone into a situation that might possibly get them hurt or killed.

"We have to hope that Logan finds out something on Avdacal that will help us." Royanna sips at her juice before setting down her glass. "I heard from Roushta and Thurda after you both left us this afternoon. As far as they can tell, all of the creatures that they got on tape may well be some of the missing people. They do agree with Logan that the two that died were your parents Shey. I'm sorry."

Sheyome looks down at her lap for several seconds before looking up again. When she does Cassie and Royanna notice the tears in her eyes, that she still refuses to let fall. "I agree with him too Anna. The female's cry sounded to much like my mother, and my father would never be far from her side when she was that distressed."

"At least we know that the couples are staying together. We'll have a private service for your parents when this is all over Shey." Royanna assures her placing a hand over Sheyome's and giving it a gentle squeeze. She just wished that there was something more that she could do for her to heal her grief.

The chamber door opens and Logan walks in. The three woman look up in surprise and then Cassie jumps up from her seat. "Logan!" She cries out and runs to throw herself into his waiting arms, nearly knocking him to the floor.

Catching her and his balance, Logan hugs her close and brings his mouth down on hers for a long hard kiss. When he finally releases her lips, he smiles down into her eyes. "You didn't happen to miss me did you?"

"Oh you!" Cassie punches him in the shoulder. "What happened? Why are you back so soon? You're not hurt are you?" She looks him over carefully.

"Whoa there, one question at a time. I'm fine and things went better than I could have planned." He puts Cassie to his side and looks at Royanna and Sheyome. "Good evening."

Walking over to the sitting area he invites them to sit back down and then seats himself and pulls Cassie down onto his lap. "We'll discuss what I've found, but not here. I've sent Libre to get a carriage ready. We're going to meet father at Roushta's where we're less likely to be interrupted." He looks up at Cassie. "Go and pack up our things sweetheart. After our meeting we'll be staying with my father and sister until I find us our own house."

"But...but what about Tru and Kim? They'll be returning in less than a week." Cassie stammers knowing that Thurda's home isn't big enough for a maid with a small child.

"They'll stay with Tru's mother until we find our own place. Don't worry, we'll have room for them. And if father and Chev agree, Tru can come and help out at the house while we're there."

Pacified Cassie stands up and goes to pack their things. After she leaves the room, Logan looks at Sheyome. "Was there any trouble?"

Sheyome tells him about everything that had happened since he had left that morning. About the Timeless One and her warning to Cassie and the mark she had left on Cassie's hand. She also tells him what she had done to protect her.

"All right Shey. From now on she's never to be left alone. I want you with her at all times. Unless she's with me, my father, or Royanna." He tells her. "Can you sense when Firnap is around?"

"I think so Logan. Whenever he's close I tense up."

"Okay, we'll have to get the others to raise up their psi to detect a higher pitch of psi. They'll have to raise it about three points. If Firnap is one of the creatures like I suspect, they should be able to sense him at that level. We'll know for sure tomorrow or sooner if he should come around. I'm all ready set to pick up on him."

Cassie comes out of the bedchamber and closes the door behind her. As she comes into the sitting room the others stand.

"Got everything love?" Cassie nods and Logan takes the bag from her. "Libre should have the carriage ready by now. We'll drop this off at father's before going to Roushta's place." He opens the door and Sheyome steps out first.

Royanna and Cassie follow her, while Logan brings up the rear, closing and locking the door behind them. He nods to Sheyome and she leads them down the hall checking well ahead of them as they go through the palace. They reach the carriage at one of the side entrances without meeting anyone. Logan helps Royanna and Cassie into the enclosed carriage and then climbs in after them. Sheyome climbs up next to Libre, while the others climb onto the back and sides. Once everyone is ready, Shey touches Libre on the arm and he pulls away from the palace at a slow pace so as not to draw unwanted attention to them.

After dropping their bag off at Thurda's, Logan has Libre take an ever changing route before having him head for Roushta's.

When they reach the house, Logan has him and the other guards stand watch at different positions around the house. "Put the carriage in the stables and keep in constant mental contact with each other. If you spot anything unusual, let me know immediately." He looks at each of them.

Knowing that his orders would be followed to the letter, Logan enters the house and closes and locks the door, then turns to face the others. "What I'm about to tell and show you must stay between the six of us at all cost. Whenever any of us are at the palace, we will need to protect our minds. We may even have to do it outside the palace as well."

Everyone looks at him gravely before nodding their agreement. Roushta leads them into his private study where they sit down. Logan ports the holo recorder from the ship before taking his own seat. "I have positively identified two of the missing people from the group of botanists." He stops and looks at Roushta. "They are Chiero Culato and his mate Shama."

Roushta gasps at the news of his granddaughter still being alive, but being one of the creatures. Thurda reaches over and grasps his shoulder tightly. Roushta takes a deep breath and then nods that he is all right.

Though he would rather have broken this news to Roushta more gently. He had realized on the way back to Manchon that they didn't have time for gentleness right now. "Chiero still has the power of speech, but there's no way of telling for how long. I found a clutch of five eggs in the botanist camp. That was how I found Chiero. Right now they have a hatchling about the size of Kimtala. I believe that the clutch I found was also theirs." Logan stops again as Roushta gasps and turns pale.

Royanna and Cassie move quickly to Roushta's side. Royanna touches his forehead to calm him and Cassie places a hand over his heart. Instantly she feels his pain and gasps herself. Logan quickly stands and rushes to her side.

"Don't touch her Logan!" Royanna warns him sharply but quietly. When Logan stops a couple of feet from Cassie, Royanna nods and then looks at her. Speaking just as quietly she tells her what she needs to do. "Block his pain from both of you Cassie."

Nodding jerkily, Cassie tries to block Roushta's pain from both their minds. When the pain subsides she nods and Royanna asks her what she sees. "It looks..."

"Tell me with your mind. Show me what you see."

'It's like someone is squeezing his heart in a heavy fist every couple of seconds, using more and more pressure with each squeeze.'

'All right, I see it. Use your mind to massage it. Get it to relax and slow down to a normal rhythm Cassie.'

Cassie does what she can as she continues to project the image to Royanna. *'It's beginning to relax. I can feel the tension going... going...it's gone.'*

'Okay, now, think of it as undamaged, the walls are strong healthy tissue and the main arteries are clear and unclogged.'

Cassie pictures a healthy heart beating and pumping naturally. When the beating is back to normal, she pulls herself back and slowly opens her eyes. When she removes her hand from Roushta's chest she collapses and Logan catches her and carries her over to the couch and lays her down gently.

After making sure that Roushta is feeling better, Royanna quickly mixes up an herbal drink for Cassie, and makes her drink it down slowly. With Logan's help, Cassie sits up and looks over at Roushta and gives him a shaky smile.

"Are you all right now?"

"I'm fine now, thanks to you." He returns her smile. "When you first touched me the pain lessened and then it went away completely."

"I'm glad." She gives him a stronger smile.

"As am I. I'm just sorry that it happened. I guess it was just the shock of hearing that my first great grandchild was born as one of these creatures, and that five more are in eggs buried in the ground."

Logan sits down beside Cassie and takes her hand in his. "I'm sorry too Roushta. I just didn't think how much of a shock the news would be to you."

"Don't worry about it son. No matter how you had told me, it would still have been a great shock."

"At least Royanna and Cassie were here to help you through it." Thurda points out, relaxing now that his friend was out of danger. "Cassie will make a good healer on day. She's not afraid to help when its needed or to do what is needed." They all smile as Cassie blushes.

"Okay. Let's finish this out so that we can find a way to help my granddaughter and the others." Roushta tells them sitting straighter in his chair.

After looking over the tape and listening to Logan's report, Sheyome offers to get them all something to drink from the kitchen. Royanna stands by the study window looking out into the night. She knows that Roushta is counting on her to find a way to reverse the transformation of his granddaughter and the others up on Avdacal. She's just not sure that there is a way, and if there is, will they be able to change everyone back?

"If we do find a way to reverse the transformation, one of the creatures will have to volunteer for the first attempt." Royanna tells them still looking out the window. "We'll also need one of the first ones to be transformed. There may be a time limit to when the transformation can be reversed."

"Then we're going to have to search for them. I'm pretty sure that the ones with Chiero were also part of the botanist team." Logan tells her.

"What do you think our chances are of finding the others?" Thurda asks his son, watching Royanna.

"By ourselves, not good father. I think that if we can reverse the transformation, Chiero might be willing to help us." Logan looks at Royanna not wanting to put her on the spot, but having to know. "What about the children Anna? Will we be able to change them also?" He didn't want to go back on his word, and he felt that if they couldn't the others would refuse.

Royanna turns to face them and looks sadly at Roushta. "I honestly don't know." She looks at Logan. "From what you've told us, they lose whatever part of them is human before they ever emerge from the eggs."

"Isn't it possible that somewhere in their genetic makeup a human gene could still exist, but lay dormant? After all they start out as human even in the egg. Wouldn't that mean that some part of them could stay human, but be hidden?" Cassie asks with a small frown.

"Not necessarily Cassie. It would depend on the strength of the dragman genes." Royanna explains as she returns to her chair. "For the degree of change done to the adult body, and in such a short amount of time, it would appear to be very strong." She frowns a little in thought. "Then again, it is possible since they are human in the eggs even for a short amount of time. It would mean using a totally different type of procedure on them then we'll be using on the adults."

Sheyome comes in carrying a tray with a pitcher of juice and a bottle of flincen. Logan stands and takes the tray from her, setting it on the table. She thanks him and pours out drinks, then hands them around. "While I was getting the drinks I thought of something." She tells them taking her glass and sitting down. "Why can't we just pull the strand out? If we remove it the transformation should automatically reverse itself."

"That would be the logical thing to do." Roushta admits having thought of it himself. "But chances are that some of their nerves are now attached to the strand as well. If we were to try to remove it, we could either kill or cripple them."

They all sit quietly trying to figure out some way to help the people trapped on Avdacal. Cassie looks around at the others thinking about how the people of Manchon were so different from those on Earth. These people truly cared about what happened to others and were not willing to risk those lives unnecessarily. It didn't matter that they weren't related, but that they were human and that they needed their help.

"What if we could look into their bodies and 'see' what had to be done? It would make it easier to treat them and be less dangerous."

"It would be less dangerous for them, but not for the person that was doing the 'looking'." Logan points out to her. "They're aggressive creatures Cassie. For all that they were once human, they could still turn on us with no other reason then it being a natural response."

"Not if we were to mind sedate them first." She points out reasonably. "We couldn't use any drugs on them, but we could use a mental sedative. As soon as they agreed to cooperate, we would sedate them and go from there."

"There's another problem with that plan." Royanna says as she sets down her glass and sits back. "None of our healers can 'see' specific organs or nerves, and only a few can even see at all. It would take considerable concentration and stamina to follow the paths and then the 'looker' would also have to sever anything connected to the strand and repair the damage immediately. Plus we would need a second person to do the sedation and remove the strand."

"I could do it." Cassie tells them quietly. "It would be just..."

"No!" Logan interrupts her shaking his head in denial. "You will not do it. When this is done, it will have to be done on Avdacal. I don't want you anywhere near that place until it is completely safe and no longer a danger."

"How much safer is it here with Drogen Firnap running around, always watching me, and Nicca plotting against me? Besides, I can 'see' what Royanna and the others can't. I've already done it twice today." Cassie argues and then takes Logan's hand and holding it against her cheek. "Please let me do this Logan. Let me help to bring these people back to themselves, back to their homes and their families. I may not know them but I don't want to know that I could help and didn't and they are lost to everyone. I couldn't live with myself knowing that."

Logan looks at her, at the pleading in her eyes. He wants to protect her from the danger that he feels creeping into their lives. He turns to look at Roushta as he clears his throat.

"I know that you wish only to protect your mate Logan, but you must also look at it from the view point of the people she would be helping. She may well be their only hope of ever being human again." Roushta points out not thinking of what it would mean to himself. "Are you willing to deny them this one chance of returning home where they belong?"

"No, of course not. But..." Cassie squeezes his hand and Logan looks down at her again. Closing his eyes, he sighs. "All right, but before we try it, I want you to practice with Royanna and Chevala until you can do it without passing out or getting dizzy. I don't want you taking any chances."

Cassie smiles up at him. "I will atmo."

Logan returns her smile reluctantly and then looks at the others. "Since we've covered everything, I think that we should call it a night and get some sleep. We all have to be at the Council meeting in less then nine hours." He stands up and pulls Cassie to her feet.

Roushta stands and stretches while Thurda stands and holds out his hand to Royanna. She takes it and stands slowly, using the time to speak privately to him. *'You must tell him now Thurda, before we leave here.'*

'I know atma.' Thurda looks at his son. *'Why don't you take Cassie to the front parlor while I tell him?'*

Royanna nods and holds out her hand to Cassie. "Come my dear. Thurda needs to talk privately with Logan before we leave." She raises her hand to stop Logan from objecting. "We'll wait for you both in the front parlor and go no further."

Cassie bites her lower lip and then reaches up to kiss Logan's cheek. *'Stay calm love.'* She warns squeezing his hand and then releasing it to take Royanna's. She lets the older woman lead her from the room with the others. Logan watches them leave and then turns back to his father with a raised brow.

Thurda clears his throat and turns a little away from his son. "What I have to tell you is very important son and...and concerns Royanna." He looks at Logan and sees him frowning. "There's no easy way for me to tell you this, so I'll come straight out with it. Royanna is at present my dium. I'm hoping to convince her to become my life-bond mate."

Logan looks at his father for several moments. "I see." Though he says this, he didn't see it at all. How could his father, who had always told him while he was growing up that love meant beyond forever, even when one's mate died? Was he now telling him that had all been a lie? "What about mother?"

"My relationship with Royanna takes nothing away from what I feel for your mother Logan. My love for her is just as strong now as it was when she and I were first lifemated. But I also love Royanna, though it's a different love, it's strong too."

"How does she feel? I thought that she loved Thayer's father?" Logan sneers in contempt and pain for both himself and the betrayal he felt for those that weren't here. "Or was he just a distraction for her? Is that why she wouldn't take him for her lifemate? Did she know that one day she could get her hands on you when mother was gone?"

Thurda strikes him across the face with an open hand. "You will watch your tongue and show more respect!" Thurda snaps furiously. "Royanna loves Robus as much if not more than I love your mother young man. Both Royanna and Robus knew that his mind wasn't strong enough for a lifemating to take place. It tore them apart to know that they could never totally share themselves like your mother and I could. Knowing that they would never have that most wonderful of gifts." He tells him sharply holding nothing back, and going so far as to share his memories with his son of that time. "We knew exactly when Robus took his last breath. Royanna felt his loss immediately and it took all the skill your sister and I have for healing to keep her from following him on his final journey. So don't you dare ever belittle what she felt for Robus Starhawk. Do you hear me?!"

Logan closes his eyes and rubs his cheek and then his temples. "I'm sorry father." He says quietly opening his eyes and looking at him contritely. "You're right, and I have no right to judge. I'll stand by you and your decision."

"Thank you son. I'm sorry for striking you."

"Don't apologize father. You had every right for doing it, and I deserved a lot more then a slap across the face for what I said. If it had been Thayer, I would be a bloody heap on the floor right now, and he would not be apologizing for giving me exactly what I deserve."

"It still doesn't excuse my having done it. You were up set and lashing out for something you didn't understand. Royanna has been worrying about how you would react. I guess she should have been worrying about how I would react to your reaction. When you told her about coming to stay at the house, she wondered what you would say or do when she stayed at the house instead of returning to the palace."

"I didn't mean to worry either of you. I've just never thought of you with anyone except for mother. She's probably been uncomfortable around me since I came home, and I apologize for that." Logan says now understanding the looks and touches that had past between the two since he had returned home. He was just surprised that no one else had told him before now.

"I don't believe that son. Besides, I don't think an apology is necessary. I should have told you about us when you first came home. Just let her know that you approve and that you won't hold our relationship against her."

"I will and I don't." He assures his father, and looks at him. "Does Cassie know about you and Anna?"

"Yes, she knows. I think she had already guessed soon after you both arrived. We confirmed it this morning when she came to breakfast." Thurda turns to the door. "We better head back to the house now. Chevala will be wondering where we've gotten to. She had a date with Libre's brother Nacari this evening, and I promised not to interfere or interrupt. I think that she's planning to end their relationship."

"Have they been seeing each other long?" Logan asks as they leave the study.

"A couple of years now. He wants more out of the relationship then your sister does." He stops and places a hand on Logan's arm. "Are you going to explain the mark on Cassie's hand to her?"

Logan looks ahead of them to where the others are waiting between the parlor and the front door. "Yes, I'll tell her about it before we go to bed tonight."

Thurda nods and they continue down the hall. Watching them come down the hall, Royanna and Cassie keep their eyes on the two men.

'It's going to be all right Royanna. Logan's accepted your relationship with his father.'

Royanna nods and smiles shakily at Logan. Returning her smile Logan hugs her. "I welcome you into our family Royanna." He kisses her cheek. "Please forgive me for any discomfort I may have caused you unintentionally."

"No forgiveness is needed Logan." She assures him as he steps back.

Logan turns to look at Roushta. "Remember to put a shield up before entering the palace. I don't want Nicca or Firnap to even suspect what we've learned and have planned."

"I'll put it in place before I even walk out of the house in the morning."

"That sounds good."

"Libre and the others are ready with the carriage Logan." Sheyome informs him.

"All right, you go first and than father and Royanna will follow. If you notice anything unusual Cassie and I will port into the carriage."

Sheyome nods farewell to Roushta and steps outside. Seconds later Thurda and Royanna follow her. After seating Royanna inside the carriage, Thurda signals to Logan that everything is secure. He and Cassie walk out of the house and climb into the carriage. Thurda climbs in after them and as soon as the door closes behind him, Libre starts them off for the Knightrunner house. None of the guards leave anything to chance, they continue to search the areas around them for any hidden threats.

CHAPTER EIGHT

The next morning everyone is quiet at the breakfast table as Royanna tells Chevala which of her patients she wants the younger woman to see when she goes on her morning rounds. "If I'm unable to make my afternoon rounds, I'll contact you about who you'll need to see. Are you sure that you'll be able to handle the extra people?"

"I'm sure. There aren't that many and most of them are already in the area I'll be checking on today."

"All right, contact me if you run into any problems with any of them. I've already informed them that you are coming in my place." Chevala nods and continues to push her food around on her plate.

'Sis, are you all right?'

'I'm fine Logan. Just feeling a little down right now.'

'Your date with Nacari didn't go very well did it?'

'No, it didn't go very well.' Chevala stands and picks up her plate. "I think that I'll get an early start this morning. I'll see all of you tonight." She gives them all a smile and then turns and walks from the room.

'If you need to talk sis, Cassie and I are here to listen any time.'

'Thanks little brother. I appreciate that.'

Thurda looks at his son, but Logan only shakes his head slightly. Sighing, Thurda finishes his coffee, wishing that he could protect his children from ever feeling such emotional pains.

"When should we approach Nicca about taking the exam? Should we do it before or after the council meeting?" Royanna asks pouring more coffee for Thurda and Logan.

"It might be best if we waited until after the meeting." Logan tells her taking a sip from his coffee. "That way we don't take the chance of her anger reaching out to anyone else. Our combined abilities should be able to defuse it more quickly if we don't have to worry about the others."

"Maybe I shouldn't be there for the examination Logan. Nicca doesn't care for me and my being there might anger her more." Cassie says looking at each of them her eyes coming to rest on Logan.

"That may be dear, but you're Thayer's ambassador, and there for his eyes and ears." Royanna points out to her. "When he asks how his cousin is doing you will be better able to tell him having been present for the examination. You will know her first reactions and you may even pick up on something that I miss."

"She's right Cassie. Though Logan also represents Thayer, only you have the right to report Nicca's condition to him."

"But Thayer has known Logan for years. He knows that Logan would tell him everything he needed to know about what is happening."

"He also knows about my former relationship with his cousin Cassie. That's one of the reasons he made you his ambassador. There will be little or no doubt on who influenced who when all is said and done. No one can claim a bias should things not go to their way of thinking. You have nothing to gain and are as Royanna stated his eyes and ears here on Manchon."

Cassie looks into Logan's eyes and sees the truth, faith, and wisdom in Thayer's decision to send her. She also knows that he did it so that she and Logan could stay together and be able to strengthen their bond before they were lifemated.

"We should go now. The meeting will start in less than an hour." Thurda mentions as he stands. "Roushta will meet us outside the council chambers."

Logan and the women stand and they all walk to the front door. Cassie and Royanna put on their shawls and then they all put their mind shields up before leaving the house. Just before they step out, Logan strengthens Cassie's shield even more and kisses her briefly.

⌒

"And who would be the High Leader of the Alliance Mistress Blackwood?" Queen Niccara asks after all points for the Alliance have been gone over again.

"Majesty, his Majesty King Thayer and Queen Leyla feel that all of the royal houses of the Alliance should share equally in the leadership. That no one person or world should have power over the others." Cassie states firmly looking straight into Nicca's eyes. "They feel that this will help to keep all things in perspective for everyone. The Federation is losing their own perspective in the fact that only one people are seen as the major leaders."

"Then why do we not just join the Federation and become members of their council?" Someone down the table asks.

"Yes, why not? It would be easier then starting a new Alliance. Once a part of their council we could then stop things before they could get started or out of hand." Someone else adds and others begin to murmur their agreement.

"Ladies and gentlemen." Logan stands and holds up his hands for quiet. "It would take at least ten years maybe more before we could achieve such a position on their High Council. By doing so, by joining the Federation, we could no longer remain neutral. They would then have the right to use our planets and people as they choose." He stops and looks around the room. "Is that what you want for our children, our people, to become fighters and destroyers? Because that is what they will become if the Federation ever gets control of us." He sits back down and nods to Cassie to finish what she has been trying to tell them. Privately he tells her to tell them everything that they can expect and to hold nothing back. They had to be made to understand what they could look forward to should the Federation take control.

"What Logan has said is all true, it had already started on Earth. The children will be expected to train with other Federation children. Any young men and women over the age of eighteen will be assigned to combat training. Then there's always the chance that they'll just be expected to use their abilities to kill the intended target or to control them." Cassie looks around the table at the council members and then back at Nicca. "Is this what you want for your people your Majesty? That they become killers for someone who doesn't care about their spiritual well being, doesn't care that such actions will be killing them little by little, day by day? That's why we need this Alliance, why Thayer and Leyla are working to join us all together. So that all our children, all our people, don't have to be put through these things."

Once again the murmuring begins as Cassie sits down still looking at Nicca. Several seconds later, Thurda stands up and the chamber quiets down. "Your Majesty. I for one do not wish to see my grandchildren turned into slaves by the Federation or anyone else. I do not want to see our people suffer at the hands of people who will only use them to manipulate and destroy others."

"Thank you Lord Thurda for stating your stand on this matter." Nicca says quietly nodding for him to sit down. "Lady Royanna, what are your feelings on this matter?"

"I to, do not wish to see my grandchildren turned into slaves. Neither the children or anyone else deserves that type of life. As the ruling body, it is our duty to our people to see that this doesn't happen. Now or ever." Royanna looks around the room. "If any one of us allows such a thing knowingly, than that person does not deserve his or her position." She looks at her niece for only a minute, then looks away.

There is silence throughout the room as everyone thinks about Royanna's words. Roushta clears his throat and stands. "I think that we should adjourn for now and think over all that has been said here today. We have learned more that should not be taken lightly."

"Yes, I agree Lord Roushta." Nicca says quietly and then stands. "We will adjourn until tomorrow morning, when we will again meet and discuss this further."

Everyone else stands as well, and then Logan and the others in his group follow Nicca from the chamber. Royanna approaches her quickly. "Nicca, I need to give you another examination."

Nicca stops and turns to face her with a narrow look. "Why? You just examined me a short time ago. Nothing has changed since then."

"True, but it has to be established that there is no physical or mental reason for your decision to be questioned. Some of your actions of late have been questionable to some of the people." She tells her truthfully. "Even I question some of what you have done. As your Chief Advisor, and the Master Healer, it is my duty to establish your stability for this very crucial decision." She tells her knowing that she is placing the majority of the decision to do the exam on her own shoulders to protect the others should the younger woman become angry.

Nicca looks around at the others with her aunt. A frown appears when she sees Cassie standing beside Logan. "I can understand Thurda and Roushta's presence, and even Logan's to some degree, but why Miss Blackwood?"

"Cassie has to be present because she is Thayer's representative, and she will be the one to report to him on the results." Logan points out to her.

Nicca frowns more deeply. "And if I refuse to have this examination?"

"Then I will have to remove you from the throne of power." Royanna tells her looking her straight in the eye so that there is no doubt that she will do just that if she has to. "A refusal will be taken as a sign that you are attempting to hide something that could be dangerous to one and all."

"Very well. When do you want to do the examination?"

"Right now will be fine."

Nicca nods and leads the way to the palace healing room. Drogen walks beside her and whispers in her ear. "This is not good. You should have refused this examination Niccara."

"I could not. You heard what she said. To do so would mean losing the throne of power." She hisses back at him.

"Better that then them discovering our Mistress." Firnap whispers sharply. "If that other woman touches you she could feel the Mistress' presence within you."

"She won't. There is no reason for her to touch me. She will observe, nothing more."

They finally reach the healing room, but before anyone enters, Royanna steps forward. "Mr. Firnap may not enter. He must remain out here."

"You ask too much my Lady Aunt. He is my personal guard and is always with me." Nicca protests beginning to worry about this examination.

Royanna shakes her head that Nicca would feel it necessary to have a guard present. "That does not matter now Niccara. You will be amongst family and friends, and are in no danger. None present would do you harm and you know this to be true."

Wanting to avoid any questions being asked about his constant presence, Firnap nods his agreement. "The Lady Royanna is correct your Majesty. I will remain here until you are done." He tells her quietly causing Nicca to look at him sharply. He nods his head once and steps to the side of the door.

"Very well then. Let's get this over with!" Nicca says coldly and leads the way into the room.

"Your physical body is not in very good shape. You've lost more weight and your skin tone is more sallow." Royanna tells Nicca as she helps her put her robes back on. "I don't understand why you're still losing the weight."

"I've been eating and drinking the extra meals and teas you told me to. Daemon even brings me fruit pastries to eat before we go to bed each night."

"We may have to try some stronger herbs to decrease your metabolism, so that you don't burn up the fats and calories so quickly." Royanna tells her and waves to a chair. "We'll do the mental exam now."

Nicca goes over to the chair and sits down. She looks around at the others. "Who is going to assist you since Chevala isn't here?" She asks looking over at Logan.

"Cassie will be helping me. I'm training her, to improve her healing abilities." Royanna tells her stepping behind her chair and pulling her hair back away from her temples. "Now relax Nicca." She urges her when she feels Nicca's body tensing. Cassie steps up beside Royanna. Not wanting to upset her niece any more, Royanna talks to Cassie telepathically. *I want you to do the contact. Tell me what you see and feel as you did with Roushta.'*

'Won't she know that it's me doing the contact?'

'No. You make the contact and I'll join with you quickly. She'll feel my presence and it will distract her while you search. She won't know for sure which of us is doing the searching.'

'How far should I go?'

'As far as you comfortably can. Remember to keep your shields up at all times while your searching. Never forget that Nicca is one of the strongest psi's on Manchon.'

'I'll remember.'

"All right Nicca. Now I want you to totally open your mind and try to stay as relaxed as you can so that I don't cause you any pain. It shouldn't take me any more then fifteen minutes to complete the exam. Keep your shields and defenses down Nicca. I don't want to be hurt any more then I want to hurt you."

Nicca closes her eyes and nods when she's ready. Cassie steps forward and places her fingers gently on Nicca's temples. Royanna places her right hand on Cassie's shoulder near her neck and joins their minds together.

While waiting for Royanna to distract Nicca, Cassie tightens and strengthens her shields to where only Royanna should be able to penetrate them. As soon as Royanna gives her the okay, she begins to search through Nicca's mind and memories. After only a couple of minutes, she feels the other presence and pulls back from its malevolence. *'There is definitely another mind present Royanna. It is a vicious and evil mind.'*

'Can you continue?'

'Yes, I think so.' Cassie says taking a deep breath both physically and mentally before continuing. She goes on, following the malevolence through Nicca's mind. All the time reporting to Royanna what she sees and feels. *'There is a lot of fear and anxiety going through her Royanna. She's also in extreme conflict with herself.'*

'Can you tell if the other mind is controlling her?'

'Yes, I'm sure that it is in some way.'

She goes a little further only to stop suddenly when she feels the malevolence trying to push it's way into her mind. Her body stiffens slightly in reaction.

'Do you think you can stop me Earthling? This one will soon be mine as will you.'

Cassie shivers as the other mind speaks to her. Though she tries to block it out, the voice continues, and she wonders if Royanna can hear it as well.

'This world and all its people will be mine Earthling. I will have all of them and then we will spread to other worlds. My people will grow stronger once again until we rule all of your so called humanity.'

'We won't let you do that. We will find some way to stop you. You can't control people and expect to get away with it. None of us will let that happen. Not even Niccara.'

'You can try, but you will not succeed. This one is more mine with each day. None is strong enough to defeat the Dragman.'

'You're wrong, and we will stop you.'

Cassie finally pulls back, leaving the malevolence of the Dragman to wonder at her brave, if empty words. They had to find a way to stop this creature before it hurt any more people, and before it gained complete control of Nicca. She suddenly becomes aware of Royanna mentally calling to her, and she can hear the panic in the call.

'Cassie answer me! Are you all right?'

'I'm fine Royanna. We're finished now.'

'But what...?'

'Later, when we're away from here and can discuss it with the others.'

Though she wants to insist, Royanna knows that she is right. She does not like it that she had lost contact with Cassie's mind, even though it was only for a few seconds. She tells Nicca that they will release her in just a moment, that she had one more thing she had to check. When Cassie steps away, Royanna touches Nicca's left temple and quickly checks her thyroid for any abnormalities.

'What is the decision on her state of mind to be Cassie?'

'Leave her in control for now, but we must keep watch over her at all times.'

They completely release Nicca and step back. Thurda helps Royanna, while Logan puts an arm around Cassie's waist. Cassie leans into him, grateful for his support. Before anyone can ask questions, she speaks first startling them all, including Niccara.

"As far as I am concerned, Nicca is fit to remain in her position, unless or until she shows signs of physical or mental stress."

Nicca frowns up at her over her shoulder for a minute and then slowly stands to face her. "Thank you Cassie. Now, if you will all excuse me, I wish to go and lay down. Such exams are a bit wearing on the mind and body."

"We understand. We'll see you at the meeting tomorrow morning. Drink some pinsang tea when you get up again. It should help with the weariness." Royanna tells her as she walks with her to the door. She opens it and nods to Firnap and then watches them walk down the hallway. Turning back to the room, Royanna closes the door and looks at Cassie with a raised brow.

"Not here, not now. I think that we should return to the house for our discussion." Cassie says to her quietly.

———————/———————

"She knows of our Mistress' presence. I told you if she touched you she would know. You should have stopped it from happening." Firnap snaps at Nicca.

"I couldn't. She was Royanna's choice to assist. I didn't think that Royanna would have her do the mind search." She snaps back at him. "Besides, I don't think the Mistress was too concerned about it."

"She should not have had anything to be concerned about, but now we must send the Earthling to her to deal with. You must deal with Knightrunner. He must not go looking for her."

"He'll look for her Drogen. Their bond is very strong and not so easily broken."

"Then we'll have to make sure that it is broken painfully. Nothing must get in the Mistress' way. She must continue at all cost. Even if it means killing a few of these weak minded fools."

Nicca says nothing more. In her last private spot in her mind, she rails at herself for ever letting this happen. It wasn't her people that were weak minded, it was herself, and the people were being made to suffer because of it. She wished that Cassie had not chosen to let her continue as Queen. If she hadn't then maybe her people would have had a better chance. At least then they would have some idea of what they were dealing with. It would have forced the Golden One to leave her lair and deal with the people herself instead of through her.

Niccara didn't know how much longer she could hold out against the Golden One. After so many years, she was tired of fighting it. If only she could have told her aunt what was going on, maybe none of this would be happening now, but she hadn't wanted to put her in any danger. If something should happen to her aunt then the people of Manchon would be lost. She had been protecting her as best she could, but soon there would be no way to protect any of them.

CHAPTER NINE

"Part of the Dragman's mind is within Nicca. Though I'm not sure how. It claims that it will soon have complete control of her." Cassie tells them once they are all settled into Roushta's private study. It had been agreed as they left the palace that they would go there instead of the Knightrunner home. "It plans on taking over all of Manchon. It's going to change all of the people into those creatures and then go out to other worlds. All it cares about is the domination of humanity."

"Why did I lose contact with you?" Royanna wants to know.

"When it was communicating with me, it seemed as though it was trying to surround my mind. I think it may have been trying to leave a part of itself inside my mind."

"It didn't did it?" Logan asks looking into her eyes.

"No it didn't. My shields kept it out and I had made them stronger just before I entered Nicca's mind. I allowed for Royanna's touch, but when I felt the other I had to strengthen them even more and had to cut her off from me." She assures him. "There is something else you should all know and understand. Nicca has been fighting the Dragman's control over her." She looks at

Royanna. "That's why she isn't gaining any weight. All her energies are being put into keeping some control of her mind. Drogen is her watch dog, and any time she gives him trouble the Dragman causes her some kind of pain either mentally or physically. It's slowly wearing her down and I'm not sure how much longer she can hold out against them."

"What about the people that have been taken?" Roushta asks. "Do you know why they were chosen?"

"Most were taken to become breeders. Others were taken to be workers. The workers care for the Dragman, seeing to her comfort. Those will be the hardest ones to get when we start the reversal."

"How many care for the Dragman?" Thurda asks thinking that they may be able to do them one at a time.

"I'm not sure, possibly ten or fifteen. There are two that stay with her at all times." Cassie tells him.

Thurda nods and looks off into the distance. With that many they could change more of them at once, but they would have to make sure that they weren't being monitored for it to work.

"When will you be speaking to Thayer?" Royanna asks.

"Sometime this evening. They should be getting ready to head for Panthera to further discuss the Alliance with the Pantherian and Aquilian leaders." Logan tells her. "I think that we should have them come here before they go though. We may need their help to deal with the Dragman."

Cassie nods her agreement. "I think so too. If the Dragman is capable of such control of Nicca at this distance, it's power could be more than we can handle." She warns them quietly.

"In the ships they brought to Earth, they could be here in less than a week. But I think that we should have them wait until we've reverted as many of our people back as we possibly can before they make their presence known."

"Is that wise though?" Roushta wants to know. "If Thayer and his queen can deal with the Dragman, and destroy it, we may not have to reverse the change. They may change back after it's destroyed."

"They may also stay that way forever or die upon it's death Roushta." Royanna points out to him. "No, first we must see to our people. We can't take any further chances with their lives. We could be their only hope to becoming human once again."

"Let's wait and see what Thayer and Leyla think about this whole thing." Cassie suggests running a hand through her hair. "Either way, we will need their help to change the children. There is still a human element in them that only Leyla and Thayer will be able to reach."

'That's what we're up against Thayer. Nicca is fighting, but I don't know how much longer she can hold out against it.'

'What do you think we should do Cassie? Should we come now and show our support or wait?'

'Truthfully Thayer, I think that you should wait. We don't know if the Dragman would be able to sense your power or not. If she can, she may do something to Nicca and the others before any of us could stop her.'

'What about you Logan? What do you think?'

'I agree with Cassie, Thayer. Until we know the true extent of the Dragman's power, we need to treat her with the thought in mind that she could cause more problems once a stronger power is present. I'd like to get our people safely away if possible before you make your move on her. That way she can not use them against you and possible sacrifice them to save herself if things go against her.'

'What about the children? There is a chance that once we destroy this Dragman, they will remain as they are.'

'I don't think so Thayer. I believe that it will be easier once the Dragman is gone, to change the children to human form. The human part of them is something that the Dragman did not count on. She

couldn't remove all of the humanity from them, and this makes them different from her.'

'All right, we'll wait here until you need us. If we sense anything before then we'll be there immediately.'

'We don't expect any trouble until after we start changing people back to their human forms.' Logan informs them.

'All right Thayer. Please tell my family that I said hello, and that I'm doing fine here. Everyone's been wonderful.'

'I will Cassie, take care. May the Great One bless and protect you.'

Cassie collapses back in her chair as Thayer ends their communication. She rubs her temples to relieve some of the pressure caused by channeling her thoughts for so long. "I hope that I can get used to that soon."

"You will. Channeling your thoughts will become easier with time and practice. Don't forget, until recently the only one's that you've communicated with have been within a ten mile radius at the most." Logan explains handing her a cup of tea.

There's a knock at the door followed by Thurda and Royanna entering the room. "How did it go?" Royanna asks taking the chair next to Cassie.

Cassie sips at the tea before answering. "Fine. They're going to wait until we need them to deal with the Dragman before they come. Thayer agrees that the Dragman may sense their power and do something to Nicca and the others." She tells her. "He also said that if they sensed anything wrong before we contact them, that they'll come immediately."

"How are things progressing back on Earth?" Thurda asks getting himself a drink. "Have they gotten Leyla's parents settled to deal with the Federation for the people?"

Logan steps to his father's side and gets his own drink. "Yes, but they still want to make sure that they have everything under control before they leave." He tells him. "They're talking about keeping Earth under Calidon and Manchon protection. Since it seems that a lot of our people settled there in the past, and most of the telepaths there can prove blood ties to Manchon."

"How far back are their ties?" Royanna asks thinking of the past hundred years and the hundreds of their people that had left for other worlds.

"As far as they can tell, as far back as ninety to a hundred years, possibly more. There are of course more recent ones, but there's no doubt to the blood ties. Each one has proof of their Majichonie blood."

"Would any of them care to come to Manchon now?" She wants to know.

"I don't think that Thayer has asked any of them yet." Logan says looking at her closely. "But even if they do wish to come, wouldn't the law keep them from doing so?" He asks wondering out loud.

"Not if we change the law." Thurda puts in. "None of us really feel that the law is very fair to the families still on Manchon. We all have the right to know what is happening or has happened to family members that are no longer living amongst us. They in turn have the right to the protection of their birth world."

"Why was such a law ever made in the first place?" Cassie asks having wondered about this since she had first found out about it. "Why would you want to cut your own people off that way? Without such a law things might have been different on Earth. Your people could have let you know what was happening, and you might have been able to stop it."

"The law was made to protect us from outside influences. The Federation wasn't that old and was always at war. Always looking to strengthen their forces. When we refused to join, they convinced some of our people to go with them. They promised them all kinds of things. Things that we didn't have here." Royanna tries to explain. "When those that had left returned, they brought back with them all the negative attitudes that they had picked up from the people they had been with. After their return, criminal activity increased at a frightening rate. Everyone that was involved was taken into custody and reprogrammed. The ruling family, my family, then made the law that any Majichonie wishing to leave Manchon could not return. It was further decided that their descendants could not return either, because they would be just as likely to bring back those same negative traits."

Cassie shakes her head at the finality of such a law. To never be allowed to see one's family again, or one's home would be too much for her. She suddenly looks around to the others. "What about Logan and I? Will we have to stay on Manchon until the law can be changed?"

"The law will be changed before you ever have to make such a decision my dear. I promise you, it will be changed." Royanna assures her reaching over and gently patting her hand.

"I don't know about the rest of you, but I'm ready for some sleep." Thurda says stretching. "The meeting will start at eleven tomorrow, instead of nine. Nicca is meeting with Tacara first thing in the morning. It seems that Tacara's mate is still missing and she is insisting that Nicca to send out trackers to find him. She can't understand why she hasn't already done so. Family is all she has for support now. She won't let anyone else help her during this time."

"I just hope that she doesn't upset Nicca to the point of her doing something she will regret later on." Royanna says worriedly. Standing she moves to Thurda's side. "We better get some sleep. I want to be at the palace early to give them both my support, and maybe waylay any trouble between them. Good night dears. We'll see you at the meeting if we don't see you at breakfast."

They leave Logan and Cassie and head up to bed. Logan stands up and walks over to the window. He looks outside and thinks about what could happen tomorrow. He turns back to Cassie. "I'm going to go with Royanna tomorrow and try to help keep things under control."

Cassie looks up at him. "Are you sure that's wise Logan? Nicca might resent you being there since its a family matter."

"I don't think so. She just might control herself if I'm there."

Though she doesn't like the idea, and she feels that something major is going to happen tomorrow, she agrees that his presence may just keep Nicca from doing something crazy or stupid. "Well if you're going, I think that I'll go and visit with Tru and Kim. I'll meet the rest of you in time for the meeting."

"All right. I'll tell Shey and the others before I leave in the morning." He walks over to stand beside her chair. "Are you ready to go up to bed?"

"Yes. I feel as though I've just spent the day mind wrestling with Merri and Colt and came up the loser."

Logan reaches down and takes her hand to pull her to her feet and into his arms. He kisses her and then ports them up to their room. He knew how draining the distance mind contacts could be, and was proud of her for never giving up. Her mind was getting stronger with every touch Leyla and Thayer had with her.

⸻

Nicca wraps her robe tightly around her waist and looks back at her bed where Daemon is sleeping. Quietly she leaves the room, closing the door gently behind her. Stepping into her private sitting room, she turns to face Drogen. "What do you want? I'm tired, and have to be up early in the morning to talk to Tacara about Raude. You weren't suppose to take anyone from my family until we had control of the others."

"He was asking too many questions about me and my activities. I caught him following me after one of my returns. I am to do whatever I deem necessary to keep my movements from being discovered." He reminds her curtly. "What I came here to tell you is that the Earthling will be gone very soon. You must break her bond with Knightrunner. The Mistress is not ready for him yet. If he shows up before she's ready, she will destroy him."

"But she has promised him to me! She can't do that!"

Drogen slaps her, knocking her onto the small sofa. "Do not ever presume to question the Mistress' decisions about anything again, or what she can or can not do! Do you understand?" Nicca holds her hand to her cheek and nods slowly. "Good. Start breaking their bond tomorrow. If you don't Niccara, he will pay the price for your failure with his life." Turning, he walks from the room.

Nicca stares after him and starts to shake all over. She wraps her arms around her waist and hugs herself tightly. After several minutes she turns to return to her bed and gasps when she sees Daemon standing in the open doorway.

"I'm sorry atma, I didn't mean to startle you." He assures her walking to her side. "What's the matter?" He stops in front of her. When she turns away from him, he gently but firmly turns her back to face him. "What happened to your face atma? Who struck you?"

"Nothing, it's nothing Daemon. Please don't worry about it. I couldn't sleep that's all. It felt like there was something crawling on my cheek and I slapped at it, that's all." She tells him, not quite meeting his eyes as she lies to protect him.

Daemon frowns slightly, sure that she wasn't telling him the truth. "Well, if you're sure. Are you ready to come back to bed now? Tacara will be arriving early to talk to you. You look as though you could use a lot more sleep."

"Yes, I am still very tired. I hope that I don't have to go through any more of those examinations. They're very draining."

Wrapping an arm around her shoulders, Daemon leads her back into the bed chamber. He helps her out of her robe and into bed. Going around to the other side, he climbs in beside her and pulls her into the curve of his body. "Rest now atma. You'll find you feel better in the morning."

Sighing, Nicca snuggles up closer to his side with her head on his shoulder. Slowly her body relaxes and her breathing slows to that of sleep.

Staring up at the ceiling, Daemon wonders what he should do about the hold Drogen had on his love. To have her removed from the throne would cause her great embarrassment and humiliation, and he just couldn't bring himself to do such a thing to her. He wonders if she even realized that he knew what had been going on for the past few years, or what his silence was doing to his peace of mind and spirit. Though he couldn't really blame her if she didn't. Whomever or whatever was controlling her, wasn't giving her a chance to think about anything or anyone else and they were slowly killing her. Knowing that there was nothing he could do at the moment, he relaxes and lets sleep finally reclaim him. In the night, Nicca whimpers, and Daemon reaches out to her automatically to give comfort from the demons that plague her.

CHAPTER TEN

"Cassie, I'm having a bad feeling about this visit." Sheyome says looking all around them as they walk to Truloka's family home. "It feels as though something is going to happen."

"I feel it also." Libre warns.

"But what could happen? I cannot believe that anyone would be crazy enough to attack royal guards." Cassie says with confidence. "Besides, they should know that it would not be wise to anger Logan. When he gets angry, you don't want to be around him when he blows. It could be very dangerous to your health."

"And if something should happen to you, Shey and I will be held responsible." Libre reminds her.

"Nothing is going to happen to me Libre. You won't let it. Besides that, I'll stay in the house the whole time that we're there. All right? You, Shey and the others can stand watch outside."

"All right, but make sure that you stay in mind contact with Shey at all times. She doesn't have to know your thoughts, she just has to feel them." Libre warns her as they finally come to their destination.

"I will." Cassie smiles at them and goes up the steps and knocks on the door. She walks in and the door closes behind her without any of them seeing who opens the door. Once she's safely inside, the guards take up positions at each corner of the house to wait not concerned by what they had not seen.

/

"You have to send someone to look for him Nicca. He wouldn't just up and leave without a word to anyone." Tacara begs her sister. "Emira will have her first transition soon. Raude must be there to help her through it."

"And where do we start looking for him Cara? He could be anywhere on Manchon." Nicca points out reasonably. "Unless they know where to begin searching, it would be a waste of their time and energy."

"Damn it Nicca! If it were Daemon who was missing you wouldn't care how much time and energy it took. You would do anything to find him. Well Raude means just as much to me!" Tacara cries out, whirling away from her older sister and falling into Royanna's arms.

"Tacara, you know that Nicca cares about you and your mate. If there was a way to find him, don't you think she would do whatever she could to do so?" Logan asks touching the weeping woman's shoulder.

Tacara looks up at him. "How can I believe that Logan? She won't even look for the botanist sent to Avdacal. She knows and cares about a lot of them too, but she's never sent anyone up there to search for them."

"And I've told you, like I've told all the others that have questioned me about my decision, that there was no psi trace of them from those that took up supplies. There's no way to locate them without some form of psi to follow. You know that." Nicca tells her for what seems to be the hundredth time. "With Raude its doubly difficult because we don't know where he was when he disappeared."

"But we know where he was going, and which way he took. The trackers could start from there." They all hear the pleading in Tacara's voice as she turns to look at Niccara. "Please Nicca. Won't you at least try?"

Everyone looks at Nicca and she frowns slightly before turning away from them. She wishes that Drogen were there now. With him around she would know what to say, though it would not be what her sister wanted to hear. Slowly she turns back to face them. She would give in because she knew that Drogen would never leave any trace of his victims for anyone to find.

"Very well Cara. I'll send someone out to search. You must accept whatever their findings may be. Many people have gone that path since Raude's disappearance, and the tracker may find nothing of him at all."

Tacara runs to her sister and hugs her tightly. "I will accept. Thank you Nicca."

Hesitating only slightly, Niccara returns the hug, then steps away. "Now go and see to my niece. I'll let you know when the tracker has anything to report."

"All right." She hugs her once more and then turns to Logan and Royanna. "Thank you both for being here."

"Your welcome dear. Come, I'll walk you out." Royanna says placing an arm around her niece's shoulders and guiding her to the door.

Logan watches them leave, grateful that things have worked out. He turns back to face Niccara who is now standing near her chair rubbing her temples and watching him. "You've relieved her of a lot of her worries by agreeing to the search Nicca."

"A lot of good that's going to do Logan. You and I both know that the odds of a tracker finding anything are a thousand to one. What am I suppose to do then?" She asks shaking her head not really expecting an answer. "Sometimes I wish that I had never been made queen."

Logan walks over to her and places his hands on her shoulders. "From what I've heard since my return, you've been a good queen.

You've just had a lot on your mind lately. Which is completely understandable with all the disappearances."

She smiles at him slightly. "That's true. Your return hasn't exactly made things any easier either. When I first learned that you were coming back I thought that maybe..."

"You thought that we would continue where we left off." He finishes for her.

"Yes. Though Thayer neglected to mention that you were involved with his ambassador." She says bitterly staring at his chest. "Even so, I've been thinking that it could still work out for us." She wraps her arms around his waist and lays her head against his chest. "It could work Logan, I know that it could. We would be perfect to rule Manchon together. The two strongest families joined together. No one could defeat or control us." The last is said with even more bitterness.

She looks up at him then and Logan notices a feverish light in her eyes. He slowly shakes his head as he feels a mental push for him to accept her words. Carefully he unwraps her arms from his waist and steps back. "I'm sorry Nicca, but there can never be anything more than friendship between us now. Cassie and I are meant to be together." He gently assures her still holding her hands in his.

"NO! You can't know that for sure Logan." She denies him squeezing his hands with more strength than he thought she possessed. "You've been away a long time. You need to get used to being around your own people again, that's all."

Logan sighs. "Nicca, you must believe me. Cassie and I are lifemates. Our minds and spirits are as one. They have burned with the 'fire' for a long time."

"No, I don't believe it! I won't allow it!" She shouts at him. "You will become my mate Logan Knightrunner or...or I'll not agree to this alliance. I'll close down the planet. No one will be allowed to come or go and your precious Cassandra will be reprogrammed as a criminal to Manchon should be."

Logan stares at her, not recognizing this person standing in front of him. "You can't do that Nicca. Cassie is under Thayer's protection as well as mine. Your abilities may be equal to mine, but believe me, you're no match for him or Leyla. If you should do anything to harm her in any way, there would be nothing that anyone could do that would save you from their anger, especially Leyla's. Cassie is like a sister to her, and she would do whatever she wanted to get revenge against you for hurting Cassie."

Nicca completely pulls away from him and turns her back. "You know my wishes Logan. Either agree, or Cassandra Blackwood will pay the price." She walks to her private door before stopping and turning back to him. "You have until the meeting to decide. I will then publicly express my wishes. Deny me and within the hour she will not even remember your name." With that she walks out and slams the door behind her.

Running his fingers roughly through his hair, Logan curses and leaves the room. He needed to talk with Royanna and to check on Cassie. They couldn't put it off any longer. Nicca had to be removed from the throne. If she did something to Cassie, she wouldn't live long once Leyla found out.

⌒

"Where's Kimtala Tru?" Cassie asks looking around the room that Truloka leads her into. Something was very wrong here. The house was too quiet, and Kimtala should have greeted her by now.

"She's...she's still abed Mistress. She was up late with the babe last evening telling him about the palace and...and things." Truloka tells her nervously, twisting her hands behind her. The Great One forgive her, she didn't want to hurt Mistress Cassie, but they would hurt her sweet Kimtala and the rest of her family if she didn't do as they said.

"Oh, well we can discuss your new duties then." Cassie says signaling the other woman to sit down and reaching out to the child. She had to be sure that she was really all right. "Since we're staying with Logan's family, there isn't much room. If you wish, you can come there to work while you're staying here, or you're free to find another position. We still want you to come to us when we find our own home." Finding the child unconscious and not merely asleep, she knows that something is very wrong and quickly plants the thought for her to awake only when Logan touches her mind and she knows that she is safe. She can feel the evilness in the house close to her.

"That...that would be...would be fine Mistress." Truloka says nervously noticing the shadowy form moving behind Cassie. "I...I..." The shadow stops behind Cassie and Truloka jumps up from her seat. "NO!" She cries out.

As Cassie looks behind her, Drogen spits his venom into her face as she jumps to her feet. Within moments she collapses into a heap on the floor. As soon as she hits the floor, Drogen's man stuns Truloka and steps over her fallen body. He picks up the Earthling and looks to Drogen, who uses a personal transporter to get them out of the house seconds before Sheyome and the others break in.

They quickly check the house finding the rest of the family in a back room, all but the baby have been stunned. Sheyome calls out to Chevala and Royanna, then waits for Logan to appear, knowing that they would not have to wait long. Within two minutes of Cassie's disappearance Logan appears in front of Sheyome looking around the house as if searching though he knows that Cassie is no longer there.

"What happened Shey? Where's Cassie?"

"I don't know Logan." She tells him looking around the room again. "There's no sign of her or a struggle, and there's no way out of the house that one of us wouldn't have seen her."

"What about Tru and her family?"

"We're waiting for Royanna and Chevala to come and revive them. All of them were stunned except for the baby, which is lucky, because it probably would have killed him."

121

Soon Royanna and Chevala rush in. They examine everyone before reviving them. Within minutes they're all awake except for Kimtala. Royanna sits back on her heels and frowns. "I don't understand why she's not coming out of this Logan. I can't find any reason for her to still be unconscious."

Logan frowns down at the little girl. "Let me try. You had better go and try to calm Tru. She's beginning to become hysterical." He tells her nodding his head to their left. Royanna nods and stands to walk over to where Truloka is. Logan looks down at the small child in front of him. He carefully picks her up and places her on his lap.

'Kimtala, can you hear me sweetie?' He mentally calls to her and listens closely. *'Come on Kimmybird. It's time to wake up now.'* Again he waits and listens. All he can pick up from her is fear. *'It's okay sweetie, you're safe now. Logan's here now. I won't let anyone hurt you again Kimmybird. I need you to wake up now Kim. Cassie needs you.'* Logan watches her face and soon a small frown appears. *'That's it sweetie, come on.'*

'Ca...Ca...Cassie.' Kimtala's mind calls out weakly. *'Ca...Cassie. Have to help...Cassie.'* Slowly her eyelashes flutter and she takes a deep breath. Her lashes flutter again before opening. It takes a few seconds before her eyes can focus on Logan's face, when they do she cries out and wraps her small arms around his neck crying softly.

"It's all right baby, you're safe now. Shh." Logan assures her patting her on the back gently as he embraces her.

"Bad man take Cassie." Kimtala tells him between sobs.

"What bad man Kimmybird?" Logan asks looking up as Royanna and the others step forward. "Who was he Kim?"

Kimtala looks up at him and then around at the other adults standing around them. Her eyes stop at Sheyome and she sends her the mental picture of Drogen Firnap. Sheyome gasps and closes her eyes at what the little girl is showing her. Several seconds later Kimtala collapses against Logan and Sheyome sways slightly.

122

Catching herself, Sheyome opens her eyes and looks at Logan. "Firnap." Is all that she says.

Logan stands carefully and hands Kimtala over to Chevala and then turns to Truloka. "What happened here Tru? How did Drogen Firnap get into your home and how was he able to take Cassie without any of the guards knowing anything about it until it was too late?"

"I don't know my Lord." She says quietly looking down at her feet instead of at him.

"You don't know?!" He exclaims. "How is that possible? You let Cassie into the house. How could you not know how he got inside?" Logan demands taking a step towards her.

Royanna steps in front of him and places her hand on his chest to stop him. *'She's telling you the truth Logan. All she remembers is a great fear for her family and Cassie. Nothing more.'*

Logan takes a deep breath before stepping back. "Then how could Kimtala know what had happened?"

"I think that before she was knocked out, Cassie put everything into Kim's mind." Shey tells him stepping forward. "That's probably why it took so long for her to come out of it. Cassie probably suggested that she awaken only for you. She couldn't be sure that something hadn't happened to me and the others."

"Then why didn't I pick up on what she sent to you?" He asks running his hands through his hair in frustration.

"Kimtala's mind is still only attuned to send to other females Logan." Royanna explains. "The only males that she can send to are those in her own family. Your bond with her isn't yet strong enough for her to send to you."

"But I don't understand, I heard her as she was waking." He tells her with a frown before shaking his head. "Okay." He turns to Sheyome and looks deeply into her eyes. "Show me what she showed to you Shey."

Sheyome is slightly stunned by the sharp contact, but she opens up to him. After he receives the images Logan looks at

Truloka who is trying to stem the flow of tears down her cheeks. He steps up to her and gently places a hand on her shoulder.

"I'm sorry for snapping at you Tru. I know none of this is your fault." He assures her. "My fear and anger caused me to speak to you as I did."

Truloka nods and looks up at him. "I would never willingly do anything to hurt or harm Mistress Cassie my Lord. Never."

"I know that Tru. I know. We'll leave you to tend to your family. When you're done, I want you to go to Lord Roushta's and stay there until I summon you, understand?"

"Yes my Lord." Tru nods and curtsies before taking her daughter from Chevala and rushing from the room.

Logan watches her go and then turns to the others. "Shey, I want the other two guards with you to stay here and wait for Tru and Kimtala, then escort them to Roushta's. Send to the palace for a half dozen more guards to watch over their family. Pick only those that you would trust with your own life."

"I know just who to get Logan." She assures him and closes her eyes to contact the people she needs.

Logan turns to Royanna. "Father will meet us at the house. We need to plan how we're going to proceed. We know that he's taken her to Avdacal and what will happen. We have at most three days before Leyla and Thayer show up and then all hell will break loose."

"All right. Chevala can stay here and keep an eye on the others, especially Kimtala." She looks at Chevala. "You may have to help her through some mind pain caused by Cassie's transfer. No doubt it was done quickly and she didn't have time to prepare Kimtala's mind for it."

"I'll do what I can. You go and start making plans. I'll join you as soon as I can."

Sheyome opens her eyes and focuses on Logan. "They're on their way. They'll stay with the family until you or I dismiss them."

"Good, then let's go. I don't want to wait too long before we move." He leads the way out of the house and down the path.

"We should contact Nicca and let her know that we won't be at the meeting." Royanna mentions climbing into the waiting coach.

"At this moment I don't care what she thinks about our missing the meeting. No doubt she already knows." Logan snaps and climbs up beside her. "I can't believe that she was stupid enough to allow this to happen. I've warned her what would happen if something should happen to Cassie. Now she'll find out that I wasn't exaggerating about Thayer and Leyla's reaction. She'll find out only too soon."

"What do you mean you warned her? Why would you have to warn her about anything?" Royanna asks in confusion swaying back as they start off.

Logan tells her about his conversation with Nicca after she and Tacara had left them alone. How when he refused her, she had threatened to have Cassie reprogrammed within an hour if he refused her at the meeting. "That's when I warned her about Leyla and Thayer. I just hope that Thayer is now strong enough to prevent Leyla from hurting Nicca. If he's not, then Nicca could very well die. There's also the possibility that Thayer himself could destroy her."

Royanna stares at him in shock, unable to believe what he is telling her. "Do you really believe that Leyla would kill Nicca? That Thayer might? Even knowing that her actions are controlled by the Dragman?"

"I don't know Anna. We'll have to do some quick talking or else get Cassie back before they get here."

They stop at the Knightrunner home and Logan gets down and turns to help Royanna down as Thurda comes out of the house. "Nicca is throwing one of her tantrums because you both left and Roushta and I followed. She's canceled making a decision indefinitely." Logan looks at Royanna and raises a brow as if to say 'See what I mean.'.

"Let's go inside." Royanna takes Thurda's arm and walks to the front door with Logan close behind them. Roushta meets them in the entryway.

"Firnap's ship took off seventeen minutes ago." Roushta tells them as they enter the house.

"That's about three minutes after I lost contact with Cassie." Logan confirms.

"Then we need to move quickly before the Dragman has a chance to change her into one of it's creatures."

"But how do we find her? I have no mental contact with her at all."

"There's still your physical connection, which is just as strong." Royanna points out leading the way into the sitting room. "It should be strong enough for you to reach out to her that way."

"I'll try..." He stops suddenly and closes his eyes.

'What's happened to Cassie Logan?!'

'She's been taken Leyla. I'm getting ready to...'

'Who's taken her?'

'Drogen Firnap. I'll be going after her soon.'

'We'll be there in fifty-two hours. I had better feel her mind before I reach Manchon Logan.'

'I'll do my best Leyla, you know that. But you must give me time.'

'You have until we get there Logan. Then I handle things my way, and queen or no, family or no, Niccara Rican will pay for what she's done.'

'Leyla, you can't just blame Nicca for what's happened. She's not in total control of her mind. The Dragman has more control then she does.' He waits for a response and after several seconds calls out to her. *'Did you hear me Leyla?! You can't blame this all on Nicca.'*

'I can and do Logan. But I will wait an extra twenty hours. If I do not feel or physically see Cassie in that time, Niccara will pay dearly for what has happened.'

'I understand Leyla. But you need to understand too. Nicca has been fighting this thing alone for a long time, and it's almost killed

her. Cassie was...is willing to give her a second chance. Will you do any less?' Logan knows that he is taking a chance, that Leyla is upset and worried about Cassie, but he also knows that he has to get her to think about what Nicca has gone through and is still going through.

'All right Logan. I will give her a chance, but you have to get Cassie back. We're leaving now.'

'Okay Leyla. We'll see you in fifty-two hours.' Logan opens his eyes and looks at the others. He sits down and rubs his temples. "We have two and a half days to find Cassie before they arrive. Less if we plan to save Nicca from Leyla's anger and pain."

Royanna frowns and paces around the room. "We are all going to have to go with you to Avdacal. Without Cassie's help the removal will be a little more difficult, but I believe that with Thurda and Chevala's help, I can still do it." She looks at Roushta. "You will have to keep a close eye on Nicca while we're gone."

"Do you think that she'll cause any problems?"

"No, at least not while Drogen is gone. I've noticed that when he's not around she's calmer and not so agitated."

"We won't have to worry about him after this trip." Logan assures them as he stands up. "He won't be returning from Avdacal."

"What will we be needing to take with us?" Thurda asks looking from Royanna to Logan. "We need to get started."

"I've got most of what we'll need on my ship. You and Anna may want to bring some environmental suites to wear though."

Just then Sheyome and Libre enter the room. "The other guards are in place Logan." Sheyome says as they stop just inside the door. She looks to Roushta. "Truloka and Kimtala will arrive at your home mid afternoon my Lord with four of my best guards to watch over you all while we're gone."

Roushta nods and then looks at Logan. "I'll make sure that they and their family stay safe while you're gone."

"Thank you." Logan looks back at Sheyome. "I wanted you and Libre to come to Avdacal with us and I see that you've already decided to come. But do you think that you can handle the situation Shey? If not, I'll understand."

Sheyome takes a deep breath and considers everything that is at stake. "Yes, I can handle it Logan. What do you want us to do?"

"For the moment you will be guarding my father, Royanna, and Chevala while they do the removal. If I should need any help in my search, one of you will stay with them while the other helps me."

Chevala enters the room stepping around Sheyome and Libre. "Klinwa is with Tru's family now and Kimtala is doing fine."

"Good. I suggest that we leave now then." Logan tells them turning to Roushta. "If you need us use code one-zero-nine. The computer unit on the ship will pick it up on the scrambler. Only use mind contact if its extremely necessary. Everyone will be using most of their mental powers for the removal and transformation."

Roushta nods and then shakes Logan's hand. "Good luck my boy." With that he nods to the others and leaves.

Logan faces the others and notices that they all have their environmental suites in their arms. "I'll teleport us directly onto my ship." He tells them and then touches his wrist communicator to contact the ship. "Ali, come in."

"Yes Logan."

"Start the engines and set course for Avdacal. I want to get there as soon as possible."

"All right Logan. What's wrong with Cassie? Her bio-rythums are extremely erratic and there is very little brain activity."

"I'll explain everything to you in a minute Ali. Get the ship ready, we'll be there in a few seconds." He looks up. "Let's go." He holds out his hands and his father and Royanna each take one, holding out their free hands which Sheyome and Libre then take. Chevala finishes the circle and Logan closes his eyes to concentrate on porting them all safely. Within seconds they arrive on the ship and drop their hands. Logan hurries to the control room.

"Let's go Ali. Top speed once we've cleared Manchon." The ship lifts off and their speed increases the higher they get from the planet's surface.

"Where's Cassie, Logan? She's not one of those that came with you." Ali asks him worriedly.

"She's been taken by Drogen Firnap. We have to reach her before the Dragman has a chance to change her into one of it's creatures." He tells her checking the monitors. "Did you observe Firnap's ship leaving the planet?"

"Yes, but it disappeared from my monitors and all my sensors."

Thurda and Royanna enter the control room at that point and Thurda frowns. "Could a ship that small have a cloaking device of some kind?"

"Possibly, but highly unlikely." Ali states. "There would be an energy discharge of some kind that could be tracked. I picked up no such discharges."

Logan continues to watch the monitors for several more seconds. "What about a mental cloak? Thayer and Leyla used one when they were gathering the last of their people to escape detection from Earth Security. They were able to control it for several hours."

"It's possible Logan, but I don't believe that Drogen has the power to carry it out." Royanna puts in. "Though his psi is on a different level and pitch, it still isn't strong enough for such an action. Even if he could do it, he wouldn't be able to maintain it for very long."

"Which means that either we're missing something or the Dragman is able to transmit high energy from it's lair." Logan concludes.

"How long before we reach Avdacal?" Thurda asks looking at the monitors.

"Three hours and forty-two minutes." Ali replies.

"Well, I suggest that we go over the removal procedure before we arrive on Avdacal."

"You're right father. Ali, keep monitoring and let us know if any ships land on Avdacal. We'll be landing at the same site as we did before."

"All right Logan. Cassie's bio rhythms are weak but steady. We'll find her."

"I hope so Ali. I truly hope so."

CHAPTER ELEVEN

Cassie fights to clear her numbed mind. Her body feels as though it's weighted down. After several attempts, she manages to open her eyes to mere slits and then to a more normal opening. The chamber she's in is very dark at first and then her eyes begin to adjust to the darkness. She notices several long tube shaped bundles across from her.

"You're awake at last Earthling. This is good." A female voice says coming from somewhere to Cassie's left.

"Who's there? Where am I?" Cassie asks moving her eyes in the direction of the voice.

"You know who I am Earthling, and you know where you are also."

A tall shadowy form moves into her line of vision causing her to gasp and draw back as the Dragman steps closer and lowers it's face closer to hers. "I told you, you would soon be mine. You will soon see that my power is without equal anywhere in the universe."

"You won't get away with this. My mate will come for me."

"He may come, but he will never find you. This mist has closed your mind to all. Once I place a part of myself within you, no one will be able to mind talk with you ever again except for me."

The Dragman reaches up and plucks one of its golden hairs from the back of it's head near it's neck, and bringing it forward so that Cassie can see it. At the end that was pulled from the skin, Cassie notices movement and strains her eyes to see it better.

"Now you will be mine and will serve me as the others do. Though I do not yet know if I will make you a breeder or a worker." The Dragman says with a frown looking at the hair in it's hand.

Cassie is still watching the movement of the hair and realizes that it has a life of it's own. She thinks to herself that this must be how the strand is placed so easily into the victims. It burrows itself into them. Concentrating as hard as she can, Cassie tries to send Logan this new information, knowing that it is important for Royanna to know. When she begins to feel weak she stops and prays that it had worked.

"Now you shall join my people to serve me. You will make a good breeder." The Dragman tells her looking up from the hair. "I will put you to my strongest breeding male. Though he already has a mate and has produced six young, so far only one has hatched. You should both give me good dragmen."

The Dragman nods and two dragmen servants step forward and unstrap Cassie from the stalagmite she had been placed against. Each of them take an arm and lead her to a stone table near the tube shaped bundles. Seeing their true size for the first time, Cassie realizes that these are the cocoons of the people taken within the last week or so, and that she would soon be joining them. Not knowing if she has any chance of succeeding, but needing to try, Cassie forces herself to brake the restraint of the two dragmen's hold on her arms.

Stunned by her attempt and an unexpected electrical charge, the dragmen release her arms and step back, right into the path of the Dragman. Blocking her path to Cassie.

Taking advantage of the situation, Cassie quickly runs around the table and heads for the corridor that looks to be lighted by the sun. Though her body feels weak, she forces herself to keep moving. In her flight from the transformation chamber, she passes several of the worker dragmen busily cleaning and moving things around. The dragmen stop what they're doing and watch as she makes her way to the entrance of the cave.

Blinded by the light outside, Cassie stops just inside the entrance and briefly closes her eyes. All of a sudden she hears a roar behind her and spins around. The Dragman is lumbering into the outer chamber, pushing her way past the workers that are blocking her way.

"Move you fools! She must be stopped!" The Dragman roars at them.

Not waiting to see what happens, Cassie runs from the cave and looks around for a way to go. She also memorizes the location of the cave so that they'll know where to find it later. Quickly she heads off into the trees using the skills she learned at the stronghold to cover her trail and make it difficult for anyone or anything to follow her.

"Are you sure it was Cassie, Logan?" Royanna asks across the table from him where they are eating a light meal. "After all, none of the others have ever been able to communicate after being taken." She points out.

"I'm sure Anna. It had to be her, no one else knows that something like this would be important to us."

"Could it be that something within Cassie can fight off Drogen's mist?" Chevala asks looking from one to the other. "After all, she's not Majichonie, and doesn't have the same type of bio rhythms that we do. Even her thought process is slightly different from ours."

"That could be it." Royanna agrees.

"Yes, but how are we to find her?" Sheyome asks looking around the table. "Even if her mind fought off the mist, the Dragman has probably implanted that hair and no doubt has full control over Cassie now." She voices not wanting them to forget who now had her and what they were up against.

"I don't believe so." Thurda disagrees setting his cup of coffee on the table. "Don't forget, Cassie has spent time with the Starhawk family and has no doubt learned some things that may assist her in some way."

"Only if she can get away father." Logan says and then tells them about the type of training Cassie had received. "So you see, unless she can get away from the Dragman, none of her skills will do her much good."

"I believe as Lord Thurda, that Cassie will find a way to escape before it is too late." Libre puts in his own thoughts on the subject. "I think we should all believe that she will."

After a couple of hours on the run Cassie stops to rest. She climbs up into the highest tree and finds a branch that will allow her to see in all directions. Not knowing what abilities she still has, she tries a basic kinesis test by trying to bring one of the broad leafs closer to her. Though it takes a great effort, she finally succeeds. Setting the leaf down, she rubs her temples to relieve the pain and pressure caused by the attempt. Taking a look around she notices no movements other than those of small animals. She watches a couple of cattila birds gathering grasses to build their nest. Soon she begins to feel tired and braces her body in what feels like a natural seat on the branch close to the trunk of the tree. Its deep enough where she can feel safe going to sleep without worrying about falling.

Examining the leaves around her, she feels certain that her hiding place is secure from all eyes. To be on the safe side though, she puts up a shield that will block her thoughts, breathing, and scent from being picked up by anything. Though she's not certain that it will work, Morning Star had told her it was always a good defense just in case.

Several hours later she awakes hearing barks and growls coming from off to her left. The sky is darkening, but it won't be completely dark for a couple of hours more. She wonders if she should try and find Roushta's granddaughter and her mate. She knows that even if Logan and the others follow, that would be where they would go first. Carefully she checks the area below for any signs that the dragmen have been in the area. Once she's sure that its safe, she climbs down and looks around, trying to decide which way to go.

First she looks back the way she had come and then looks up through the branches to the sky. Not being able to tell direction from the stars, she looks at the tree, looking for a growth of moss. She remembers Logan telling her that on Avdacal, moss grew on the west side of the trees. Once she locates the moss she figures that the Dragman's cave is northeast of where she is now. In the report that Logan had given them, he had found the clutch of eggs southeast of the high mountains. Knowing that the Dragman's cave was definitely located on a mountain, she decides to head southeast and hopefully she would find Chiero and Shama before the Dragman found her.

Just before total darkness falls, Cassie begins to feel as though she's being watched and followed. Though she reaches out, she can feel nothing. Coming to a small clearing, she looks across to the trees on the far side. She is just about to step out into the clearing when a clawed hand reaches out and grabs her arm, pulling her back. Before she can scream, another clawed hand covers her mouth.

"Shh y...y...ou a...a...re sss...afe." A strange voice hisses in her ear. "Dra...g...ma...ma...n wa...it f...f...or y...y...ou. Ma...ma...ny lo...ok f...f...or o...o...ne n...n...ot ch...ch...an...ged." Chiero Culato pulls the female back away from the clearing so that the others do not see or smell her and call to Debrory. Even though she has offered him this female, he has no wish to see her become as he and Shama. She is free and he will try to keep her that way as long as he can. The man Logan has returned, but he can not meet with him until Debrory was not so close. "Y...y...ou c...c...ome w...wi...th mm...e. T...ta...ke y...y...ou sss...afe c...c...ave."

Cassie nods her head quickly and is released. When she opens her mouth to speak, Chiero shakes his head and points to his ear. Understanding that he wants her to listen, Cassie concentrates on the sounds around them. Now that she is listening more intently, she can hear the heavy foot falls of several dragmen.

Taking her gently by the arm, Chiero leads her away from the clearing and then heads in an easterly direction. Cassie worries because she is sure that they are traveling in the wrong direction to go to the caves Logan had told them that Chiero and Shama were living in.

"N...n...ot sss...afe th...th...ere." Chiero tells her easily picking up on her thoughts. "G...go t...to n...ew c...c...ave. Dra...dra...g...man n...ot kn...ow wh...wh...ere."

Cassie looks at him in surprise. "You heard my thoughts."

"Y...y...es."

"But how? Your psi is higher then... Has my psi been changed?" She asks, realizing that this was the only explanation.

"O...n...ly sm...a...lll ch...ch...an...ge. N...n...ot a...lll."

A few minutes later he leads her into a small cave entrance. It widens after a couple of feet and they step into a larger chamber. There are about eight female dragmen and about twelve young sitting around the cave. Chiero leads Cassie over to Shama and tells his mate to keep the female safe, that she is some how connected to Logan and possibly her grandfather. To Cassie's ears it sounds like barks and growls, but she understands that it has something to do with her.

"Y...y...ou ss...st...ay Sh...Sh...am...ma. Ss...afe I re...t...t...urn." He says turning back to Cassie. "Mu...mu...sst g...g...go n...n...ow Dra...Dra...g...ma...n m...mi...sss."

Before leaving Chiero warns the others to help Shama hide and protect the female, that she may be one of those that could help them. After assuring himself that they understood, he quickly goes back to the clearing. Five minutes after his return, the Dragman flies into the clearing. As her wings close, Chiero and the others step forward. Each of the dragmen reports that they have found nothing.

The Dragman turns to Chiero and waves him closer. "What of your search Lato? Did you find any sign of the female?"

Barking and growling his answers to her questions, Chiero slowly steps closer. Debrory leans down to him and sniffs the air around him. Suddenly she rears up and stands over him. "You have lied Lato. The female's scent is all around you. Where is she?" Chiero again answers her with barks and growls telling her that he hasn't seen her, that he could have rubbed up against something that the female had already touched. The Dragman hisses at him before knocking him to the ground.

"I am no fool Lato. Unless you moved from this area, you could not have picked up her scent. Since none of the others carry her scent, you had to have left this place. You will tell me where she is now or your mate will suffer until you do."

Chiero sits up and wipes the blood from his mouth. He then stands and faces the Dragman not moving or saying anything. He was sure that Shama and the others were safe and that Debrory could not reach them in the new cave. There was something in the cave walls that protected their minds from her power. Anything stronger then a telepathic message could not reach those in the caves.

Debrory glares at him for his insolence and sends out the mind pains to Shama, knowing that Lato will feel her pain and suffering. After several minutes of getting no response from him she strikes out, once again knocking him to the ground. Looking around at the others she glares at them. "Where has he taken the female?!" None answer her and she roars at them. "You will answer me or all of your mates will suffer!" Again none answers her and she sends pain out to their mates. When there is no response, she sends the pain to all of the dragmen in a fit of temper. The dragman around her fall to the ground, twisting and writhing in great pain, as do the others on the rest of Avdacal. After several minutes she releases them all one by one, but continues to torture Chiero, and therefore his mate..

In the cave, Cassie watches in horror as all of the adult females collapse onto the floor clutching their heads as if in pain. Then one by one they stop, and slowly sit up, all except for Shama, who continues to cry out in pain. Not knowing what else to do, Cassie rushes to her side and places her hands over Shama's and draws the pain into herself. At the first contact she nearly collapses, but then she gathers her strength and quickly finds out what has been happening. With great effort she creates a barrier around Shama's mind and then helps her to sit up.

"I'm sorry that this is happening Shama. I'll stop it as soon as I can." She stands up, but Shama grabs her hand, stopping her before she can step away. Cassie looks down at her and Shama shakes her head. "Don't worry Shama, I'll be fine." She pulls free and walks towards the entrance. Before leaving she turns back to Shama and the others. "Logan and Royanna are coming to help all of you. We've figured out how to change you back. Trust them Shama as I have trusted you. All will soon be as it should be." With that she rushes from the cave before any of them can try and stop her.

Before leaving she makes sure that her scent is covered so that not even the best hunters could follow it back to the cave. Not wanting the Dragman to discover where she's been, Cassie goes far-a-field and then heads back to the clearing. Just before she reaches the clearing she releases the protective shielding and rushes forward. She stops quickly when she sees the Dragman standing over a fallen dragman. Her entrance pulls Debrory's attention away from the downed dragman causing her to stop torturing him. Cassie stands there and stares, not moving a muscle as the Dragman walks towards her.

Stopping only a foot away, Debrory looks down at her for several seconds before roaring and knocking Cassie to the ground with one swipe of her clawed hand. "Turn her over." she orders pulling a hair from her head. Two of the dragmen carefully turn Cassie over onto her stomach and then quickly step back as Debrory squats down beside her. "You will become mine now Earthling. Though it would be better to have you with me at my cave, this will have to do. Besides..." Debrory looks back at Chiero who is now on his feet. "Besides, I'm sure that your new mate will enjoy seeing you transform to look just like him." Debrory continues to look at Chiero for several more seconds before turning back to Cassie.

Carefully, almost gently she moves the hair away from the back of Cassie's neck, then holds the hair from her own head above the back of Cassie's neck. The living end of the hair begins to wriggle wildly and sends out a small blue light of electrical current, which makes a small hole just above the shoulders into the spinal column. Slowly Debrory lowers the hair to Cassie's neck and watches as it wiggles and twists itself into the hole. As soon as its well in she releases it and watches it finish burrowing its way in. When its completely inside she turns Cassie over and checks her eyes.

"Good, it has taken well. Soon your new mate will be ready Lato. Get many young from her or I will give her to another." She looks up at Chiero before standing. "Make sure that she lives Lato, or I will take your first born." With that she spreads her wings and flies off to her cave.

Chiero slowly approaches Cassie's still form and kneels down beside her. He pushes the hair from her face and gently touches her cheek. The others move in closer and look down at her. Looking up at them Chiero tells them to go back to the cave, but to take separate directions and to make sure that the spies don't follow them back.

After they've gone, Chiero looks around the clearing and then up into the night sky. He could not understand why she hadn't stayed in the cave like he had told her to. She would have been safe from the Dragman. Minutes later he carefully picks up her limp body and stands. Looking once more at her face, he shakes his head at her for choosing to suffer such a fate as him and the others of his group.

CHAPTER TWELVE

Logan returns to the ship an hour after full darkness falls. Royanna meets him at the door. "Anything?"

"Nothing. The eggs are still there but the caves are all empty. I couldn't pick up anything from the caves. They must have moved within hours of my leaving them." He tells her as they walk back to the lounge area where the others are waiting.

"But why? Chiero must have believed that you would come back. Why move from the area you would come back to?" She asks puzzled by such a move.

They enter the lounge and Logan sits down in one of the chairs. "I'm not sure Anna. There may have been a problem with the Dragman after I left." He nods his thanks to Libre who hands him a drink. "I doubt that they've gone very far though. They're very protective of their eggs, so they'll want to stay close enough to watch over and protect them."

"How will we find them son? We don't have much time before Thayer and Leyla arrive."

"I know father, but which direction do we start looking?" Logan asks him in frustration. "They could be anywhere within a ten mile radius of the eggs."

"What about sending out a message to Chiero?" Chevala asks. "We know his level of alpha. Send a message to him telling him that we're here and to meet us."

"We could, but we don't..."

"Logan, Cassie's brain pattern is beginning to change and weaken." Ali interrupts them.

"What about her bio rhythms?" He asks jumping up from his seat.

"Those are changing also. It's as though..."

"As though what Ali?" He demands.

"It's as though she was changing from the inside out." Ali finishes.

Logan walks over to the wall and punches it several times. "Damn! We're too late!"

Thurda and Libre look at Logan and then at each other. Chevala steps closer to Royanna, while Sheyome looks out the portal with tears running down her cheeks. She tries not to draw attention to herself, keeping her mind calm so that the others won't pick up on her distress.

"I don't believe that Logan Knightrunner, and neither should you." Royanna says patting Chevala's shoulder before stepping away from her and moving closer to Logan. "Something isn't right here Logan. Don't you see? This change has taken too long. If anything, Ali should have detected it hours ago instead of just now."

"Yes that's right son. Remember that Chiero said that the hair was placed shortly after they awoke? Cassie was able to get that message to you, so she had to be awake to do it." Thurda points out walking over and grasping Logan by the shoulders. "Don't you see? She must have escaped and only recently been caught again."

Logan looks at his father and then at the others. He notices Sheyome standing alone by the portal looking out. He suddenly realizes that he is not the only one to be affected by Cassie's change. "All right, we have to try and find her quickly before she finishes the transformation." He says to the room at large but continues to look at Sheyome. He had to know that she was mentally capable of handling this.

Sensing his regard Sheyome carefully wipes away her tears before turning to face him. "How do we look for her when we have no contact with her?"

"I'm not sure Shey, but we will find her." He assures her.

"What about Ali?" Chevala wants to know. "She's picking up on Cassie's brain pattern and bio rhythms. Couldn't she give us a location to start looking?"

"Ali, you heard Chevala. Could you give us a general direction to start looking in?"

"All I can tell you Logan is that she is or was northeast of us. Several miles below the mountain."

"How far is the mountain from our present location?"

"Approximately eighteen miles." Ali informs him. "When I noticed the changes in Cassie, she was at least nine miles from us."

"Which would mean that she either came from the mountain or near it." Logan says almost to himself thinking quickly. "Are there any clearings or meadows in that area?"

"Checking." Ali says and within seconds she confirms that there are two small clearings in which Cassie could be located.

"All right, we'll port three to each clearing and check them over." Logan decides and turns to his father. "Father, you and Libre go with Chevala to the first, I'll take Shey and Anna to the second. If either group finds something we contact the others and meet at that location. Agreed?"

Everyone nods their agreement and starts gathering up the supplies they'll need to reverse the transformation of Cassie and the others.

"Remember to stay alert at all times. We don't need to be taken by surprise." Thurda reminds them. They double check their supplies and then Thurda and Logan teleport their groups to each of the clearings after assuring themselves that they won't be appearing in the middle of a trap set by the dragmen.

Chiero and Shama watch over Cassie as she starts her transformation. Her eyes were the first to change, but now her skin is taking on the color of the female dragmen. Though it is not their true coloring, because Cassie's is showing signs of gold coloring as well as the blue and green though those colors begin to fade to gold as well. Having removed her clothing, they notice when the skin changes stop. Though the coloring is all over her body, Cassie's skin doesn't have the scaliness of the others. She has scales, but they are finer then any other. Suddenly she sits up causing both Chiero and Shama to jump back in startled surprise.

Cassie looks around her in confusion and then looks at Shama and Chiero. Everything looks different to her and she wonders what is wrong with her eyes for several moments before everything comes rushing back and she looks down at herself. She notices the change in her skin and the beginnings of claws on her hands and feet. Shakily she gets to her feet and places her hands over her face. It is then that she discovers the minute changes to her face. Dropping her hands she lets out a howl of such pain and anguish that all of the dragmen drop to their knees and cover their ears.

A mile away, Logan and the others also hear the howl. Logan can almost feel the pain and anguish in that cry. He bends back down to show his father what they had found, but suddenly he straightens up and looks in the direction of the scream, which he now realizes is what it was. "Cassie." He whispers to himself. Not waiting to see if the others follow, he sprints off in that direction. His only thought is to reach his mate and comfort her.

'Logan, where are you going?'

'That was Cassie father. I have to get to her.'

Thurda and the others look at each other before following him through the trees.

Though he's not sure where he's headed, Logan continues on and then comes to a sudden stop about twenty feet from a cave entrance where several male dragmen are standing. He takes a few more steps forward but stops again when the dragmen begin to growl and bare their teeth at him in warning.

Several seconds later the others stop beside him panting and out of breath. Royanna leans heavily against Thurda for support as she looks at the dragmen. Just as Logan is about to step forward again she reaches out to him. *'No Logan, wait. If you go any closer they'll attack. Whatever or whoever is in that cave, they plan to protect it at all cost.'*

'But Cassie's in there Anna. I can still feel her. She needs me.'

'Yes, she needs you. But she needs you alive and in one piece. These dragmen will tear you apart before you get anywhere near that cave.'

'Then I'll port myself inside.'

'You can't port in there blind. Besides, there are probably more of them inside. They would attack you before you knew it.'

Logan growls in frustration and glares at the dragmen blocking his way to Cassie. "Now what?"

Royanna lets out the breath she hadn't realized she'd been holding and steps to Logan's side. "Call to Chiero. From what you've told us, he's the leader of this band. I believe that he's our only way into that cave safely."

During their conversation the dragmen have moved closer to the cave's entrance and each other. They keep a careful watch on the humans, not trusting their reasons for being there. Knowing only that Chiero had said that they must protect the new female from all harm.

Logan holds up his hands and takes a single step forward. "I am a friend. I wish to speak with Chiero Culato." He looks around at the different faces and remembers a few of them from the last time. "I came before, talked to Chiero about helping you to return to your true form, to return home."

The dragmen look at one another and then one of them goes into the cave behind the others. After a few minutes the dragmen separate and Chiero steps out. He stops halfway between the two groups and looks at Logan before looking at the rest of the humans with him. He recognizes the Master Healer and Logan's father and sister, but he's not sure about the other two.

"Lo...ga...gan fr...fr...ien...end."

"Yes Chiero, I am your friend. We've come to help you as I said we would. But we need your help also." Logan tells him stepping closer. "My mate was taken this morning Chiero, and brought here. We know that the Dragman has already put the hair into my mate. This was done only a short time ago. We must get to her now Chiero, before the full transformation takes place."

Chiero shakes his head sadly. "I...I...ss dra...dra....g...ma...na n...n...ow."

"But that's not possible Chiero. It takes at least three or four days for the full transformation to take place. How can she already be one? She can't have changed so fast." Logan says in a panic.

"C...C...ome I ssh...ssh...ow." Chiero turns back to the cave and barks to the others to move and do nothing.

Thurda and the others follow closely behind Logan and Chiero past the males and into the cave. As they all enter the females and young start to fuss and make whimpering sounds. Chiero barks at them to be quiet. All fall silent except for the two smallest children.

Stopping in the middle of the cave, Chiero points to a darkened corner. "Ssh...Ssh..ee i...i...sss th...th...ere."

Logan takes a step towards the shadows and notices movement edging away from him. He stops and holds out his hands to her. "It's all right Cassie. You know that no one here would hurt you."

The figure moves even further away. Logan hears a gasp from behind him as one of Cassie's arms and legs is revealed by the light of the fire in the center of the cave. There is a green tint to golden skin and claws can be seen on the hand and foot that are revealed.

"We know that you've been transformed Cassie. It doesn't matter atma. You're still the same person to us. To me. Let us change you back sweetheart." He takes another step toward her and Cassie again steps away. This time though she steps completely into the light.

"N...no Lo...gan. Do...n't co...me ne...ar me." She pleads with him and tears run slowly down her cheeks. Her speech is less jointed then Chiero's and is more understandable.

Logan sees the sadness and despair in her eyes, he also sees the longing and hope that still shines deep within their depths. Not caring any longer what might happen to him, he rushes to her and takes her struggling form into his arms.

Cassie fights him for several seconds, then stops, not wanting to hurt him in any way. She collapses against him and weeps silently. She couldn't understand how he could still care for her with the way she now looked.

Holding her close, Logan rubs his hands over her back and murmurs to her that everything will be all right. Slowly they lower to the floor and Logan cradles her close to his chest. He closes his eyes and rocks her gently, trying to control his emotions.

Carefully and quietly, so as not to startle her, Royanna approaches them and kneels down beside them. Gently she touches the top of Cassie's head. Though she doesn't know if it will work, she sends out comfort and love. Slowly Cassie calms down and then sighs softly, then looks up at the older woman. Their eyes meet and hold for several seconds before Royanna gives her a gently smile. "We'll have you back to yourself in no time dear. I promise."

Cassie slowly nods her head and then looks at the others. Seeing Sheyome, she holds out her hand to her. Sheyome rushes forward and kneels down taking the hand and placing it on her cheek.

"It'sss no...t yo...ur faulll...t Ssh...ssh...ey. Knew it wou...ld hap...pen. I ha...d to pro...te...te...ect yo...ou ffrr...om Dro...gen." She tells her.

"But I was suppose to protect you Cassie, and I failed to do that."

"On...ly be...cau...se I pre...ven...ted yo...ou ffrr...om do...ing ss...ooo. Yo...ou co...me be...ffrr...or Lo...gan or I. Th...Tha...yer's wi...ssh an...nd I un...der...sst...ood th...isss."

Sheyome's eyes open wide and she stares from Cassie to Logan and back again, not understanding why Thayer would ask such a thing of them.

"She's right Shey. We both agreed with Thayer that you would be protected at all cost, including at the cost of our own safety. You are just as important to us as we are to each other."

"We need to hurry now Logan." Royanna interrupts them. "Thayer will be arriving sooner then we planned. Leyla felt Cassie's cry earlier and is now teleporting them here in jumps. We have less then twelve hours before they arrive."

They all stand and Cassie looks at Chiero then at Royanna. "Te...st me fir...st."

"N...n...oo, mu...mu...sss...t n...n...ot. De...br...or...ry fff...eel y...y...ou ch...ch...an...ge. I d...ooo ffir...st."

Cassie and Chiero stare at each other for a few moments and then Shama steps up to Cassie and touches her arm. Cassie looks at her and then slowly nods. Looking at Logan and then the others, she smiles slightly before teleporting outside the cave. She sends the others into the cave and then places a barrier over the entrance to keep everyone inside, just as Logan rushes to stop her. He falls back in surprise when he runs into the barrier.

She wasn't sure if she could reach him mentally but she knew that she couldn't waste any more time trying to explain it all to him. *'You'll be safe while you work my love. They need you now. I will return, but first I must do something for myself. Don't worry about me.'* With that, great golden wings appear on her back and lift her from the ground. *'Leyla and Thayer will know what to do when they arrive. I will send the other dragmen to you shortly.'* She flies up and away.

Logan watches as she flies towards the mountain knowing that she was going to face the queen Dragman in her lair. He waits until she's out of sight before turning back into the cave. Though he wanted to stop her, he knew that there was nothing he could do. He knew that there was something happening that he didn't understand, but he would trust her to return to him. Her mental communication with him had also startled him. Her mind felt stronger in some way.

⁓

As Cassie flies up into the sky, her mind is confused by the memories and emotions she is seeing and feeling. The memories are her mother's, but yet not the mother that she remembers.

Debra Rose Blackwood had been a planetary researcher for the Galactic Federation of Planets. Only a year after Colt and Merri's birth, she left on a mission to explore a planet that the Federation felt was ideal for colonization. Six months later the Blackwoods were notified that the research team had disappeared and were presumed dead. No bodies could be found, and there was no trace of their ship either.

The memories that are going through her mind are of her mother and the other researchers on that planet. They looked at the plants and animals, took samples of soil and rocks, all to be sure that they could support human life. They had even checked out caves and valleys, never seeing any sign of intelligent life.

Suddenly after being there for three months, members of the team started to disappear. Everyone that is left becomes worried when they can find no trace of them. Then on a day that they went on another search, they returned to where their ship was, only to find it and the three people they had left with it gone. It was never a possibility that they could have taken off without them. None of the three knew how to fly the ship. Even though she tries, Debra can pick up no sense of the ship or the missing members of their team.

A couple of weeks later, though she knows that she shouldn't go off by herself, she sets off to explore an area that showed signs of regular animal use. Sweeping the area, she discovers a large clutch of eggs that had not been there two days before. Checking the size visually, she then picks one up and discovers that there is an embryo inside. She is surprised by the human feel of the life force she is holding in her hands. All of a sudden a shadow falls over her and she looks up. Standing before her is a creature that appears part human and part dragon. Very carefully she places the egg back with the others and slowly moves back before just as slowly standing. She makes sure that none of her actions appear threatening. Slowly she begins to back away, but suddenly she runs into something behind her. Two clawed hands come up and grab her arms. The hands have a bluish green color to them and are shaped as the creature in front of her, the only difference that she can see is the coloring. The one in front of her is gold in color.

"I meant no harm to the eggs." She tells them. All the time watching the golden one, knowing that any danger came from it. When it steps around the eggs she starts to draw back only to come to an abrupt stop by the one behind her.

"You do not belong here. This is the world of the Dragmanie. You will be made as one of us and give us many young." The golden one tells her.

Debra struggles with the one holding her, but can not free herself from it's grip. She finally gives up and stares straight ahead. "I don't know how you plan to make me like you, or if its even possible. Even if you do, the one thing that you will not change is my humanity. With that I will never be like you."

"Others have said this human, and they are now only dragman. You too will be only dragman in time." With that it spits a mist into her face which causes her to blackout.

When she regains consciousness, Debra notices that she's in a large cave and that the rest of her team is there also. They are all secured to stalagmites and surrounded by the blue-green dragmen. She's not sure how much time passes before five of the golden colored ones come into the chamber. She watches as one by one the others are taken to a stone table and held down while a gold dragman plucks one of it's hairs and places it against the back of their necks. After that the blue-green dragmen carry them to the side of the cave and lay them on pallets. Finally they come for her, but Debra does not fight and struggle as the others had. She knew that there was no way to escape what was going to happen. She shrugs off the hands that take her arms to lead her to the table. With her head held high she walks to the table and lays down. Before turning onto her stomach, she looks up and stares at the golden dragman that had captured her. Turning over, she pulls her hair away from her neck and closes her eyes. Why fight what she couldn't change? She would bide her time and then she would escape.

When she awakens again she's in a different cave that is lighted by a luminous formation in the walls themselves. There is a dampness to the air around her. She moves and feels something move beneath her. Looking down she discovers that she is on a grass pallet. Sitting up she looks around the chamber and notices that its being used as living quarters. Raising her hand to her face, she gasps when she notices that she has physically changed. Her hand is now clawed and her skin is scaled and golden. Tears run down her cheeks as she realizes that she will never see her husband or children again. The golden dragman that captured her enters the chamber and stops to look at her. There is shock on it's face and she glares at it.

"What are you staring at? You said that you would change me to look like you, and you have. Go away and leave me alone!"

"That is not possible. You are to be my mate, but first I must take you to the Queen. She will want to see you. You have not changed as the others have."

Debra is taken before the Queen of the dragmen and both physically and mentally checked over. It is found that something in her genetic makeup is extremely compatible with that of the dragmen. It is then decided that she would be trained in the leadership of the dragmen since there were now very few golden females born.

These memories and thoughts along with others through the years, runs through Cassie's mind and she watches as her mother quickly loses her humanity. Soon there is nothing left of Debra Rose Blackwood but faded memories of her former life and those she had loved.

Landing at Debrory's cave, Cassie folds her wings and slowly enters. As she walks into the first chamber, she sees the worker dragmen laying on their pallets sleeping. Before any of them can wake or become too alert to her presence, she ports them to Chiero's cave. Walking deeper into the cave she calls out to the Dragman. "I'm here mother!"

Walking into the transformation chamber, she studies the cocoons laying within. Some are only a few hours from opening, while others will not open for a couple of days yet. Hearing a sound to her left, Cassie turns towards it and sees the two dragmen that have been her mother's personal servants for the past several years. "I know that you're here mother. Why won't you face me? Can't you face what you've done to your own child?" She shouts turning around in a circle ignoring the servants.

"I can face you Cassandra." Debrory states coming into the chamber. "You have changed faster than I did when Mastory placed his hair within me." She stops in front of Cassie and looks her over. Walking around her Debrory notices her wings and frowns slightly. This was not a normal development. She should not have developed her wings for at least two years.

"Why mother? Why would you do this to me?" Cassie asks turning to face her mother. "How could you plan to do this to your whole family? By the Great One, we've mourned you for almost twelve years. Now you return to us and plan to change us into monsters that don't care for any other life form but it's own. You told Mastory that he could change you, but that he would never change your humanity. You lied to him and to yourself mother. When it came down to it, you willingly gave up your humanity, the part that all of us loved in you the most. Now you can know that we will all hate you for the rest of our lives."

As she speaks Debrory's eyes are getting redder and redder as her anger builds. "Do not speak to me of love and hate or of humanity." She snarls and whirls away. "Yes I gave up my humanity willingly. After humanity gave up on me and those with me. You have some of my memories but not the ones I've tried to forget. Like the fact that the Federation never sent anyone to find us. Like my loving husband not trying to contact me. Where was their humanity for us? Love, I had love from Mastory. He showed me love at the most basic level and was always there for me. If I was not back from going somewhere, he came looking for me. As for hate, I've had a long time to let it grow."

"So everyone pays for what you saw as abandonment by the Federation and Father. You'll condemn all of your children for something that we had no control over and could do nothing about."

Debrory whirls back to face her again, though her eyes are still red, they're not as red as they were at first. Cassie wonders if she sees sadness and regret in her mother's eyes, but knows that these emotions are no longer a part of her in regards to humans.

"I don't see it as damning you Cassandra, I see it as getting my children back. All of my children have been taken from me. First you and your brothers and sisters, and then the children that I had with Mastory were taken from me. Is it so wrong for me to want my children with me?"

"Yes mother, it is. Especially when that wanting takes something away from us." Cassie tells her sadly. "You've taken away my freedom of choice in how I wish to live my life. I won't let you do that to the others."

"There is nothing that you can do to stop me Cassandra. You may look like me, but you don't have my powers."

"I wouldn't be to sure of that mother. There are things about me that you don't know. Things that happened over the years you've been gone, things that have changed me greatly, have changed all of us. If anything, you have enhanced those changes and made them stronger." Cassie looks down at her feet and then her head suddenly snaps up. "Don't take another step Drogen." She warns him still looking at Debrory. "You may do my mother's bidding, but I do not. It would give me great pleasure to life-end you this very moment, but my mate would like that honor for what you have helped to do to his people."

"I do not fear the Majichonie cub, and I do not fear you. No Dragmana can harm me in any way that I must fear." Suddenly he goes flying through the air to crash into the far wall. He slides to the floor and sits there stunned by the throw. Cassie doesn't even bother to look, but Debrory turns her head slightly to frown at Drogen.

"While Drogen proves to be no challenge for you Cassandra, you will find that I am an entirely different matter." Debrory tells her turning back to face her. "Now you must excuse me. I must go and see to some discipline problems." Debrory places a barrier around Cassie and then turns fully to Drogen who is now on his feet. "You have become very arrogant and over confident Drogen. If I did not still need you to bring me the humans I would have life-ended you myself years ago." With that she turns and walks from the chamber.

Cassie watches this and waits until her mother leaves before removing the barrier. Quickly she puts up a barrier of her own over the cave's entrance and waits for a response. She doesn't have long to wait.

"Cassandra!!" Debrory roars.

Drogen makes the mistake of stepping into Debrory's path as she returns to the transformation chamber and is knocked to the ground. Debrory stops just inside the chamber and glares at Cassie. Cassie smiles at her and then walks over to the stone table. She notices the start of surprise on her mother's face and shrugs her shoulders as best she can.

"Remove the barrier Cassandra."

"No mother. It stays in place until I know that the others are safe."

Debrory laughs and starts to walk around the chamber. "I see, and what others do you expect to be safe? Lato and his other mate? The other dragmen that follow him in his defiance of my will?" She asks stopping on the other side of the table. "Or maybe you mean the Majichonie humans that came after you?" She smiles and nods at the surprise on Cassie's face. "Yes, I know that they are here. I've known since the second that they landed. No doubt they thought that they could reach you before I had the chance to transform you."

"That's where you're wrong mother." Cassie informs her. "Oh they knew you would change me, but the main reason that they're here is to change the dragmen back to their human forms."

"It can't be done. Once the transformation has taken place it can never be reversed."

"It can and has been. Right now, all but ten have been changed back and those ten will be done shortly. You won't be allowed to continue doing this to innocent people mother."

"How do you plan to stop me Cassandra? Do you think that you can change me back as you supposedly changed the others? I don't want to be changed back."

Cassie looks at her and frowns. Even if it was possible, she doesn't feel it would be a good idea to change her back. Without her humanity she would just be another human monster that would hurt and destroy others. "I wouldn't want to change you

155

back mother. There is no quality that you have now that would benefit anyone."

"So you plan to life-end me. You can try, but you won't succeed. You will die before I do and then I will finish what I have started."

"At least I would have died protecting those that I love and care about. What would you be dying for mother?"

They stare at each other for several minutes and then Cassie turns to the cocoons. The three that were only hours from opening crack and fall apart. Cassie sends them to Chiero's cave and looks at the others and decides to send them too. Debrory roars at the disappearance of the cocoons and sends Cassie flying across the chamber.

Cassie stops herself from hitting the wall and lands on her feet. They stare at each other and Cassie sees the intent in Debrory's eyes. She realizes that to protect Logan and the others, she will have to fight her mother. Though she does not wish it to be this way she knows that there is no other way. She would not let her loved ones suffer if she could help it.

CHAPTER THIRTEEN

Royanna removes the last strand from the last dragman and steps back. It would take fifteen to twenty minutes for the reversal to finish, but at least they know that it works and doesn't take as long as the original transformation.

Chiero had been the first to undergo the removal. After finding the ease of the removal, Royanna decides that Chevala will be able to do some as well, which will make everything a lot quicker. Over the next several hours they work steadily to remove the implanted hairs before Leyla and Thayer reach them. They're not sure what will happen to the dragmen should the Queen be destroyed.

"Royanna, you had better come in here." Libre calls from the front of the cave.

Standing, Royanna stretches and looks around the chamber at the people still recovering from the removal. Raude is not among those that have been changed back. She walks out to the other chamber. Logan, Thurda, Chevala, and Sheyome follow closely behind her. As they enter the chamber, they notice the cocoons and the three dragmen standing in the middle of them.

"They just arrived. These three came out just as they materialized. They've just been standing there not moving." Libre informs them.

"Have they looked at each other or at themselves yet?" Chiero asks walking up to stand beside Royanna.

"No, they've just been standing there."

"Then they haven't yet realized what's happened to them. I would suggest that you move now to remove the hair. Once they come out of this trance they'll be very violent for several hours."

Royanna looks at the three closely, trying to figure out who they might be. She looks at each for several minutes always returning to the one in the middle. *'Thurda, look at the one in the middle.'*

Thurda studies the male in the middle for a long time. *'Yes, it looks like him atma. Let's get those hairs out of them before we have a fight on our hands and someone gets hurt.'*

Royanna nods and signals for Chevala and Sheyome to come and assist. Quickly they move behind them and Thurda moves to assist Royanna while Sheyome helps Chevala. Logan bends down to check on the unopened cocoons. From the looks of them and the ones that are already open, he figures that they won't open for a couple more days at least. He looks up at Royanna. *'It looks like three of these may be females. The size indicates that they could be very young.'*

'I don't know how we're going to change them before Leyla and Thayer arrive. It could be dangerous to try and do anything while they're still inside the cocoons.'

'But if we do nothing, they'll surely die when Debrory is killed, and she will be killed.'

"We need to lay these three down in the other room." Chevala says stepping from the last one.

Logan looks up and then teleports the three into the other chamber. He then stands and walks to the entrance which is still blocked by the barrier. "We need to worry about Cassie too. With this barrier still up we can't even help her if she needs us."

"Your mate will be all right Logan." Chiero assures him. "She's different from what we were. I think that in some way she may be connected to Debrory. Her transformation was too quick and she became gold instead of the greenish blue of the other females."

"How long before we got here had the hair been implanted?" Royanna wants to know.

"Between thirty and forty-five minutes, maybe less."

Royanna nods and kneels down beside the unopened cocoons. She places a hand in the center of one of the cocoons and closes her eyes to concentrate. She links with the mind inside and picks up confusion and fear. Doing the same to the others, she finds the same confusion and fear.

Logan's wrist-comm buzzes and he answers. "Yes Ali."

"I just received a message from Thayer Starhawk. They will arrive here within the hour."

"Are they coming straight to Avdacal?"

"Yes. I also heard from Manchon. Queen Niccara collapsed an hour ago and they have been unable to revive her."

"All right Ali. Contact Manchon and tell them to make her as comfortable as possible, and to contact us if there's any change."

"Affirmative."

Drogen watches as the two golden Dragmana fight a mental battle within the confines of the cave. Never had he seen such a battle before.

Cassie dodges as Debrory throws another stalactite at her. She retaliates by hurling the stone table at her. Debrory puts up a shield from which the table bounces off and flies to the side. Not moving quickly enough, Drogen Firnap is caught under the table as it lands, crushing his legs and back. Both Cassie and Debrory ignore his screams of pain, knowing that if they loose their concentration now it could cost either of them their life.

Knowing that there are still two dragmen in the cave with them, Cassie decides to take their fight outside. Logan and the others were safe inside the cave, and Debrory didn't know it's location. Slowly she pushes Debrory into the outer chamber and forces her off to one side of the entrance so that she has a clear path out.

With her back to the entrance she allows Debrory to force her towards it. With a subconscious thought the barrier drops and Cassie steps through the entrance. As Debrory follows her out, Cassie spreads her wings and lifts off the ground. Debrory hesitates and then follows.

"Now you will see how the Dragmen really fight." So saying Debrory spits fire at her.

Cassie feels the heat of the flames on her skin for a few seconds before putting up a shield to hold them off. When the flames stop, she lowers the shield and sends flame back, catching Debrory off guard.

Screaming out in pain at the attack, Debrory dives for Cassie with claws out. She gets close enough to claw Cassie's left shoulder. When Cassie falters, she attacks again but is stopped in mid-dive when Cassie sends several lightening bolts at her. Once again she is shocked by the attack not understanding how she was able to perform such things that had taken her at least a year or two to learn how to do.

While Debrory is dodging the bolts, Cassie notices the last two dragmen standing just outside the cave and quickly ports them to Logan, subduing their minds so that they cause no trouble. Her shields go up as Debrory sends some bolts back at her.

Suddenly Debrory brakes off the attack and flies off. Puzzled by this move, it takes Cassie several moments to figure out where her mother is headed. Quickly she follows, knowing that if her mother reaches the egg clutches first she will either destroy them or hold them as hostages.

'Logan, hear me. Tell Ali to place a shield around the eggs and the ship. Debrory is headed that way right now.'

'Cassie, where are you? You have to come back now so we can change you back. Leyla and Thayer...'

'I know, but I can't return yet. Don't worry about me, just have Ali put up those shields. Debrory will be there in two minutes.'

Cassie places a barrier wall in front of her mother and watches her slam into it. She then dives down and lands on Debrory's back trying to force her to the ground.

Logan contacts Ali and she puts up the shields around the ship and clutches. Since she is not sure of the Dragman Queen's power, she puts maximum power to the shields.

Debrory sends an electrical shock through her body which knocks Cassie off and slightly stuns her. Once Cassie is off her back she dives down to land near the clutches. As she steps up to the first one she is knocked back by the shield. Growling she tries again and is again knocked back. Roaring she goes to another clutch and is once again knocked back. As it happens at every clutch her anger builds until she releases it in a burst of flame and lightening directed at the clutches.

Cassie watches her for several moments, but when she heads for the ship Cassie lets out a roar and dives down to claw at Debrory's chest. Staggering back from the attack, Debrory quickly recovers and returns the attack. They fight furiously for many minutes. All the time they are fighting Cassie can feel Leyla and Thayer getting closer. When she's sure that they are close enough, she calls out to Leyla.

'Leyla, you must put up your shields to cover your approach. Debrory will pick up your power soon and I think that she will head for Manchon as soon as she does.'

'We'll put up the shields. What's happened to you Cassie? Your mind feels different.'

'I've been changed Leyla, but don't worry about me. Don't let father or the children get off your ship. They will be in great danger if Debrory sees them or feels they're presence here.'

'Why would they be in danger?'

For several moments Cassie cannot answer because of Debrory's increased assault. Slowly driving her back, Cassie tells Leyla of her family's connection to this Dragman queen. *'That's why you must keep them safe. I don't want them to know that this creature is or was Debra Blackwood. You must totally destroy her, leave nothing to be passed on to the family.'*

'What about you? Can we destroy her without harming you?'

'Yes, I'm separate from her. Before you come here to face her, go to the cave where Logan and the others are trapped by my barrier. There are seven cocoons inside with Majichonie inside them, changing into dragmen. You and Thayer must change them back before destroying Debrory. The children and the eggs will be safe.'

'All right. We'll join you as soon as we finish.'

Just as they break off, Debrory sends bolts of lightening at Cassie, but they only bounce off to strike the ground. "Your time is almost up mother. Soon you will be a threat to no one ever again, and the people of Manchon will forget that you ever existed or caused them grief. Daniel and the other children will never know what you have become. They won't have to grieve a second time for someone who died long ago. Father will never have to know that the woman that he loved for so long, and was willing to die for, was going to kill him for not being more than he was and is."

Debrory laughs harshly and flies above Cassie. "It is you that they will not grieve for. When I'm done, they will not remember you or your father." Diving at her, Debrory knocks Cassie off her feet and slashes her with her claws. They roll around on the ground tearing at each other with teeth and claws. Cassie lashes out and tears several holes into Debrory's wings which will prevent her from flying. With a great heave Cassie sends her flying against the ships shield. Jumping back to her feet, Debrory snarls and lunges at Cassie sending them both rolling around on the ground again.

Suddenly a bright light appears over them and they are forced apart. They stand and look up to see two fiery entities hovering above them. Cassie smiles up at them and then looks at Debrory.

"Now I will say good-bye to you mother. Your evilness ends here and now. The Firestar and Starhawk will finish with you. Even though you are now totally evil in intent, you are still my mother and I will not take your life."

"Then you are not my daughter and it will no longer matter to me if I kill you." So saying, Debrory sends a barrage of bolts at Cassie, striking her with three of them. Cassie collapses to the ground and the Firestar screams in rage. She puts up a fire-shield to protect Cassie while Starhawk attacks Debrory forcing her to her knees. They both look down at her as she struggles against the force keeping her on the ground.

'Your struggles will do you no good Debrory of the Dragmanie. You will remain in that position until sentencing is carried out.'

"You can not punish me. You have no say in what I do or what happens with those of Manchon."

'You are wrong Debrory, we have a say in what you have done here, and with what happens with those of Manchon. My family rules Manchon, and Firestar as my mate has a say in what has been done not only to the Majichonie, but to the one she calls sister as well.'

'And I Firestar say that for your crimes against Manchon and Cassandra Blackwood, that you should die. You have enslaved people and changed their physical bodies without their knowledge or consent. It is also known to us that you planned to continue to do this on other worlds. We can not and will not allow that to happen.'

Cassie stirs and slowly sits up holding her head. Firestar removes the protective shield to allow Cassie to stand. Slowly she rises to her feet and shakes her head. When her eyes clear, she sees Debrory on her knees and her eyes flashing red with hatred and loathing. She knows that nothing she can say will change the outcome.

'Remove the barrier at the cave Cassie. Bring Logan and those that came with him here.'

Releasing the barrier, Cassie ports Logan and the others to the site. When they appear, Logan rushes to Cassie's side and hugs her close.

"Are you all right atma?" He holds her at arm's length and sucks in his breath when he sees the cuts and bruises covering her body. "By the Great One, I will kill her with my bare hands." Releasing her he turns to Debrory.

Before he can move Firestar places a barrier in front of him. *'No Logan, we will take care of the Dragman. You and the others are here to give witness to her destruction. No part of her will be left to poison or corrupt anyone ever again.'*

Thurda and Royanna lead the others over to Logan and Cassie. They all stand together and look up at Firestar and Starhawk. They watch as they move to either side of Debrory and their body's grow brighter with each passing second.

Debrory begins to shake and her eyes never leave Cassie's. Slowly Cassie walks forward, stopping a couple of feet away. As she watches, a dark light comes down from Firestar and Starhawk. Just before the light touches her, Debrory lets a single tear roll down her cheek and says quietly, for Cassie's ears only. "I'm sorry. I love you Cassandra."

"I love you too momma." Cassandra whispers softly just as the light touches Debrory and in moments she's gone.

Seconds later Leyla and Thayer appear and stand on either side of Cassie and wrap their arms around her and hug her tightly between them.

"I'm sorry there was no other way Cassie." Leyla tells her softly with tears of sorrow for what her friend has had to go through.

"I am too Leyla. But there was nothing really left of the mother I once knew. It's better this way for all of us."

Royanna walks up to them and looks at Cassie. "We should remove the hair from your neck now Cassie."

With a nod, Cassie steps away from the comfort of Leyla and Thayer's embrace. She folds in her wings and kneels on the ground. Royanna steps behind her and moves the golden hair away from the back of Cassie's neck. She searches the back of her neck from the base of her skull to the top of her shoulders, but can not find the hole where the hair entered. "I can't find where it entered." She says looking at Leyla and Thayer in confusion. They had no trouble with locating the others.

Leyla and Thayer look at each other and then step up to Cassie again. They hold hands to the front and back of her head and close their eyes. A white light envelops their hands and then travels over Cassie. As the light passes over her neck the entrance hole appears as a blue mark on the back of her neck. At first there is no sign of the hair, but as the light travels all the way down her body and then back up again, the hair begins to move. When it reaches the hole Royanna grabs it with a pair of tweezers. When it is finally out, she holds it up.

Unlike the other hairs which when removed had caught flame, this one writhes with life at the end of the tweezers trying to get back to Cassie. Releasing Thayer's hands, Leyla looks at the hair and then takes it from Royanna. Within moments of her taking it, it bursts into flames.

Logan comes forward and lifts a swaying Cassie into his arms. "Ali, lower the shields and open the hatch." The shields go down and Logan carries Cassie into the ship and down to their cabin. Gently he lays her on the bed. Brushing the hair from her forehead and looks at her face. He can see the small changes as she starts to return to her human form. Covering her with a light sheet he leaves the cabin. The others are in the lounge waiting for him. Thayer hands him a drink and then sits down beside Leyla. Logan walks over to the portal and looks out.

"Chiero and the others want to know if the young in the clutches can be made human. If not, is there some way to help them retain their humanity and remove the aggression. Though they're dragmen, they're still their children and they love them." He says still looking out the portal.

"It should work to give them human forms, but the parents should realize that the ones from the eggs will all be the same age." Leyla points out. "Depending on their sizes, the others will vary in age. They'll be from about two to five years old by my estimation."

"When do you want to do the changes?" Royanna asks.

"We should probably start first thing in the morning mother. The one's with clutches should stand beside theirs so that we know whose is whose." Thayer tells her. "We'll do the first hatchlings before we start on the clutches."

"I think that we should return the others to Manchon." Chevala suggests. "If you don't need us, I think that Royanna, father, and I should return too. Nicca still hasn't regained consciousness and it appears that her physical condition has worsened. We need to try and get her stabilized as quickly as possible."

Leyla frowns and stands up to pace the room. "I have to tell you all that as far as I'm concerned, she can rot for what she has done."

"No Leyla. You can't blame Niccara." Everyone turns to look at Cassie as she walks slowly into the room. "Debrory's control over her was more than she could handle. It wasn't her that choose who was to be taken, but Drogen."

Logan quickly walks to her side and helps her to one of the empty chairs. After seating her, he gets her a drink and sits down beside her. After taking a swallow of the drink, she continues.

"Whenever she attempted to protect the chosen one, she received quick and sever pain. She had nothing to do with my being taken Leyla. Debrory had already decided that it was time for me to join her and it wouldn't have done Niccara any good to try and stop it. I don't blame her for what has happened because I believe that it was meant to be. If Royanna can't heal her, I want you to heal her for me. She needs your help more than anyone. Her heart, mind, and soul need to be healed Leyla." Cassie tells her letting her eyes show her depth of concern. "I don't believe that all that's happening to her now is just because of Debrory. I believe that it's also because she's blaming herself. She no longer feels that she has the right to live because of what she thinks she allowed to happen. We have to let her know that she isn't to blame and to help her to forget all that has happened because of Debrory's control."

Leyla frowns again and Cassie reaches over to take her hand. Taking a deep breath, Leyla smiles at her and nods. "We'll do all that we can for her Cassie, but she will have to want to live more than die. If she doesn't, nothing we do will change the outcome."

"I understand. I'm sure that when it's necessary, she will know that her place is with the people that love and care about her."

"Yes, and the one to give her the strongest feeling to stay with us is Daemon." Royanna puts in quietly. "Now I think that we should go and tell Chiero and the others about tomorrow and then turn in. It has been a very difficult day for all of us and we need the rest."

"Leyla and I will return to our ship and meet you at the clutches in the morning." Thayer says standing. "We'll bring down one of the shuttles and have the pilot take mother and the others back to Manchon while we finish up here."

"That sounds good to me." Logan agrees standing and shaking his hand. "Sheyome and Libre will stay here with us until we're done."

"All right. We'll see you in the morning." Thayer leans down and kisses Cassie on the cheek and gives her shoulder a gentle squeeze. "Do you want us to bring your father when we come back?"

"No, just tell him that we'll see them back on Manchon when we're done here." Cassie smiles slightly up at him.

Leyla kisses her cheek as well and tells the others goodnight. Thayer kisses his mother and then they teleport back to their ship.

Cassie stands and looks around at the others still gathered. "There's something that I need to tell all of you before we turn in. Debrory was..." She stops and takes a deep breath and lets it out again looking down at the table in front of her. "Debrory at one time, a long time ago, was my mother." There are gasps from everyone in the room and Logan begins to frown. She goes on to tell them about Debra Blackwood and her disappearance twelve years ago. Then she tells them of the memories that she was given by the implant of what her mother's life had been after she went through the change.

"That's why I feel that Nicca should not be held responsible for anything that has happened. No matter who had come into contact with Debrory, we would still be here now." The room is silent for so long that Cassie turns away. "I'm sorry that a member of my family has caused the Majichonie so much pain and grief. I...I...excuse me." She rushes from the room unable to continue.

For several moments no one moves and then Logan stands up and looks at the door. He then turns back to look at the others, unsure of what he should do.

"You had better go after her son. Tell her that we understand and that we don't consider Debrory as a part of her family. As far as we're concerned, her mother died on that distant planet twelve years ago." Thurda tells him standing also.

"Yes, I think you should go to her Logan. Our silence has made her feel that we hold her personally responsible in some way for what's happened." Royanna adds frowning in concern, knowing that none of them felt that way at all.

Logan nods looking at the door once again. "We'll port up to the cave and tell Chiero and the others about tomorrow after we've talked, and I've reassured her. Goodnight." He quickly leaves the room and goes to their cabin, but when he doesn't find her he asks Ali to locate her.

"She's out near the clutches Logan."

"Thank you Ali." He leaves the cabin and walks off the ship. Quickly he walks to the clutches and stops just under a tree to watch Cassie kneeling in the middle of the clutches.

"I know why you're here Logan. I know that you and the others don't blame me, but it doesn't change the fact that at one time she was the woman that gave birth to me. That she has hurt your people greatly. She also hurt someone I've come to care a great deal about. There's nothing that I can do to make up for that hurt or lose." Cassie turns her head slightly to look at him over her shoulder.

Logan notices the tears in her eyes and running down her cheeks. He walks over to her and kneels down beside her. Reaching over he wipes away her tears and puts his arm around her shoulders, taking one of her hands in his free one. "Cassie, atma, it's not for you to make up to anyone for something you didn't do. Debrory was not your mother. Your mother died the day she gave up her humanity, the day she stopped believing in your father and his love for her."

"In my mind I know that, but in my heart I remember Sheyome's grief at losing her parents. After I told all of you about my connection to Debrory, it occurred to me that you would all have a reason to hate me, especially Sheyome. Then, when no one said anything I guess I just let it get to me."

Logan hugs her close. "That's understandable sweetheart, but as you said, we don't blame you and you need to stop blaming yourself." He stands up and pulls her to her feet. "Now lets go tell Chiero and the others about tomorrow and then get some rest."

Gaining her feet Cassie nods and wipes the tears from her eyes and smiles up at him. Returning her smile, Logan holds her hand and ports them to the cave.

Early the next morning, after Leyla and Thayer arrive with the shuttle, Cassie takes them, along with Logan, Libre, and Sheyome, up to Debrory's cave to make one last check that all the dragmen have been changed back. As they enter the transformation chamber, they cover their noses because of the foul stench emanating from the chamber. Without a thought Cassie kinetically moves the table covering Drogen's body.

"I had meant to leave him for you Logan, but he got in the way during my fight with Debrory." She explains looking down at the body.

"What was he?" Thayer asks squatting down for a closer look at the body. "He doesn't appear to be either human or dragman."

"He was specifically made to serve Debrory. When they discovered that an unknown virus was killing off their people, and Debrory wasn't affected, it was decided that she would leave the planet and begin a new and stronger line of dragmen. To make it easier for her to get the people necessary, Drogen was changed only enough for her to be able to control him and for him to still be accepted by humans. While alive, you couldn't tell that he was not completely human."

"Well he won't be helping anyone do anything any longer." Thayer says standing up and backing away. He holds his hand out over the body and it suddenly bursts into flame and is gone.

They check the rest of the cave, but find no sign of any other dragmen. What they do find is the equipment and some of the supplies that were a part of the biological expedition. Logan teleports everything back to his ship and asks Ali to check everything over. "Check to see what's there and what's been used. The expedition's manifest should still be in your memory."

"All right Logan. The others are waiting for you near the clutches."

"Thank you Ali. Tell them that we'll be there shortly." They check all of the chambers a second time before leaving.

⌒

"After we do the young that are standing with you now, we'll do the clutches. As Logan and Cassie have already told you, the ones in the clutches will all be around the same age." Leyla reminds them and then looks at each of the couples. "I must ask you now if you wish for all of the eggs in your clutches to be hatched? Are you all sure that you're ready to accept the full responsibility of three to seven children?"

The couples all look at each other and then at their own mates. After several minutes they face Leyla and Thayer once again. Chiero and Shama are the first to answer, saying that they want all of their children. Two of the other couples agree that they too want all of their children. The other eight couples vary, wanting only one or two of their other children.

Over the next few hours, Leyla and Thayer go from child to child, changing them to human form. With each child the time for the change varies, but they don't rush. By noon the fifteen children are now in their human forms and being examined carefully by the med-techs that came with Leyla and Thayer.

"We need to stop and rest for a while. After we've eaten and relaxed, we'll get started on the clutches." Leyla informs everyone.

"There's food over by the ship for everyone." Cassie announces and points to the tables set up along the side of the ship in the shade. "Go and eat, feed your children. When you're finished Sheyome and Libre will show you where the children can lay down and rest."

The couples and their children move towards the tables while Cassie and Logan go to stand near Leyla and Thayer. "Are you sure that you can finish this today?" Logan asks in concern looking at Leyla's pale features. "They'll understand if you want to wait until tomorrow to finish. We don't need you making yourself ill over this."

"I'll be fine Logan." Leyla assures him and then frowns slightly as she looks at the nearest clutch. "I'm not so sure about the eggs though. If we were to wait I don't think that they would last. I've been feeling a weakness from all of them for the past half hour or so."

"I've felt it too." Cassie admits and kneels down beside Chiero's clutch. She places her hand on the dirt mound and closes her eyes. Seconds later she opens them again and tears slide down her cheeks. She looks up at Leyla and the others and shakes her head. "They do not wish to be born. They're too weak to make the transition, and do not wish to cause their parents further pain."

"How do you know that Cassie?" Logan asks with a slight frown.

"I can feel their minds and they can feel their parents thoughts and love. If Chiero and Shama were still dragmen they would feel theirs as well." She tells him looking deep into his eyes and letting him feel their thoughts.

'We will not survive if they change us. Mother will hurt for us when we die. It would be better if she doesn't see us when we do. We can not hurt them anymore.'

Logan hears the children's thoughts and nods his understanding. He looks over to Leyla and Thayer. "Is there anything you can do to help them, or at least spare the families further pain? I would rather none of them went through any further distress over all of this."

Leyla and Thayer look at each other and then Thayer nods. "We'll have to do it quickly so that Chiero and the others don't realize what's happening and attempt to stop us."

"I think that we should take care of the families first." Leyla suggests to him. "It will be easier once they have no memory of the clutches."

"What about Roushta?" Cassie asks looking at Logan. "He knows that Chiero and Shama have a large clutch. Its going to upset him when they return with only one of their children." She points out to them.

"Yes, you're right, and he'll start asking questions. He'll want to know what went wrong." Logan agrees looking over at Chiero and Shama. "And they would have no idea what he was talking about."

"What is Roushta's connection to Chiero and Shama?" Leyla asks and Thayer answers.

"Roushta is Shama's grandfather, and only living blood relative. He's also a member of the High council."

"He's also my godfather." Logan puts in. "We almost lost him when he first found out about Shama, Chiero and their clutch."

"We should be able to include him, but we'll need someone that has recently been in mind touch with him." Leyla assures them. "It will probably have to be you Logan. You're probably the only one here that has touched his mind recently enough. With your bond to him it will make it that much easier to reach him."

"You had better get started then. They'll be finished eating soon." Cassie warns them nodding to the group at the tables.

Leyla and Thayer stand facing each other while Cassie and Logan step back. Firestar and Starhawk quickly appear and within moments Chiero and the others have no memory of the clutches or what they contain. They then use Logan's mind to reach out and touch Roushta, Chevala, and Thurda, to take away their memories of the clutches as well. Minutes later they reappear and nod to Cassie.

"They have no memory of the clutches. It would be best if you get them into your ship now. They don't need to be present for this, they won't know what we're doing or why." Thayer tells them.

"I want to stay...need to stay here until you finish." Cassie tells them looking from one to the other.

"Cassie I don't think..." Leyla begins, but Cassie interrupts her.

"This is something that I have to do for myself Leyla." She tells her looking into her eyes.

"All right Cassie. Logan will you see to the others? It shouldn't take us more than a half an hour to take care of things here."

Logan nods and then kisses Cassie gently before walking over to the tables. Slowly he leads Chiero and the others onto the ship and closes the door behind them.

Slowly and carefully they remove the eggs from their clutches, laying them gently down on the ground together. Just before they transform Leyla and Thayer both receive images of a planet that appears peaceful and serene. They also receive images of the dragmen eggs on the planet hatching. Suddenly they hear a strange yet familiar female voice in their minds.

'Send the children to this planet Firestar. They will be safe and have a good life. It is their destiny to be more than what they were intended for. Their humanity will guide them to a better life. Starhawk, you must protect this planet for the next ten years. When they are old enough they will be able to protect themselves and they will be an asset to all of mankind in the years to come.'

They look at each other and then turn to Cassie. Leyla looks at her with a smile. "They will be born Cassie. We'll strengthen them and then send them some place where they can grow. In time they'll be all that Debrory never was and all that you have wished for them to be."

Cassie just stands there and stares blankly at them. She too had heard the strange voice and it had told her that the children would not pass from this life, but would have a new and better one. The voice had also told her that because of her humanity, she would be blessed in many ways.

Leyla and Thayer transform and within seconds all of the eggs begin to glow. Minutes later there is no sign that the eggs had ever been there. Returning to their human forms, Leyla and Thayer notice a golden light surrounding Cassie. As they watch, the light slowly fades away until there is only a small amount of the light outlining her body. Walking over to her, Leyla takes her hands and smiles when she feels the love and warmth flowing through her friend. "The Great One has blessed you Cassie. Now you will be and are, all that you were meant to be."

Cassie returns Leyla's smile and then hugs her close. "I'm glad that we're friends." They stand there and look at each other for several seconds before Thayer clears his throat.

"I think that we should get going. We have a lot of people to return to their families."

"Yes...yes we do." Cassie says stepping back from Leyla. "Are you two going to ride back with us to Manchon or...?"

"No, we'll port back to our ship. Yours is a bit crowded right now." Thayer reminds her with a smile. "Besides, we have to let the others know that everything is all right now. Especially your family. They've been worried about you, and we haven't said anything to them about what's been going on."

"All right. Thanks for not saying anything to them. I'll figure out what to tell them, without causing them any hurt or confusion." She tells them with a small frown not really knowing what she was going to tell them that wouldn't hurt them. Whatever it was, it wouldn't be about how Debra Blackwood had changed so much after she left them.

CHAPTER FOURTEEN

Flying back to Manchon, Logan and the others explain to Chiero and his group that no one on Manchon except for those with them, knows for sure what happened to them.

"How are we to explain our children?" Shama asks holding her daughter close. "None of us were gone long enough to explain our having children as old as they appear to be."

"We'll have to wait and see how things go when we get all of you home Shama." Cassie smiles at her gently. "If we have to explain it to anyone, we'll tell them that there was a time displacement which caused them to grow at an accelerated rate."

"But we would be lying to our families and friends." One of the others points out with a frown.

"No, you wouldn't be lying. A normal pregnancy would last nine months, whereas a dragman pregnancy lasts only a week and then the eggs are buried in the soil. Normally it would take the eggs three months to hatch. Something in Avdacal's soil caused a time displacement causing them to grow at an accelerated speed." Logan tries to explain Cassie's meaning to them.

"Because the dragmen age differently, Leyla and Thayer stopped the age acceleration so that they will now age at a normal human rate. They used their physical size to determine what their human ages would be." Cassie tells them.

"But what about their minds Logan?" Chiero wants to know. "Their minds have been those of teenagers and young adults. Are their minds now that for children of their ages?"

"For the most part they are Chiero. Though their minds are stronger, they're as every other child. They also have no memory of how they were born or what they looked like. Soon all of you will have forgotten what you have been through."

"Logan, you're needed in the control room for an incoming message." Ali announces over the intercom.

"I'll be there shortly Ali." Logan stands up and Cassie follows suit. "We'll arrive on Manchon in a few hours. Your families will meet you at the palace and take you home. We'll let you know within fifteen minutes before we're ready to land so as to give you time to prepare yourselves and the children for that meeting. There are replicators in the cabins that you can use to get yourselves new clothing if you wish. Now if you'll excuse us, we need to see about this message."

Taking Cassie's hand in his, Logan leads her from the room and they hurry to the control room. Sheyome and Libre turn from the monitor as they enter the room. "What's happened Shey?" Logan asks stopping in front of her and the monitor.

"Lord Roushta contacted us. Niccara's condition has gotten even worse. Royanna needs Leyla and Thayer as quickly as possible. She says that she can not touch Niccara's mind and is afraid that she may have already given up."

Cassie steps up to the monitor. "Ali, put us through to Leyla's ship with visual." Within seconds Leyla's image appears on the monitor and Cassie quickly explains the situation to her and suggests that they go ahead. "We'll follow as quickly as we can."

"Hold on Cassie, let me check with Stephen. I think that there may be a way to take your ship with us." Leyla turns away for a moment to talk quietly with Stephen, then turns back. "There's room in our docking bay for your ship. Stop your engines and we'll tractor you inside. Once your secure I'll port us all directly to Manchon."

"All right Leyla, we're shutting down now." She nods to Logan and he turns off the engines. "We're ready." In minutes the cruiser is within the large flagship and seconds later the flagship appears and lands on Manchon. Thayer ports the cruiser out of the docking bay and sets it down beside the flagship. Shortly after that Logan and Cassie join Leyla and Thayer in front of the ships. They leave Sheyome and Libre in charge of getting Chiero and the others off the ship as soon as they are all ready.

Thurda meets them at the side entrance and leads them to Nicca's private chambers. As they enter, Daemon Heorte is demanding that Royanna do something to bring Nicca back to him.

"You can not let her stay this way!"

"I don't plan on leaving her like this, but right now I can not reach her mind. It's closed off from me. I've sent for someone to help her, but you have to be patient. They'll heal what they can, but you will have to call to her. You will have to make her want to stay alive Daemon." She turns to face Cassie and the others as they enter.

"Has there been any response at all Anna?"

"None Cassie. I've tried many different types of stimulants, but nothing has worked. Daemon hasn't been able to touch her either. Its almost as if there is a wall surrounding her mind."

Cassie turns to Leyla. "Will you see what you can do for her?" Leyla nods and steps forward and moves over to the bed. Placing her right hand on Nicca's forehead, she closes her eyes. She remains that way for a couple of minutes and then opens her eyes with a frown of confusion.

"There is a wall, but I can't even seem to get past it. I can feel a strangeness within her too." Leyla says to Cassie and then looks over at Royanna. "Did you examine her for any unusual marking? Something that would give us an idea of how Debrory was controlling her?"

"Yes I did. Chevala and I checked her from head to toe, front and back, but we couldn't find anything."

"Did you 'look' into her body for anything?" Cassie asks.

Royanna shakes her head. Since neither she or Chevala were very good at 'looking' that way, they hadn't even tried. Cassie walks over to the bed and gently places her hand on Nicca's head and closes her eyes. She finds the wall and feels its completeness. Carefully she follows it until she locates it's source behind Nicca's left ear. Using her other hand, she places her index and middle fingers over the spot where Debrory had placed one of her scales. Within moments she dissolves the scale and feels the wall collapse. When the wall is completely down, she calls out to Nicca. Though there is no answer, Cassie can feel some impulse from Nicca's mind. She removes her hands and opens her eyes.

"The wall is down now. Debrory placed one of her scales behind Nicca's ear. That's how she was able to control her and punish her if she didn't do what they wanted her to do when they wanted. It was placed in such a way that it would cause the most pain, but could not be picked up by any means. The scale had been joined to her skull. A med. unit wouldn't have been able to detect it."

Daemon forces his way past Leyla to get to Nicca's side, knocking her slightly off balance. Thayer growls at Daemon's action and takes a step forward only to stop as Leyla holds up her hand.

'No Thayer. It's all right. We need to establish some kind of link with Niccara and right now he's the best choice to establish that link. You can't hurt him.'

'Link or no, that does not excuse his rudeness.'

'It does if his emotion is strong enough to get her attention and brings her mind to a point that we can reach her.'

Reaching down, Daemon gently touches Nicca's cheek while talking to her both verbally and mentally. "Atma, come back to me. All is forgiven. You are no longer under the control of Drogen or the Dragman Queen. They are both dead now and will never hurt you again."

The others in the room watch as there is no reaction at first to Daemon's words, then slowly Nicca frowns and moves her head slowly from side to side. "Yes, atma yes. They are gone and will never return. Your cousin Prince Thayer and his mate have made sure of it."

Niccara's head moves faster from side to side and her body begins to shake. Daemon looks at Leyla and Thayer with pleading clearly showing in his eyes. He then looks across the bed to Cassie. *'Please my Lady. Let her know that you do not blame her for what has happened.'*

Cassie takes Nicca's hand gently in hers. "Nicca, there are no bad feelings between us." She assures her caressing her hand. "I understand your need to protect your people and I'm proud that you held on for so long. Now we want to help and protect you, but you have to open your mind to Leyla and Thayer. They'll heal and strengthen you. You're going to have to want it Nicca, you have to want to live. Not just for your family, not just for Daemon, and not just for the people of Manchon, but for yourself. You have a lot to offer to everyone Nicca, don't give up on yourself now." As she speaks, Nicca's head turns towards her and Cassie knows that she is listening. Moments later Nicca's body relaxes in acceptance. Quickly Cassie signals for Daemon and Royanna to move back. Thayer takes Cassie's place and looks across to Leyla and holds out his hands.

Leyla holds out her hands to him, and even though they don't physically touch the link is made. Closing their eyes they concentrate on healing Nicca's body from the inside out. They then proceed to heal her mind and restore it to a more stable consciousness. While doing this they remove all memory of what she has been through and that she had ever been queen. This at Royanna's request. The only advanced memories that she has now are those of a healer capable of becoming a Master Healer. As they do this, Thayer comes up with a plan that will ensure that no one will remember this time or what has happened.

When they finish, Leyla and Thayer step away from the bed and Royanna quickly checks Nicca over. Once assured that she will recover, Royanna removes everyone from the room so that Nicca could rest undisturbed.

 /

"So what you're saying is that none of us will remember any of what has happened in the past several years." Daemon asks Thayer as he paces around the private sitting room.

"Except for the normal things in their lives. With the exception of Cassandra and Logan, my wife and myself, everyone will forget what has happened since Niccara was made queen. No one will remember her as queen or any misjudgments on her part. My mother will be queen and when everyone awakes in the morning everything will be as it should be." Thayer assures him.

"Very well your Highness. If you will all excuse me now, I would like to go and sit with Nicca." Thayer nods and Daemon bows to them all before returning to the bed chamber. After the door closes behind him, Thayer turns back to face the others.

"Leyla and I will return to the ship and rest for a while before we take this next step. In the morning it will be as if we have only just arrived." Thayer faces his mother. "It will also give me the chance to make up for our improper greeting when I first arrived."

Royanna smiles up at him. "I will be so pleased to see you again."

"What about the talks about the Alliance Thayer?" Thurda asks stepping forward to stand beside Royanna. "Won't that be forgotten as well? If it is forgotten, how will you explain Cassie and Logan's presence here before you?"

"Only the negative things that happened while Nicca was queen will be forgotten. Therefore any positive things she did will be attributed to my mother and there will be no need for explanations." He looks to Sheyome who has stayed standing at attention since joining them a few hours ago. "The only thing we can not change that I wish we could is Sheyome's loss." He watches her closely. *'Come to me Sheyla.'* He calls to her. At first she doesn't move, but then Thayer holds out his arms to her and she rushes into them. *'We'll make your loss easier in your mind little one. It will be something that will lessen the pain and sorrow you have already suffered.'*

'Thank you.'

He hugs her close a little longer and then slowly releases her and smiles down at her. "We'll be talking soon about what you wish to do. Though you won't remember me saying this in the morning, we will discuss it."

Sheyome nods and then steps back from him and wipes the tears from her cheeks. She returns to her place next to Libre and once again stands at attention. She wasn't sure how they could make her parents deaths less painful, but she would not fault them if they could not.

"What about the living arrangements?" Cassie points out looking at everyone in the room. "After all this is the Queen's chambers. All of Nicca's belongings are here, and Royanna's things are all at Thurda's. We'll need to transfer their belongings before everyone wakes up in the morning or there will be some confusion."

"Yes, Cassie's right. We will have to move Nicca's things to one of the other chambers. Her presence in this chamber can be explained by her illness." Royanna tells them as she looks around the room. "We can then bring our things in and have everything set so that it will be familiar when we awake." She looks at Thurda.

"We can set up Nicca's chambers the same way she has these so that it will be familiar to her and Daemon." Thurda looks over to Logan. "You and Cassie can stay at the house with your sister."

Logan nods and then turns to Thayer and Leyla. "Why don't you two go and get some rest while we take care of moving things around? I'm sure that we can handle everything."

"All right Logan. If you should need anything, or need some help, just contact Sarah and she'll find someone to give you a hand." Thayer tells him and then looks over at Cassie. "We'll make sure that your family doesn't remember the reason for us being called here so early."

"Thank you Thayer." Cassie smiles up at him.

With a final nod and farewell, Thayer and Leyla port back to their ship. Once they're gone Logan and the others begin getting things ready for in the morning. They find a chamber close to the Queen's that is setup with the same floor plan and is already empty. Slowly and carefully they transfer Nicca and Daemon's things to the other chamber. They put everything in exactly the same place and position so that the rooms will feel familiar.

After removing all of Nicca and Daemon's things, they start moving in Thurda and Royanna's belongings from the house into the Queen's chambers. As they bring the things in, Royanna starts putting them where she feels they will feel most comfortable. She checks with Thurda about his personal items. Within a few hours they have everything in place. After double checking everything one last time, Royanna goes into the bed chamber to explain to Daemon what they have been doing all afternoon.

Logan looks around the room and then faces his father. "I think that Cassie and I will go and make sure that all of the families got safely back to their homes and that their children are being accepted. Though it won't matter tomorrow. They could have some emotional problems today."

"That sounds like a good idea son. Let us know of any problems they may be having. If we have to we'll bring them to the palace until later this evening, and then we can return them back to their homes. I don't really believe that there will be any problems though."

"Let's hope that you're right father. We should be back in time to join you and Royanna for the evening meal."

~

Back on the Calidonian flagship, Selina and Brockton Centori discuss the plans to erase Niccara's time as queen from the minds of the people of Manchon.

"I still don't believe that they should try this Brock. Not on a worldwide scale at least." Selina tells her husband as they sit alone in the lounge. "They've metamorphosed almost a dozen times in the past month. Whose to know what its doing to their unborn child?"

"Sweetheart, you know that Leyla wouldn't do anything to harm her child. She would protect it any way that she could." Brockton takes her hand and gently squeezes. "I believe that the metamorphosis is only strengthening the baby. I can not believe that such a natural part of Leyla would hurt her child in any way."

Selina frowns a little, but then agrees that it would be unlikely that something that was such a major part of her friend would harm the child. She still worries that such a large undertaking is not a good idea for them to be doing without more rest. "I still think that they should do it in stages instead of all at once." She tells him squeezing his hand and standing to pace around the room. "They could do those within say a fifty or a hundred miles first. Then do other areas of the same distance every few days until they cover the whole planet."

"Something like that would take months to finish Selina." Brockton points out watching her pace the room. "We can't spare that much time. Don't forget we still have to meet with the Aquilians and Pantherians before we can return home. We don't know how long that meeting will take."

"You're right, maybe it won't be as bad as I think. Still they won't be able to do the whole planet tonight. They'll only be able to do about half the planet, because of the time differences." She points out. "While everyone is asleep here, the other side of the planet will be awake."

"That's right. We'll have to remind Thayer of that when they get up." Brockton stands up and stretches. "In the mean time, I think that we should go and see if the Blackwoods need any help getting ready for tomorrow."

Logan and Cassie check on the families, and find that everything is going well. Everyone has accepted the children and are helping the missing members to get back to a more normal way of life. After checking on the last family, Logan decides to take Cassie to a small meadow for some time alone with her. Laying his cape on the ground, they sit and Logan takes Cassie into his arms and holds her close. "How are you doing atma?" He asks dropping a kiss on the top of her head. For the past couple of hours he has felt that something was bothering her, but he wanted to give her the time to tell him on her own what was wrong.

"I'm doing all right." She sighs looking across the meadow to the trees on the far side. "It still bothers me that Debrory has caused so much pain to the people. Its hard to believe how much she changed from the mother I remember. The woman I remember would never hurt anyone or anything."

"Yes, I know its hard, but you need to put it behind you now. Remember her only as she was when she was a physical part of your family. The creature that you met on Avdacal was an unbending and cruel form of what humans would become if we were ever to lose our humanity."

"I know that you're right, and I'll try to remember that, but..." She pulls a little away from his embrace to look up at him. "Though the hair is gone and I'm physically myself again, I'm different in some ways."

"In what ways are you different?"

"My abilities are a lot stronger than they were before and I think that I may have a few more then I did before." She smiles at him slightly, and Logan notices the unease entering her eyes. "I also think that I may still possess something of the golden dragman that I became."

"Like what?" Logan asks her frowning.

Cassie pulls completely out of his arms and stands up. Stepping a few feet away from him, she closes her eyes. In seconds the golden wings appear on her back, unfolding and spreading out behind her. Though they are no longer the leathery form of the dragman, they are still golden but now feathered. Opening her eyes, she looks over her shoulder, Cassie catches sight of what she thinks is a look of horror and fascination on Logan's face. Their eyes meet for a few moments and then Cassie turns away and closes her eyes once more. The wings fold and grow small before once more disappearing into her back. When she opens them again, Logan is standing in front of her.

"With the hair removed, there should be no physical proof of your once being a dragman. How can this be possible?"

"I don't know Logan." She looks at him and tears begin to flow down her cheeks.

Logan pulls her into his arms and holds her tightly against his chest while she cries. He murmurs softly in her ear that everything would be all right. After a few minutes Cassie sniffles and pulls back to wipe her eyes. "Why don't we go and talk to Royanna about this?" He suggests tipping her head up so that he can look into her eyes. "She may have some ideas of why you still have the wings."

Cassie looks at him for several seconds before slowly nodding her agreement. Though she doesn't doubt the loving concern in his eyes, she can not forget the horror she had glimpsed earlier. After picking up his cape, Logan takes her hand and they begin the walk back to the palace.

"They are a physical part of her Logan." Royanna tells them after she does a thorough examination of Cassie and the wings. "I can only guess at the reason why she still has them though."

"And what reason would that be?" Logan asks watching as the wings once again disappear into Cassie's back leaving no trace of their existence.

"I would say that somewhere within her essence or genes, that she was meant to have them. That somehow during the transformation, that part of her was awakened and is now a more natural part of her." She pats Cassie on the shoulder. "The best way to check this out would be to use one of those medic boxes on your ship. Have it check each of her family members. If its a natural part of her, it will show up in the others as well."

"But what if none of them have this unknown gene Royanna? I don't want to be any more different then anyone else." Cassie tells the older woman chewing on her lower lip.

"My dear, just because you have those wings doesn't make you any more different. It makes you special and unique in your own way." Royanna takes her hand in hers. "There is something different in each of us that makes us all just as special. Some find that difference sooner than others, and some never find it at all. What really matters is that to the Great One, all of us, human or not, are special to Him in one way or another."

CHAPTER FIFTEEN

Leyla and Thayer sit in the lounge and listen as Selina explains her worries about what they are about to do and what they have come to realize. After listening Thayer explains to them that the other side of the planet is only used during the spring and summer months for the planting of food crops.

"Now that its winter over there, its too cold for living. Everyone has already returned to this side, but even if they had stayed there it wouldn't have caused any problems for us to reach them. We would have been able to reach them through their families who were still on this side." He assures Selina as he stands and stretches. "As for the baby, it's totally safe. It becomes one with the Firestar whenever Leyla transforms."

"Then what you're saying is that it will only take you this one night to remove Niccara's time of rule from everyone's memory and then replace it with your mother's instead?" Brockton asks shaking his head at the strength of their abilities. It amazed him how powerful they were, yet how they didn't let that power take control of their lives.

"That's right. Once Nicca is removed from their memory as queen, along with the negatives, we'll place mother's image in their place. Since there are not that many negatives in their minds, what gaps are made will soon be filled with new positive memories."

"Will you be putting in any of those positive memories?" Selina asks watching Thayer walk around the room.

"No, those will fill in themselves in time." Leyla tells her. "The best memories are those we experience for ourselves. Besides, it would be to hard to place any type of personal memory which would not cause confusion. The gaps in their memories won't cause any undo alarm because they won't remain empty for very long."

"Leyla, sorry to interrupt, but Cassie and Logan wish to speak to you."

"Thank you Sarah, I'll be there shortly." Leyla stands and looks at Selina. "Thank you for showing your concern Selina. I hope that we've been able to ease your mind some about everything."

"You have Leyla. I just wanted you to think about the possible dangers to the baby and even to yourselves if you were to over do it."

Leyla nods and excuses herself to go to the communications room. As she enters Stephen Seven is telling Cassie about her family. "And it appears that Merri is still jealous of Colt's friendship with Princess Salis. Though they are getting along better then when they first met."

"As long as Merri understands that this is something that will happen more and more over the years as they get older and meet new people. I think that she still thinks of Colt as hers instead of belonging to himself."

"Yes, well, I'll have another talk with her, but as your father has said, she'll have to learn to let go sooner or later." Stephen looks over his shoulder and then back at the monitor. "Leyla is here now. I'll check our med-units and prepare them to receive the information." He steps aside for Leyla to come closer to the monitor.

"Evening Cassie. Are you having any problems?"

"No, not really, but I need you to do something for me." Slowly she tells her about the wings and Royanna's ideas about why she still has them. "I've already entered the med-unit on our ship, and Ali was able to isolate the gene. As soon as Stephen has your units ready she'll send the information to Sarah to do a check on the rest of my family for the same gene."

"All right Cassie. Will you be able to handle this if it comes out that none of them has this gene?" Leyla asks in concern for her best friend's peace of mind.

"I think so Leyla. Anna says that I should look on it as something that makes me a little more special in my own way." She says giving her a wobbly smile.

Logan's image comes onto the screen. "I'll help her to get through it Leyla no matter which way the results should go."

"I'm glad to hear that Logan. Okay, have Ali go ahead and send Sarah the necessary information and we'll run the tests. I think we should wait to tell them what the test is for until after we get back the results and you're all together. It would be easier to learn of this from you or I'm sure that Royanna wouldn't mind explaining it if you don't think you can."

"We'll wait until the results are in Leyla." Logan assures her. "Tell Sarah that Ali will send the information shortly. We'll see you in the morning. Goodnight."

"Goodnight Logan, Cassie. Rest easy, everything will work out for the best."

They end the communication and Leyla returns to the lounge and Thayer meets her at the door. Quietly she tells him about Cassie's call. "We still have a while before everyone is asleep. I'll go and speak with Denral about the test. Stephen will run them while we take care of Manchon. I've been thinking that we should remove their memories of this time too Thayer. I don't think that Cassie should have such a memory as the last one of her mother."

Thayer frowns at her words since he had been thinking the same thing. "I don't think that it should be her last memory of her mother either Leyla, but it's not our decision to make. It was her decision to keep what she knows and we can't interfer with her free will." He reminds her of the most basic law of any telepath. "Do you want me to come with you to see Denral?"

"No I can do it alone. Why don't you go and check on Salis before we get started though. I've been feeling energy surges from her again so she may be going through another transition. See if you can judge the strength and frequency of the energy going through her this time. We may have to isolate her this time if they're stronger then the last."

"All right, I'll meet you at the hatch in an hour." He looks over his shoulder at Selina and Brockton. "Don't bother waiting up for us. We'll be going slowly and carefully so that we don't miss anyone."

They both nod and then watch Thayer and Leyla leave the room. Since its getting late, Selina and Brockton decide to go and make a last check with the guards and to make sure that the people in the special hold are all comfortable.

After checking Nicca, Cassie and Logan say goodnight to Royanna and Thurda, then go to their chambers in the palace. As the door closes behind them, Logan pulls Cassie into his arms and kisses her slowly and deeply. Without releasing her mouth, he swings her up into his arms and carries her into the bedroom.

Slowly he lowers her to the floor and silently undresses her, never once releasing her from their kiss. Once all of her clothes are removed he picks her up again and gently lays her down on the bed. Only then does he release her lips. Cassie then watches as he removes his clothing just as slowly and his eyes never leave her face. When the last of his clothes land on the floor, he climbs into the bed beside her. Without saying a word, he slowly begins to make love to her. Kissing her, he runs his hands over her body, touching her in the places he knows will excite her. Carefully he turns her over onto her stomach and begins to kiss and caress her back.

At first Cassie stiffens when he touches the area on her back where her wings come out, but begins to relax when Logan refuses to let her pull away. When she doesn't sense any sign of revulsion as he touches her there, she relaxes more fully. His lips travel from her shoulders down her back, covering every inch. He runs his hands over her, caressing and rubbing. When his hands squeeze her buttocks, Cassie pushes herself into his touch. After a few more seconds he turns her over again. As she turns to face him, a tear slides down her cheek and Logan kisses it away. He strokes her cheek and looks deeply into her eyes before moving above her. Sliding between her legs he caresses her thighs and smiles as they relax.

Logan groans as Cassie takes him into her hand and caresses him before guiding him to her private place, all the while watching him and then she moans as he enters her. Releasing him, she places her hands on his shoulders and lifts herself up to meet him as he moves more fully into her. They both gasp in surprise and shock as Logan comes up against a barrier. They look at each other as they both realize that her maidenhead has grown back. Logan starts to withdraw but Cassie grabs his hips to keep him inside her.

"No, stay with me." She pleads.

"I don't want to hurt you atma."

"The pain doesn't matter Logan. Before...before I...I thought that I was in love with the man I first gave myself to, but I know now that I wasn't. I'm being given a second chance to give it to the man that I truly love and want to spend the rest of my life with."

"We could wait until our lifemating. It would make it that much more."

"Do you want to wait?" She asks moving her hips and causing him to groan and stiffen.

"No sweetheart, I don't want to wait."

"Then don't." With that she raises her hips and wraps her legs around him, pulling him down to her. Because his body is so stiff, he penetrates her deeply and tears through the maidenhead quickly. Cassie cries out as it tears and clutches Logan even closer to her while taking deep breaths as the pain radiates through her for several seconds before beginning to ease. When the pain stops and the pleasure begins, she smiles up at him and he returns it fully.

He begins to move deeply within her. He watches as Cassie's breathing becomes shallow and her head rolls from side to side on the pillow. Wanting to prolong her pleasure, Logan keeps his thrusts slow and deep, but Cassie does not want that and arches into him forcing him to move faster and harder within her. Just as they reach the highest point of their physical union, their minds reach out and touch. They both feel each others release. As the last waves of pleasure go through them, they collapse and fall into an exhausted sleep.

While Stephen is running the tests on the Blackwoods, Leyla and Thayer step out of the ship and look around into the night. For the first time, Leyla gets a good look at Manchon even though it is during the night.

"It's beautiful Thayer. I can't wait to see it all during the day. With everything that was happening earlier, I didn't get a chance to look around."

"It is beautiful at night, but you can't see the colors as they should be seen, with the sunlight shining down on everything." Thayer tells her looking around at the palace grounds and at the parts of the city that he can see from where they are standing.

Closing his eyes, he sends his mind out to touch those of the people of Manchon. Leyla stands beside him waiting patiently for him to see that everyone is asleep. Ten minutes later he opens his eyes and nods. "Everyone is asleep, even the palace guards.

Mother must have planted the suggestion that it would be safe for them to sleep tonight. We'll do them first and then wake the ones that need to be on duty. Even though everyone's asleep, I don't like the idea of the palace being unguarded for too long."

Leyla nods her agreement, then takes a step back from him so that they are facing each other. Closing their eyes, they concentrate on their other selves. Within moments they are the Firestar and Starhawk once again. They fly up above the palace, each going to opposite sides to cover the whole palace at once. The guards are done first and then they continue on to the rest of the people within the palace. After that they move out over the city.

Several hours later they finish the last area and change back to their human forms. Once again Thayer closes his eyes and reaches out his mind to make sure that they haven't missed anyone. When he opens them again he smiles over at Leyla. "We've gotten everyone my love. Now all we have to do is get back to the ship and get some sleep before everyone else wakes up."

"You sound as tired as I feel. Luckily we don't have to get back on our own. While you were double checking I called Stephen and asked him to send us a speeder. It should be here soon to pick us up." she tells him looking into the sky.

"Good, I wasn't looking forward to trying to port all the way back. I don't think I could even do a small port right now." Thayer admits with a sigh.

"That's why I called for the speeder. With any luck we won't have to metamorph for a long time. Now I understand Selina's worry that we might over do it." Just then she hears the approach of the speeder and looks up. "Here it comes now. How long do we have before sunrise?"

Thayer looks up at the sky. "About four or five hours. We should be able to get about seven or eight hours sleep before we have to be at the greeting chamber."

"As long as Salis lets us you mean. You know how she is, and she's been cooped up in the ship since we arrived without any chance to leave it."

"She'll let us sleep. I explained to her that we would be very busy tonight and that she must let us rest. I told her that when we woke up we would take her to meet her other grandmother. She agreed to wait, though she says that it will be very, very hard to wait so long."

They watch as the speeder lands a few feet away, Stephen steps down and walks over to them. "I thought that it would be best if I came to fly you back. Sarah detected the fatigue in your voice when she talked to you and mentioned it. I figured that Thayer would be just as tired if not more so."

"I for one am glad you came Stephen." Thayer says slapping the android on the shoulder. He takes Leyla's hand and leads her over to the speeder. "Get us back as quickly as you can without too many bumps please."

"Right. I'll have you back in less than fifteen minutes with little or no bumps." Stephen assures them stepping into the speeder and up to the controls.

When Leyla and Thayer sit down, Leyla leans into Thayer's side as he puts his arms around her. They both close their eyes and relax as the speeder lifts off the ground. Within seconds both are in a deep exhausted sleep.

"Sarah, prepare to transport Leyla and Thayer directly into their bed as soon as we land. They're both out of it for the rest of the night and since they're locked in each others arms, I won't be able to carry either of them myself without disturbing them, and it would be too difficult to carry them together."

"All right, I'll be waiting. Should I have one of the servants waiting to disrobe them?"

"No, I'll take care of that after I deal with the speeder. We'll arrive in seven point three minutes." He shuts off the communicator and looks over his shoulder at the sleeping couple. Being in their service was never going to be dull that was a fact. Then if Salis was anything like Leyla as she was appearing to be, then he was going to be very busy for a very long time to come. Already she had gotten herself and Colt Blackwood into some sticky situations in the past couple of weeks. Like her mother she had convinced him several times not to tell of the things he's had to get her out of. He didn't really mind though, since it gave him more time to study her interactions with others and the things around her. Each day it was becoming harder and harder to tell that she wasn't Leyla's biological daughter. She had begun picking up Leyla's mannerisms and speech patterns almost immediately. Soon you wouldn't be able to tell that Leyla hadn't given birth to her.

Landing the speeder he turns and watches as Sarah transports them to their room. Turning back to the controls, Stephen checks that everything is shut down. After securing the speeder he heads up to Leyla and Thayer's cabin. Stepping into the chamber, he notices that they have moved away from each other. It would make his task of undressing them a lot easier. Moving carefully so as not to surprise him, he does Thayer first. Moving around the bed he begins to remove Leyla's clothing. As he reaches to unhook her belt he receives an energy surge from the unborn child. For several moments Stephen's systems shut down and then come back on. Slowly he draws his hand back and looks at it in surprise. Frowning slightly he turns his hand over and looks at it front to back. Blinking his eyes, he continues undressing Leyla and then covers her and Thayer with a light sheet. Dimming the lights, he leaves the room after taking one last look at the sleeping couple. Closing the door, he quickly goes to his own chamber to do a thorough systems check. He could not understand why there had been a power surge and wanted to rule out any malfunctions that could put the family at risk.

CHAPTER SIXTEEN

Nine hours later Leyla and Thayer lead their group into the palace and then to the greeting chamber. Salis walks between her parents followed by Trocon Damori, Selina and Brockton Centori, and then by Cassie's father and brothers and sisters. Finally six of the Calidonian royal guards bring up the rear.

As they walk through the palace, guards stand straighter and servants step out of the way bowing and curtsying. Thayer acknowledges all of them with nods and with some by their given names. Coming closer to the greeting chamber the doors are opened before them and they notice the gathering of people within the chamber. As they enter the room all conversation stops as the people turn to watch them.

Walking up to the dais, Thayer bows to his mother and then kisses her hand. Leyla steps forward next and curtsies and kisses her hand as well. They both step to Royanna's left and Thayer makes the formal introductions. He pitches his voice so that all of those present will hear him.

"Queen Royanna. I your son Prince Thayer Robus Starhawk of Manchon, King of Calidon, do bring before you and those gathered here, my lifemate Queen Leyla Aeneka, and our daughter Princess Salis Chandelle."

Salis steps forward then, curtsies and kisses her grandmother's hand as she had seen her parents do. Straightening up she smiles shyly and then quickly steps to Leyla's side and takes her hand.

"Also with us is Lord Trocon Damori, our High Chamberlain." Trocon steps forward and bows. "Brockton Centori, our High Councilor, and his mate Selina who is our High Advisor and Chief Communications Officer." Brock bows and Selina curtsies.

Cassie steps to Royanna's right. "Your Majesty, the gentleman and young people with them are my father and younger brothers and sisters." Denral and his family step forward and bow to Royanna.

"You are all honored guests and I welcome you to Manchon." Royanna speaks loudly so that all can hear her. "I welcome my son home and acknowledge his position as King of Calidon and his lifemating to the Queen of Calidon. I accept her as my daughter and this child as my granddaughter."

Cheers go up from the crowd. Royanna allows it to continue for several moments before she holds up her hands for quiet. Once all is silent again she dismisses everyone. "We will have a celebration this evening to welcome my son and his family and friends. Until then you may continue with your normal plans."

The people nod and bow before slowly working their way out of the chamber. Murmurs can be heard of how well Prince Thayer looked and of how beautiful his queen is. There are also murmurs that can be heard of Cassie's family, of how unusual it was to see so many twins in one family. Didn't the father look like one of Queen Royanna's advisors?

After all of the people have left and the doors are closed, Royanna pulls Thayer into her arms and hugs him close. They stand that way, holding each other, until Thayer feels a tug on the hem of his jacket. He looks down at Salis.

"May I greet grandmother that way too?" She asks shyly looking from her father to Royanna.

Everyone laughs a little and Royanna smiles down at her. "Yes you may greet me in the same way if you wish." She bends down and holds out her arms and Salis steps into them.

After a few moments Salis steps back and smiles up at Royanna. "You smell nice, just like grandma Neka." She tells her causing everyone to laugh again.

"I will take that as a very high compliment. Thank you." Royanna smiles back at her and then turns to Leyla and opens her arms to her also. Leyla walks into the embrace. "I am delighted to finally meet you in person my dear. Cassie shared some of her memories of your friendship with me and I am glad to know that my son's choice was such a good one."

"Thank you Majesty. My mother felt the same way upon meeting Thayer in person."

While Leyla and her family are getting acquainted with Royanna, Cassie and Logan go to greet the Blackwoods. They all hug and laugh together before Thurda comes over to meet the family that will soon be added to his own. Cassie takes her father's hand and introduces him to Thurda. The two men shake hands and Thurda frowns slightly looking closely at Denral's facial features.

"You know Cassie. I believe that some of that murmuring could be true. Your father does look like someone on the council." Thurda tells her never looking away from Denral. "In fact I'm sure that there's a resemblance. Except for maybe the hair and eye color of course."

"Father, what are you talking about? Resemblance to who?" Logan asks frowning at his father in some confusion. Denral looked as he always had and he wasn't sure who his father could be thinking of.

'Roushta, you're needed in the greeting chamber.'

'Yes, yes Thurda. I'm on my way. I meant to be there on time, but Shama isn't feeling too well this morning.'

'What's wrong? Is she better now?'

'*A little, but she's still a bit pale. Chevala said that she would stop by later this morning to check on her just to be sure.*'

'*Good, good. Well hurry up and get here. This could be very important to you and your family.*'

'*I'll be there in a few more seconds.*'

"Father?" Logan calls to Thurda when he doesn't answer.

Thurda shakes his head a little and then looks at Logan. "Sorry son. My thoughts were somewhere else. What did you say?"

"I wanted to know..." Just then the doors open and Roushta rushes in apologizing for being late. He looks over to where Thurda is standing and comes to an abrupt stop staring at Denral. Slowly he walks forward, never taking his eyes from the other man. He stops less than three feet away and the two of them stand there staring at each other.

Cassie and her siblings gasp at how much the two look alike. Cassie's head turns from one to the other and back again. She now realizes why she had felt so drawn to Roushta when she had first met him.

Quietly, where it is almost a whisper, Roushta says something in his own language to Denral. Hearing the words, Denral's eyes blink twice and then he begins to smile. Suddenly he bursts out laughing and the two men hug each other tightly. Cassie frowns at Logan and Thurda. Logan shrugs his shoulders in confusion while Thurda stands there with a large grin on his face.

He turns to look over at Royanna. '*Roushta's family has just grown from five to thirteen my love.*'

Royanna looks over at them and sees Roushta and Cassie's father in a brotherly embrace. Thayer and the others follow Royanna's look and notice the two men hugging. As one they move nearer to the other group to find out what has transpired between the two. As they come closer, the two men step back from each other, both still smiling. Everyone moves closer and their movements finally draw the men's attention from one another to those around them. They turn to face the entire group. Royanna notices tears in Roushta's eyes, but knows that they are tears of joy and excitement.

"What have you to tell us Roushta of this unusual happening?" She asks as he wipes away the tears before clearing his throat.

"Your Majesty, I have just found the lost family members of my great-great grandfather's line." He tells them with a slight tremble in his voice. "As you know, my great-great grandfather left his family almost one hundred and thirty years ago. He left his mate, a son, and a daughter to find something he felt was missing in his life. He told his mate that if he should ever take another and have a family, that he would make sure that when the time came, blood would call to blood. The new family would not know until the first one spoke the words of welcome and greeting. Those words have been passed down from generation to generation so that each one would be able to say or hear them when the time was right. Now blood has called to blood and our family is once again whole."

Royanna nods her understanding and smiles at the joy and peace that are radiating from her old friend. "I'm glad that you have finally found what your family has been missing." She turns to Denral and smiles at him. "I am also glad that you were able to find that which could and has made you whole again. You are doubly welcome to Manchon."

From a side entrance Chevala comes in and walks over to Royanna and whispers to her quietly. "Nicca is awake now and is asking for you."

"Thank you dear, I'll be there shortly." She turns to Thayer and Leyla. "Your cousin Niccara's been ill for some time. I've had her in my chambers so that I could keep a closer eye on her myself since she got worse. Chevala's skills are very good, but even I've had a hard time healing her. She seems to have gotten better during the night, but I still don't know what caused her illness in the first place. It was all very strange." She shakes her head. "Well, I need to go and see what she needs. Would you like to come and see her? She's been looking forward to seeing you again, and to meeting your mate."

"If you're sure that she's ready for visitors, I'd like to see her. We won't stay long though. We need to discuss what Cassie and Logan have already told you and the council before your meeting this afternoon."

"That will be fine dear. I just wish we didn't have to have it so soon after your arrival. If your cousin is well enough, we'll be able to move her back to her own chambers later today and have a little more time together."

Thayer nods and then looks at Logan and Cassie. "We'll meet you in your chambers in about an hour."

"All right. We'll see to chambers for Trocon and the others while we're waiting." Logan agrees.

Thayer holds out his arm for Leyla to take. After taking his arm, she takes Salis' hand in hers and they then follow Royanna and Thurda from the chamber.

"Cassie, your family can have my chambers here in the palace." Roushta volunteers still smiling. "It's large enough for all of them to be comfortable."

"Thank you Roushta." Cassie tells him and kisses him on the cheek. "Are you sure you won't be needing them though? With all the meetings scheduled...?"

"No its all right. With Shama not feeling well, I want to be home if she should need me. Chiero has his hands full with Vonia."

"Would you like me to send Tru over to give you a hand until Shama's feeling better?"

"Let me think about it and talk it over with Chiero and Shama and see what they say." Cassie nods and then she and Logan lead the way out of the greeting chamber.

After settling the others from Leyla's group and agreeing to meet with her family as soon as the afternoon meeting is over, Cassie hugs her father and each of her brothers and sisters before leaving them. She and Logan head for their chambers.

As they enter their chambers they hear Kimtala laughing in her room and exchange smiles. Cassie goes to the door of the room and smiles again as she watches Truloka tickling Kimtala as they wrestle on the bed. She waits a few seconds and then knocks on the door. Kimtala looks up first and squeals when she sees Cassie.

"Cassie back, play too!" She cries scrambling off the bed and running over to her.

Picking her up, Cassie kisses her cheeks and then slowly shakes her head. "Not right now sweetie. Logan and I are expecting some very important guests in just a little while. Maybe we can play later, all right?"

Kimtala pouts a little, but then nods her head. "Promise Cassie?"

"Yes honey, I promise." She gives her another kiss and then sets her back on the floor and turns to Truloka. Kimtala runs from the room to look for Logan. "Tru, I'd like you to arrange with the kitchen for refreshments to be sent up. Then you and Kim can go and visit your family. We won't need you again until later this afternoon."

"All right Mistress Cassie. Is there anything special that you would like the kitchen to send?"

"No, just the usual drinks will be fine, and maybe a fruit plate."

"I'll go down and get the tray myself then so that you won't be interrupted."

"Thank you Tru. Why don't you go ahead and leave Kim here with us. We'll spend some time playing with her and take her mind off not being able to spend more time with her."

"You don't have to do that Mistress Cassie."

"I know Tru, but I like spending time with her and so does Logan. It gives us something to look forward to when we have children of our own."

Truloka smiles and nods her understanding. "I'll go now and bring something back in about ten minutes."

Cassie nods and leads the way back into the sitting room where Logan has Kimtala sitting on his knee and is bouncing her up and down. Truloka goes out to get the refreshments and closes the door quietly behind her. For the next few minutes Logan and Cassie play with Kimtala, laughing as she tries to tickle them and wrestle them to the floor.

Just after Truloka returns and sets up the refreshments tray, Thayer and Leyla arrive. Cassie introduces Leyla to Kimtala while Truloka welcomes Thayer home. Shortly after that Truloka and Kim leave for their visit with their family.

Logan pours them all drinks and then sits down after handing them out. "Where's Salis?" He asks taking a sip of his drink.

"She stayed with mother and Thurda. They're showing her around the palace. When we're done here we're going to join them for lunch." Thayer leans back in his seat. "While we're at the meeting she'll stay with your family Cassie."

"That's good, at least she'll be with people she knows." Cassie turns to Leyla. "What about the tests? Were Sarah and Stephen able to locate the gene in anyone else in my family?"

Leyla sits forward. "Yes, they found it in your brothers and sisters, but not in your father. It must have come from your mother's side of the family."

"So all of the kids have this wing gene?" Logan asks reaching over to take Cassie's hand in his.

"Yes, all of them have it." Leyla nods looking closely at Cassie. "I've asked Sarah to do a genealogy check on your mother's family. She'll go back as far as she can to try and find where the gene entered. Something tells me that whatever she finds will be very important to all of us. Not just you and your family, but to our new Alliance as well."

"Does Sarah have any idea of how to prevent the gene from being activated?"

"No. Unless we know how to activate it first, there's no way to know how to prevent it." Thayer tells her. "We know that with you it was the physical change that activated the gene. For the others it could be done by anything or nothing."

"I think that we need to explain to your brothers and sisters what may happen sweetheart. This way if it does happen, it won't come as such a shock to them." Logan says squeezing her hand to get her to look at him.

"You're right I know, but how do we explain it's already happened to me?" She asks looking at each of them.

"Why don't we just take everything one step at a time?" Thayer suggests standing up. "I'm sure that when the time comes, you'll know just what to say." He walks over to the refreshment tray and pours himself another drink then turns back to them. "Now, how far did you get in the discussions about the Alliance? Do you think that the council will be in favor of it or against it?"

"We've discussed everything several times, and by the last meeting I think that everyone was pretty much in favor of making the Alliance. There were a few at first that thought that we should join the Federation, but we were able to convince them that such a move would not be of any benefit to any of the telepathic worlds that would be a part of the Alliance."

"Then we'll do a quick review of what you've already told them and add what we've discussed with the Aquilians and Pantherians since you came here." He paces around the room. "Whatever we do, this Alliance must happen soon. There is something going on with the Federation that could at some point draw us in. Saitun and Aeneka will keep an eye on things through his contacts in the Federation."

"Did you find out if the Federation was still going to fight you over the governorship of Earth?" Cassie asks thinking that if the Federation was going to take over the Earth, she would convince her family to stay on Manchon instead of returning to Earth.

"They've agreed that both Manchon and Calidon have the right to claim Earth as a surrogate world since our people have integrated into the society there. A lot of the people have some type of tie to either planet and may claim our protection. At least those from Calidon can. We need to get the law changed here to fully push the Federation into fully releasing Earth to Manchon and Calidon control."

"Royanna has already said that she was going to change the law." Cassie informs him. "Now all we have to do is set up a better communication system between all the planets that will be a part of the new Alliance."

"Yes, and it will have to be able to keep the Federation from tapping in whenever we need secrecy." Logan points out.

"Selina is already working on just such a system with Stephen." Thayer tells him no longer pacing the room. "Hopefully they will have something figured out before we have to leave in a week's time." He closes his eyes as he receives a message from Royanna telling him that their ready to go to lunch, and to have Logan and Cassie join them. He tells her that they'll be there shortly and opens his eyes to look at the others.

"Mother says that lunch is ready and that they're waiting." He sets down his glass and walks over to Leyla's side, then looks at Cassie and Logan. "She also requests that both of you join us. She's already invited the others. We'll be eating in the private dining hall."

Logan and Cassie agree to join them and lead the way. Cassie offers to show Leyla around when Thayer asks Logan about going to some of their old private places. It is agreed that on those days that the men were gone, the women would spend time together and that Leyla would learn more about Manchon and the people.

CHAPTER SEVENTEEN

"As part of the Alliance, each of the member planets will send groups of their people to each of the other worlds. There will be at first three groups since we will only have the four worlds to start with. Each of these groups will consist of ten families and ten singles. These groups will familiarize themselves with the worlds they are on and with its people. This is so that we will all learn about each other while strengthening our alliance." Thayer speaks while walking around the council chambers. He looks at each of the council members and gauges their reactions to his statements. Several nod in agreement, but a few frown. He waits knowing that some type of objection would be voiced.

"How long will these groups be gone?" One of the female councilors asks.

"They will be gone a minimum of three years. If they wish to, they will be allowed to stay longer. It will be their decision." Leyla answers her.

"And how will these people be chosen?" Someone else asks.

"It will strictly be on a voluntary basis. The people will be told what they need to know to make a decision." Thayer tells them, once again walking around the chamber. "We would like people from all areas to participate in this. Anyone going will receive equal what they have at home, with what they will have there."

"Why the single people? Why not all families?"

"The reason for the singles is to see if its possible for more lifemates to be found." Leyla says looking around the chamber. "In the past few hundred years the number of lifematings on both Calidon and Manchon have dropped to less then fifty a year. That means that the bonds on our own planets are decreasing. We need to find a way to change that decline. Aquila and Panthera are also having the same problems and agree that we need to try to correct this as soon as we can."

"What happens if these people do find mates? Do they stay where they find them, or do they return to their birth homes?"

"That will be up to the couples that become lifemated. No one will be forced to do anything." Thayer stresses strongly looking at each council member. "Everyone must realize that this is important to all of us. If mates are found, it will only strengthen the bonds that we hope to make with this alliance."

"When would the groups be expected to leave?"

"We will announce tomorrow that we need volunteers and what we need them for." Royanna tells the council. "Everything will be explained in detail so that they can make their decision. We will ask to have that decision in three days time. As far as any couples that are joined during their absence or presence, anyone that causes them pain or grief will be heavily fined." She looks at each of the council members that had voiced their objections to outside unions.

"Outside matings can only strengthen our people as it already has with myself and my son. As it will with Logan and Cassandra. I want to hear no more further objections on the subject." Royanna intones unwilling to tolerate any more arguments. "We will be a part of the Telepathic Alliance, and give our full support to all of the people involved." For several moments the council chamber is silent as Royanna and Thayer look at each of the members.

When no more objections are made, Royanna nods to Thayer to continue.

"As of today, the old law that has kept our people from returning home has been lifted. Any Majichonie wishing to return home may now do so, along with their family and anyone else with Manchon blood." Thayer announces. "Those that have never been to Manchon, will be taught about their ancestors and how our world is run for the benefit of all."

"Don't we risk the same dangers as caused the law to be made in the first place?"

"Not really." Cassie speaks up for the first time. "Those with Majichonie blood have some type of psi ability that caused them to be used on Earth. Once they know that they will not be used again, they will return to their peaceful lives." She assures them all. "As Queen Leyla will tell you, most of the psi on Earth lived peacefully and avoided the more aggressive emotions whenever possible. Until the President started using them for his own personal gain, the psi reacted the same as anyone would have in any given situation."

"All of the psi's on Earth have been, and are being helped to deal with what they were forced to do." Leyla informs them. "Just as a child that knows it's done wrong and needs assurance that we will forgive them for what they had no control over, so do these people."

"There's also the possibility that they will not want to come to Manchon. If that should happen, they will still need our support and assurances. No matter what, we must always support our people, even if their blood ties are very weak." Logan puts in.

When there are no more questions or objections, Royanna concludes the meeting. "Since we have covered everything that was of main concern, we'll end this meeting now. I would like all of you present tomorrow when I make the announcement. We need to show the people that we all believe that this is what is needed to keep us from being used and abused by others. If you should still have doubts about this please refrain from voicing them to the people. Take the time to work through your doubts without involving and possibly influencing others."

Everyone nods their agreement and Royanna dismisses them. As they leave, they nod to Leyla, Thayer, and their councilors. Once the last of the Manchon council leaves, Royanna looks at Leyla and Thayer.

"By tomorrow they'll have completely accepted everything and help the people to accept it as well. I think that a couple of them will even volunteer to go to the other worlds."

"That will help to put the people's minds at ease." Thayer agrees with a nod. "The Pantherians and Aquilians are already preparing their people for the moves. We've contacted our people on Calidon and they're preparing things there as well."

"What about the people on Earth? Are they going to be included in this?" Cassie asks looking at her friends.

"Not just yet Cassie." Leyla says sitting back in her chair. "We think that for now, the people on Earth need to get use to the new freedom they've been given. There's also the problem of knowing who would be compatible for a telepathic union. We know that matings with Majichonie and Calidonians is possible, but we don't know enough yet about the Pantherians or Aquilians."

"What about the matings between our people and theirs?" Logan asks.

"As far as physical matings are concerned, we're compatible. Mentally we seem to be equal." Thayer informs them.

There is a knock at the door and Royanna calls for them to enter. Sheyome and Libre step in and close the door before bowing to Royanna, Leyla, and Thayer. "Excuse our interruption Majesties, but Cassie's father wishes to see her most urgently." Sheyome explains looking at Cassie.

"Thank you Shey. If you will excuse me Anna, I'll go and see what's wrong?"

"Yes, go ahead my dear. We'll see you this evening at the celebration."

Cassie nods and curtsies before turning to leave. She doesn't hear Logan excusing himself as well. He walks to her side and takes her hand. They walk together to the Blackwood's chamber and Cassie knocks on the door.

Denral opens the door and ushers them inside. "I'm sorry to have interrupted your meeting honey, but there seems to be something wrong with the children. They're all complaining of pain and itching in their backs and shoulders."

Cassie and Logan exchange glances and then Cassie asks where they're at. Denral leads them down the hall and opens the door to one of the bedrooms. Inside the room Merri, Colt, Dessa, and Davena are laying on their stomachs moaning in pain. Walking over to where they're laying, Cassie gently places her hand in the middle of Colt's shoulders.

'Relax darling, the pain will go away soon.'

'It hurts real bad Cassie.'

'I know little one, and I promise it will stop hurting soon.' She touches each of the girls in the same way and then turns to her father. "I need to have Daniel and Mark in here too. We'll explain everything then."

Denral looks from her to Logan and then nods. "I'll need your help to bring them in Logan."

"Just tell me where they are and I'll port them in here."

"In the bedroom across the hall. Daniel on the bed, Mark on a palette at the foot."

Logan nods and closes his eyes picturing the room. Seconds later they appear next to Davena and Dessa on the floor. Cassie kneels down beside them and gently touches each of them. Denral sits down in the chair Logan places near the children.

"Now, what I have to tell you may sound crazy, but its true. Each of us has a gene that came from our mother. Sarah checked all of you, including father. Since she didn't find the gene in him, that means it came from mother. Sarah's checking to see if she can trace mother's family line to find out where the gene may have entered."

"But what's happening to us now Cassie? Is this gene what's making us hurt so much?" Davena asks looking up at her sister.

"I think so sweetie. The gene we have gives us wings. What you're feeling now is your body's adjustment to the changes that are necessary for the wings to come out." She stands up and turns around so that they can see her back. Facing Logan, she sees him nod. Dropping her shawl, Cassie closes her eyes and in seconds her wings appear and unfold. She opens her eyes and stretches out the wings. Davena and Dessa gasp at the sight of the golden wings, while the others exclaim over them.

"Will our wings be gold like yours?" Merri wants to know.

"I don't know sweetheart. They may or may not be, but whatever color they are doesn't matter. What matters is that you accept them as a natural part of your body. A natural part of who and what you are."

"Will they just appear, or do we have to think of them?" Colt asks looking over his shoulder at his back.

"Well, so far they've only come when I've thought of them. They may come if we're under a lot of stress too, but I don't really know. We'll have to wait and see what happens."

"How do you feel about Cassie's wings Logan?" Daniel asks looking up at him with a grimace.

Logan steps over to Cassie and lightly runs his hand down one of her wings. "I think that they're very beautiful Daniel. Like she says, they're a natural part of her and I wouldn't change anything about her."

Merri and Colt both begin to moan loudly, and rock on their stomachs. Cassie folds in her wings and goes over to kneel beside them. Carefully she removes Colt's shirt and checks his shoulder blades. She then parts Merri's shirt and checks hers as well.

"Your wings are ready to come out for the first time. Think of them budding out like a flower or a leaf." She instructs them and mentally shows them what she means. "Once they're out, think of them growing and spreading. You're going to need to stand up and away from each other so that you have room to spread them."

Luckily the room was big enough for them to do this or else they would have to move out to the palace gardens and Cassie didn't want to chance anyone seeing them yet.

Slowly and carefully she helps each of them to stand and then steps back. Colt goes first and closes his eyes to concentrate as he had seen Cassie do. Within moments small wings appear, then slowly begin to grow and spread out. Once they are fully out, they look at the colors which are a silvery white and a burnished gold. Colt opens his eyes and looks to his left and then to his right, looking at his wings.

"WOW!"

Merri closes her eyes and her wings appear. She has the same coloring as Colt, only in the reverse pattern.

Next Davena and Dessa bring out their wings. Davena's are a reddish brown and a pale gold, and Dessa's are just the opposite, only her gold coloring is a little brighter than Davena's.

Finally Daniel and Mark bring out their wings. Theirs are a soft mahogany and a soft yellow gold. After each of them attempts to flap them for a while, they fold them in and within moments they disappear into their backs once again. Setting their clothes back into place, they all turn to face their father.

Denral looks at each of his children with pride and a deep affection. He notices more of their mother in them now then ever before, especially the girls. He wishes that Debra could be with them to see them now. "Your mother would be very proud of each of you if she was here with us now. I'm sure that where ever she is, she's smiling with pleasure at how well you have all grown."

Cassie and Logan exchange another look and Logan hugs her close. *'At least he still remembers her in a good way. He'll never have to know what happened to her or how she was at the end.'*

'I just wish that I didn't know either. That doesn't make me a bad person or daughter, does it Logan?'

'No atma. It makes you very human. I'm sure that everyone has memories that they would rather forget, but can't because those

memories make them the people that they are today. Your memories will only make you stronger my love.'

"Can we fly with our wings Cassie?" Merri asks looking up at her.

"Yes you can sweetheart, but for now, I don't want any of you flying around where people can see you. Right now only the Queen, Logan's father, and a few others know about our family having the power of physical flight." She explains looking at each of them. "Royanna will make an announcement in a few days to inform the people of our ability. Until then, Logan and I will take you to a private place where you can practice."

"Then after her training you'll send Salis to us for further training here as well?" Royanna asks Leyla and Thayer as they sit with her in her private sitting room.

"Yes, that will be fine. I'm sure that she would enjoy it."

"We'll send her to you within a week of her eighteenth birthday mother. By then she'll be better able to understand all that you have to teach her."

"By then the Alliance will be well in hand and she can help us study how well the immigrants have adjusted to their new home." Thurda puts in. "I think we should all do that in fact, to make sure that everyone is comfortable. It will also help us to know who is easier and better able to handle such moves in the future."

"Have you decided on what to do about Cassie and her family's new abilities?" Leyla asks setting her glass on the table. "I know that she's worried about losing all of the friendships she's made since she and Logan have been here. She doesn't want anyone to treat her differently, she's still the same person as when she first arrived."

"I'll make an announcement in a few days and explain that something here has caused them all to advance in their physical development that wasn't on Earth. I'll also tell them what it is and Cassie can demonstrate."

There's a knock on the door and it opens slowly to reveal Salis. She waits for Royanna's nod before entering the room. Walking over, she stands between her parents and smiles at all of them.

"The gardens here are beautiful grandmother."

"I'm glad you like them love. Did you see any of the animals that live in the gardens?"

"Oh yes! Shey pointed out several birds and small animals. I've never seen birds with green wings before." Salis says in a voice of awe.

"And how do you like Sheyome?" Thayer asks her wrapping an arm around her waist.

"She's really nice Daddy." She leans into his shoulder. "But she's really sad and misses someone a whole lot."

"Yes, we know sweetheart. She's missing her parents. They died in an accident several months ago." He tells her very softly. "Would you mind if she came to live with us on Calidon when we return?"

"Could she really? I know she would like it there, and I could show her around and take her on picnics, and..."

"Hold on a minute honey." Leyla says holding up a hand to stop her. "First we have to find out if she wants to come with us or not. Don't forget that she has a life here and a special relationship with Libre. She may not want to leave her life here or him, and he may not want to leave Manchon."

"Oh." Salis looks down at her father's shoulder. "Can I ask her if she wants to come home with us?"

"I'm sorry sweetheart, but not for this. I have to talk to her about something private first and then I'll ask her about coming with us."

"Don't worry dear," Royanna smiles at her. "I think that Sheyome is ready for a change and will gladly accept your offer to move somewhere new."

"I hope that she comes with us. I really like her and I think that she needs to be with us for at least a little while. Maybe we can help her not to be so sad about losing her mom and dad." she tells them remembering vaguely how she had felt when her birth parents had died. It had helped her a lot when she found her second mother. She didn't think that they would find Shey a second mother, but they could be her family and be there for her when she needed them.

All of the adults look at her with pride that she is showing such great concern for someone that she had only just met. Her heart was open and willing to accept another into her life with no reservations. They were sure that one day she would make a great leader with her love and compassion.

CHAPTER EIGHTEEN

"You need to stiffen your wings more Merri, to get them to support your weight." Cassie advises and tries to show all of them what she means. "After you've done it a few times it will happen without any thought at all."

Spreading out her own wings, Cassie begins to move them, making them more and more ridged with each movement and slowly rising off the ground. Going up several feet, she flies around them a couple of times to show them the movements that are necessary. Landing near Merri, she smiles encouragingly. "Now you give it another try."

Merri tries again, but still cannot get her wings to support her weight. "I can't do it Cassie. It's too hard."

Logan steps up beside Cassie. "Why don't you give them the memory of how to do it? It would make it easier for them to understand and less frustrating."

Merri looks from one to the other. "Please do it Cassie. Otherwise it will take us forever to get it right." She pleads.

Cassie looks at each of them and they all nod their agreement. "All right. You'll have to open all the way up for me to plant the memory deep enough into your subconscious so that it will stay with you." She tells them looking at them. "I'll do Colt and Merri first, then Davena and Dessa, and then Daniel and Mark."

Facing Colt and Merri, she looks deeply into their minds and places the memory deep within their subconscious minds. She carefully does each of the others and then they wait for a few moments for the memory to plant itself deeply enough before trying again. Within ten minutes they're all in the air and the boys are attempting to do acrobatics.

After a couple of hours, they all land and fold in their wings. Logan brings out the picnic hamper that Cassie and Truloka had packed for them. Spreading out the blankets and putting out the food, everyone sits down to eat. They all eat in silence for a few minutes and then Daniel asks, "What purpose do we use our wings for Logan?"

Looking up at him for several moments, Logan finally shrugs his shoulders. "That's really up to you Daniel. You can use them to help in rescues or help someone to move something up high that you can't use kinesis on. If you plan to return to Earth, I think that those would be the best uses."

"Until the people on Earth are reeducated to the true nature of telepaths, its best not to use psi abilities unless absolutely necessary." Cassie puts in. "Right now, non-psi's are very leery of us because of what happened in the past."

"But won't they be just as leery of us because of our wings?" Dessa asks after wiping her mouth.

"I doubt it Dess. It's not as if we have claws and a beak that might hurt someone." Colt points out.

None of them notices Cassie's sudden paler. Logan takes her hand and gently squeezes it reassuringly. *'He's just stating a fact atma. Don't worry, they'll never know.'*

'I hope not Logan. I couldn't stand for them to know that part of our mother's legacy. It would hurt them, possibly cause them to resent this change, to hate her. I don't want that.'

The color returns to Cassie's face and she pours out more juice for everyone. Sitting back she leans against Logan's shoulder and looks closely at each of her siblings. She wonders which ones will stay on Manchon, and which will return to Earth. Though she would like them all to stay, she knows that they must all make their own decisions. Even Colt and Merri must be allowed to decide where they wish to live.

"We had better head back to the palace now. The celebration will be starting in a couple of hours." Logan reminds all of them.

"Do we have to get all dressed up for this thing?" Colt asks with a slight frown.

"I'm afraid so little brother." Cassie smiles at him knowing how he hates to get dressed up in his Sunday bests. "Life here is a lot different from that on Earth. Most celebrations are dress affairs especially at the palace."

They all help to clean up the picnic area and put everything back into the speeder. After everything is put into place, they all take their seats for the ride back to the palace.

／

"Your parents made me your guardian until you have found your lifemate. You have been of age to seek a lifemate for several years now Shey, and you still haven't found one." Thayer points out as they walk through the gardens. "Unless you've decided to take Libre as your lifemate?"

"No, I care for him, but he's not the one." Sheyome tells him quietly.

Thayer leads her over to one of the benches to sit down. "Would you be willing to leave Manchon and come to Calidon with us? You wouldn't be considered one of the volunteers, but part of the royal party, part of our family."

"I don't know Thayer. What would I do? Most of my life here has been served with the royal guard. Would I be able to do that on Calidon?"

"If that's what you want to do, then yes, you could do that. Though if you're willing, we would like you to become Salis' companion." He watches Sheyome's eyes light up. "Salis enjoys your company Shey, and would like you to return with us. You would have more time for yourself to do what you want to do. You wouldn't have to spend all of your time with Salis."

"Do you think that I'll find my lifemate on Calidon?"

"It's always possible Shey. Even if you don't, you may find him on Panthera or Aquila. We'll be traveling to both planets regularly over the next couple of years, until the Alliance is well established." He looks around the garden and then back at her. "You can take a couple of days to think it over. We plan to leave at the end of the week. If you decide to stay, I'll hand over your guardianship to Logan and Cassie, if that's all right with you."

"I don't have to think it over Thayer. I'd love to come with you to your new home. Though I would miss Manchon, I no longer have any family here, now that mother and father are gone. Technically you and your family are my family now." She looks up at him and smiles a little sadly.

Thayer hugs her close and kisses the top of her head. "No matter what, you will always have a family and be a part of our lives Shey."

They sit there silently for a while, and then stand to go back into the palace. As they turn, Thayer notices Logan and the Blackwoods coming through the garden towards them. Waiting for them, he asks Sheyome what she thinks about Cassie and her family's ability to fly.

"It makes them different and special in their own way. Cassie was a little worried at first, but that's only natural since it was a surprise to her as well as to the rest of us. I don't think that anyone will think any less of them because they have wings. In fact I think that some will envy them. Besides, they're only human. With all the different people in the universe that makes them just like everyone else deep down."

Hugging her again, Thayer laughs softly. "Yes Shey, they are only human. I'm glad that you've learned not to judge people by their appearance."

As Logan and the others join them, Thayer asks how the lessons went. Cassie and Logan let the others tell them all about their first time of using their wings. Walking through the palace, Cassie asks Sheyome if she would like to help her pick out dresses for the girls while Logan helps the boys with their clothing.

"Well, as long as Thayer doesn't mind?" She says looking up at him.

"Of course not Shey. In fact, while you're helping with their clothes, you can pick out some new ones for yourself as well."

"Oh, but I don't need any new clothes."

"Don't you? Remember that as of today, your status has changed." He reminds her.

"You mean I'm no longer a part of the royal guard?"

"That's right. Now that you've agreed to come with us, you are fully a royal ward of Calidon and Manchon. As such you will no longer be expected to perform your former duties."

She looks at him in complete shock for several moments and then nods slowly. "I'll have to tell Libre." She says almost to herself, not sure how he was going to handle it.

"If you would rather, I could speak to him for you." Thayer offers sensing a slight unease in her mind.

"No, it would be better if I told him myself. He would be terribly hurt if I didn't." He would probably be hurt any way, but there was nothing she could do to change that. She had made her decision, and Libre would have to accept it. If he truly cared he would understand.

Thayer nods his understanding and is very proud that she is ready to accept her responsibilities, no matter how much pain it may cause her. He also knows that her parents would be proud of her too. She would be the perfect companion for Salis in the coming years.

When she's done taking Cassie and her sisters to the palace dressmakers, and finding each of them something nice to wear to the celebration, Sheyome excuses herself so that she can talk with Libre before things begin. Walking to their chambers, she wonders if maybe she should have let Thayer tell him, then shakes her head. It was her decision to leave and it was her responsibility to tell Libre of that decision. To do anything else would be to lessen what they had shared over the years.

Entering their chamber, she doesn't sense his presence and breaths a little easier that she doesn't have to tell him right this minute. Taking her new dress, she goes into the bathing chamber to cleanup and get dressed. Running her bath water, she hangs the dress up so that the steam would take out the wrinkles caused when it was wrapped. Climbing into the tub, she lays back and lets the hot water relieve the tensions from her body. Ten minutes later she senses Libre entering their chambers and her body begins to tense again. She takes a deep breath and tries to relax again. *'I'm taking a bath Libre. I'll be done in about twenty minutes.'*

'Did you have your talk with Thayer?'

'Yes. I'll tell you about it when I come out.'

'Would you like a drink or something to snack on.'

'No thank you.'

Closing her eyes Sheyome blocks the gentle probe he sends. When he pulls back, she begins washing her hair and body. After rinsing off, she climbs out of the tub and wraps a bath blanket around herself. Drying her hair, she looks at her new dress and debates on whether or not to put it on now or later. Since there wasn't much time left before she was to meet Thayer and Leyla, she decides to put it on now. Libre would know when he saw the dress that something had changed. She shrugs her shoulders both in acknowledgment that there is nothing she can do about the knowledge and to drop the bath blanket.

Noticing that she's forgotten fresh undergarments, she ports what she needs from her dresser. She pulls on her clothes and then puts on some light make-up. Checking her reflection in the mirror she knows that there is nothing more to delay her talk with Libre. Stepping over to the door, she takes several deep breaths before opening it and walking through.

Libre stands as she enters the room and looks at the dress she's wearing. Frowning slightly, he looks down at the drink in his and then takes a large swallow. He sets the glass down before looking at her once again. "Thayer has decided to invoke his authority as your guardian, hasn't he?"

Sheyome walks further into the room and stops behind one of the chairs. "His authority as my guardian has been since my parents death Libre. While he was away, Royanna was my guardian in his stead, and then Logan was by Thayer's order. We all knew that when he became the Starhawk, that he would return. Under the laws of guardianship, when my parents died, if I didn't have a lifemate, he could care for me as he saw fit."

"If you had agreed to become my bondmate, you wouldn't have to be worried about leaving your home and friends."

Sheyome looks down at her hands gripping the back of the chair and forces herself to relax. "That's not exactly true Libre. Thayer has always known that I would only take a lifemate. I want that total bond Libre, just like my parents had." She tells him gently. "Anything else and I would not be true to myself and what I wish for in my life."

"So you're going to go with him to Calidon? What about us? We've been together for a long time. Can you just walk away from what we have and not feel anything?"

"Of course not! Do you think this is easy for me!? You have known yourself that I wanted to be lifemated. I'm not just walking away from what we've had, if I were I would have let Thayer tell you that I was leaving." She turns slightly away from him. "It is because I care that I wanted to tell you myself. I thought that if I told you, it would be less painful for both of us. If you can't be happy for me and wish me luck in finding my lifemate, then it's not me who doesn't care about anyone else's feelings, it's you."

Looking at him, all she can sense from him is anger and pain. Porting in one of her shawls, she puts it on and takes a deep breath. "I have to meet Thayer and Leyla before the celebration. I hope...I hope that you will still come tonight and that you will remain my friend Libre." She waits a few seconds for him to say something, and when he doesn't speak she walks to the door and opens it. "Don't blame Thayer for my leaving Libre. He gave me my choice. It is my decision to go with them to Calidon. If he hadn't asked me, I would have asked him." With that she closes the door behind her.

"Now Salis, you have to treat this celebration as any other royal function. Until all of the formalities are over, you must stay with me and your father. After that you can go off with your friends for awhile."

"Will Shey be there?"

"Yes she will." Thayer tells her pulling her carefully onto his lap so as not to wrinkle her dress. "From now on she will be a part of our family."

There is a knock at the door and Leyla kinetically opens it to admit Sheyome. As she enters the room Leyla notices the redness of her eyes and the slight slump of her shoulders. *'Are you all right Shey?'*

'I will be in a little while Leyla.'

Thayer looks up as she comes in and frowns as he sees her face. "You've told him."

"Yes."

Salis looks at Sheyome and then climbs off of her father's lap and walks over to her and takes her hand. "Please don't be sad Shey. We want you to be happy. If you don't want to come with us, that's okay."

Sheyome smiles at her and then hugs her close. "Don't worry love, this sadness will go away. I'm happy to be going with you. I'm sad right now because I had to hurt Libre so that I could be happy. All he can see right now is that I'm leaving him and he doesn't want me to."

"But he should be happy for you." Salis says pulling back a little to look up at her. "If he really cared about you, he would want your happiness before his own. Wouldn't he mother?" She asks looking over at Leyla for reassurance.

"I'm sure that once he's thought about it, Libre will realize what this means to Shey and will wish her well honey." Leyla assures both Salis and Sheyome. "Right now he's just in shock and a little confused."

"Your mother's right love. After Libre has thought about it for a while, he'll realize that this is what I need to make me happy." Sheyome agrees.

Thayer and Leyla exchange glances and then Thayer stands up and walks over to Sheyome and Salis. "No matter what happens with Libre, we'll make sure that she never regrets coming home with us won't we?" He places a hand on Salis' shoulder and gently squeezes.

"Yes daddy." Salis agrees looking up at him and smiling.

"Good. Now, let's go to the great hall so that we're ready when all the guest arrive." Thayer turns to help Leyla up from her chair. "We'll also let mother know that Sheyome will be going with us when we leave."

Cassie takes the girls back to her chambers to get ready, while Logan stays with her father and brothers. The men will pick them up when its time to go. While Davena and Dessa take their baths, Cassie and Merri lay out all of the dresses and other things that they will need. After setting everything out, Cassie takes Merri into the sitting room. Pouring them each some fruit juice, she sits down beside Merri on the couch and hands her a glass.

"What do you think of Manchon?"

"It's beautiful here Cassie. The people seem really nice too." Merri sips at her juice. "Thayer's mom seems younger than how he described her to us though."

"That's because life here is more peaceful and less stressful on the mind and body. For years, except by special permission, no one was allowed on Manchon that might cause unrest in the people."

"But aren't they taking just such a chance now with the Alliance? I mean none of us really knows anything about the Pantherians or the Aquilians." She points out.

"I can't see where they would cause such problems sweetheart. To all intents and purposes they're the same as us. Their physical appearance is slightly different, but they have the same abilities and beliefs as we do."

Merri thinks this over for a while and then nods. "I guess that would make it difficult for them as well. If you don't mind though, I'll wait and see what happens."

"If that's what it takes for you to feel comfortable, that will be fine honey." Just then Davena and Dessa come out of the bathroom laughing and giggling and flicking each other with their towels. "All right you two, that's enough. Go into the bedroom and start getting ready while Merri and I take our baths. Don't put too much make-up on either. The women here don't wear very much of it."

"Okay Cassie, but it will be hard for Dessa. You know how she has such a heavy hand when it comes to making up her face." Davena says and receives a snap from her sister's towel.

"Not like you when you have a date Davena."

"Girls, that's enough. Do it right or I'll do it for you, and don't take too long. The men will be here in a little over an hour."

The girls nod and go into the bedroom while Cassie and Merri step into the bathroom. While Cassie starts the water, Merri disrobes. Once the double tub is full, Cassie disrobes and follows Merri into the water. Cassie washes Merri's hair for her and then Merri returns the favor. Rinsing the soap from their hair and bodies, they climb from the tub and quickly towel off. Entering the bedroom, Cassie smiles as she notices the elaborate hair styles that the girls have made. She carefully covers up the laugh that slips past with a hand over her mouth and a cough.

"I'd try something...less with your hair girls. Such styles are too much for the people here. A simple style will be fine and it will suit you better. Those styles are a little too old for you."

"Aww Cassie. We spent a long time on these." Dessa complains.

"And it will only take a few moments to take down again. You don't have to impress anyone, just be yourselves. The only thing that needs to be different about you tonight, is your clothes nothing more."

As they're talking, Cassie and Merri are getting dressed. After buttoning Merri's dress, Cassie fixes her hair in a style that suits a young girl of thirteen. Merri smiles at her reflection and then reaches for the make-up.

Cassie fixes her own hair in the light weight style that Truloka had showed her that most of the ladies wore for special occasions. By the time she's finished with her hair and make-up, Davena and Dessa have redone their own hair to something more suitable for sixteen year olds. After double checking that everyone is properly buttoned and snapped, Cassie leads them into the sitting room to wait for the men.

"Now, there's one more thing that I have to tell you. None of you will be left on your own until you are completely familiar with the people and then only within the confines of the palace. Until then you will each have a personal guard who will make sure that you don't have any trouble from any of the males."

"I don't need a guard Cassie." Merri informs her with a frown. "Just after you left, I became a full fledge warrior." She states with great pride in her success.

"That may be Merri, but it is by the Queen's order that you all have guards until she deems it no longer necessary."

"But Cassie..."

"No Merri. You will accept it like everyone else."

Merri throws herself down on the couch and crosses her arms over her chest. Dessa starts to giggle, but one look from Cassie and an elbow from Davena stops her. Before anyone can say anything more there is a knock at the door and Cassie goes to answer it. Pulling it open, Cassie's legs are almost knocked out from under her as Kimtala launches herself at her.

"Whoa Kimtala!" She exclaims hugging the child to her while trying to keep her balance.

"I going to party Cassie. Momma says we have to say 'lo to Anna's son again." Kimtala looks up at her and holds up her arms for Cassie to pick her up.

Obeying the gesture, Cassie picks her up and kisses her cheek. "That's right sweetie. He's been gone for a long time and we're celebrating his coming home." She looks at Truloka and smiles fondly. "You look very lovely this evening Tru."

Truloka blushes and looks down at her dress. "Thank you Mistress. Kim wanted to come and show you her new dress and shoes for the party."

Setting the little girl down again, Cassie looks her over front and back and then lifts up the little hem to look at the shoes. "Oh, they're beautiful Kimmybird. Anna is going to be very pleased that you got all dressed up just to say hello to her son again."

Kimtala smiles up at her and then looks around the room looking for Logan. "Want to show Logan too." She spots the other girls and shyly smiles at them.

"Logan's not here right now sweetie." She tells her and then turns to introduce them to her sisters. "These are my younger sisters Kimmy. This one is Merri and she's thirteen."

Merri's pout disappears as she looks at the little girl. "Hello Kimtala." She holds out her hand and Kimtala takes it in her smaller one and shakes it several times as she had seen the adults do.

Cassie turns her slightly. "This is Davena and Dessa. They're sixteen and are twins." She tells her pointing to each as she says their names.

Kimtala looks at each of them with a small frown forming. "They look the same Cassie."

"That's what twin means sweetie. Actually Davena and Dessa are what is known as mirror image twins. They're identical, they are also opposites. Merri also has a twin, only hers is a boy instead of a girl. They are what we call fraternal twins."

"Hello Kim, its nice to meet you." Davena and Dessa say together and Kim's mouth drops open in surprise.

The door opens and Logan comes in with the others. Kimtala runs to Logan and he picks her up to give her a hug and a kiss on the cheek. "Hello Kimmybird. Did you have a good time at grandma's?"

"Yes. See my new dress Momma gotten me?"

"Oh yes, it's very pretty sweetheart. Are you coming to the celebration in your new dress?"

Kimtala nods and then looks over Logan's shoulder at the others. "Look Mommy, more twins." She points to Mark and Daniel and then looks at Denral and Colt. "You not twins." She says accusingly.

"No, I'm Cassie's father and this is her little brother little lady. And who might you be?" Denral asks.

"Me Kimmybird." She tells him looking into his eyes as Logan and Cassie start to laugh.

"Da, this is Kimtala and her mother Truloka."

"I'm pleased to meet you both." Denral says and takes Truloka's hand and kisses it, which causes her to blush.

"If you ladies are ready, I suggest that we get going." Logan tells them still holding Kimtala. "Tru, you and Kim can come with us."

"Oh, but my Lord..."

"I insist Tru. You're more than a servant to us and we want you there with us." Logan tells her gently.

Truloka bows her head and Cassie puts her arm around her shoulders. "You're family Tru, and family doesn't see station or position."

Guiding her to the door, they prepare to leave. Colt goes to Merri's side while Daniel goes to Davena and Mark goes to Dessa. Denral holds out his arm to Truloka and she blushes again before taking it. Cassie takes Logan's free arm and together they lead the way to the great hall.

CHAPTER NINETEEN

Cassie and the others meet up with Thayer and Leyla just outside the great hall. The women compliment each other on how they look while the men shake their heads at them. Together they all enter the great hall and move to the dais. Royanna and Thurda greet them and then Royanna takes Kimtala from Logan.

"Don't you look pretty Kimtala. Is this a new dress that you're wearing?"

"Uh-huh. Momma just gotten it for me." Kimtala smiles up at her. "And some new shoes too." And she pulls up the hem of her dress to show Royanna the shoes.

"Oh, they're just lovely little one." Royanna kisses her cheek and then hands her over to Thurda before turning to Truloka. "You look lovely too Truloka. I'm glad that you came with Logan and Cassie."

"Thank you Majesty. Its an honor to be included in such a way." Truloka curtsies to her.

"You're more then welcome Tru. Have you introduced Kimtala to Thayer yet?" Royanna asks and Truloka shakes her head. Before she can say anything Royanna continues. "Well then, Thayer, I would like to introduce you to the youngest member of the palace staff. This is Kimtala, who keeps everyone on their toes and was the first to totally accept Cassie to Manchon. Kimtala, this is my son Thayer who is here for a visit."

Thurda steps forward with Kimtala in his arms. Kimtala looks at Thayer for a long time and then looks at Royanna. "He's a Fireman Anna."

For several moments everyone just looks at her and then Royanna answers her. "Yes he is. Do you see his fire?"

"Uh-huh. It's all around him. That lady is a Firelady and she has a little baby in her belly." Leyla looks at Kimtala in surprise and then looks over at Royanna.

"We've noticed lately that she can see just about anything in any body. I've been thinking about having Chevala and Niccara begin to train her as a healer. With such insight, she could help a lot of people."

Salis touches Leyla's hand and Leyla looks down at her. "She's like grandmother Rachael. Grandmother can see what no one else can too."

Kimtala looks at Salis and after a few seconds Salis looks back at her. For several minutes the two girls look at each other and then Kimtala grins and begins to squirm in Thurda's arms until he puts her down. She walks over to Salis and takes her free hand. "You have fire too. Will you be my friend too?"

"Yes, I'll be your friend too." Salis squeezes the little hand in hers gently she wasn't surprised that Kimtala had seen her fire as well. Grandmother Rachael had already told them that she would have the same abilities as her parents.

The doors at the front of the great hall open and the people begin to file in. Royanna and Thurda move to the center of the dais, while Leyla and Thayer stand to Royanna's right with their group, and Logan and Cassie stand on Thurda's left with the Blackwoods and Truloka. Though they must insist that Truloka stay by their side.

Once the room is full, Royanna holds up her hands for silence, and has to wait several minutes for everyone to quiet down. "I would like to thank you all for joining us in welcoming home my son and celebrating his lifemating." She stops as cheering begins around the room. When it is quiet again, she continues. "This is also a welcome to a missing part of one of our great families. Soon others will return and we will celebrate their return as well." Again the crowd cheers and Royanna takes the opportunity to contact Roushta.

'I am here Anna. It's just so packed in here that I can't seem to get more then a few feet at a time.'

'Where are you now?'

'Maybe ten feet from the door.'

'Wait there and I'll get Thayer to port you up to us.' She tells him and turns to Thayer. "Roushta is stuck near the door. Could you port him to us?"

Thayer shakes his head. "Not without knowing his physical mass. What about Logan or Cassie? They're both familiar with his physical mass."

Royanna looks over at Cassie and Logan, but before she can ask, Roushta appears in front of Cassie.

"Thank you my dear. I was beginning to feel quite anxious for a minute. I think that we should open the doors to the smaller halls."

"It might not be a bad idea if we did. I had to nudge a few people a little before I could safely port you." Cassie agrees looking out at the press of people. "The people can barely move right now, and it won't be easy for any of us to move amongst them."

Royanna frowns slightly as she looks around the hall and gauging the movements of the people. Seeing that there is hardly any physical movement, she signals for the guards to open the doors to the smaller halls. While they're getting into position, she holds up her hands for quiet.

"It has been brought to my attention that we are a bit over crowded, and so I am having the doors to the smaller halls opened. It will give us all some extra room to move about. Once we are all more comfortable we will continue."

The guards open the doors and slowly some of the people begin moving into the other halls. Once things settle down again Royanna tells them about Roushta's ancestor and then about the Blackwoods. "As you have already learned with Cassandra Blackwood, these missing family members bring with them a newness that will be refreshing to all of us." She looks around the room. "When and if these people decide to come, we can all accept them with open arms in welcoming them home. Anyone wishing to, after things are settled on Earth, may go and visit and encourage their families to return." She looks at Thayer and nods before stepping back.

Thayer steps forward and looks around the room. "I wish to thank you all for coming here this evening to welcome me and my family and our friends." Cheers go up at this and he waits for quiet to return. "Though we can not stay for long, we will return whenever possible. Right now we are trying to form a special Telepathic Alliance with two other planets which is very important right now. This Alliance will make life a lot easier and safer for all of us and I hope it will help to bring all of our people closer together."

Murmurs can be heard around the halls wondering just how this alliance will be of benefit to the Majichonie. Thayer waits for their attention to refocus on him before continuing.

"You will all learn more about the Alliance tomorrow. For now I hope that you will accept my lifemate and our daughter as you accept me. It is also my hope that you will accept the Blackwoods just as readily. We are all proud of our Manchon blood, and will always honor it's ties."

Again cheers go up and Royanna must wait for the people to quiet down. As she waits, she signals to the guards who are to stay with the young Blackwood females. When they are close enough, she warns them once again to make sure that none of the girls is ever out of their sight.

"Now we will all move among you and you can give your own personal welcomes and be introduced to all here. The servants will bring refreshments around to all who wish them and food will be served out in the gardens in an hour." With that she nods and leads the way down from the dais.

As they move through the crowd, Thayer says hello to those he remembers and introduces Leyla and Salis. Though many wonder about Salis, none ask.

Logan and Cassie introduce her brothers and sisters while Roushta takes Denral around. After a while Daniel and Mark go off on their own followed a short time later by Davena and Dessa. Merri and Colt stay with them for a few more minutes and then they too go off on their own. Though Colt is with Merri, Logan nods for the two guards assigned to Merri to stay with them. Cassie watches the guards move closer to keep her youngest sister in sight.

"I hope that she doesn't become too irritated with them. She's upset because Royanna insists on their presence. She and Colt were made warriors just after we left. I think she may be a little insulted that we should think that she needs a guard."

"None of them will need them for more than a day or two atma. It's only to show the people that they are to be respected and protected as anyone else on Manchon."

"I just hope that it doesn't alienate her from all that she could have here. She's already having problems with Salis because of her jealousy of her relationship with Colt."

"Don't worry atma, I'm sure that she will work things out for herself. She's coming to terms with the fact that neither she nor Colt really need each other any longer. Even though they still have their special bond, it's changing to accommodate them as individuals."

Cassie nods slightly in agreement and looks around. "Oh, look Logan. Chiero and Shama came too. She looks a little pale but she seems to be feeling better." She points to the couple standing a short distance away. Together they go over to say hello and to make sure that Shama is all right.

"Yes, I'm fine. Grandfather just over reacted a little. I'm sure it's only a stomach bug and will go away in time." She shrugs her shoulders. "Chevala gave me some herbs to help with the nausea. Though it doesn't bother me too much unless I get up too fast or eat some foods."

"She also told us that she didn't think that it was infectious. She put up a special viro shield that should keep it contained if it is." Chiero assures them.

Just then Truloka and Kimtala join them and Cassie picks the little girl up and gives her a hug. "Are you having fun sweetheart?"

"Yes. My new friend going to play with me tomorrow." She informs her.

"You really like Salis don't you?"

"Uh-huh. She's pretty inside and she has some fire too."

"What do you mean Kimmybird?" Logan asks her touching her hair lightly.

"Like her mommy and daddy, she has fire too. It's real pretty, like a fire petal."

"What is she talking about Logan?" Chiero asks bewildered.

"She can see Thayer and Leyla's other selves. It sounds like Salis may be the same."

Kimtala looks at Chiero and Shama. While looking at Shama she begins to smile, and points to her belly. "Shama has baby inside Cassie."

Looking totally shocked, Shama places her hand over her lower stomach. Chiero frowns slightly and before he can question the child's statement, Cassie quickly looks into Shama's womb to confirm it.

"She's right Shama. You are definitely pregnant, and I would say that you're about six weeks along, maybe eight." Logan and Cassie exchange glances while the others are looking at Shama.

'She must have just conceived shortly before she was transformed back to her human form.'

'*Do you think that it will be a normal pregnancy Logan? I mean, since she was changed wouldn't the child be changed too?*'

'*It should be a human child atma. There's no way to know for sure for at least a few months.*'

'*Maybe, maybe not. I think that in a couple of days I'll take a closer look. We need to know before Leyla and Thayer leave in case we need them to change the child.*'

"Do you think that we should tell grandfather Logan? It might let him rest easier knowing that it's not an illness after all, but a natural body function." Shama asks after recovering from her shock.

"I think that would be a good idea."

"Oh Cassie, I wanted to welcome you to the family. Grandfather told us earlier that your father is a direct descendant of his own great-great grandfather."

"Thank you Shama. We are glad to have more family, especially Da. Since his twin Lenral died several years ago, he's been looking for a lost part of himself. He's found it now and there's so much more joy and purpose in his life now." Cassie tells her grinning and looking towards her father and Roushta.

"Will he and the others be staying on Manchon, or will they return to Earth?"

"I'm not sure Chiero. We haven't really talked about any of their plans yet. I do hope that at least some of them decide to stay here though."

"The servers are coming in now Mistress." Truloka points out quietly. "If you don't mind, I think that I will see if they need any help."

"Oh Tru, don't work tonight. We've given you the night off to enjoy yourself, not carry around trays laden with food." Cassie pleads, but seeing that Tru would like to help, and knowing her nature to do so, she finally gives in. "All right, but only if they really need the help, and only for a little while. We'll keep Kim with us until you're done."

"Thank you, I'll be back as soon as I can." She promises and then takes Kimtala's hand. "You be a good girl for Mistress Cassie while I'm away Kimtala. You stay with her and Lord Logan, no running off."

"I promise mommy." Kimtala assures her mother and kisses her on the cheek, then wraps her arms around Cassie's neck.

"Don't worry Tru, she'll be fine." Logan assures her. Truloka nods and moves off making her way to one of the servers. After talking to the girl for a few moments asking if they could use some extra help, she heads for the outer doors.

After agreeing to meet with Cassie in a couple of days, Chiero and Shama move off to talk to others. Cassie and Logan go through the crowds and work their way back to Leyla and Thayer's side. While Logan and Thayer talk about their first trip together, Cassie mentions Shama's pregnancy to Leyla. She keeps a close eye on Kimtala while she sits nearby petting one of Royanna's dogs.

"I'm going to do a deeper probe in a couple of days to see if the baby is human or dragman. If it should be dragman, do you think that you can change it to human form while it's still in the womb?" She asks quietly.

"It's hard to say Cassie. I don't believe that it will be necessary though. There is every indication that all of the dragman genes were totally removed from all of them when the hairs were taken out. I'm sure that the child will be human. From what I could tell from my short contact with the eggs, they didn't start their change until sometime after being placed into the clutches. While in the womb they were still human. There shouldn't be any problems with the pregnancy or delivery." Leyla tries to assure her. "How did you figure out that she was pregnant?"

"Kimtala noticed it when she looked at Shama. I just confirmed it."

"Did Kimtala say anything that would indicate that it wasn't a normal baby?" She asks with a frown, but Cassie shakes her head. "Then it probably is, otherwise she would have said something about it being different."

"I still want to be sure Leyla. I want to save them from any shock when the baby's born."

"All right Cassie. If you notice that it will be a dragman, I'll see if there's anything that can be done. Just don't worry to much about it or you'll give yourself an ulcer."

"I'll try Leyla. Oh, I almost forgot to tell you, Kimtala says that Salis has fire inside her too."

Leyla nods slowly. "I thought as much from the surges she's been having lately. We'll have to keep a close eye on her to see how it will manifest itself. Grandmother Rachael had mentioned that Salis had fire but she wasn't sure what form her fire would take. She thought that she might be a pyrokinetic."

By the end of the evening, most of the Blackwoods have made new friendships with the people they have met. Though she has tried, Merri has had a hard time accepting her status on Manchon. She feels as though her hard won title of warrior has been taken from her just as Colt was being taken from her.

Though no one has said anything yet, she is sure that most of her family plans to stay on Manchon instead of returning to Earth. She knows that Daniel will return to be with Dawn Flower, but none of the others really have any strong ties left on Earth. Even though the rest of the family will remain here, Merri knows that she could never live here for very long and act like a lady. She wants to live the life they had found at the stronghold.

All of these thoughts are going through her mind as she walks back to the chambers she shares with her family, with the guards close behind her. When she reaches the door she turns to the guards and tells them that they can go.

"We must make sure that one of your men are present before we can leave you Mistress."

"That's ridiculous. I will be perfectly safe by myself in our chambers. I'm sure that there is somewhere or something else you both would rather be doing."

The guards look at one another and then back at Merri. "We're sorry Mistress, but we must follow the Queen's order. Unless one of your men is present, we are not to leave you alone."

"What if I were to give you no choice in the matter?" So saying, she ports herself to Leyla's ship and sits down in the lounge. Five minutes later Stephen Seven walks in and sits down beside her. They sit there quietly for several minutes before either one speaks, and then it is Merri to say something first.

"I want to go home Stephen. They treat me like a regular female here and put guards around me." She complains to the android. "I'm a warrior now and can take care of myself."

"What makes you think that they don't believe that you can take care of yourself? Are you the only female with guards?" Stephen asks her with a slight frown.

"Well no. Davena and Dessa have guards too, but they don't have the same training that I do. I'm sure that Thayer told his mother that I could protect myself if I had to. He was there when I was made a warrior."

"I don't think that the guards were placed with you so much to protect you, as they were to show that you and your sisters are to be respected. That your family's position here is very high. Placing guards is to show the people that even though you and the others were not born here, you are still protected by the laws of position. The guards are meant to show that position, nothing more."

Merri looks down at her hands. She could understand that a little, but it still didn't make her feel better. "Okay, I'll go along with all of that, but why wouldn't the guards leave me alone at the rooms that we're staying in? There was no one around to care what my position on Manchon is."

Stephen's processor works out the best way to explain this without offending her. "Though you're a warrior on Earth, here they see you as a young girl that is very beautiful. It's possible that they want to protect you so that you won't have to protect yourself. They also may not know how good your skills are. Don't forget, they have never seen the type of training you went through."

Merri thinks about this for awhile and Stephen just sits quietly beside her. Thinking it over, she realizes that he's right. Just being told that she is a warrior is no proof that she can defend herself. On Earth most of the people are norms with little or no psi abilities. Here on Manchon everyone is a psi and their strengths could be less than hers, the same as, or even stronger. No doubt the guards know everyone's strengths and weaknesses.

"I still want to go home. I feel restricted here, and I miss my friends at the stronghold."

"There's no reason why you can't make new friends here as well Merri. I'm sure that there are young people here that would like to have you as a friend. You could probably teach them things you've learned, and they could teach you a few things as well." Stephen tells her getting up and getting her a drink. "I know that Salis would like to be your friend, but you don't seem to acknowledge any of her attempts to do so. I know that it hurts her."

Merri looks down at the drink he handed her and remembers all of the times that the other girl had tried to talk with her, or to include her in something that she was doing with Colt or Davena and Dessa. She hadn't been very nice to Salis, and still she had tried to be her friend.

"I guess I haven't been very nice to her. I don't mean to be mean to her Stephen. It's just that I get this funny feeling when I see her with Colt and I get angry because...I don't know why I get angry. It feels like she's taking him away from me, and there's nothing that I can do to stop it."

Stephen sits back down beside her and puts his arm around her shoulders and she leans against him. "She's not taking him away from you Merri. It's just that you and Colt are growing apart. You're both becoming your own people now and that's what frightens you. Instead of accepting that, your mind has changed from the fear to anger and placed that anger towards the one that is most acceptable to the cause of your separation."

"I want to be her friend Stephen, but those feelings keep getting in the way."

"Then you need to let go of those feelings Merri. You have to accept that you're growing apart is a natural part of growing older and that no one is responsible for it happening."

Merri looks up at him with a tear running down her cheek. "But why Stephen? Why do we have to grow apart?"

He gently wipes away her tears. "Because neither of you would ever be able to reach your full potential or follow your true destiny. Would you deny all that the Great One has planned for you just to keep Colt with you? Would you deny him his destiny, his chance to find what Logan and Cassie have? What Leyla and Thayer have? Would you deny yourself that chance?"

Shaking her head she wipes at her cheeks. "No. I'll try harder Stephen, but I still want to go home. I think I understand how Colt is starting to feel about Salis. How when he's not with her he misses her and wishes to be at her side. I've been feeling the same way without Little Bear near. Has Colt felt what I did towards Salis towards Little Bear do you think?"

"I don't know for sure Merri, but I'm sure that he probably has. Maybe not as strongly as you, but no doubt he's felt some of the jealousy. My programming and memories tell me that at times like this, the emotions tend to run stronger in females rather than males."

"That was a sexist statement Stephen. Some males are more emotional than any three females put together."

"All right, I'll fix that statement. Now, don't you think that you should be getting back to your chambers? Your family know where you are, but I think that you owe them and the guards an explanation for your disappearance. You'll also have to explain to Royanna that it was not the guards fault so that they will not be punished for what you did." He tells her gently.

"Yeah. I really need to apologize to them. I don't think I would like myself too much if they were to suffer because of my temper." Standing up she turns to face him as he too stands, and gives him a hug. "Thanks for talking and listening to me Stephen."

"Any time Merri. Even when I'm not around, you have plenty of family around that will gladly listen if you let them. You also have all your friends back on Earth that will listen if you need someone to talk to. I'm sure that if you really need to you can talk to Saitun and Aeneka. They are always there if you need them."

"Thank you Stephen. Goodnight." She reaches up and kisses his cheek. Stepping back, she ports to the sitting room of her family's chambers. When she appears she notices that her whole family is there including Logan and Cassie. "Hi." She says softly looking quickly at each of them before looking down at her feet after gauging their moods.

Denral stands up and places his hands on his hips. "You have some serious explaining to do young lady."

"I know Da." She looks up at him then back down at her feet. "I'm sorry that I left the way I did. All I can say in my own defense is that I was feeling trapped and that I had to get away. When the guards said that they were going to stay with me if none of the men were here, I just had to get away from them."

"Do you realize that because of your actions, your desire to get away, that those two guards now face punishment for allowing you out of their sight without having your family present?" Logan asks her very sharply. "They will spend the next two weeks with no contact whatsoever with their own families."

Merri looks at him and then at Cassie. She sees the disappointment in Cassie's eyes and looks down again. "I didn't mean for that to happen Logan. Tomorrow I'll go to Royanna and explain to her what happened, that it wasn't their fault. Before I ported, I blocked out all thought so that they couldn't follow me."

"No matter how trapped you were feeling Merrilynda Blackwood, you knew that they would be punished if they did not fulfill their duty as they were ordered." Cassie reminds her with great disappointment in her voice at her sister's actions. "Even knowing that, you still left them to suffer for your actions. You held no regard or respect for them as warriors."

"Back off Cassie, she's said that she was sorry." Colt demands with a growl having stood up and moved to his twin's side to give her his support. "She's said that she'll explain to Royanna tomorrow. We all knew that she wasn't all that thrilled about coming here in the first place. She's gotten use to being outside and fending for herself. We bring her here and tell her that she has to have guards following her around like she didn't know anything. I don't blame her for wanting to get away, I would too under the circumstances. Now, whether you mind or not, we're going to bed." So saying, Colt takes Merri's hand and leads her into the bedroom they're sharing and closes the door with a slam behind them.

Merri collapses into Colt's arms and cries softly. Colt wraps his arms around her and lets her cry it out, feeling her pain at Cassie's disappointment in her. "Don't worry Merri, I understand. Cassie will to after she thinks about it and you explain everything." He assures her running his hand over her hair.

"She was right though Colt. Even knowing that they could be punished, I left them. All I could think about was myself and getting away."

"Don't be so hard on yourself sis. I'm sure that once they know the whole thing they'll understand why you did what you did. We should never have made you come when you didn't want to."

"It's not that I didn't want to come Colt, I did. I just have a lot of feelings that have been giving me a lot of trouble lately and I haven't been able to deal with them very well." She tells him stepping back and wiping away her tears.

"My friendship with Salis is giving you trouble isn't it?" He asks and she nods looking at the door to the sitting room. "I thought that it was. Merri, no matter how my feelings for Salis may go, you will always be a part of me, and I a part of you. I feel us growing a part too and it's as scary for me as it is for you, but I know that you will always be there for me. Just as I will always be there for you." He assures her.

Merri looks at him and smiles slightly. "That's just about what Stephen told me tonight. He says that we're becoming our own people."

"He's right. Just remember that we'll always be a part of one another no matter what other relationships we may have in our lives. Nothing and no one can take that from us."

"Thanks for understanding Colt."

"Hey, what's a twin for? If I couldn't understand you who could?" He asks with a grin and then ducks when she throws a pillow at him. They horse around for a few minutes, and then he straightens up. "Come on, let's go to bed. We're going to have to get up early so that you can go and talk to Royanna."

Nodding, Merri goes into the bathroom to change into her night clothes. She hopes that Royanna will understand as well as Colt had. She had a lot to make up to the guards, she just hopes that they will be able to forgive her.

CHAPTER TWENTY

Early the next morning, before Royanna makes the public announcement about the Alliance, Merri requests to speak with her privately. Waiting in the small sitting room off the council chambers, she wishes that she had let Colt come with her instead of doing this alone. She could really use his moral support right now. Sitting in one of the chairs, she chews on one of her fingernails and fidgets around nervously. When the door opens she jumps to her feet and turns to face it.

Salis slips quietly into the room, closing the door softly behind her. Looking at the other girl, she bites her lower lip as she moves closer. "I know that you probably don't want me here Merrilynda, but it seems that since most of what's been happening lately is my fault, I thought that I should be here to take most of the blame for what happened last night." She says in a rush coming to a stop a couple of feet in front of Merri.

For several moments Merri just stands there in shock staring at her, then recovers. "What are you talking about Salis? You haven't done anything."

"Yes I have. I've come between you and Colt, though I never meant to. Somehow I've managed to make you uncomfortable and angry." Two tears slide down Salis' cheeks. "I didn't mean to do anything bad, I swear. I only wanted to be your friend."

Frowning, Merri realizes that her treatment of the other girl has deeply hurt and confused her to the point that she has started blaming herself for all of Merri's actions, even ones that had nothing to do with her. Before she can say anything though, Salis continues.

"I'm sure that if I explain to grandmother, she will understand that none of this is your fault. That I..."

"Wait a minute! None of this has been your fault. Not on Earth, and certainly not here."

"But if I hadn't come..."

"It would have happened whether you had come or not. If it wasn't you, it would have been somebody else. Salis, Colt and I are growing apart, becoming our own separate people. I've been acting the way I have because my feelings and emotions are confused. I also didn't want to accept that I was no longer the center of Colt's life anymore." Slowly she takes the few steps that put her right in front of Salis. She looks at her for several seconds and then reaches out to take one of her hands. "I want to be your friend Salis. You've done nothing to deserve the treatment I've been giving you since you came into our lives. I hope that you can forgive me and that you will accept my unconditional friendship from this day on."

Salis looks down at their joined hands and then back up at Merri and smiles. "I don't know this un-con-di-tion-al, but I would like to be your friend. I do understand what you have been going through. I've been having problems with my emotions too. Though different from what you're going through, they still confuse me. Stephen says that it is a natural part of growing up."

"Yeah that's what he pretty much told me last night. It would suit me just fine if we just skipped the growing up part and went right to being adults. It would be less painful for all those concerned and less confusing."

"I agree." Both girls laugh and giggle but stop abruptly when the door opens and Royanna walks in. "Grandmother." "Your Majesty." The girls speak together and curtsy.

"Stand girls." Royanna looks at both girls and then walks over to her chair. "I didn't know that you would be here Salis. I thought that this was to be a private audience for Miss Blackwood."

Both girls notice the formal name that Royanna has used and look at each other. Salis is the first to speak. "Yes it was to be so grandmother, but Merri is my friend and I wished to be present to give her my support. I know that it is not easy to confess to a wrong done to others when other things have been weighing upon your mind."

"I see." Royanna says knowing from Leyla and Thayer that until today, the girls had not considered each other as friends. She indicates that Salis should sit beside her and that Merri should remain standing in front of them. She notices Salis squeezing Merri's hand before taking her seat. "If you are going to stay, you must remain quiet. Is this understood?"

"Yes grandmother."

"Very good. Now, what did you wish to speak with me about Miss Blackwood?"

Merri casts a quick look at Salis who nods slightly and takes a deep breath. "The guards that you assigned to watch me are innocent of any wrong doing Majesty. I gave them no chance to stop or follow me. When they refused to leave me alone at our chambers, I blocked their gentle links and ported myself to Leyla and Thayer's ship."

"Though you should not have been able to do this, I wish to know why you did so." Royanna asks with a raised brow.

"I was feeling trapped and..." She stops and looks at Salis and then down at her feet. She wasn't sure how to say it without insulting the Queen.

"And..." Royanna prompts with a slight frown.

"And insulted Majesty." Merri tells her and then rushes on when Royanna's frown deepens. "I felt insulted because it was as if my attaining warrior status had been stripped from me without thought. Though I know now that the guards were not meant as an insult but as an honor. I couldn't see that at the time. The guards were meant to show the status of respect and protection you wished to convey upon myself and my family. Knowing this, I now ask that you not punish my guards. Any punishment should be mine and mine alone. My emotions lately haven't been very stable and I let them control my actions to the point where others have been hurt. I don't want that to happen any more." This last she says looking at Salis.

Royanna frowns a little and she too looks at her granddaughter. Noticing Salis' smile and the understanding in her eyes, Royanna decides that something more is happening then what she has heard. "Very well, I will discuss with your father and Cassandra what punishment should be given you for your offense. What ever it will be, it will be done in such a way as to atone to both guards for what they suffered in thinking that they had failed in their duty." Merri looks at Royanna and nods. "It will last no longer than two weeks. Whether or not it last the full time will be up to the guards that you have wronged."

Merri nods again, knowing that if they were back at the stronghold, Nightstorm would issue the same punishment. In fact, she is getting off lightly with only two weeks. Nightstorm would have given her a month and would not have bothered to discuss it with her father or anyone else.

"Now I suggest that we go and meet the others so that I can make the announcement about the Alliance." Royanna stands followed by Salis. "I will have my discussion with your father and sister this afternoon after the noon meal."

"Yes your Majesty." Merri looks down at her feet. "Do you wish me to be present during your discussion with them?"

"No, I think that part of your punishment will be in wondering what is to happen. I will call you when it has been decided." Opening the door, Royanna leads the way and the girls follow close behind. Salis once again takes Merri's hand and gives it a squeeze.

'You did very good Merri. I don't know how you managed to stay so calm. I would have been shaking the whole time, especially with some of the frowns grandmother was giving you.'

'I was shaking the whole time. I just didn't let it show.'

'Are you all right now?'

'Yeah. I'm getting off easier then if I was back home. If I was there Nightstorm would have me doing hard service for a month and wouldn't bother talking it over with Da or anyone else before carrying out my punishment. He would argue with any one that tried to interfere.'

'But how could he? Wouldn't your father and Cassie object to such an action? After all they are your family.'

'Under normal circumstances they probably would, but during my training to become a warrior, Nightstorm became my adoptive father. Even now he has all the rights of a real parent.'

'Like mother and father?'

'Yes. At the stronghold punishments are hard because everyone is responsible for the well being of everyone else. To disrupt that well being is to hurt the community and cause disharmony. Until that harmony is restored, the offender can do nothing that does not help or bring peace to another. Not even sleep.'

They meet the others and after thanking Salis, Merri goes to stand with her family. After assuring Colt that everything was all right, she looks at her father. Seeing his frown, she looks down at her feet. She knows that whatever Royanna decided, her father and Cassie would agree to. She'll be lucky if Cassie or Logan don't contact Nightstorm and tell him what she's done. If they do, when she gets home she'll be lucky if she only gets one month of service.

Since there isn't enough room on the balcony for all of them, the Blackwoods stand in the double doors to watch and listen. Cassie and Logan take their places beside Leyla and Thayer.

After checking to make sure that all of her councilors are present, Royanna looks out at the people gathered in the courtyard. As far as she can tell, except for the very old and the very young, everyone from the town and the surrounding area is present. Those in the out laying areas would be told the announcement by special messengers soon after Royanna speaks.

Stepping up to the microphone that Leyla's android has setup for this, Royanna clears her throat and the sound gets everyone's attention. Thayer mentally instructs his mother to speak in her normal voice.

'The speakers will make it possible for all of them to hear you with no problem mother. Stephen has placed the speakers at intervals around the courtyard to be sure that all can hear you.'

"As many of you already know, my son and his mate have contacted two other telepathic worlds. They have decided to combine these worlds as well as our own in a special alliance to protect telepaths and others with psychic abilities from being exploited by the Federation or anyone else. The council and I have decided that Manchon will join this new Alliance and help out in any way that we can, others like ourselves that are being used. We will give other telepaths sanctuary from all who would enslave and abuse them. We all need to get to know each other better to be able to help each other. It has been decided that each world will send ten families and ten singles to the other three worlds. These people will live on those worlds for at least three years learning about the people and customs. After that time the decision to stay or return home will be decided."

She stops for a moment to let her words sink in and to take a sip from a glass of water that Thurda hands her. Her throat felt as though it hasn't had very much use, but she knows that she has made several speeches over the years. After taking another sip of the water, she hands the glass back to Thurda and continues.

"Now, instead of ordering some of you to take part in this, you will be allowed to volunteer of your own free will. The worlds you have to decide on are Aquila, Calidon, and Panthera. You will

251

have the same positions and status on these worlds so you won't lose by going. For those of you wondering, yes you can look for your lifemates on these worlds. These matings will be accepted and we will all rejoice in your finding your true mates. As you know, my son and his family will be leaving in five days time. When he goes he will be meeting the rulers of Aquila and Panthera. I would like him to be able to tell them that the Majichonie are ready to fully participate in this Alliance and that when the time for the transfer comes our people will be ready. Therefore I ask that you go home and talk it over with your family and friends. Please let us know as soon as possible who will be going." She looks over at her councilors and three step forward. Two have mates and the other is single. They look to Royanna for permission to speak to the people and tell them of their decision to participate in the move. The last one to speak is the single council woman.

"We need this Alliance to strengthen us and bring us all closer together. Calidon is our sister planet, but who is to say that Aquila and Panthera are not a part of us as well? I plan to go to Panthera to try and find my mate. In my heart of hearts I know that is where I will find him. All of you who are still looking for your one true mate need to get in touch with your inner selves and ask yourselves how important it is to find that mate and be with them no matter what. Don't let fear of the unknown keep you from finding total happiness."

"Thank you Lady Glorita." Royanna nods to her and then looks out at the people. "You have heard from those of the council who have decided to take part in the move, and their reasons for doing so. Now it is up to you to decide if you're willing to follow their example. Go and think it over. When you have decided you can let us know." She steps back and Leyla steps forward.

"By this time tomorrow there will be several tents set up with computer monitors that will display all the information we have on Aquila and Panthera. You will be able to study this information so that it can help you to make a more informed decision. If you have any questions, just ask the computer and she will answer you as best she can with the information she has."

Royanna nods to the people and then leads the way back inside, thanking her councilors for their support. After agreeing to meet the following evening before last meal of the day, they all go off on their own. As they walk back to Royanna's small personal reception room, Royanna asks Trocon what he thinks the people of Manchon will decide.

"I think that at first none were too keen on participating, but Lady Glorita has most definitely swayed the singles into trying it. The hardest ones to decide will be the families, especially those with older children."

Royanna frowns slightly. "Why do you say that Trocon? Do you think that they won't want their children involved?"

He shakes his head in the negative. "The older children, the ones thirteen and older may not want to go with their families. Then there are those who may want to go and their parents do not. Who will decide what is right for them? They are at the point where their emotions are confused and they are entering adulthood." He points out with a frown of his own. "They have already been given the right to be responsible for the decision on deciding what is right for them as well as others. Should that right now be taken away at this point and they be forced into doing what full adults decide is right? Or should they be allowed to decide on their own what will make them happy? They are their own individuals in their own right. Can we tell them now that it is no longer so?"

Trocon finishes as they enter the reception room. Everyone waits for the royal family to sit before taking the remaining seats. Merri, Colt, and Salis stand off to one side and listen quietly to what is being said.

"He has a point mother. All of the children have been raised to decide their own fates when they reach the age of thirteen. The right to decide what they wish to do with their lives. To take that right away now could very well damage many family relationships, not to mention relations with other adult figures in their lives."

"But what types of arrangements would have to be made for those who stayed or those who decide to go alone?" Selina asks looking at the others. "Though they have the right to decide, they still need to be cared for on a basic level. Especially those that still need some type of guidance."

"Yes, though they make their own decisions, they are still basically children. This type of move cannot be taken lightly." Leyla agrees with what Selina has not voiced out loud. "I think that for this, it should be left for the parents to decide..."

"NO!" Merri cries out taking a step forward even though Colt places a hand on her arm to stop her.

'Merri, no. This doesn't concern us.'

'Doesn't it Colt? Do you want Da making your decisions for you until he thinks you're old enough to make them?' She tells him still looking at the adults. "Thayer's right. If you take this decision away from them, I can guarantee that there will be damage done to relationships with the young adults. They will feel betrayed and insulted by your actions whether they understand them or not."

Everyone turns to face Merri, and Denral frowns deeply at her, still upset over what she had done the night before. "This discussion does not concern you Merrilynda. You have made enough trouble..."

"It does concern me father. Just as it concerns Colt, Salis, Davena and Dessa, and all the others our age. That's exactly what I mean. You think that just because we don't have a high age number that we don't know what concerns us and what doesn't. That just because we've made past mistakes that we haven't learned from them." She looks from her father to Royanna and steps closer to the older woman. "Your Majesty, this is what I was talking to you about earlier. Though you didn't mean it as an insult, your assigning me guards was both an insult and a humiliation to me, a kind of betrayal. That's how these young people will see your taking away their right to decide their own fates."

Closing the distance between them, Merri kneels down in front of her and places her hand lightly on one of hers. "This morning when I came to speak to you, it was my decision to do so not my father's. It was also my decision to take whatever punishment you decided on. Were either of my decisions wrong? Did they show that I have no sense, no honor, no respect for others and the decisions they make? I admit that what I did before these decisions was wrong, but I made those decisions based on the way I was taught and raised. Your young people will make their decisions on what they have been taught and how they were raised. Unless you have some doubt about how that was done and you don't believe that they have learned those things?" She shrugs her shoulders to indicate that she had no way of knowing the answer.

Royanna looks at her and then over at the other four young adults standing quietly in the room. They had not said a word the whole time that Merri was speaking or before. "Do you all agree with what she has said?"

They all nod and then Salis steps forward. "May I speak grandmother?" Royanna nods and Salis takes a deep breath. "Why couldn't we start a fostering program for those young adults who stay and those that go? That way they would have the guidance they need, and they would still be able to make their own decisions. It would ease the minds of their parents as well."

Royanna and Leyla exchange looks and then Royanna looks down at Merri who is still kneeling before her. "Do you think that they will accept the fostering if we allow them to make this decision for themselves?"

"Yes your Majesty, I do."

"Thayer, do you think that we can work this into the exchange agreement and that the others will accept it?"

"I don't see why not mother. No doubt they will have the same situation and will welcome any solution we can come up with." Thayer looks at his daughter and then at Merri and the other three. "I think that since it was their idea, that these young adults should be the ones to handle the details."

Royanna begins to nod and indicates that Merri should stand and beckons the others to come forward. Standing, Merri steps back and Colt and Salis stand on either side of her. "You two as well." Royanna says to Davena and Dessa. They look at each other and then move forward to join the others.

"You five are now responsible for finding out who, between the ages of thirteen and nineteen, wish to go or stay. You are also responsible for finding families or couples to do the fostering for all eligible young people. After lunch today, we will expect to know how you plan to approach both the young people and the foster families. It will also be your responsibility to explain to the foster families that they may be asked to foster off world young as well. Do you all accept the responsibility that is being given to you?"

Salis, Merri, and Colt all nod at once, while Davena and Dessa look at each other once again before nodding their agreement.

"Good, then I suggest that you all go to Salis' private rooms and begin discussing how you plan to go about your duties." Royanna dismisses them and Salis leads the way to her own chambers.

As they go, Merri looks at her father and sister. Though Cassie nods, Denral doesn't acknowledge her. Merri sighs and follows the others from the room, sure that it would be a while before her father listened to her. She would be glad when it would be time to return home. She didn't think that she could stand to live with him knowing that he was so disappointed in her and felt that she had embarrassed him beyond what he could tolerate.

CHAPTER TWENTY-ONE

Waiting for the maid to leave, Salis gathers up some paper and a pen and carries them over to Merri. "Will you write down the ideas we come up with?"

"Sure, but Davena or Dessa can write neater than I do."

After setting out a tray of drinks and cookies, the maid curtsies to Salis and then leaves the room.

"All right, so how do we explain to the young people that they will be allowed to decide whether they go or stay?" Colt asks handing each of the girls a glass of juice. "How do we convince the adults to foster those who stay and those that come?"

"We'll have to talk with the parents too." Davena points out. "If they object, what good will it do for the young people to make their decision? The parents are the final authority when it comes right down to it."

"Then we have to convince the parents how important it would be for their young people to make this decision and how much the experience could mean to their self-esteem." Merri tells them after taking a swallow of her juice. "They should be the first ones that we talk to about fostering. Both for those going and those staying."

"First we have to meet with all the young people and find out how they feel about the move." Dessa tells them taking a cookie from the tray. "For all we know none of this may even be necessary."

"I don't believe that Dessa. If anything the young people will see it as an adventure, whether they go or stay." Salis tells her. "But I agree that we should meet with them first and find out how they feel about it." They all agree that this is necessary and Merri writes it down on the note pad along with the decision to talk with the parents.

"Okay, we have to let them know that the Queen is agreeable that they can make this decision for themselves, but they also have to know that their parents have to agree before that decision is put into action. They need to consider their parents' feelings as well as their own." Dessa says and Merri writes it all down.

"I think that we should have some rules of conduct to go by too." Colt looks at them, especially Merri. "Rules that will give them an idea of how they should act and conduct themselves and the consequences of not following those rules."

Merri looks at him for several seconds and then nods and writes it down. "Ten rules to go by should be enough. Any more and they would feel pressured by authority."

"We'll also have to make sure that the rules will be understood by the other young people as well, especially those from Aquila and Panthera." Salis points out. "We should make the consequences of breaking the rules strong enough to stop bad behavior before it starts."

"Yeah, and there should be a limit to how many times someone breaks the rules." Colt suggests, standing and walking around the room. "I think that anyone breaking three of the rules in less than a year, should be sent to their parents."

"But that would be going against the purpose of letting them make this decision. If they make the decision, they should be dealt with by the laws of whatever world they're on. Our punishments should be for minor things. Anything major should be dealt with by the proper authority of that world." Dessa points out to him. "What better way for them to learn about another culture than to be placed within the restrictions of their laws?"

"I agree with Dessa. They're making the decision and they should know that they are under the jurisdiction of whatever laws govern the world they're on." Davena looks at each of them. "They have to understand that they will be treated just as an adult and as anyone else that goes. They can't think that just because they weren't born there, that they can take advantage, that they're above the laws of the land. Earth's history has many areas where people from other countries did bad things in the country they were visiting, and then claimed diplomatic immunity so that they wouldn't have to suffer the consequences of their actions. We need to make sure that it doesn't happen now with anyone, adult or child. We all have to accept responsibility for our actions. If anyone does do something like that, it should be put before a set council of all the worlds to deal with fairly and justly. If the Alliance is going to work, such a system will have to be set up."

The other three Blackwoods look at her in shocked surprise. It was the first time any of them had ever heard Davena say so much. Dessa continues to stare at her twin in amazement. She had taken her thoughts and put them into the words that she herself couldn't think of.

"Maybe we should suggest that? I don't think there's been any mention of such a council." Salis tells them oblivious to the others silence and shock.

"Yes, and have a junior council as well, made up of young people from each world." Merri agrees taking it one step further. "Then we can have one of the adults sit in to make sure that everything is done right and fairly." Everyone nods their agreement and she writes it all down adding many of Davena's words so that the adults would better understand their reasoning.

After she finishes writing, Merri reads back to them all that they have come up with and asks if there's anything they've forgotten. They all agree that they've covered everything except what the rules should be.

⁓

"I met with Merri before the announcement, and she has taken all responsibility for what happened last night." Royanna explains to Cassie and Denral. "She has also asked that she be given the punishment instead of her guards. I've agreed that this will be done and that it will last no longer than the two weeks that would have been the length of the guards punishment. Will you agree to this?" She looks first at Denral and then at Cassie.

Denral frowns slightly, but nods his agreement, while Cassie takes longer. She realizes that Merri is getting off very lightly for something that caused great disharmony in the two guards. "I agree with your decision Anna, but I must admit that I feel it is too light for the offense."

"How do you mean Cassie?" Royanna asks with a slight frown.

"Well, back on Earth, such an offense at the stronghold would have been given a harsher punishment to make sure that the same offense didn't happen again."

"I see. That would explain her look of surprise." Royanna says almost to herself. "But there is no way to change the decision now. Besides, the law states that the true offender must serve his time in the service to the wronged person for no longer then their penalty time and no harder then their punishment would have been."

"Yes, well...If you don't mind, I will be contacting her adoptive father and letting him know what has happened. He will include a punishment of his own when she returns home."

"Do you really think that's necessary Cassandra?" Her father asks frowning at his oldest child. "After all, the guards..."

"Yes it is necessary Da. As Nightstorm's adopted daughter, she was representing him if not in name, then by the training he has given her. She has dishonored him no less than she has dishonored you or me by her actions."

"All right, you've made your point." He tells her, not wanting to get into a discussion over Nightstorm. He still wasn't sure why he had agreed to allow the adoption of his two youngest children to stand when he reached the stronghold and had recovered his health. There was no changing it now, it had all been made legal.

Seeing that Denral had no objections, Royanna nods her agreement. "Very well Cassie. You may contact Nightstorm and inform him of what has happened. But you must also tell him what punishment has already been given and the final results of that punishment."

"I will Anna." Cassie agrees. She didn't plan on making it any worse for Merri, she just felt that if her sister wanted to be treated like the warrior she had become, like a true member of the stronghold family, then she must abide by all the rules and laws even when she was away.

"The guards will decide on what she should do for them to atone for her actions. It may be helping their families or taking their place during a guard shift." She explains what would happen to them. "Whatever she does for the next two weeks will be something in their service or for me personally."

"What if the guards should not want her to be punished?" Cassie asks knowing that this too was a possibility.

"Then her service will be completely to me. If that happens, she will move into the small maid's chambers within my own chambers until her time of service is over with."

—

"All right Merri, that should be ten. Though their natural rules, it should help everyone to focus. Read them off and lets see how they sound." Colt says finishing off his third juice.

Merri flips through the last of her papers and begins reading. "Rule one: Behave with honor and respect at all times. Rule two: Report to the proper authorities all wrong doings that harm, hurt, or endanger another. Rule three: Always report anything unusual to the proper authorities. Rule four: Never probe without consent unless it is a life threatening emergency. Rule five: Protect all children and elderly at all times. Rule six: Help anyone in need unless it should place you into danger; call for help in either case. Rule seven: Accept an adult's authority in all things unless you know that it will cause harm. Rule eight: Never take or steal from another. Rule nine: Complete all tasks you are asked to immediately and to the best of your ability. Rule ten: Always admit to any wrong that you have done, don't let another take the blame."

"I think that covers everything. It reminds everyone of the important things." Dessa says when Merri is done. "It should also help them to remember others that are just as natural."

"Did you read them in order of importance Merri?" Davena asks looking over at her.

"Yeah. We'll have to write them in order though." She tells them looking down at her notes. "We'll have to write out how we plan to organize everything else as well. Put them in the order that we plan to do them."

"That's a good idea sis." Colt agrees then looks at his watch. "It's almost time for lunch, and we need to have it ready by the time lunch is over."

"I think that we should have lunch here and finish up." Salis suggests looking at the others. "Grandmother will want everything done in an orderly fashion. We want to prove that we are serious about this project if she is to allow it to become a part of what they are doing."

"Couldn't we have Sarah or Ali print it all up for us?" Dessa asks. "It won't take either of them that long to put it into order for us."

"No Dessa, we couldn't." Merri glares at her sister. "We agreed that this would be our responsibility. We have to see it through all stages for Royanna to accept it."

Dessa pouts while the others agree with Merri. It would be like doing only half a job and leaving it to someone else to finish. She didn't really like that idea. When the others look at her she finally agrees. "All right! First we have to get permission to eat here instead of joining the others."

"I'll contact grandmother and explain it to her." Salis offers and closes her eyes. Several seconds later she opens her eyes and looks at the others. "She's already arranged for our lunch to be brought here. Cassie's servant will be bringing it in about fifteen minutes."

Merri gathers up her notes and carries them over to the desk. Davena follows her and lightly touches her shoulder. "I'll write it all up Merri. You take a rest."

"Thanks Vena. My hand was getting a little sore."

Davena smiles and gently squeezes her shoulder before turning her back to the others. "Go and sit down and I'll get started."

Going over to the couch, Merri sits down and picks up her glass. Dessa goes over to the desk and sits down to help Davena. They divide the notes and start writing. While they're doing that, Merri explains to Colt about her meeting with Royanna.

"And I'm sure that Cassie is going to let Nightstorm know about what I've done."

"Probably." Colt agrees feeling sorry for his sister. She thought that Cassie's disappointment was bad, Nightstorm's would be worse. Though he had adopted both of them, Colt knew that the ties between his sister and their adoptive father were stronger then his. Even though she has feelings for their friend Little Bear, Colt knows that her feelings for Nightstorm are a lot stronger. He's sure that her feelings are nearly the same as his for Salis. Though he's not sure how he feels about that, he is sure that in the years to come Merri and Nightstorm would become mates. He didn't think that they would become lifemates like Cassie and Logan, or

Leyla and Thayer, but possibly life-bond mates. In less than five years the adoption could be set aside and they would be free to become mates. He hopes that things will work out for them.

"Are you going to accept whatever punishment he comes up with?" He asks her standing behind Salis' chair.

"Not that I have much choice in the matter, but yes, I'll accept whatever he decides." Merri looks down at her hands. "In fact I'm thinking of contacting him myself." She looks up at him. "I think that it would be better if I did. Don't you?"

"It might be. It would show him that you respect his position in your life and his authority over you." Colt agrees. "It may even lessen your punishment."

"Yeah, but either way I won't be able to sit down comfortably for a while." She smiles slightly and then looks at Salis who had gasped and turned pale at her last comment.

"You mean he would beat you over this?" Her face going even paler.

"No Salis, he wouldn't beat me. He would just warm my bottom a little." Merri assures her sensing that the thought of a beating disturbed her greatly. "If he doesn't, it will mean that whatever punishment he gives me will be a lot worse."

"I don't understand." Salis looks from her to Colt in confusion.

Colt walks around her chair to sit next to Merri. "What she means is that, if Nightstorm doesn't spank her, the punishment will be very hard and last a very long time. If he does, it will be a little easier and last about three months tops."

Salis still doesn't understand, but is glad that she is not in Merri's place. Just then there is a knock at the door and Colt gets up to answer it.

Truloka comes in with a large floating tray and two smaller ones. Salis nods to the table that has just appeared in one empty corner of her room, and Truloka takes the food over and begins setting it out so that they can serve themselves. "Will there be anything else Princess?"

"No thank you Truloka. I believe that we have everything that we will need. You can go if you wish."

"Thank you Princess." Truloka curtsies and leaves the room after returning Colt's smile.

"Dessa, Davena, take a break and come and eat while its still hot." Colt calls to them.

"We're almost done. You three go ahead and start, we'll be over in a few minutes." Davena tells them never once looking up from what she's writing.

Colt sees Merri and Salis seated at the table and then takes the chair between them. After dishing up their plates, they eat quietly for several minutes. "I'm glad that you and Salis have become friends at last Merri."

"Me too Colt." She smiles at him and then at Salis. "I've already apologized to Salis for the way I treated her. I need to apologize to you too. I didn't mean to be so mean to you either."

"That's all right sis, I understand. It's over now and that's all that matters. I just wish you could have been friends longer though. They'll be leaving in five days."

"It doesn't matter Colt. Now that we are friends, we'll stay friends no matter what. Right Salis?"

"Yes, friends forever." Salis agrees smiling at Merri and then including Davena and Dessa too when they finally come to the table.

"We're done." Dessa says sitting down and filling her plate with fish and vegetables. "Now all that's left to decide is who's going to do the presentation to Royanna and the others."

"Since I was the one that got us into this, I'll present it." Merri tells them.

"No, we all accepted responsibility for this project." Davena reminds her. "We should divide it between the five of us and each take a turn explaining a part of our plan."

"Yes, that sounds fair." Salis agrees and then frowns. "But how do we divide it up?"

"Merri can explain about the young people. Salis, you can explain about the law councils. Davena can explain the rules and Dessa the consequences. I'll explain about the parents and the fostering." Colt looks at each of them. "That will show that we have all agreed to do our part in developing the Alliance." They all agree and then hurry to finish their lunch so that each of them can go over the notes that involve them, before they have to meet with the adults. They wanted to be sure that they had everything perfect.

<center>~~~~~</center>

"They're eating their lunch in Salis' chamber so that they can finish up what they're doing." Royanna explains to the others about the young people's absence from the dining hall. "According to Salis, they want to get their ideas into order and on paper to show what they have in mind."

"Do you really think that they will have a workable plan mother?" Thayer asks sipping at his drink.

"Yes I do dear. They all have sharp minds and given the chance will make great leaders some day. Especially the three youngest. Merri is outspoken and bold, but accepts responsibility for her actions. Salis is quiet and peaceful and very observant, her loyalties once given, remain strong and true. Colt is also quiet, with an inner strength that you would not expect in one so young. He too has strong loyalty and a need to protect that will get him far. They will all be a blessing to us in the coming years."

"But should they have so much responsibility so soon Anna?" Logan asks her with a frown of concern. "When it comes right down to it, they are still children with a lot to learn about life and being responsible on such a large scale."

"How else will they learn Logan?" Royanna raises a brow at him. "Sooner or later they must learn. Why not see if they have learned anything already?" She suggests looking at each of them.

"We all had to learn some type of responsibility that only an adult would have at their age."

"She's right Logan. If they're ever to be all that they are meant to be, we have to give them this chance." Cassie touches his hand. "You were given a great responsibility at eighteen and even before that when you trained to become Thayer's personal guard." Logan looks from Cassie to Thayer and then at his father.

"They're both right Logan. Though I was not sure if you were ready, or of your commitment, you convinced me that I should at least give you the chance to prove yourself. We can do no less with these young people then we did with you." Thurda tells him and Logan nods his understanding and agreement.

"So, if everyone is in agreement now, we will finish lunch and meet with our young people and hear what they have come up with." Royanna watches as they all nod and then finish their meal. When they are done she contacts Salis and tells her that they are to meet in fifteen minutes.

Salis tells the others and they gather up their notes.

"Do we all know what we're going to say?" Colt asks and the girls all nod. "All right, we go in the order I mentioned earlier. Merri, Salis, Davena, Dessa, and then I'll finish up." Opening the door he lets the girls go out first and then follows closing the door behind him. At first none of them speak, but then Dessa asks who was going to explain what they were going to be doing with each of them speaking.

"I will since I'm speaking first." Merri tells her.

They reach Royanna's private meeting chamber and Colt knocks on the door, waiting for permission to enter. When it comes he opens the door and Salis enters first followed by Merri, Davena and Dessa, and then Colt, closing the door behind him. The girls all curtsy and Colt bows at the same time. Something that they had not practiced, but happens automatically.

Merri steps forward and tells the adults what they plan to do to explain what they have come up with. When Royanna nods, she tells them her part of the plan, about meeting with the young people and explaining to them about being given the opportunity to decide what they wanted to do.

Next Salis steps up and explains about the need for law councils for both the adults and the young people. Davena then steps forward and tells them about the ten rules that every young person will be expected to live by whether at home or on another world. Dessa tells them about the consequences that would be a result of breaking those rules.

Finally Colt steps forward and tells them the plans for getting the parents involved both in letting their young people decide and in the fostering program. Then how they plan to get others to help foster those who stay and those who come from the other worlds.

Royanna looks at each of them when they are all done and nods her approval. "You have all done very well. I'm very proud of each and every one of you. What you have come up with appears well thought out and well organized. Tomorrow you will begin putting your plans into action." She tells them and smiles at their looks of shock. "It is your responsibility to get the ball rolling so that Leyla and Thayer can present this to the Aquilian and Pantherians during their meeting. Thank you. You may go now." She dismisses them knowing that they would now have to plan their presentations to the young people and their parents. Watching them as they leave she notices them already talking and planning what they would do next.

After they leave the Queen's chambers the children agree to meet in a couple of hours to finish up what they had started. They all need some time to themselves to think about what they have gotten themselves into and how this decision will effect their futures.

CHAPTER TWENTY-TWO

The next day, Royanna tells the people of the Blackwood siblings having wings. Cassie and the others bring out their wings and show them, and then with a nod from Royanna, they fly around for the people to see that they are functional. At first the people are very quiet, but then suddenly cheers and shouts can be heard from all gathered.

When they land, they go down in the open area that the guards have made in the middle of the crowd. Slowly, one by one, the people step forward and reach out to gently touch the wings and ask questions about them. After a while the people step back and they fly back up to stand with Royanna and fold in their wings.

Royanna then asks that all of the young people between the ages of thirteen and nineteen, go to the small meeting hall to meet with her granddaughter and the younger Blackwoods. "Everything will be explained to you once you're there. Please listen carefully to all that they have to tell you. It is very important to all of you." She looks out at the crowd. "After the noon meal I would like the parents to meet with them as well."

Logan steps forward. "This evening Cassandra Blackwood and I will be lifemated. We would greatly appreciate your prayers in it being completely successful." He can see the nods and smiles of many of the people. "Thank you all." He steps back and Royanna nods that the gathering is over.

The parents talk to their children and then send them into the palace for their meeting. While they are entering the palace Royanna leads Cassie and the others inside. The adults all excuse themselves and Royanna continues on with Salis and the others.

"I will stay only long enough for the young people to understand that they will have my support." She assures them when she notices their nervous glances at her. "After that it will be up to you to explain all of the other things to them. I will come back when you talk to the parents and confirm that their children have royal support in making the decision to stay or go."

They reach the Queen's entrance to the small meeting hall and Colt opens the door. Royanna leads them in followed by Salis and then the others. She indicates that they should sit at the table provided. Salis takes the center chair with Colt and Merri on her right and Davena and Dessa on her left. Standing to Salis' right, Royanna nods for the doors to be opened. As the young people come in, they each stand near one of the seats that has been provided for them. For this meeting, one thousand young people are present. They will be asked to inform their peers of what they hear.

"What you hear here today has to do with volunteering for the Alliance exchange. All young people in your age groups will be allowed to decide whether they wish to stay or go. You will have the support of the royal house in whichever choice you make." Royanna announces in a clear voice. "Now I will leave you with the Princess Salis and the Blackwoods, who will explain every detail to you." Nodding she touches Salis' shoulder and then leaves the room.

After her grandmother leaves, Salis smiles and nods and tells the young people that they may sit. They look at each other and then take their seats. Once their all seated, Merri nods for the servants to begin handing out the papers that Sarah and Ali had printed up for them while Salis explains what is happening.

"The servants are handing out to you all a set of papers that covers everything that we will be discussing with you."

Merri stands up and picks up her copy of the papers. Looking around the hall she notices that most of the papers are handed out and clears her throat. "The papers you have include the Queen's agreement, a paper that your parents must sign agreeing to allow you to make this decision along with their personal mental seal. Without these your decision will not hold. The next page has a list of ten rules that all young people must follow and the consequences of breaking those rules. If you go or stay, you will be expected to sign this paper and abide by the rules if your parents are or are not on the same world that you are. The next page is about a law council that will be setup for adults and one that will be setup for young people. The last page is for your parents. It is an agreement to act as foster parents for those of you staying, and those who come. Whether they go or stay, we would like for them to be foster parents."

By now they all have the papers and are looking through them. Giving them time to read over the pages, Merri sits back down. *'Salis, how many young people did Sarah say there are between thirteen and nineteen?'*

'She figures that there are about thirty-five hundred.'

'I think that we need to set up a different exchange program so that everyone has a fair chance of going.'

'But how do we make it fair sis?' Colt asks looking around. *'With that many, at least a third will be of age by the time its their turn.'*

'I know, but we need to find a way for them to all experience it.'

Looking out at the group, Merri decides that they should wait and see how many want to go before coming up with a plan that will be fair to everyone. Standing up, she explains that each of them will discuss different parts of the agreement with them.

⁓

While the young people are meeting, the adults are finding out about Aquila, Calidon, and Panthera. Some of the parents already know what the young people are hearing and some already know what their young ones plan to do. Though they themselves do not wish to go, they can't see the harm in letting the young people take part in the Alliance.

The parents that know about the fostering program think strongly of signing up for it even if their young ones don't go. They want to do their part to help with the Alliance in any way that they can, even though they can't see themselves leaving their homes.

Sarah answers all the questions that she can and tells them that Logan's computer will try to answer the unanswered questions as soon as she has the information. In the meantime she tells them about the weather conditions and foods. She also explains to them the customs and laws that they have on file and how the worlds are run.

⁓

In the council chambers, Royanna announces that she and Thurda will be life-bonded at some time after Cassie and Logan's lifemating. "There is no need to put it off any longer. Since Thayer is now King of Calidon, Thurda and I will try for another heir. It is still safe for me to conceive and deliver a child. It will also be a joy and a pleasure to give Thurda another child, and to have a second child of my own." She looks around the room. "If it is not the Great One's will that we have a child, then Chevala and Logan will become the heirs through Thurda. Is there anyone here that would object to that likelihood?"

No objections are made so the council goes on to discuss what is happening with the young people and the plans that they have come up with. They too ask how it will be fair to all, when some will soon reach full adulthood.

"In all probability, only about sixty percent will want to go on their own." Cassie announces looking around the room. "About ten percent will go with whatever their families decide, and twenty-two percent will want to stay."

"What about the other eight percent? What will they do?" One of the councilmen asks.

"It's hard to say." Logan answers looking at the man. "Right now the percentages Cassie has mentioned are probabilities and nothing more. The last eight percent will raise any of the other percentages to a little higher point that's all. Right now it's only speculation on our part."

"Whatever the young people's decision, we must try to find a way to follow through for them. Their decisions are just as important as any adults."

"We all agree about that your Majesty." Lady Glorita assures her. "How many will be allowed to go at one time though and for how long?"

"I think that if Aquila and Panthera will agree, we should send forty to each world." Cassie suggests. "Their time there can be for eighteen months instead of three years. We can send a new group a month before the others return so that those already there can help the new ones to adjust to the change. They will probably be the first to really pick up on the customs of their host worlds."

"Will they still have the option of staying?"

"Only the older ones will have that choice. The ones that will be twenty within three months of their time to leave." Royanna informs them. "If when their time is over they will be twenty in three months or less, they will be given the choice of staying. The others can re-volunteer later when they come of age. When they return after their year, they will act as junior ambassadors to whoever comes from the world they visited."

They all nod at this plan. It will keep the young people involved and interested, and it may help them to decide what they want to do. It will also let them know that they are useful.

"Then we are all agreed that we will send forty young people and that they will stay for eighteen months. When they return they will become junior ambassadors and help our visitors to learn and adjust." They all nod once again as Royanna looks around the room. "Is there anything else that we need to discuss or explain to anyone?"

"Yes there is one more thing your Majesty." A junior councilman stands. "How often will we be sending people and for how long?" He asks then sits back down.

"We will send people every three years for the next twelve." Thayer tells him standing up and then explaining further as he walks around the room. "To fully understand the others, and for them to understand us, we need as many observers and opinions as possible to reach that understanding. Every adult will be expected to fill out a report each month as will the young people. By the time we start the move, each world will have several computer buildings setup for the filing of those reports. Special scramblers will be used to make sure that no one else picks up on those reports, especially the Federation." He returns to his seat.

"Until we are secure in our Alliance, the Federation can not know too much. The Alliance Council will decide what is safe for the Federation to know and when." Leyla informs them all quietly.

"Queen Leyla, what will happen about those traveling to Calidon?" The same young councilman asks. "From what I understand, Calidon is quite a distance from all of the other planets in the Alliance, especially Manchon."

"That's true, and right now my computer is working on a viable solution to that problem." She informs him. "She is trying to come up with a transportation ship that will make the travel time less then it is at present. Hopefully we will be able to make the trip from Manchon to Calidon in roughly two weeks or less when we finally find the solution."

"Until that time, one of our large cruisers will be sent back to Manchon after we return home. It will take the people from here and pick up the others on Aquila and Panthera and bring them to Calidon." Thayer explains. "It should only take a month's travel. As Leyla has said hopefully Sarah will come up with something even faster."

After going over everything two times and assured that everyone understands, Salis closes the meeting. "Go over everything with your parents over lunch so that they will fully understand as well. Then afterwards, meet with your friends and discuss it with them. As you leave the servants will give each of you three more packets of the agreement. Give these to those who were not here to look over. When we meet with your parents we will ask them to talk to the other parents."

Merri stands up. "Also if you know of any adults that may like to be foster parents, please talk to them. The more foster parents we have, the better it will be for this program. Without enough, the Queen may not allow our plans to go through." She looks around the room. "If this is to work, we all have to work together. All of us are new to Manchon, and don't know too many people very well. Though this program touches our lives, it will greatly involve yours. You now have to decide how involved you're willing to be."

The room is completely quiet, and then Salis dismisses them in groups of one hundred. As they pass the servants, they are handed the extra packets. Within half an hour the hall is clear and the doors are closed behind the last group. The servants bow to Salis and then leave the room as well.

"I think that we did pretty good." Dessa says standing and stretching. "There didn't seem to be too many that didn't want to go it on their own."

"Yeah, and most of them liked the idea of becoming junior ambassadors after they return home." Davena stands and twists herself at the waist. She straightens up and looks at the others. "What about the ones that go to different worlds then their parents? When their time is up, they have to join their parents."

They all frown at this, and then Colt smiles. "They can still be junior ambassadors. They don't have to return to their home worlds to share what they have learned. It would help to strengthen the Alliance as well. Not only would each world learn from their own people but from others as well."

"That's true Colt. We should bring it up to grandmother though, she may not have realized that part." Salis warns him.

"I don't think that's possible, but we can still mention it at lunch." He assures her. Royanna didn't seem the type to not have thought of all the possibilities. "They might have thought of something else that could be added. After all, they did come up with the suggestion of making the young peoples time for a year and a half, not just a year."

The private doors open and Royanna comes in followed by Thayer, Leyla, Cassie, and Logan. "How did it go children?"

"It went very well grandmother. They've accepted everything." Salis tells her with a large smile. "And they'll help to spread the word to the others and to find adults to act as foster parents."

Merri steps forward and looks at Royanna. "We explained that since none of us really knows the people, that they may know of some adults who would volunteer to be foster parents. It was also explained to them that if the program was to succeed, that they would have to help it to work."

"They've agreed to everything in the agreements that Sarah and Ali printed up for us." Salis adds again. "They'll give all the other young people the extra agreement packets and explain it to them. They'll discuss everything with their parents over lunch, which will make it a little easier for us when we meet with them after lunch."

"Very good my dears. We are all very proud of each and every one of you." Royanna smiles at all of them. "Now, let us go and get something to eat before your afternoon meeting."

Several hours later the two groups meet again to discuss the outcome of the meeting with the parents. Of the one thousand-three hundred and sixty parents, four hundred and forty-eight have agreed to let their young people go, and to act as foster parents to others. They had all agreed to speak to others about fostering.

After going over everything, they all go to get ready for the evenings activities. Thayer tries to convince his mother and Thurda that they should go ahead and become life-bond mated when Logan and Cassie are lifemated.

"It would be a double blessing to all of us mother."

"But this is to be Logan and Cassie's special night Thayer."

"And what better way to make it even more special then sharing it with both of you?" He points out convincingly. "Logan wouldn't mind mother, and neither would Cassie. In fact they would be honored if you did share this night with them."

"But the people are not expecting us to be mated tonight Thayer." Thurda puts in. "Your mother is right. This should be Logan and Cassie's night alone."

"But they want to share it with you Thurda. Logan wants to say his vows at the same time as you do. He wants the two of you to share that special bond of giving to a mate that not many others share."

For several moments Thurda has a thoughtful frown, but then it disappears as he remembers one of his great uncles telling of the feeling of love and joy he experienced when he shared his mate night with his father. He looks back at Thayer and then at

Royanna whom he shared that memory. Royanna nods slightly and smiles back at him.

"If Logan really wants to share this night with us, then we agree to share it with them."

"What about Cassie? Does she realize that we too will be sharing as the men will?" Royanna asks wanting to be sure that Cassie understands what will happen during the ceremony.

"Yes mother, she understands, and wishes to share with you as well. She has come to see you as a mother figure and would feel blessed to share this special day with you."

Royanna smiles and nods her pleasure. Later, at the evening meal, Thurda and Royanna tell Logan and Cassie that they would be blessed to share this night with them. Before they finish the meal, Royanna sends out a telepathic message to the people that she and Thurda will become life-bonded this night in a special sharing ceremony with Cassie and Logan.

After dinner they all go out to the garden where the tent for the matings have been setup. The walls of the tent are transparent and as the two couples walk in, a brilliant white light illuminates the inside and their clothes change. Royanna and Thurda are now wearing white flowing robes, and Cassie and Logan are wearing gold flowing ones. The priest turns to face them and in each hand he holds a blue crystal goblet. Thurda and Logan stand to one side of the priest while the women stand on the other.

"You come to me, a servant of the Great One, to be joined in all things. Lord Thurda, you have been lifemated, do you now wish separation from that mate?"

"No, I do not wish that Presbyteros. The Queen and I would share even that link of all others. We wish to become life-bonded."

"And do you agree to this Royanna Riccan-Starhawk, knowing that you can never share his spirit?"

"Yes Presbyteros, I agree to this. Though my bond mate and I could share no more than our bodies, in our hearts, minds, and spirits, we were lifemated. Thurda and I will share even this."

The priest looks deeply into their hearts and sees the truth in them. He nods and turns to Logan. "Lord Logan, you have chosen this woman to become your lifemate. How do you know that she is the one to share everything that you are?"

"I know that she is my chosen because all that I am burns for her. When I touch her the burning eases for a while but it still burns strongly. She is the other half of myself and my spirit Presbyteros."

"And you Lady Cassandra, do you too feel this burning for Lord Logan?"

"Yes Presbyteros. I too feel the burning. It is eased only when we are together. He is the mate of my mind, my heart, my body, and my soul. There is no other but him."

He looks deeply into their hearts as well and not only sees the truth but feels it as well. He pulls back quickly and nods. "Yes, you are truly meant to be lifemates. There will be no problems for either of you." He smiles slightly, but then sobers.

"Lord Thurda, Lord Logan, you will now speak your vows and drink from the goblets of Light and Truth."

Thurda and Logan face the women and then begin to speak in unison. "I stand here in the Light of the Great One and His servant, to pledge my all to my chosen," Thurda says life-bond mate, while Logan says lifemate, "for all time. We will share all that is meant to be shared by mates. All that I am, all that I have, I freely give into your keeping. We will be as one."

They each take a goblet and drink half of its contents. The priest takes back the goblets, holding Thurda's in his left and Logan's in his right and turns to the women. "Queen Royanna, Lady Cassandra, speak your vows and drink from the goblets of Light and Truth."

As the men had done, Royanna and Cassie speak their vows in unison. "I stand here in the Light of the Great One and His servant, to pledge my all to my chosen," Royanna says life-bond mate, while Cassie says lifemate, "for all time. We will share all that is meant to be shared by mates. All that I am, all that I have, I give freely into your keeping. We will be as one."

They reach out to take the goblets but stop before touching them. Cassie looks up into the priest's eyes, but does not probe. She sees in his eyes that she must decide if the goblets are true or false. Though she saw him place Logan's goblet in his right hand, the feeling from the goblet in that hand is not Logan's. Looking over at Royanna, she reaches out to take the one from his left hand, but waits for Royanna to reach for the one in his right. They both smile and take the goblets. The priest nods in acknowledgment of her correct choice and they drink. When the goblets are empty the men place their hands over the women's and then the priest places his over theirs.

"Your love is based on the Light and Truth, and you are as one. Go now to the caves of light and become mates in the presence of only the Great One. He will guide you through all that is necessary." With that he removes his hands and the two couples disappear. When they are gone the priest steps out of the tent and the light within goes out. Facing those gathered, he smiles. "Their choices were true and strong. When next we see them, they will be mated with the blessings of the Great One. Go now and celebrate their matings with joy and love." So saying, both the priest and the tent disappear.

Appearing in the caves, both couples stand still for several minutes absorbing the tranquility and love. After that, Thurda leads Royanna off to the left, while Logan and Cassie go to the right.

Entering the private chamber, Logan removes Cassie's robe and then she removes his. Hand in hand they walk into the pool of water at the back of the chamber. Slowly they wash each other, never once speaking aloud. When they're done, Logan carries

Cassie out of the pool and over to the cushions where he gently lays her down and then lies down beside her.

'Everything we do from now on will be with our minds, our bodies, and our spirits. Are you ready to finish our mating atma?'

'I'm ready atmo. Join with me and become one with me as I will become one with you.'

'I join my mind with yours, I join my body with yours, I join my spirit with yours and we are one in mind, body, and spirit.'

Then they come together and join their lives together for all time.

Logan brings their bodies together and they open their minds completely to each other for the first time, sharing all their thoughts and memories. As they touch each others subconscious minds they begin to feel what the other is feeling. They gasp in surprised shock and look into each others eyes, only instead of seeing each other, they see themselves through the others eyes. Their joining is so complete that they can not stop and as they climax, their spirits mingle and become one. Together they soar through and up into the light which binds them completely. Even in death they will never be alone. Should one die before the other and there still are things that must be done, the other will carry on still attached to the spirit of the other for support and strength until their time to be together again. If all is done when one dies the other will immediately follow and they will enter the presence of the Great One together as they have lived their lives.

Hours later both couples return to the palace and to their chambers. For the next few hours, before dawn, they lay in each others arms sleeping, but still sharing thoughts and feelings. The bonds between Thurda and Logan are now stronger and they better understand each other. The new bond between Cassandra and Royanna brings peace to both and brings them a new joy as they now become mother and daughter in a bond that can never be broken.

CHAPTER TWENTY-THREE

In the morning the people gather outside the palace to see the newly joined couples. Together Royanna, Thurda, Logan, and Cassie walk out onto the front balcony and the cheering begins. Thayer and Leyla step out, and Thayer steps forward to announce, "I present to you, Queen Royanna and her life-bond mate King Thurda."

More cheers go up and then Leyla steps forward and announces, "I present to you, Lord and Lady, Logan and Cassandra Knightrunner."

After things quiet down, Thayer invites everyone to a breakfast feast in the outer gardens. While the people are moving towards the gardens, Royanna and the others go back inside and are met by Cassie's family. Davena and Dessa gush over how radiant Royanna and Cassie look causing both to blush.

"Was it what you expected Cassie?" Dessa asks blushing slightly thinking of how her words might have been taken.

"That and a whole lot more Dess. It makes you feel whole and complete." Cassie smiles at all of them. "I hope that all of you find your lifemates so that you can see for yourselves what I mean."

"We had better get going before all the food is eaten." Mark says pulling Dessa with him down the hall. The others laugh and follow.

"Does it matter how old you are when you get lifemated?" Colt asks watching Mark and Dessa. "I mean, say you find your lifemate before your twenty? Can you be lifemated before you turn twenty?"

"Only under certain circumstances would anyone under the age of twenty be allowed to lifemate Colt." Thayer tells him with a slight frown. "A lifemating is a very serious step. Not only is the couple joining their bodies, but they're joining their minds and spirits as well. Both the mind and the spirit have to call to each other and when that happens, there is what is called a burning. When the burning starts, only by touching physically or mentally is it eased, and it can only be stopped by lifemating all of what you are with your chosen mate.

"Special care is needed then because both the man and the woman must be mentally and spiritually strong equally. If they are not, great harm can be done to one or both of them. Should a person find their lifemate before they are mature enough to go through a lifemating, a priest can put up a special barrier to stop the burning until it is safe. If the parents are willing though, the young couple can be bonded in a special ceremony that will change only when both are ready and then it will only take the slightest of touches for them to become lifemates." Thayer squeezes Colt's shoulder. "Does that answer your question well enough?"

"Yeah, it does. I may not have understood it all, but it does answer the question." They all laugh and walk out into the garden.

Denral looks around at his children gathered to decide what they are all going to do. He wishes that they would all stay here together, but he knows that they all have to make up their own minds and not be forced into something that they are not comfortable with. He clears his throat and sits a little straighter in his chair. "I have decided that I'm going to stay on Manchon. Whether or not you decide to stay, I will go along with your decision." He looks at each of them. "You are all capable of making this decision and of knowing what will make you happy. You will all be welcome in my home no matter how old you get. I love you all and want only your happiness. Daniel, what do you want to do?"

Daniel looks at his father and then at each of his siblings. "I want to return to Earth." He tells them and then looks at his father. "Dawn Flower is there and I want to be with her. I don't know if she's meant to be my lifemate, but she is very special to me."

Denral nods and then looks at Mark. "I want to go to Aquila." He tells them. "I want to learn about mother's people and maybe find more of our family. Since Sarah found out that mother's line came from there, I've felt a pull to go there and find something."

"I have too." Dessa speaks up. "I want to go with Mark to Aquila. I feel that there is something we have to do there. Not just find mother's people, but help them in some way. It's like if we don't go, we'll all be losing something."

Denral nods and looks at her twin. "Davena, what do you want to do?"

"I want to stay here with you Da. I have no wish to go back to Earth, or to travel further into the stars right now. Besides, with Cassie married, who would cook for you?" She smiles at him and the others laugh. All of them knowing that if left to cook for himself, their father would more than likely go hungry.

"All right, all right. Colt, what will you do?"

"I haven't decided yet Da. It depends on a few things happening before I make my decision."

Denral nods his understanding and then looks at Merri, already knowing what her decision will be.

"I'm going back to Earth Da. To the stronghold and my friends." She looks at him with a hint of sadness. "I love you Da, but I don't feel comfortable here. To live here I would have to act like a lady most of the time. At the stronghold I can be completely myself and not have to worry about offending someone all the time or doing the wrong things."

Smiling at her, Denral stands and walks over to her and takes her into his arms, hugging her tightly and kissing the top of her head. "No matter where you go or what you do, you will always be a lady when it matters most.

"Thanks Da." She says and returns his hug just as tightly.

"All right then. We'll let Cassie and Logan know our decision soon. Why don't you all go and find something to do. I have to meet with Roushta to go over my new duties as Lord of Acquisitions. He's invited us all to lunch, so try to be on time. If you should get another invitation let us know ahead of time."

"Mark and I are going to go over the information Sarah found on mother's people, and see if we can find anything more that will help him and Dessa on their search. We'll have Sarah remind us when its time for lunch." Daniel says with a look at his twin.

They all leave together and then separate once they reach the main hall. Davena and Dessa go off with Leyla and Cassie to look around the shops. Merri and Colt meet with Salis and Sheyome to go to the swimming hole.

While they swim, Sheyome tells them about some of the animal life that can be found on Manchon. They discover that a lot of the animals on Calidon and Earth are very similar. "Some people think that a few of our animals didn't originate here, but were brought here at some time in the distant past." Sheyome tells them thinking that from what they have told her it could very well be possible.

"It's possible Sheya. Father and mother said that at one time, long ago, Calidonians and Majichonie traveled back and forth between our two worlds. Then one day a strange space storm hit both worlds and Calidon disappeared and reappeared where it is now."

"Yeah, and Thayer's father came form Earth." Colt reminds them. "Isn't it possible that some earlier travelers from Earth could have brought animals with them and left them here to start new and maybe stronger breeds?"

"It could be Colt." Sheyome agrees having never thought of it before. "But I couldn't say for sure. I'm not up on our history, so anything is possible."

Just then several of the palace guards go rushing past the swimming hole, headed for the Mystic Forest. Sheyome calls out to them to find out what was happening and one of the men stops.

"One of the Usoni children is lost in the Mystic Forest and no one can reach her mind, or feel her physical presence."

"Are they sure that she's in there?"

"Yes. Her and one of the boys were there gathering wood for their father. One minute she was beside him, and the next she was gone." He tells her looking over his shoulder as he starts moving away. "Someone else said that they had seen Nuary gypsies near there a couple of days ago. It's possible that they were waiting for just such an occurrence."

"If they've taken her, the Queen will lock them all up this time. You go ahead, I'll join you shortly for the search."

The guard nods and rushes off. Everyone knew that if anyone could find the Usoni girl, it would be Sheyome. She knew the Mystic Forest better than anyone on Manchon, and she never got lost.

"Colt, would you and Merri take Salis back to the palace? It would be better if I start looking right away." She tells them pulling her trousers on over her wet swimsuit.

"Merri and I could help Shey. We could fly over the trees and look down. That way we'd cover more ground and find her faster."

"But Salis..."

"I can port myself back Sheya. Please let them help you look for the little girl." Salis pleads knowing how scared the girl must be.

Sheyome looks at her. "Do you promise to go straight to the palace?"

Salis nods and picks up her dress. "I'll go straight to grandmother and let her know that you and Colt and Merri are helping in the search." Without waiting she ports herself to Royanna's chambers.

Sheyome sighs and finishes getting dressed. Looking up after tying her shoes she notices that neither Colt or Merri has put on their clothes.

"It will be easier for us without the bulk of our clothes." Merri tells her as their wings come out and stretch. "We'll carry you to the edge of the forest and you can give us an idea of where to start looking." With that they each take one of Sheyome's arms and lift off the ground. Sheyome gasps in shock as they go up.

Colt and Merri quickly fly the short distance to the forest, and set Sheyome down by the guards that are already there. They then fly back up and head towards the center of the forest. Colt circles to the left, while Merri circles to the right, keeping in constant contact with Sheyome. After a while Merri notices a flash of white moving through the trees slowly. She reaches out and gently touches the girl's mind.

'Don't be afraid, I won't hurt you. My name is Merri Blackwood. Are you lost?'

'Yes. Some people are after me too. I've never seen them before.'

'Where are they now?'

'Somewhere behind me. Not too far away.'

'Can you climb one of the trees?'

'Yes.'

'Okay, climb as high as you can. What are the people following you wearing?'

'The man...is...wearing black...pants and a...dark blue...shirt. The woman is...wearing a...dark dress..., green...I think.'

Merri picks up on the images of the people chasing after the girl and sends it to Sheyome. She then signals to Colt to join her. Together they fly over the tree that the girl is climbing.

'Juna, do you know who I am?'

'I think so. You're Lady Cassandra's sister, aren't you?'

'Yes I am. My brother Colt is with me and we're flying above where you are now. If you can get to the very top of the tree, we can fly you to safety.'

'I'll try, but the branches don't look very strong.'

They wait and watch, seeing Juna test each branch against her weight before leaving the one she's on. Colt notices movement in the tree a couple of feet below her.

'Juna, I'm Colt. Don't panic, but I want you to look below you and to your left. What do you see?'

'It's the man, and he looks very angry.'

"We can't wait for her to climb any higher Merri. He'll catch up to her in a few minutes."

"But how do we get to her? Unless she can port herself up to the top of...No she can't. The forest neutralizes all but telepathic abilities."

"We can port her up together. Like we did with the Albertson's dog when he fell in that hole. You've felt her mind, and I've felt her build. Together we should be able to do it."

"All right, we'll give it a try, but we'd better warn her first."

'Juna, we're going to try and port you to the top of the tree. Be ready to catch yourself if we don't make it.'

'I'm ready Colt.'

Linking their minds, they concentrate on Juna, getting all of her physical dimensions. Just as the man's hand reaches for her ankle, they port her to the top of the tree. Quickly, they fly down and take her arms.

'Shey, we have Juna. The man is in the tree.'

'Good. We've got the woman, we'll get him when he comes down. Take Juna back to the palace. Her family is waiting for her there.'

"The guards have the woman and will get the man as soon as he comes out of the tree." Merri tells Juna. "You'll need to identify them, but you don't have to be afraid of them any longer."

"Thank you both for helping me."

"There's no need to thank us Juna." Colt assures her. "We were happy to be of help."

They fly straight to the courtyard, and land amongst the royal family and several of their guards. As they release Juna, an older man steps forward and takes her into his arms, squeezing her tightly.

"I'm fine Papa, I'm fine." Juna pushes back from him a little to look at his face. "No, they didn't hurt me, they just scared me. Merri and her brother got me out by porting me to the top of a tree. No I wasn't scared to fly with them, they were very careful."

Juna's father looks over at Colt and Merri. *'Thank you both for saving my daughter and bringing her back to us.'*

"You're welcome Sir." Merri and Colt say in unison.

'Come to my shop later this afternoon and I will have something for you both to better show my appreciation.'

"That isn't..." Merri begins, but stops as Royanna touches her shoulder.

"That will be fine Pautorin. Sheyome will bring them down later. Go now and take Juna home to Galena so that she can see for herself that her daughter is safe and unharmed." Royanna tells him softly. "We will need Juna to identify the couple and make a statement tomorrow if they do not confess when they are brought before me."

'She will be ready Majesty. Thank you for sending the guards to find her so quickly.'

"I would do no less for any child, then I would my own granddaughter were she missing and in danger." She assures him.

Ten minutes after the Usoni's leave, Sheyome and the guards come in with the man and woman that had been chasing Juna.

289

They are taken to the viewing chamber where Royanna, Thurda, Leyla, and Thayer are waiting with Merri and Colt. Sheyome brings the prisoners forward and forces both to their knees. "Majesties, these are the two captured below the tree were Juna was rescued."

"What do you have to say for yourselves?" Royanna asks with a hint of anger. "You are charged with the attempted kidnapping of a young girl of eleven years of age."

The woman looks over at the man and then up at the royal family. "I beg mercy for myself and my bondmate Majesty. We meant no harm to the child, only to ask her of the possibility of her having an older sister that would be willing to...to..." She falters and hangs her head.

"To what?!" Thayer demands strongly. "What was so important to you that you chased a child through the Mystic Forest? So important that this man," he points at the man who has not yet said a word, "would follow that child up into a tree, where she might have fallen to her death? Tell us that!"

Leyla touches his arm and sends calming thoughts to him and warns him, *'Wait Thayer. What they have to say may very well be very important to them. We can't judge that importance ourselves without knowing everything.'* He takes a deep breath and nods.

"We only meant to ask the child if she had an older sister that might consider carrying a child for us Majesty." The man finally speaks up. "Like my mate has said, we meant the child no harm. When we saw her she was walking towards a hidden man-creeper. We called out to her to stop her stepping into it's range, and she began to run from us. We only went after her to make sure that she came to no harm. I swear to you on my oath as the Master Healer and Seer of the Nuary clan. I followed her up the tree because she was so distraught that she wasn't picking up our thoughts of peace."

"Why was there anger in your face when you were climbing towards her?" Colt asks him with a frown.

The man looks at the young man standing with the royal family. "The anger was not directed at the child my young Lord. It was for the fear placed in her for our clan." He looks back at the royal family. "Majesty, we have never taken a child into our clan and never will. They come to us looking for something that they did not think they had at home. Most of the time we persuade them to return home, others we contact their parents and get permission for them to stay with us for a while. Even with doing this, falsehoods are spoken against us. Whenever guards have stopped us, if they would only ask we would have told them this. Instead we are detained and our belongings are searched. Some accuse us of stealing things that they have never found in our possession, and never apologize for their false accusations. There are never any trace vibrations of whatever they are looking for either." He stops and looks down again, not sure if it was doing them any good to mention the treatment of his clan. "That was the anger that she saw, nothing more."

"Why do you need someone to carry a child for you? You are not that old." Royanna asks quietly looking at the woman.

The man looks over at his mate and nods for her to answer the question. "I do not seem able to conceive Majesty. We have tried many herbs and potions, but nothing has helped me to conceive. I fear that I am barren and will never be able to give my mate a child." She begins to cry softly and her mate reaches over to take her hand in his, his own eyes tearing.

Royanna and Leyla exchange looks and talk privately. *'I'm going to send for Kimtala and have her look into the woman. If what they say is true, we will have to carefully explain all of this to Pautorin.'*

'I can feel only sincerity in all that they have told us Anna.'

Royanna nods and then contacts Truloka and asks her to bring Kimtala to the viewing chamber. Within minutes she enters the room carrying her daughter. She takes her to Royanna and then steps back.

"Kimtala, I want you to use your gift to look at the woman there." She points to the Nuary woman. "Tell us what you see in her belly. Can you do that for us?" Kimtala nods and looks at the woman's belly.

Looking at everything, a frown forms on her small face. The color of the place where babies sleep is all wrong. Instead of the red like her mama's, or the pink of Shama's, this one is brown and kind of green. Shaking her head she looks up at Royanna. "Her baby place is sick Anna. No red or pink, only brown and green. It looks yucky. The tube things look like knots too."

Royanna frowns not knowing what this condition could be or how to correct it, if it can even be corrected.

Leyla, noticing Royanna's frown offers, "I'll have Sarah send our medical unit and we can use it to find out what the problem is. It has the latest diagnostic programs." She looks down at the woman and smiles slightly. "It's a machine that knows the subtle differences of Majichonie biology. If the problem can be fixed, it will do it automatically."

Royanna nods and Leyla contacts Sarah. Within seconds the med-unit appears and Leyla goes over to it and programs it for the examination and treatment. Turning back to the Nuary woman, she explains to her the units full purpose, and that all she has to do is lay down inside. "If it can repair the damage, it will do so right away. You have to remain as still as you can, but if you wish, it can also give you a mild relaxer to help."

The gypsies look at each other and then the man nods for the woman to do as they ask. She gets up and walks over to the box. For several seconds she looks at the unit and then looks at Leyla. When Leyla smiles encouragingly, she climbs inside. Leyla closes the plas-glass and then pushes a few more buttons and steps back.

"This could take as little as a couple of minutes, or as long as a couple of hours." Leyla informs everyone looking over the readouts. Since they had never really had to use it for something like this there was no way of knowing how long it would take.

Ten minutes later the unit opens and Leyla helps the woman to sit up on the edge. After a few moments she stands and smiles at Leyla. "Thank you Majesty. The box has made me feel better then I have in a very long time."

Leyla nods and then turns back to the unit to check its medical report. After reading over it carefully, she prints up a hard copy and returns to Royanna's side. "According to the med-unit, her uterus had been infected by a fungus that was causing a slow deterioration. Her tubes had knotted up as the uterus shrunk in size. The unit gave her a slight radiation treatment and administered strong antibiotics to kill the fungus. They will release into her body over the next seven days at six hour intervals. It also gave her an injection that will increase her egg production for a while, at least until she conceives her first child." She turns to look at the Nuary woman. "Given a little time, you will carry your mate's child."

Royanna nods and stands up. "I believe that you intended no harm to Juna, so I will release you. If in the future your people need something or someone for whatever reason, you are to come to the palace." She warns looking from one to the other. "If you don't want the children, or even the adults to fear you, then you are going to have to start interacting with the rest of the population. How can we learn to trust you when there is so little contact? We don't wish to control you or your ways, only to be able to get to know you and trust you. When you return to your people, speak with your elders about sending someone to come and join the royal council. Add the voice of the Nuary to that of the other Majichonie. All of our people have a right to be heard. You may go now."

The Nuary bow to all of them and then leave the room. Royanna quickly contacts Pautorin and tells him everything that they had learned and what had been done about the situation. He agrees that no harm was meant and that he bears the couple no grudge.

CHAPTER TWENTY-FOUR

Cassie sits on Leyla and Thayer's bed and watches her friend pack up their belongings to be taken back to their ship. Though they will be seeing each other again in a few months time, Cassie wishes that they had more time together now.

"Are you sure that you couldn't stay for another week? It would give Thayer a little more time with his mother and give you more time to get to know about your father's family here."

"I wish that we could Cassie, but right now the Alliance has to come first. We've already stayed longer then we originally intended." Leyla stops her packing to look at her friend. "Once we have everything well underway we'll come back for a longer visit. Besides, you'll be coming with the first groups and be staying with us for three months."

Cassie looks down at her hands. "Yes, I know, but that isn't why I asked. Royanna needs some more time with Thayer. She hasn't seen him in fifteen years and there's no telling how long it will take to get the Alliance on sure footing. Thurda loves her, but she still needs to know more about her son." She points out standing and walking over to the dresser.

Leyla frowns slightly and walks over to stand beside her. "Did Anna tell you this Cassie? Does she want us to stay but can't tell us?" She couldn't see the older woman not stating what was on her mind, especially when it came to family.

"No, she hasn't told me. It's just something that I've been picking up on for a day or so. She believes as you and Thayer do, that the Alliance comes first. She won't ask for anything that would hurt the people in any way, even though it would save her from being hurt."

Leyla puts an arm around Cassie's shoulders and hugs her close. "I know that this is hard for you to understand right now. The extent of what we're giving up, but it's the same as giving up something for your family. You do it so that their lives can be better and happier. Both Thayer and I would love nothing better than to stay here longer and visit, but first we have an obligation to finish what we've started. When that's done, then we can think of ourselves a little and do something to make us happy."

"How long do you think it will take to get this going where you can take time off for yourselves?"

"Within a year at least, but we're hoping not that long because of the baby. We'd like both Thayer's mother and Thurda, and my parents to be present for the royal christening."

Cassie gives Leyla a hug and then steps back. "I hope that it will work out that way. I'd better go. I promised Sheyome that I would help her pack."

"All right. Any news about Libre?"

"No. He hasn't talked to her since she told him that she was going with you. Logan doesn't think that he'll see her before you leave, but I think that he will. Even if he doesn't say anything, I think he'll want to see her one last time."

"I hope that you're right. I wouldn't want her leaving to be so painful. Maybe he won't either."

Cassie nods and leaves the room, heading for Sheyome's chambers.

"We'll be back as soon as the Alliance is on a firm footing mother. Leyla and I both want you two and her parents at the christening of the baby."

"But won't the people of Calidon feel slighted if you have the christening here?" Royanna asks frowning.

"I don't think so. We plan to explain to them why we want to do it this way. Selina says that the new power generators will be strong enough to receive the images Sarah will send back so that the people can see the christening."

"Well, if you're sure. It will be good to see you when neither one of us has other things on our minds."

"Yes, and we can get to know each other again." He smiles at his mother and then looks at Thurda. "It will also give me time to get to know my new father as well. I'm glad that you will be at her side from now on Thurda."

Thurda nods as he takes Royanna's hand in his. "So am I Thayer. I am also pleased to have another such fine son as you. Robus would be as proud as I am if he were here."

"Thank you. That means a lot to me." Thayer bows his head slightly at the compliment. "I'm sure he would be pleased to know that mother has chosen such a worthy mate and is happy." Thurda bows his head in acceptance of Thayer's words.

Cassie and Sheyome are nearly done packing Shey's things when Libre comes in. Quietly Cassie excuses herself and leaves them alone.

Libre waits until the door closes behind her before looking around the room at all of the boxes. He still found it hard to believe that she was going to leave him. "So, you're really going to go."

"Yes." Sheyome nods and places the last of her knic-knacs into the box. "I didn't think that I would see you again before we left."

"I know. It hasn't been easy for me to accept that I was losing you." He moves around the room noticing the things that she has left for him. "The Queen gave me some time to get my emotions under control. I went up to the Zenal mountains for a while and did some meditation." He stops his wanderings a couple of feet away from her. "I realized that I wasn't being fair to you by trying to keep you here. You're right about trying to find your lifemate. I'm sorry for the way I acted, and for hurting you."

"I'm sorry too Libre. It was never my intention to cause you pain. When Thayer asked me about going, I thought of the possibilities, but not the sorrows. I don't want to leave you, but I need to go with Thayer. There is something or someone waiting out there for me, and I need to find it to be complete."

Libre steps closer and takes her into his arms as she wipes away a few tears. "It's all right Shey, I understand. One of the things I relearned on the mountain is that we have to follow where the Great One leads us. He is leading you away from Manchon, away from me, because it is your destiny. Now that I have accepted that you're leaving, I have also accepted that I will always be a part of you in a very special way, as you will be a part of me."

Sheyome looks up into his face and sees that he really accepts this and that he is happy for her. "You're right Libre. You will always be a special part of me no matter what the Great One has planned for me." She steps out of his arms and takes his hand, leading him into the bedroom. For the last time they would join their bodies in an act of love and for a final good-bye.

Merri and Colt are standing near the rear entrance to the palace gardens and Colt has just told her his plan to stowaway on Leyla and Thayer's ship.

"But why Colt? All you have to do is tell Leyla and Thayer that you want to go to Calidon with them."

"I did Merri, but Thayer says that I have to wait. He said that if I really wanted to come, I could come with Cassie and Logan in three months."

"Then why don't you? None of us are leaving until then anyway." She reminds him.

"You just don't understand." He looks out the gateway towards the ship. "I have to go now. Three months is too long." He looks over his shoulder at her, and she looks into his eyes and frowns slightly at the fire she can see there.

"It's Salis isn't it? You want to go so that you can be together."

Colt nods his head and then looks at the ship again. "Knowing that we have to be apart even for a short time fills me with a great sadness and dread Merri. It's like a part of me is being ripped away and that I'll lose it or never find it again."

Merri steps to his side and puts her head on his shoulder. Colt puts an arm around her waist and sighs softly as he receives her comfort. If he did this, chances were that he wouldn't see his twin for a very long time. Though this causes him sadness, not being with Salis would be even worse.

"What I'm feeling is so strong Merri that I know that it would be wrong for me not to go with her now. It's kind of like the burning that Thayer was telling us about I think." He looks at her. "It's sort of how you feel about returning to Earth, that a part of you is missing. I don't think that I could deal with it as you have, and why should I? There's plenty of room on the ship, and I could be Salis' companion like Sheyome is."

"Even if you did get aboard, Sarah would pick up on your life signs and tell Leyla and Thayer." Merri points out to him.

"No she won't. I'll do like I did with Ali and scramble my pattern so that all she picks up on is an extra chair or something. The only one that will know that I'm on board is Salis, and she won't give me away. If I'm lucky, no one else will find me until we're nearly to Panthera and then it will be too late for them to bring me back."

"When are you going on board? They'll be leaving in a few hours."

"I'll get on only a few minutes before they do. That will give me a better chance of not getting caught right away. They won't be expecting anything like this so everyone's guard will be down, including Sarah and Stephen's. There's enough room under Salis' bed, that if anyone walks in they won't be able to see me."

"I hope you know what you're doing Colt. Thayer and Leyla are not going to be happy when you're found stowing away. Especially Thayer."

"I know." He frowns and wonders what punishment he'll have to deal with. Since Thayer and Nightstorm were raised together, he knows that it won't be an easy punishment. "Come on. I need to be seen for a while before I disappear. I think that you should disappear for a while after I do. I'll let everyone see me port and you can say you're going to see if I'm all right or something like that. If you're not around they can't question you about anything and you don't have to lie to them." They turn back to the palace.

"Okay. I'll try and give you enough time, but if they turn up the heat, you're on your own. Especially if it's Royanna putting on the heat. I'm in enough trouble with her as it is and I don't want to add to my punishment list." She tells him and then smiles.

"Deal." He assures her. He wished that he didn't have to involve her.

⁄

"I'm sure that everything is fine between them Thayer. If I had felt any anger from Libre I wouldn't have left them alone." Cassie assures him after telling of Libre's return. "All I felt from him was love and peace. He's accepted that this is something that Shey has to do."

"Yes, but he's probably still hurting and he may say or do something to upset her."

"Darling, they're both hurting." Leyla reminds her mate gently. "Don't forget that they've had a personal relationship for a long time, this decision hasn't been easy on either one of them."

"I know, I just don't want Shey to be hurt anymore than she already has been."

"None of us do love."

There's a knock at the door, Sheyome and Libre walk in when Leyla calls for them to enter. All three notice that the couple are holding hands when they come in.

"Majesties, Lady Cassandra." Libre bows to them.

They all nod to him and then wait for one of them to speak. Sheyome squeezes Libre's hand to encourage him to speak up and he returns the gesture.

"Majesties, I would like your permission to visit with Sheyome each year for one month's time until one or the other of us finds a lifemate. I understand and accept her need to go with you. We would like to keep in touch with each other and keep some parts of our relationship open."

Thayer looks at both of them for several seconds and then nods. "If that is what you both wish, it will be arranged."

"It is Thayer." Sheyome assures him, knowing that it's only his wish to protect her and make sure that she's happy and can live with her decision.

Thayer smiles at her and then looks at Libre. "If you wish to at any time, you will be welcome on Calidon."

"Thank you Majesty, but I plan to remain permanently on Manchon. My visits will be enough to make us happy. If we were together again on the same world, we might resume our relationship again and then we may end up hurting each other again. Neither one of us wishes to do that."

"Very well. We will look..." Another knock at the door stops him and he calls for whomever to enter. Opening the door Salis comes in and looks at the adults.

"Everything is loaded onto the ship father. Sarah says that we can leave any time now."

"Okay sweetheart. Why don't you go and tell your grandparents that we're ready to leave then?" Thayer smiles at her and Salis gives him a half smile before leaving the room.

"I don't think she's to happy about us leaving." Leyla says frowning as she watches her daughter leave the room.

"No, she's not." Thayer agrees with a frown. "Both she and Colt are upset that I won't let him return to Calidon with us."

"They have become very attached to each other Thayer." Cassie tells him.

"I know, that's why I think that it best that Colt wait and come with you and Logan with the first group. They need some time apart for a while. If they still feel the need to be together then, then we'll see about Colt staying on Calidon." Thayer tells them as he stands.

"It's possible that they are meant to be together Thayer. Don't forget what Colt asked you the other day about lifemating." Sheyome reminds him. "It's possible that they are already feeling the pull towards each other. It has been known to happen, though not often enough that it has become a real problem."

"That's what I'm concerned about Shey." He agrees and shakes his head. "That was why I suggested he wait the three months. We should know from their behavior if it's more than puppy love."

Cassie smiles and shakes her head, sure that they would know a lot sooner if they were meant to be together. If they are, nothing would keep her little brother away from Salis, not even her father. She just hopes that her friends would find a gentle way to handle the situation for all of their sakes.

They all leave the chamber and go to meet with Royanna and the others. They had already said their formal farewells to the people that morning. Now was the time for them to say good-bye to their family and closest friends. As they join the others, Thayer notices Salis, Colt, and Merri standing off by themselves talking. He feels bad about separating Salis and Colt, but he sees no other way to give them the chance to get beyond their present feelings for each other. In three months he would see how things were between them and then decide how to proceed.

After hugging everyone, the adults turn to where the three youngest are standing and see Colt say something to Salis before he disappears. Salis and Merri look at each other and then walk over to the adults.

"Colt's pretty upset. If you don't mind, I'm going to go and stay with him for a while." Merri tells them. "Don't worry if we don't come back right away. He may want to camp out for a couple of days." She tells the other members of their family trying to keep her mind a blank.

They all nod and Merri hugs Salis once more and then looks at Leyla and Thayer. "Bye. Have a safe journey." With a wave she ports to her room and grabs the knapsacks she and Colt had packed earlier. Double checking the room, she ports to the mountains she noticed when they were rescuing Juna. The mountains would be one of the last places that the others would look for them since they hadn't been there yet. If she kept light and fast contact with them they wouldn't locate her for at least a week which would give her brother the time he needed and the distance to keep from being brought back.

Meanwhile, Thayer is apologizing to Salis for what has happened. "I'm sorry if Colt is upset because of my decision sweetheart, but I did what I felt was necessary. He can still come to Calidon when Cassie and Logan do. If you both feel the same way that you do now, then Colt can stay with us for as long as he wishes."

Salis frowns up at him. "Our feelings won't change in three months, three years, or three lifetimes father." She steps over to Leyla and hugs her, putting her head against her mother's stomach for a few seconds and then looks up at her. "Can I go to the ship now? I've already said good-bye to everyone."

"Sure honey. Tell Sarah that we'll be there in a couple of minutes."

Salis nods and then steps back. She throws one last frowning look at Thayer and then ports to her room on the ship. When she appears, she holds a finger to her lips for Colt to be quiet. "Sarah, mother said to tell you that they would be here in a few minutes."

"All right Salis. Everything is ready and secure. Stephen has placed the gifts to the Aquilians and Pantherians in the safe in your parent's room."

"Okay. Will you tell them that I'm going to rest for a while and don't want to be disturbed?"

"Very well Salis." There's a pause and then the computer asks, "Did you add something to your cabin? My readings show an extra solid form near your bed."

"Yes it's...it's a trunk that...that Colt gave me. It's not very big."

"Okay. Well you may want to secure it so that it doesn't move around too much."

"I will Sarah, thank you."

'We won't be able to talk aloud without Sarah hearing, so we'll have to talk telepathically until we reach Panthera.'

'Or until I get caught. I don't know how long I can keep shielding myself from Sarah. It takes a lot of energy.'

'Maybe you won't have to. Stephen's been working on a special obstructer, and he's finally finished it. He hasn't programmed the information for Sarah yet, so she doesn't know how to get past it. I'll go to his room just after we leave and get it. That should give us a couple of days.'

'But can we use it to just block me? Won't it block you as well? They'd come looking for you.'

'No. I helped him put it together, and he showed me how to program it. Sarah won't ask him about it because she won't want to admit that something's gotten the better of her. Especially something that he's designed.'

'I hope that you're right, otherwise this is going to be a very short trip for me.' He tells her with a frown.

Ten minutes later the ship leaves Manchon and Salis ports into Stephen's room and gets the device and takes it back to her room. After activating it, Colt and Salis hold their breaths waiting to see what will happen. After a half an hour they relax, and Colt crawls under the bed and closes his eyes, while Salis lays down on the bed. Both of them hope that when Colt is discovered that Leyla and Thayer won't be too mad, and that they will understand why they had done this.

EPILOGUE

Over the next several days, Merri avoids all contact with her family whenever possible. She only answers them to assure them that everything is all right and that she would see them soon. When they ask about Colt and why he isn't responding to their calls, she tells them that he isn't talking to her either.

Today she couldn't ignore the call no matter how much she wanted to. Royanna herself had called to her and was summoning her back to the palace at once. Since the Queen was calling her, it could only mean that Colt had been found. At least he was far enough away that Leyla and Thayer wouldn't be bringing him back. That still left her to face the Queen and her Da without any support.

As she packs up her gear, she shrugs her shoulders and talks to the hawk sitting on the log next to her. "Oh well. I knew that this would happen when I agreed to help them. Hopefully it won't be too bad."

The hawk turns it's head and looks at her side ways. She can feel it's sympathy for what she must go through.

"What happens to me doesn't really matter. Salis and Colt are happy and that's what really counts. I'll be happy again when I go back to Earth in a couple of months."

The hawk cries out and Merri smiles at him. "Don't worry, my sister Davena is staying here. If you want to, you can come down to the palace and meet her and her twin Dessa and my oldest sister Cassie. I'm sure that they would like to fly with you sometimes."

Again the hawk cries out and this time Merri frowns. "I'm sure the queen wouldn't let anything happen to you. As long as you promise to leave the domestic animals alone I don't see why anyone would hurt you."

'Come NOW Merrilynda Blackwood.'

Merri frowns and answers Royanna's call. *'I'll be there shortly your Majesty. I have to clean up my camp site before I leave.'*

'Five minutes no more.'

'Yes Majesty.'

Merri shakes her head and continues packing as she talks to the hawk. "I have to go she's really upset. I'll call to you in a couple of days and let you know when it's safe to come down." She reaches into her pack and pulls out the small gold medallion Juna's father had given her. "Here, wear this and it will guaranty that you reach me safely. I'll tell the queen that it shows that you are my friend."

Reaching out she lets the hawk examine the necklace and then slips it over his head when he stretches out his neck for her to do so. She waits until he's comfortable with it and then stands up. "Well, I have to go my friend. I'll see you in a couple of days. There's fresh meat in that maple oak that you can have. It should last you a couple of days. Farewell."

The hawk cries out and then sits there and watches her disappear. It looks down at the metal disc and then looks off in the direction of the palace. With a flap of it's mighty wings it soars up into the sky and soon fades into the light of the sun.

"Well young lady, what have you got to say for yourself?" Royanna asks Merri as she stands before them. "Are you proud of yourself for letting your family and friends worry about you and your brother?"

"No Majesty, I'm not proud of letting all of you worry, but if I had to do it again I would." Merri tells her unflinchingly, looking her in the eye. "Colt and Salis need to be together. By trying to keep them apart, even for three months, would have caused them both a lot of unnecessary pain and suffering. I couldn't let that happen to either of them again."

For several moments Royanna just stares at her and then nods. "Very well, but all of you should have explained this to us instead of taking matters into your own hands."

"Colt tried to explain to Thayer, but all Thayer was thinking about was separating them. If he would have given Colt a chance he would have told him that when he and Salis were not close, they felt very sad and hurt inside. I don't mean any disrespect to you or to Thayer Majesty, but it seemed quite unfair to deny Colt when Thayer didn't know everything involved."

"Be that as it may, you should have come to me and I would have done my best to convince him that they should stay together." Royanna tells her somewhat mildly. "Since they are almost to Panthera, they can not afford to bring Colt back. Thayer has separated them, if what you say is true, then he will be forced to put them back together again to ease their pain."

For the first time since this meeting had started Cassie speaks up. "Even if he separates them, they can still stay in mind contact."

"I'm afraid not Cassie." Thurda puts in with a slight frown. "As punishment for defying his decision, Colt has been put in an isolation room that blocks all psi abilities, including telepathy. Sarah has been told not to allow them to talk through the ship's comm system either."

Merri pales when she hears that Colt and Salis have already been separated. That would explain the pain she had been feeling.

"Your Majesty, Royanna, please. You must contact Thayer and tell him what's going to happen." She pleads stepping closer. "Not for Colt, he can take the pain, at least for a little while, but Salis can't. This is a different kind of pain then anything she's ever known before. If Thayer keeps them apart too long, knowing that it is and will cause her pain, she may never forgive him, or trust him again."

"What are you talking about Merri? No pain is that great for a child." Denral states with annoyance.

"Yes there is Da. Colt and I went through it on Earth, and it was very painful. Though ours wasn't that great, but this will be because Colt and Salis are meant to be lifemated in the future. Their minds are already as one. To keep them apart isn't fair to either of them. It's cruel and unnecessary."

"Are you sure of this Merri?" Cassie asks remembering the pain the twins had gone through while their minds couldn't touch. Merri looks at Cassie and she can see the tears in her eyes at the pain Colt is already in.

"Very sure Cassie. I saw them being lifemated in a dream that first night that they left Manchon. Though Colt and I aren't that close any more, I can tell that he's already starting to feel the pain of their separation, and it's getting worse every minute." She looks back at Royanna. "Please Anna, please contact Thayer. His room can block Colt from Salis, but not from me. Our minds are linked differently. Neither of them deserves this. They only want to be together as they are meant to be. Don't punish them for following their destiny."

Royanna looks into Merri's pleading eyes and not only sees but feels the truth in what she's said. Looking at Thurda, she receives his nod and closes her eyes. 'Thayer, hear me and listen. Unless you wish to lose your daughter for all time, you will release Colt to go to her NOW! Salis cannot withstand the pain she's in for much longer. Both of their lives may very well be at stake. Including Merri's.' "I've contacted him Merri, but we'll have to wait and see what happens. You will know before any of us if this is going to work. I pray for all of us that it does or we may all suffer a great loss."

For what seems like forever they all wait and wonder what would happen. Would Thayer heed his mother's warning and act accordingly, or would he see it as interference on his rights as a parent. While they wait Merri closes her eyes and concentrates on her twin willing him to hold on and not give up. She can feel him getting weaker and tries to send him her strength to get him through. She was sure that Thayer would do the right thing and take him back to Salis.

After what seems like a lifetime she feels her twin's pain easing and then his happiness as he and Salis are brought back together. Tears slip past her closed lids and she smiles as she opens them and looks at the others. "They're back together and they're going to be all right. Thayer got Colt to Salis in time."

Everyone breathes more easily and wonders what would happen to the young couple in the future if their link to each other was already this strong. What would it mean to the rest of their people if these links became common amongst the rest of the young people? How were they to handle this new and what seemed to be stronger bonding of lifemates? Only time and the Great One knew the answer to that.